EVERYONE WE'VE BEEN

EVERYONE WE'VE BEEN

SARAH EVERETT

ALFRED A. KNOPF
NEW YORK

THIS IS A BORZOI BOOK PUBLISHED BY ALFRED A. KNOPF

All rights reserved. Published in the United States by Alfred A. Knopf, an imprint of Random House Children's Books, a division of Penguin Random House LLC, New York.

Knopf, Borzoi Books, and the colophon are registered trademarks of Penguin Random House LLC.

Visit us on the Web! randomhouseteens.com

Educators and librarians, for a variety of teaching tools, visit us at RHTeachersLibrarians.com

Library of Congress Cataloging-in-Publication Data is available upon request.

ISBN 978-0-553-53844-1 (trade) — ISBN 978-0-553-53845-8 (lib. bdg.) — ISBN 978-0-553-53846-5 (ebook)

The text of this book is set in 12-point Garamond.

Printed in the United States of America
October 2016
10 9 8 7 6 5 4 3 2 1

First Edition

To all the people
who take up space
in my heart

1

On the first turn, I think about my orchestra uniform: a knee-length black skirt, soft and silky between my fingers.

On the second turn, a stack of sheet music, pieces I'm halfway through learning or planning to learn.

On the third turn, I slam into the seat in front of me. The boy three rows ahead jerks forward, too, but it's a backpack he guards instead of a viola case.

On the fourth turn, the world bursts with noise. Smattering applause of broken glass. A startled scream from a little girl. Yellow streetlight that is too bright and thick and long. The trees whirl around us; it's hard to tell whether they are gliding around on a sheet of ice or we are.

Finally we stop spinning.

There is no sound.

2

AN HOUR EARLIER
An hour earlier

About thirty miles outside of Caldwell, we pick up the last set of passengers. An elderly Asian couple and a teenage boy who looks about my age—seventeen. The couple sits in the second row closest to the doors, but the boy keeps walking through the aisle, rubbing his palms together and breathing on his hands to warm them.

He scans the bus as he enters the aisle, surveying the seating options. There are five or six other passengers, a small enough number that we're not wrestling for armrests or invading each other's personal space, which is the single worst thing about public transportation, especially on Saturdays. I'm near the back of the bus, just in case we get a surge of people.

The boy passes the drowsy-looking college student on the left whose jet-black hair flops down over his eyes. He stops a few rows from my seat, on the right side of the aisle.

Behind me, a mother shushes one of her two elementary-school-age kids.

I watch as the boy peels his backpack off his shoulders and places it on the seat closest to the window. The backpack is half unzipped, the short metal legs of a tripod sticking out. He glances up at me, catching my eye, just as I'm about to look away.

"God, it's cold," he says, rubbing his palms over his shoulders.

"I know, it's freezing," I say back disappointingly. Uninterestingly.

I notice that he's completely underdressed for this cold. His hair is tucked under a black wool beanie, but he's wearing a thin cotton shirt pushed up at his elbows. No coat, no scarf. How has he not frozen to death?

"Jackets help," I blurt out, past the acceptable response time. Then add in a slightly more normal voice, "Or so I've been told."

The boy assesses me and breaks into a grin that takes up his whole face as he looks down at how he's dressed. "Hmm. I might have to try that one of these days." His smile makes a funny feeling slide through my stomach. He hesitates a moment, then sits with his back to me, three rows ahead.

I pull out my phone to check the time and see three texts from my mom, asking how the trip is going and what time the bus arrives so she can pick me up from the station. I send her a quick response before sticking the phone back in my pocket.

"What do you play?" the boy asks a few minutes later, turning his entire upper body around to face me. He nods at the case occupying a seat next to me. The bus to Caldwell this morning got me there four hours before the concert started, so I'd brought my viola in case I found somewhere to practice and kill time while I waited.

"The viola," I say. Why do I always spend so much time hoping someone will talk to me, only to have absolutely nothing to say when they do?

Presumably just to witness my verbal ineptness, Goth College Guy rouses a little and turns back to look at me. He blinks a few times, then turns around again.

"I don't know one thing about the viola," the boy says, grinning at me. I know I'm on a concert high—"outside my lane," as my pilot father might say—because something about the grin elates me. His smile is so easy, his face so open, that I feel like he must do it a lot—which, of course, ought to put me back inside my lane. He probably smiles like this at everyone.

But staying firmly in the wrong lane, I smile back and speak a little more quietly, in case anyone is trying to sleep.

"Well, they look a lot like violins but they're not." I hear myself quickly going down the path of many Violas Are Not Violins activists who have gone before me, so I change directions. "Rumor has it that Jimi Hendrix started off playing the viola."

"Really," the boy says, and, God bless him, pretends to be interested.

"Yeah. I actually just came from watching a concert," I say, wanting to keep the conversation going. "Not Jimi Hendrix. Obviously."

"Obviously," the boy repeats, teasing, and something flutters inside me again.

"Pretty sure dead people don't have concerts."

I might be rambling, but he is playing along. "*I've* never been invited to one," he says.

I laugh. It slips out quickly, without permission, and Goth Guy rouses again to glare at me. But the boy looks pleased he's made me laugh.

I drop my voice to a whisper. "Unless it's just that they're exclusive. Think how many people would pay to see a Ghost Mozart concert," I joke. Then, sobering up, I add, "It was actually this orchestra at Samberg Auditorium."

"Were they any good?"

"They were incredible," I say.

My mind swivels back to the performance, especially to the second movement of that Bach orchestral suite. I could see why it had become famous as "Air on the G String." Through that dark, echoing auditorium, the sound stretched across all the empty space and reeled me in closer. A long musical finger, crooked at me.

I'd heard it before, but there was something about that piece. Something different and powerful. I'd clung to the armrests until the very last note ended.

Now I blink back into reality, realizing the boy is still looking at me.

"What about you?" I ask, embarrassed by my lapse in attention. "Where are you coming from?"

He looks out the dark window then and tugs on his hat. "Long story, but my piece-of-shit car wouldn't start."

He grins again as he speaks, and I wonder if "piece-of-shit" is actually code for a Lamborghini and why blood rushes to my face every time he smiles.

"That sucks," I say.

He shrugs. The kids at the back of the bus are arguing over something while their mom threatens to confiscate it. It feels awkward to keep talking across three rows, so the boy turns back to face the front and I finally force myself to pull out *Great Expectations*, the book we're discussing in English class.

We stop for gas at Riverton, and the boy gets off behind the driver. The mom, a short woman with light brown hair to the middle of her back, shepherds her kids down the aisle.

"I don't waaaanna go to the bathroom," the little girl whines, her brother following her, skipping between the seats. The girl's hair is almost identical in length and color to her mother's. The mother gives me this look I can't explain when she walks past me, then hurries her kids along.

When I squint out the window, I see the boy standing next to the bus driver, smoking. Both of them march in place, trying to stay warm, tufts of cigarette smoke intermingling with the clouds of their breath. It's judgmental of me, but the discovery of Smiling Boy's nicotine problem makes it easier to dismiss any connection we might have shared. He's a random boy on a bus in the middle of January.

The family comes back on first, and I feel the mother's gaze on me again, but this time she jerks her eyes away when I look up. As if she's embarrassed to have been caught staring. She walks to the back of the bus and retrieves a sweater and backpack, then the three of them relocate to the very front of the bus, opposite the couple.

I wonder what her problem is. I self-consciously check the

cover of my book. Does *Great Expectations* have some reputation for being super racy that I'm not aware of?

My face is back in my book when the boy and bus driver get on again, but the letters quickly blur into meaningless squiggles, and I doze on and off for the next hour.

I wake up to the spinning.

The bus sliding out of control, careening off the road. The other passengers screaming. Underneath it: the sound of sharp things breaking and blunt things—heads, elbows, backs—slamming.

Then I'm flying forward, falling. A sharp, hard pain pierces the side of my head.

Everything goes black.

3

I wake up to a light so blue and harsh its mere force seems to pry my eyelids apart. The air smells like antiseptic, and I'm lying in a bed that isn't my own. Wires extend from a machine beside me like thin plastic tentacles.

I'm in a hospital room.

When I try to sit up, it feels as if someone is plucking the inside of my skull like a string instrument, but without the relief of music. I lie back down and groan to make it stop.

"You're okay, hon," someone with a thick Southern accent says, rubbing my shoulder. "How are you feeling?"

The assault of murky, too-bright light slowly shifts into the image of a middle-aged woman in green scrubs standing by my bed.

I make an incoherent sound, but the nurse seems to be fluent in those because she nods and says, "Yes, I know. You hit your head during the crash. Do you remember that, Addison?"

My mind drifts back to the bus.

The spinning.

The boy a few rows ahead.

It takes three tries before I manage to get any words out. "Y-y-yes. Is everyone okay?"

The nurse nods. "You were all extremely lucky. Some minor injuries here and there, but everyone's going to be just fine. With how slick those roads are tonight, it could have been a lot worse. Maine in winter is no joke."

She keeps talking, explaining that we're in Greenvale Hospital, forty minutes from Lyndale, and about ten minutes from the crash site. That we were brought here by ambulance.

"Can you sit up for me?" the nurse—a tag on her shirt says MEGAN—asks a few minutes later. Her voice is soothing and maternal, and it makes me feel small and safe. The way I did in elementary school, when my mom would look after me on days I was home sick. I slide up in bed, and she adjusts the pillows behind me, then lets me lean back. It turns out I'm not connected to any of the wires by the machine, so my movement is not restricted. But there's a bandage on the top of my right arm—a cut, the nurse explains, but nothing too serious.

Nurse Megan hands me two white tablets and a small paper cup half full of water. "Those will help with your head."

The pills are huge; I can still feel them in the back of my throat after I've swallowed.

"So we've finally gotten hold of your mom. She was so, so worried on the phone, and I understand she's on her way over as we speak."

Any other time, I'd roll my eyes at that. Of course my mom is *so, so worried*. Of course she's jumped into her car,

9

ready to come and save me from a thousand unseeable dangers, but right now, I only feel relieved.

I could have died tonight.

"And"—Nurse Megan scans the room and then picks up my viola case and hands it to me—"I believe this belongs to a Miss Addison Sullivan."

"Thank you," I say, reaching for it. I've never been more grateful for the labels across the back and stitched on the inside. I open the case and immediately begin scouring every inch of my viola for scratches or dents.

"The medics said they used it to ID you before they found your proper ID."

"Oh," I say. I like the idea of that, of being found by my instrument—the same way I feel found when I play.

"What's the verdict? Will it live?" Nurse Megan asks with a chuckle, and I'm embarrassed to realize I've been holding my breath. But my viola looks fine.

"I think so," I say, shutting the case. "So, the other passengers . . . they're here, too?"

For some reason, the smiling boy's face keeps appearing in my mind. I want to ask about him, where he is, but I realize I don't even know his name. And is it creepy to do that? I mean, we had one conversation.

"They are. Brought most of you in ambulances. Are you worried about someone in particular?"

"Yes. Well, no. I mean . . . we just met on the bus tonight. It's not like we're friends or anything." Despite the water, my throat is still parched. "We talked a little. I just wanted to make sure he was okay."

If my rambling is evidence that my faculties are returning to me, I'm not sure being without them is any great loss.

The nurse gives me a weird look now. Knowing. "I'll see what I can find out for you. Do you know his name?"

I shake my head. "But he's tall. My age-ish. Big smile."

Nurse Megan is grinning at me now, like she missed the part where he's a boy *I just met,* like any second now she'll break into a soliloquy about young love or Shakespeare.

Luckily, just then the doctor raps twice on the door and comes in. Dr. Kennedy is tall and in her mid-thirties, with fashionably cropped hair and tired-looking eyes behind tortoiseshell glasses. It seems like she's been up for hours, but she smiles kindly at me and says it's nice to see me awake. I guess she saw me when I was first brought in. She has me sit up now and checks my reflexes, shines a light into my eyes, and exchanges medical-speak with Nurse Megan.

"I think we'll keep you overnight, Addison," Dr. Kennedy says. "Just to make sure you don't have a concussion and that that head is doing okay." She inspects my right temple, which is not bandaged or anything, just heavily bruised. They don't know what hit it, and I don't remember, either.

After Dr. Kennedy leaves, Nurse Megan follows her, winking at me in the doorway. "I'll see if I can find your *friend.*"

"Thanks," I say nonchalantly, but I feel my cheeks heating up. Thank God my skin is dark enough that you can barely tell when I'm blushing.

I'm curious to know what she'll find out about the boy. Does he live in Lyndale? What is his name? How injured is he?

I lean back and shut my eyes, trying to appreciate the lessening pain in my head, courtesy of the painkillers.

A few minutes later, Nurse Megan bursts into my room.

"Good news! Your young man is doing well. Broke his elbow, but they're putting it into a cast as we speak," she says.

"Oh, thanks," I say, suppressing the urge to say *not my young man*.

"His name is Bo, in case you were wondering," she says, coming around to my side of the bed. When she reaches me, I see that she's frowning. "Not that it's my place to judge, but he's a little bit sour, isn't he?"

"Sour?" I repeat while the image of his smile flashes in my mind. God, she didn't tell him I was asking for him or anything embarrassing, did she? I mean, maybe it freaked him out and that's why he seemed annoyed. . . .

"The lip rings. The black hair. I'm sure it's my bias talking because my daughter's ex—well, one of them—was exactly like—"

"Oh, Goth Guy!" I say, remembering the glare he'd given me for talking. "That's not who I meant."

"It's not?" She is visibly relieved. "I thought he seemed a little old for you, too. Who do you mean, then?"

I describe him again, the best I can. I tell her we picked him up at Raddick, where the elderly couple got on. That he's tall and has a local accent and wasn't wearing glasses.

"Hmm, maybe I missed him. I have to do some charts, but I'll check with the ER after. He might have been taken to another unit."

When Nurse Megan comes back a few minutes later, she still has no lead. "There's no record of him. He was probably well enough not to be admitted," she says, sounding disappointed that she won't get to play matchmaker tonight. "Sorry."

"That's okay," I say, feeling silly.

It's silly that I sent my nurse on a wild-goose chase to find a boy I spoke to for a few minutes at most. It's silly that the memory of his smile is stuck to my mind when I don't know the first thing about him.

Still, it feels a little sad to think that I'll never know his name.

4

"I knew something like this would happen." Those are my mother's first words when she bursts into my hospital room. "I *knew* it."

She seems to be on the verge of tears as she outmaneuvers the bandage on my arm to envelop me in a tight hug. She smells like the berry tea she loves, and I shut my eyes and breathe in the scent of her. I don't know whether it's exhaustion or the scare of the bus crash, but my own eyes prick with unexpected tears.

I blink them back quickly, because if my mother is always looking for reasons to worry, I am always looking for reasons not to worry her.

"And you wanted to *drive* tonight," she says when she finally releases me. "It's snowing now and it's coming down hard. Even getting here, I had to go at a snail's pace. You'd have been sitting alone in a ditch somewhere."

"I'm sorry," I say, technically apologizing for what could have happened instead of what did. "Where's Caleb? Did you call Dad?"

"I did," is all the acknowledgment she gives my last question. "Caleb was having car trouble again, and I wanted to get down here as soon as I got the call, so I couldn't wait for him to get home. He told me to tell you he's glad you're okay, though," Mom says, sitting on the edge of my bed.

"Thanks," I say. What Mom doesn't know is that "car trouble" is code for the rare occasions when my older brother goes to a party. They are usually high school parties, because parties thrown by people who go to the community college he attends in Lyndale are famously lame. Though maybe nothing is lamer than the fact that he has nowhere better to be on a Saturday night, despite having graduated from high school a year and a half ago. The worst thing I can imagine is being stuck the way my brother is, held in place by some invisible force, your entire life on repeat, when there's so much else out there.

"What have they done to you?" Mom asks, jostling me out of my thoughts. She's inspecting my bandage now, the thin hospital gown I'm wearing.

"Who? The aliens?"

Showing no relief that my sense of humor is still intact, Mom ignores me. "The nurse said they were keeping you overnight for observation because you lost consciousness. And that they had given you something for your head? How is it feeling now?"

"Better," I say.

"When they called, I thought . . ." Her voice is shaking

15

and she looks small in this brightly lit room, the way I felt when I first woke up. Maybe hospital rooms make everyone small. "If something had happened to you, Addie . . . I was so afraid."

"I'm okay," I tell her.

She nods, but she doesn't seem convinced. To my mother, it's always as if the worst has already happened. Or that it's always, perpetually, on the verge of happening. "Thank God you were close to Lyndale," she says, rubbing my back while I lean forward.

"Your father is in Florida tonight." She says this as if "Florida" is code for the second level of hell, and not where he always has his layovers. In fact, before my parents split up five years ago, they used to talk about us moving there permanently, since my dad seemed to spend more time there than he did with us in Lyndale. "I called him, but it went to voice mail. I had to *email* him. To tell him his daughter was in the hospital."

"He's probably sleeping off his jet lag or something," I say, but Mom just half snorts, like she can't even bother with a full one.

She settles into the rollaway bed Nurse Megan arranged to have brought in for her and turns on the TV, flipping distractedly through the channels. Naturally, she stops at Channel Se7en, the station she works for, and we watch it for a while until Nurse Megan knocks and brings Mom a blanket. I told Mom she could go home and come back for me tomorrow, but she dismissed the suggestion like it wasn't even an option.

An hour later, with the TV off, I start to feel groggy and my mind slowly hums to a stop. It's peaceful and quiet when I drift to sleep. But then, what feels like mere seconds later, my eyes fly open and every trace of sleep is gone.

In the dark, my mind is wild with thoughts of spinning buses. The foreign shadows on the hospital wall morph into ghosts.

You're awake.

You're alive.

It's okay, I tell myself.

"Air on the G String" reverbs through my mind, the whole evening reverbs through my mind, and I think of the boy again and wonder where he is tonight.

"Go to sleep," Mom says softly into the darkness.

"How do you know I'm not asleep?"

"Mother's intuition." I hear the smile in her voice. My mother told me once that with both Caleb and me, she would stay awake watching our chests rise and fall at night when we were babies to make sure we were alive. She felt almost that her watching us kept it happening—the rising and the falling of our chests, the breathing. And she'd do it until Dad dragged her away from our cribs and to bed. Knowing we were okay made her sleep better.

I hate that she still believes the closer we are to her, the safer we are. Her belief kept me from sleepovers and swing sets and the underappreciated horrors that are bouncy castles (she actually says this about them), and sometimes I'm afraid it could keep me from the rest of my life. She would wrap me and Caleb in Bubble Wrap and tuck us into her china cabinet if she could.

Usually I have no patience for her obsession with keeping us sheltered, but tonight her presence makes me feel safe and

stable, like the bus has finally stopped spinning, like everything is going to be okay.

"Night, Mom."

"Good night, Addie."

I try to fall asleep so she can.

5

"Lord in heaven, girl!" Katy says in an over-the-top Southern accent (my fault for telling her about my nurse) when she sees me on Monday, holding her arms open all the way from her locker to mine, a length of about fifteen lockers. When she reaches me, she crushes my body against hers. "I nearly had a Cardiac Event. I should have gone with you!"

I laugh, choking a little on her lavender perfume. "Why? You'd just have gotten hurt and given *your* mother a Cardiac Event."

"I would not," she says indignantly, referring to the insinuation of getting hurt—not the part about her mother, because Katy's mother *would* have had a heart attack, and Katy *would* have enjoyed it.

I peel off my coat and stuff it into my locker. "Let me take a good look at you," Katy says, clasping my cheeks in her palms. "You look like you got punched."

"I got, like, four hours of sleep on Saturday night and then three last night," I say, suddenly self-conscious about my puffy eyes. I'd been hoping they weren't obvious.

"Poor thing," Katy hums. The pain in my head is completely gone, and my thick black hair is covering the bruise on my temple. "And the arm?" She gives my bandaged arm a thorough inspection, then says, "Shouldn't affect your playing. I give you a few more decades."

"Thanks, Doctor." I pick up all the books I'll need until third period.

Katy is carrying her own violin case, even though we'll have time to go back to our lockers before orchestra; she claims to need the time to socialize between periods. Even now, as we make our way to English class, she's waving at and small-talking with people all the way down the hall.

Sometimes the fact that Katy and I are best friends seems like a minor miracle. When I changed schools after the first year of middle school, I found a small group of girls to follow around for the next two years, never fully included and never getting beyond surface-level friendship. Katy moved here from D.C. in ninth grade with her mom, and from the second she laid eyes on me in the viola section, she hated me. I realized quickly that she was jealous of my playing, and I tried not to take it personally. Mrs. Dubois *is* a little partial with solos—I've had seven in our last nine concerts, even though the viola is not the most popular solo instrument—and it wasn't the first time a fellow musicophile hadn't liked me.

I learned fast, though, that Katy's hatred was on a different level from any I'd been used to. Acting was, after all, her first passion; music was her second, her backup. I'd walk into practice and the laughter would abruptly stop, with Katy shooting me a quick look of disdain or guilt, making it seem like her group been talking about me, even if they hadn't. Or if I whispered to ask which bar Mrs. Dubois was talking about, she'd turn icily, pretending she hadn't heard.

It was three months after she'd moved here—when she found out through the grapevine that I had no intention of ever applying to Juilliard, her holy grail—that she started speaking to me. That day, Mr. Quinn had been showing us a video in bio class, something about how new memory procedures had revolutionized neuroscience and the treatment of trauma, and we were supposed to be taking notes so we could debate the ethical pros and cons. I'd just scrawled *Informed Consent* on the top of my page when Katy, who was sitting behind me, tapped my shoulder with her pencil. I turned, and she tilted her head in the direction of Mr. Quinn, dozing with his mouth open at an empty desk near us, a tiny line of drool beginning to snake down his chin. I couldn't suppress my grin, and Katy coughed to cover a laugh.

Before we bonded over music, Katy and I bonded over people. Over Mrs. Dubois and the loud, clashing patterns she wore, though she herself was timid and sweet and so quiet we couldn't hear her speak unless we were silent.

Today, as she passes us in the hallway, Mrs. Dubois is wearing one of her signature outfits, a flowing turquoise skirt with bright yellow diagonal stripes, and a brown shirt with orange polka dots. One slight lift of Katy's left eyebrow, her patented expression, and we both giggle quietly.

We bonded over Paulie Wentz, a perpetually sunburned wannabe surfer, whose presence in senior high orchestra can only be explained by Mrs. Dubois's adamant belief that music is about not how well you play but how *joyfully* you play. Paulie is joyful all right, and actually a nice kid, but there is no better description for his playing of the French horn than glorified fart sounds. Katy and I physically have to turn our bodies away from each other when he plays, or we will be gone forever.

And we bonded over Gilbert and Sullivan. Katy is Gilbert, since my last name is Sullivan, but their personalities fit us, too. Sullivan composed some of the most incredible operetta music, and Gilbert wrote the stories that went along with the music. To Katy, it is the other way around—the music molds around the story, covering it, accompanying it, but for me, the music always comes first. It has to. We argue about it all the time.

We disagree on Juilliard, too. My first choice is NYU, major undeclared, but Katy swears she came out of the womb intending to go to Juilliard for theater.

"The plan was for the doctors to cut the umbilical cord, clean me up a little, and then send me straight there. But my mother missed the memo and kept me for *seventeen years*." She says this with such solemnness that I always laugh, no matter how many times I've heard it.

I discovered the viola in fifth grade, the first year we had orchestra in elementary school, and everyone went scrambling for the flute, recorder, or clarinet. Miss Root played us short recordings of all the different instruments in an orchestra to introduce us to their "voices" so we could find which of them best matched ours. For the viola, she played Lionel Tertis's performance of Brahms's Viola Sonata in F Minor, and I fell in love with its full, heavy sound. Miss Root said it was one of the few instruments that used the alto clef, and I thought maybe that explained why it sounded a little bit lonely. Even when the melody it played was joyful, I liked that its sound was tinged with a trace of sadness and that the pockets of space between the notes were so deep, it sounded like you could hide entire worlds in there.

Katy can't understand how I could possibly be interested in another school—though the irony is that she would not have befriended me if I had wanted to go to Julliard. It's so odd, now that I think about it, how she seemed to figure that being friends with me somehow affected the probability of her getting in, or *not* getting in, as the case might be. But we'd spent hours filling out application forms together and editing the essay she sent off to Juilliard in December. My NYU application was a month later, in January, and we'd worked on it together, too.

Juilliard—being totally immersed in music—has just never been something I wanted. Music, unless you write it, is always vicarious. It's written by a composer in a particular manner with a particular style. It's somebody else's story, and even if you can relate to it or find yourself in it or *hide* yourself in it, it doesn't belong to you. When I explain this to Katy, she always says something like, "Well, write your own story, Sullivan." But you actually need a story in order to write one. You need peaks and valleys, crescendos and decrescendos, and things that wreck you and put you back together. It's not like I'm some tortured emo kid; I have a pretty happy life. But there's something in me that's always wanted a little more than I know.

I love my viola. Many times a week, I play so hard I sweat, play till all the world melts away in the heat, and hours feel like seconds, or seconds like hours. And sometimes when I stop playing, the world seems so empty and quiet that I just want to curl up at the foot of my bed and cry.

I love losing myself in the sensation of playing, in the distraction and competitiveness of orchestra, and feeling more awake than ever when I do. But I want to love something else just as much. Something that's a part of *my* story. A new place, a little street-side café, a class in college I signed up for just because, a person I haven't met yet.

The truth is, I could probably find those things at Juilliard—or anywhere else, for that matter. My mom is hoping it'll be at the community college Caleb goes to, at least for a year. But I want to go someplace where I can't hide behind anything—not the town I've lived in all my life or my overzealous parents. Not even music.

6

"So do you think Bus Boy is from Lyndale?" Katy asks, rummaging in the compartment between us for something. The mall parking lot is crowded for a weekday afternoon, but there isn't much else to do in a town this aggressively on the smaller side of medium, and I fully expect to run into half the people we've just been cooped up for hours with at school. "Check the glove box for me?"

I comply, rifling through a mess of insurance cards and hair ties and tiny bottles of lotion, despite the fact that I have no idea what we're looking for.

I told Katy that I met a cute boy on the bus, even though a minute-long conversation qualifies more as a non-story than anything else. Still, the thing about best friends is that they make you feel like your non-stories matter.

"I have no clue," I say as we both climb out of Katy's car. She stands with her hands on her hips, frowning. I can't tell whether she's trying to think of where to look next or just unimpressed with the lack of information I have on Bus Boy.

"Well, how do we send out a search party if you can't give me a less generic description than *tall and cute*? What did he look like? How tall is tall? What color hair did he have?"

"It was dark and he was wearing a hat!" I say defensively. "Anyway, he's probably not even from around here."

"That's too bad. Now, if only you'd be open to letting me find you a hot guy. Or at least letting us go to places where you could meet one." To Katy's disappointment, the fake IDs she got us almost two years ago have gone untouched—mine, Kathleen Kelly, after the character from *You've Got Mail,* one of my favorite movies, and Katy's, Beatrice Lane, Beatrice for the character in the play *Much Ado About Nothing.* "I mean, you're seventeen and you act like the freaking black widow."

"The spider or the superhero?"

Katy rolls her eyes, pulling open the trunk of her car. "Neither. You act like you're completely over love."

"Um," I say. "I think I'd have to have been under or *in* it, ever, to be over love. Pretty sure making out with Acrobat-Tongue Grant in seventh grade doesn't count as love."

"My point exactly," Katy says before her head disappears into the trunk of her car.

"What are you looking for?" I ask when she comes up for air a few seconds later.

"My silver bracelet—the one I always wear? I've told you that, like, three times," she says, irritated.

"Oh, right," I say, though I have no memory of this.

"Just the way I *told* you we were hanging out after school

26

and then I had to chase down the bus for two blocks to stop you from leaving with it. Exercise-induced asthma is no joke. And what senior even voluntarily takes the bus? God."

She's joking, but I can hear the annoyance in Katy's voice. I have been a little out of it all day. Apparently, two nights tossing and turning will do that to a person.

"It was *not* two blocks," I argue. "Anyway, I forgot. Sorry. And taking the bus is not voluntary—I told you my mom wouldn't let me have the car this morning. She wouldn't even let me out of her sight all day yesterday."

"Attachment disorder. I don't think I've seen a more severe case of it," Katy says in a know-it-all voice, shaking her head as she shuts the trunk. "When one individual is unreasonably and detrimentally attached to another." Katy's mother is a clinical psychologist, which is where Katy picks up phrases that sound like they've come from some yellowing medical textbook. It really should have turned my best friend into the best-adjusted seventeen-year-old in all of Lyndale, but it has only served as fuel for her lifelong hypochondria. Katy doesn't get headaches; she gets migraines. Anaphylaxis instead of allergies. Influenza instead of a cold. Everything is a Psychological Episode.

I've always suspected this had something to do with Katy's father leaving, remarrying by the time she was five, and sending gifts in lieu of visiting. Her mother works long, hard hours, but she does respond to crises. If Katy wants attention, she—or someone she knows—had better be On the Brink.

We maneuver our way through the parking lot, sticking close together so we don't lose each other. There is one

27

other high school in town—Meridian—and it seems their entire student population had the same idea of crashing the mall, too.

I don't really know anyone from Meridian High, while Katy can't go anywhere without seeing people she knows.

Within seconds of getting into the movie theater lobby, Katy is kicking a girl in the kneebow, and they are squealing and hugging and talking about community theater stuff. I never feel more out of place than when I'm among Katy's other friends. They, like Katy, are a certain breed of people: bright, confident, funny. They talk louder than they have to; they grab one another's shoulders and hands and cheeks. They exclaim and lunge and weep and *enunciate*. I feel lonely in such a specific way around them—like only half of me has shown up.

Some of Katy's friends are nice enough—once or twice, someone came up and started talking to me as if we knew each other, though Katy wasn't even there. I didn't want to be rude, but I could only stare at them listlessly before mumbling something and escaping. When I told Katy about it, she said it sounded like so-and-so from Meridian, and not to worry about it.

Still, these ones—a girl with white-blond hair and her boyfriend—are acting as if I'm invisible, so I tell Katy I'm going to get our tickets and then head for the concession area. I'm looking around for the shortest line to join when I see him.

A hundred-watt smile.

Tall. Skinny.

The boy from the bus.

And he's looking right at me.

Before I think better of it, I am making my way over to

28

him. He's standing behind the concession counter but not manning a register.

"Hey!" I exclaim as I reach him. "It's you!"

"Hi!" he says brightly, looking just as pleased to see me. That warm feeling twirls in my stomach again. Where does a person learn to smile like that? On anybody else, it would look goofy, but he's pulling it off.

He adjusts his black cap, the Cineplex's logo—CINEXPERIENCE—stamped across it and on the rest of his uniform.

"Are you okay? You just disappeared after the accident, and you weren't at the hospital. I was . . . looking for you."

His eyes twinkle a little bit when I say that. And they're gray, the closest to silver a human's eyes are allowed to be. I didn't notice that two nights ago. "You were?"

My face gets warm, ears hot.

"Well, kind of. I mean, *I* wasn't. The nurse . . . my . . ." *Shut up, Addie.* I need a diversion. "So you work here?"

He looks down at his black CINEXPERIENCE T-shirt, then back up at me. "How awkward would it be if I didn't and I was wearing this?"

I laugh. "Well, it seems like a fun place to work. Cheap Movie Mondays excluded," I say just as—as if on cue—someone's shoulder rams into mine, pushing me forward.

"Shit, sorry!" the person says. I turn around and see that the voice belongs to an Indian guy with short black hair and dark rectangular glasses. He is carrying about five bags of popcorn, three supersized drinks, and a bag of cotton candy. No wonder he didn't see where he was going.

"That's okay," I say, about to turn away when the boy's

expression suddenly changes. His eyes widen in something like surprise or recognition or confusion.

"Hey . . . there," he says. He's looking at me now in a way that can only be described as gaping, and it's making me uncomfortable. I want to go back to talking to Bus Boy, who is also witnessing this.

"Am I in your way?" I ask at last, because I can't think of why else he'd still be standing here. That seems to shake him out of his stupor.

"No, um, you're fine," the boy says, readjusting his grip on the bags of popcorn in his arms. Another second's hesitation. "Well, bye," he says, and takes a step backward.

"Dude, we're going in without you!" a male voice calls from somewhere across the lobby, presumably to him, and then breaks into a fit of snickers.

The Indian boy rolls his eyes, sighs, and finally turns around to head back to his friends. There are so many people clustered throughout the lobby that I lose him before I see which group he joins.

I turn back to Bus Boy, who is looking at me with an amused expression.

"Sorry, that was weird," I say to Bus Boy as a woman wearing the same black CINEXPERIENCE shirt he is reaches across him on the counter for a pile of napkins. She glances up at me. "What'd you say?" she asks, giving me a look that is both puzzled and impatient.

"Um, nothing," I say, waiting for her to realize that I was not talking to her.

She pauses a second, then narrows her eyes at me and goes

back to work. Is she annoyed at me for distracting Bus Boy from his work?

"Maybe I should let you—" I start to say, but before I can finish speaking, someone is grabbing my arm and yanking me across the lobby.

"Katy! Why are you *yanking* me?"

"And why are *you* spacing out in some corner of the lobby when you were supposed to be getting us tickets? Look how much longer the line is now!" We stop at the end of a line on the opposite side of the lobby from where I just saw Bus Boy. "I know you haven't been sleeping well and are possibly concussed and yada yada yada, but I swear it's like you're having a Psychological Episode."

"I found him!" I say, completely ignoring her previous statements. "Bus Boy! I just saw him."

Katy finally releases her iron grip on my jacket sleeve. "You saw him *here*? Why would he be here? Did you talk to him?"

I nod, unable to stop the grin from spreading across my face. "Not for long, but yeah."

"So what's his name? Did you get his number?"

"I was getting to it when *someone* dragged me away," I say.

"I didn't even see him," Katy says, a frown creasing her face. "Where is he?"

I look back across the lobby, but there are too many people in the way. "He's all the way on the other side."

"I did really want to see this movie, but we can blow it off to chat him up, if you want," Katy says, wriggling her eyebrows at me.

I give a long-suffering sigh. "No, let's see the movie." The lady at the counter didn't look amused by me hanging around to talk, and I don't want Bus Boy to get in trouble, but I act like I'm making the ultimate sacrifice for Katy's benefit. "The things I do for you."

She bumps my shoulder with hers. "The things *I* do for you. You don't even know."

As we wait, she starts telling me about how she'd been hanging out with Mitch Enns yesterday and had just driven him home—"Hanging out sounds a lot like making out," I interrupt to point out—when she realized her bracelet was gone. I feel guilty for not remembering when she first told me it was missing, because she sounds more upset about it than I've seen her about anything in months. But she lights up quickly when she recognizes someone in the line next to ours. "Addie, this is Lena from Act! Out!"

Me and the girl wearing a winter jacket over a spandex volleyball uniform exchange polite "Nice to meet yous," but she and Katy do most of the talking while our respective lines inch forward. I'm still mildly annoyed that I didn't get to say a proper goodbye to Bus Boy. Not to mention find out his name.

We are apparently doomed to minute-long conversations. Still, I'm relieved he's okay. And the fact that he lives in Lyndale means I have a good chance of seeing him again.

I replay today's conversation in my mind.

My mind hitches a little on his smile. The way it starts so slowly and then stretches, magnifying quickly across his face. Maybe I *am* having a Psychological Episode because it makes me think of physics: How quickly does the twitch of lip corners accelerate into the kind of smile that makes a stomach somersault?

Another question: Am I so starved for male attention, as Katy claims, that I overreact every time a boy smiles at me?

We reach the counter, and Katy is starting to spout off our order when I realize that it's not that I'm desperate or lame or lovesick.

His smile makes me feel something I've never felt before.

7

BEFORE
*Early July
(eighteen months ago)*

Thick air sticks to my body, hanging on so tightly it's hard to believe other seasons exist that aren't summer. I sigh with relief as I enter the air-conditioned movie store, my phone buzzing in the pocket of my dress. I try to tuck my hair out of my face, but it is prime frizz season and my hair won't be reasoned with. I inherited my mom's aversion to heat and the same tight ringlets as my father's sisters from St. Vincent, so July is always a delight.

The store looks dead, which isn't a surprise, since nobody really borrows DVDs anymore. At Home Movies is the last of its kind in Lyndale, and adults like my mom who have lived here forever and can remember the days of video stores and ice cream trucks and children playing in the streets till sundown are weirdly nostalgic and protective of it.

Though the checkout area is empty, I can hear movement, muttering going on underneath the counter. I'm enjoying the store's miraculous coolness too much to wonder about the source of the sound. I pull my phone out and brace myself for one of twenty texts from my mom, reminding me to grab one thing or the other for our family movie night. Or one of twenty texts from Katy, detailing her, by my count, decade-long road trip.

The message is a picture of four pairs of bare feet on asphalt, a crowd of toes. I pick out Katy's feet by the black nail polish she started sporting when school let out. In another picture, she's standing beside a road sign that says CURVES AHEAD, pouting seductively and holding her hands up like a show queen. The silver bracelet her dad sent her three years ago that she never takes off is catching sunlight, so it looks like she's giving off both angelic glow and sex appeal. It's very confusing.

There is no actual text. No *Missing you, boo!* or *How are you holding up?* which I don't expect from Katy to begin with. But I do expect *some* sympathy, if only out of consideration for my plight. She is exactly where I want to be at this moment. In a car, breeze blowing though her piss-straight hair (her words, not mine), on her way to New York City for three whole weeks. A trip being funded by Katy's dad, of course. New York is, like, seven hours from Maine, but Katy and her theater friends are making a whole trip out of it, stopping over at Hampton Beach and a million other places. *I,* on the other hand, am picking up DVDs for a movie night with my mom and older brother.

I spent all of April and May pleading with my parents to let me go on the trip with Katy, and all of June pouting when they refused, derailing my plans for a great summer and possibly my only chance to see New York before I move there. If they *let* me move there.

Being stuck at home is bad enough, but it was during the summer when Dad left four years ago, so July and August are famously gloomy in my family. Katy says it's like our version of seasonal affective disorder.

Maybe it makes me a horrible person—I get that it's sad my parents aren't together—but I don't feel as upset about it as everyone else in my family does. It just feels like so long ago.

Still, we rallied last week for an awkward dinner at Café Amore to celebrate my sixteenth birthday and Caleb's high school graduation a couple of weeks ago. My parents are always self-conscious when we're out anywhere as a family. We used to get a lot of weird looks from strangers, acquaintances staring too long, squeezing my mom's shoulder as they passed or patting Caleb's head uninvited. When I was younger, there were even times I wondered whether it was because my dad is black and my mom is white. But the weirdness happened even when my parents weren't around. I got strange looks from classmates' parents and the occasional special treatment from teachers; it was sympathy more than gawking. I guess my mom being on Channel Se7en makes her moderately famous in a smallish town, and the gossip about my parents splitting up was big news at some point. The odd attention happens much less now, but I remember my parents hated it then and still seem wary of it happening again. So our celebratory dinner basically consisted of uncomfortable small talk, Caleb looking like there were a million places he'd rather be, and me overcompensating to make everyone feel more at ease.

On weekday mornings for the next two months, I'll have lessons at the home of Clarence, a retired viola instructor Mrs. Dubois introduced me to last year. Mostly, it's an excuse to play for Clarence, since her arthritis prevents her from doing so now and she says recordings never sound the same. So I'll play pieces I'm working on and she'll give me notes and we'll talk music for an hour. Then I'll spend the rest of the day biding time, practicing, and reading (something off next year's reading list so I'll be ahead in English class in the fall) before doing it all over again.

The one and only relief about being home this summer is not being crushed in a car with Katy's the-*yuh*-trical friends. I was drawn to Katy for her energy, her commitment to being herself, but some ugly, secret part of me wonders whether *I'm* Katy's best friend because she needs someone she doesn't have to compete with. For Juilliard, for attention. Whether the moment something or someone better comes along, she'll move on to that. Because if there's one thing Katy is good at, it's moving on.

I push the thought out of my mind now and stare at a shelf of movies with foreign names. My mother's exact orders: "Something emotional but uplifting." Nothing against the foreign film industry, but none of these covers really scream "uplifting" to me. Maybe because I'm not fluent in Hungarian.

The last couple of weeks, Mom has unsuccessfully insisted on family movie nights with me and my brother. Unsuccessfully because we're not the kind of family that does well with bonding time and shared space and basic eye contact. Such advanced stuff is for TV families. My brother likes to keep to himself, holed up in his room, and I like classical music and imagining myself someplace far away. There's not a whole lot of overlap between us.

Right then I hear a noise from the checkout section and turn to watch a boy leap over the counter and hurry toward me.

"Hi!" he shouts, smiling, and a little out of breath. "Welcome to At Home Movies! Can I help you find anything?"

I blink at him, alarmed. "Yeah, I'm looking for a movie?"

The boy laughs, and the wave of hair at the front of his head bops. He smooths his hands over his shirt and says, "Sorry. My dad makes us greet every customer with enthusiasm, but I didn't notice you come in."

He's got the enthusiasm part, all right.

"That's okay," I say.

"What are you looking for?"

I tell him my mom asked for a foreign film that is emotional but uplifting. He frowns at the collection of DVDs on the wall.

Finally he says, "Does she like slashers?"

His response is so unexpected that I burst out laughing. "I've never asked, but I'm going to guess no."

He isn't laughing when he says, "That's too bad." He starts to walk toward another section, and I follow him, curious. "There's this Italian guy, Rinieri Ciano?" I shake my head no. I have not been indoctrinated into the world of slasher films. "He makes some of the best—like, just *sick* movies. He's a legend."

There's a good chance I'm gaping at him, because he

quickly adds, "I don't mean disturbing or scary. 'Sick' as in 'good.' In fact, I'd classify them as comedy. Satire. They are horrodies—horror comedies. It's ketchup and blue string for veins, stuffed socks for intestines."

I am definitely gaping because he laughs now. A laugh that instantly makes me feel warm all over, negating the air-conditioning, and I don't even mind. "You have to see it. Like, you know it's fake, and that's the whole point. It's Ciano's way of commenting on filmmaking and life in general."

"What's his comment, exactly?" I ask.

"I'd say art, how to tell stories." He says it so seriously, so pensively, that now even my ears are warm. As if he is telling me a secret, whispering it inside them. "Will you try one?"

"Okay," I say. Then quickly add, "Maybe not for my mom, though. I thought, er, *Le coeur est une montagne* looked good."

My face heats even more at my abysmal French.

"Ah, *oui*," the boy says, grinning at me as he reaches down to pick up a DVD case. His *oui*, which sounds like a New England boy speaking French (and by that I mean it is almost as bad as my attempt), makes me feel better. "I'd start with this one—*The Sea in the Garden*." He is back to being serious, and I realize that this boy does not play around with his slasher movies.

"I'm here all week," he says a few minutes later, when he's checking out my movies. "I want to hear what you think."

"Okay." It occurs to me then that I might hate his recommendations, *really* hate them, and then what will I say?

"If I'm ever not out front, I'm most likely in the break-room, so just ask for Zach."

Zach. It suits him somehow, an energetic, slasher-loving boy.

"Thanks," I say.

"No problem, Miss Sullivan," he says, bringing up my mom's profile on the computer.

"Addie," I correct.

"Addie." He is trying my name out, too, seeing if it fits me, fits my big, easily tangled black hair and the way I carry myself, except he is doing it out loud. He must've decided it does, because he grins at me one more time.

A bright, radiant smile that makes stepping outside and back into the heat wave on a cloudless summer day in Lyndale seem like stepping into the cool shade. I see spots as I get on my bike.

That night I watch *The Sea in the Garden* on my computer, just so I can come back the next day.

8

BEFORE
Early July

"Addie!" Zach exclaims when I walk into the movie store. He's beaming as if I am an old friend. As I get closer to the counter, though, his expression turns serious. "What's the verdict?"

"Horrible. Really, really horrible," I say, watching as his face falls.

"Really?" he asks quietly, disappointed.

"He nearly married his *sister*!" I say dramatically, and understanding lights up Zach's face.

"You're talking about *Le pontagne*!" There is visible relief in his face, and a smile crawls across it.

"*Le something montagne*," I say, glancing at the DVD case in my hand. "*Le something* shit*agne*. Though my mom loved it."

Zach laughs now, and even though it seems like something he does easily, I feel proud. He slides the movies from me and puts his elbows on the counter, leaning forward. "So the *real* verdict? I promise I won't mind. You can tell me if you hated it."

I can't. Not with his dancing eyes and his lips tilted up in a half smile, on their mark, ready to full-on sprint into a grin.

"It was good," I say carefully. "Kind of confusing."

Zach watches me, nodding slowly.

"Like, I just didn't get what made the guy snap when he'd been so normal the whole movie."

He nods again, squinting to take in what I am saying.

"And it was fake. Really, really fake." He is fully smiling now. "I think I saw the ketchup bottle in the corner of the screen once."

"I know!" Zach laughs, elated. "It's fucking fantastic."

His laugh is contagious and I laugh, too. There is a ding then as a customer, a middle-aged woman wearing a high ponytail and gym shorts, comes in to return a pile of DVDs.

"So what else do you have?" I ask. I didn't lie to Zach. The movie *was* good. Weird, but good. And different. More importantly, it gave me an excuse to come back here today.

"I could tell just from looking at you that you'd appreciate it," he says as we walk to the Horror section.

What does *that* mean? "I look like a slasher chick?" I joke.

His eyes take in all of me, and his cheeks redden the slightest bit. "Just, you know, someone who would understand."

I don't know what it means, but I like that answer.

I follow him to the checkout, and someone who looks like a carbon copy of Zach in thirty years comes out to join us. He is just as tall, his hair a reddish brown and thin on top.

"Oh, damn, I'm so sorry," the man says, addressing me. "He's pushing Ciano on you?"

"He's not pushing," I say at the same time Zach says, "She *likes* it, Dad."

The man—Zach's dad—raises both hands in surrender. "It's an acquired taste. But at least he's giving you one DVD at a time, not the whole collection." He turns to his son. "You could do that, you know. They're not exactly in high demand."

Zach keeps his eyes on the computer when he says, "I want to hear what she thinks of each one."

"Oh," is all his father says.

Oh, is all I can think as Zach hands me the DVD, signature smile in place. And then I am stumbling out the door, heart fluttering a little bit. I'm trying to figure out how other girls manage to mount bikes while wearing a skirt, praying he isn't watching me.

Hoping he is.

9

AFTER
January

Since he's just gotten back from his trip—and I guess he wanted to see me after he heard about the bus crash—I spend Tuesday night at my dad's, even though I rarely see him on weekdays.

My father lives in a tiny apartment, in the busiest part of downtown Lyndale. He isn't in it often, but even when he's home, when he's not flying, it's not my favorite place in the world. I love my dad, but I feel like we exist on separate islands. Like with my brother, whenever we are in a room together, it's as if there's this enormous gulf, a wedge between us that nothing can fill.

The sad thing is, I remember that my dad was my favorite person in the world when I was a kid. I remember him hoisting me into the air, letting me walk with my feet on top of his in the grocery store, teaching me to ride a bike in the driveway of our old house on the east side of town. He bought me my first viola. He called me Sunshine, in what remains of his lilting Caribbean accent, because he said I lit up every room I walked into. And I didn't walk, I *burst* into every room, according to him.

Some days when I've broken through on a piece I'm learning, the melody still thrumming through the tips of my fingers like an electric shock, and I feel so happy I could dance, I want nothing more than for him to see my face. To be the bubbly kid he remembers, and for him to be the dad I remember. For us to recognize each other the way you catch sight of your reflection in paneled glass. Even for a second.

"You know Dad can fly, right?" Caleb would tell me when we were really little, tricking me into thinking it was true in the literal sense. Superman-type flying with a cape and the forehead curl and the whole shebang. "Duh," I would say in whatever way four-year-olds do. Then my dad would get home from his trips and put me on his shoulders, and I always felt so high up that every time he lifted his foot, it seemed like we were teetering, picking up air.

All my memories until about twelve—right around when my parents separated—are like that, and then suddenly they are distant and different and tinged with this sadness, an uncertainty I can't explain. There's just a trace of it in every memory with my dad, like the aftertaste of something bitter you've eaten, and I'm only really sure he loves me because I remember he once did.

Dad is different with Caleb. Less distant. But maybe it's because Caleb is older; maybe fathers and sons are just different. Sometimes I think my parents' divorce split us right in half: my mother and me on one side, Caleb and Dad on the other.

My parents met at a dinner party when Mom was doing the weather for radio. Dad used to listen to the six-thirty forecast before he went up, back when he was a training pilot, and he claims he fell in love with her voice. Her calm, matter-of-fact voice, which would inch up just a little bit when there was bad news. A storm, a tornado warning, bad weather for the Fourth.

When someone introduced them, Dad exclaimed, "You're Sandy Fairweather!"

"Sandy Houston," she'd said, trying not to let on that she was pleased at the recognition.

"I didn't mind bad news if your voice was the one giving it," I remember my dad telling her as they recounted the story for the billionth time, before everything changed.

Before Dad stopped coming home and then got his own place on the far side of town.

Still, I sometimes catch him watching Mom's report.

Dad's apartment is eternally stuffy because every now and then he'll get a new piece of furniture that he won't be home to use, so the space keeps getting more cramped, the stale scent of new leather and abandoned air mixing together to form something arid and claustrophobic. When it gets bad enough for him to notice, he'll fling open all the windows and the door that leads out to the balcony, and the apartment will sound like squealing brakes, drunk couples fighting, and too-loud ambulances for the whole weekend I'm around.

I think the worst part is that the apartments are so close

together, the walls so paper-thin, that I am not allowed to practice here. We'll watch TV on opposite ends of the new leather couch he's just gotten, and every couple of hours, he'll pause the show to ask if I've seen the new lamp he bought or a new stool for the kitchen, and I'll say no even if I have.

Tonight we're watching hours of home renovation shows he's taped, eating Thai food out of Styrofoam containers.

"Are you sure your mother isn't using it?" Dad's question jolts me out of a trance, and I glance at him, confused.

"Addie?" I can tell from his frown that I have a glazed expression on my face, and I try to blink it away.

"Sorry. What were you saying?"

"I was asking about Grandpa's clock that we used to have at home. I thought it might add a nice touch to the living room. Caleb said it was in the attic somewhere—that your mother wasn't using it?"

"Oh, yeah," I say unhelpfully. "I'll look for it when I get home."

Today has been the worst day yet since the accident. I'm not in pain, but I feel like I can't concentrate on anything. Probably because the last really peaceful sleep I got was on the bus before it crashed. Katy is at her wit's end with me.

I've been tempted to mention it to my mom, but I know she'd just freak out and send me to the ER. And Dad—well, I'm not really used to coming to him when I need help. And what exactly is my issue—that I've been distracted and forgetful for three days?

I shake my head when Dad pauses the show again to ask if I've seen the new kitchen mat.

He likes the tour more than I do, the act of convincing

himself his apartment is just as full as our house used to be. Or maybe it just gives us something to say to each other. Sometimes, watching TV on the couch, I'll pull out my bow and just hold it or swipe it against the air to threaten away the sadness.

"Did you look for the exits when you got on the bus?" Dad asks out of nowhere. It's the first thing he's asked me about the accident since I got here after school today.

"Yeah, I always do," I say. For a pilot, my father has no faith in planes. He hates for any of us to fly. Years ago, before the divorce, the four of us went on vacation to visit Dad's extended family in St. Vincent—or Vincy, as he calls it. He grew up in the States, and his parents died here when I was little, but Dad always goes back every few years, and this was one of the few times we were going with him. Dad had the three of us in a semicircle at the airport, his Hawaiian shirt odd and ill-fitting on him. I remember I'd been hopping around singing every song I knew that mentioned the beach or islands or the sun. Dad looked each of us square in the face and said, "Always assume the plane is going down."

It was the last trip we took as a family.

But his warning worked, because none of us will enter a plane or bus or train without knowing where the exits are.

"Your mom says all the colleges you ended up applying to were in New York," he says now. There is no feeling in his voice, and he doesn't look at me. He never looks at me. "They have a pretty high crime rate."

"Lots of places do," I say.

He nods, then unpauses the TV. I steal glances at the side

of his face, wondering what he would say if I did tell him I'd been feeling strange ever since the accident.

Would it make him worry about me? Maybe he'd actually be able to help?

"It's asking for trouble to be so far away from family," he says, mostly concentrating on the TV now, and confirming what I suspect, which is that my mother got him to bring this up.

I bite the urge to say, *Um,* hello? *You've made a career, a lifestyle, out of being away from family.* But that feels like a low blow, so I don't answer and focus on the screen.

Even though he's not here actively *doing* anything to incite it, it's times like these I resent my brother. He's two years older than me, currently at community college—despite decent grades—and still living at home.

There would be nothing wrong with it, if it was what Caleb wanted. But I know that even if he'll never admit it, it's not what he wants. He's always been obsessed with planes like my dad, has dreamed of flying for years. But instead of doing anything about it, he stays in Lyndale, haunting parties and people he has outgrown.

The only thing my parents agree on is crushing any bit of desire Caleb and I have to go somewhere, to move, to stretch the seams of our lives. It's spearheaded by my mom, but somehow she always gets Dad to agree with her. She's convinced she can protect us from whatever dangers are out there. I'm seventeen and I have freaking *parental controls* on my computer.

As hyperbolic as Katy is about it, I know exactly what she

means when she says she feels as if she was born for a place. I think I was born for the viola, to play music on one of the loneliest instruments.

But I chose New York because I want something else. The fact that Juilliard is in the same city doesn't mean I have to go there.

I want buzzing lights and rowdy streets and the Philharmonic and Broadway and Carnegie Hall and artsy, passionate, vibrant people with places to go.

I know it's the biggest cliché, but I love the idea of a city that reminds you every day that you're alive. I love that it is different and bigger than Lyndale in every way, and I want to believe my life there will be, too.

I've worked so hard to keep my grades up, to stand a chance of getting into NYU.

Now Dad pats my knee awkwardly.

"Let's think on it some more, okay?" he says.

I nod—*Yes, let's think on it some more*—but already I am thinking of all the things that could possibly stop me from leaving, and deciding that they are all things that won't.

10

AFTER
January

The next night, I practice longer than usual to make up for yesterday, when I was at my dad's. As soon as I got home from the hospital on Sunday morning, I downloaded a version of Bach's "Air on the G String," and I listen to it now, falling in love again with the way it swoops, in and out, gently, insistently. The millions of stories I can imagine hidden in it. I've started trying to learn a viola version of the song, but it doesn't sound as full and fantastic as it should. Instead of wistful and romantic, it feels desolate. Like someone waltzing alone.

Giving up on it for tonight, I decide to work on our new orchestra pieces. I almost have "Alla Hornpipe" from the second movement of *Water Music* by Handel memorized, but according to Mrs. Dubois, there's nothing worse than teaching yourself a flawed version of a piece. Mrs. Dubois has a theory about firsts: that the first thing sets the precedent for everything that comes after. The way you first learn a song, the way you approach the first note, sets the tone for the rest of that movement and the whole piece. The first piece in a concert sets the tone for the rest of the performance. She also says the first mistake you make in a performance—and how you recover from it—sets the precedent for all the other mistakes you'll make. But since I'd rather not have any mistakes, I decide to play from the sheet music until I have it perfect. Except that I left my orchestra binder in my car, which my mother let me drive today.

It's only seven at night, but it's dark and freezing out, so I throw my coat over my flannel pajamas and pad outside. I'm still humming "Air on the G String" to myself as I dig through my car and retrieve the black binder.

I'm halfway out of the car when the sight of a person across the road, illuminated by a streetlight, nearly makes me slam my head against the roof. I climb out of the passenger seat and am waving my binder at him before I can stop myself.

"Hey!" I say, watching as he registers my presence and a smile—that smile—stretches across his face. He is wearing the beanie again, but tufts of red hair stick out from under it now.

"Hi!" he says, and then crosses the road between us so we are both standing in front of my driveway.

"What are you doing here?" I ask.

He scratches the back of his neck. "I just kind of found myself here, I guess," he says. "I was taking a walk. You?"

"I live here," I say, signaling behind me, but instead of looking at my house, his eyes travel down the length of me. Stopping at the place beneath my knee where my coat ends and my Rainbow Brite pajamas are tucked into slippers.

"You weren't just prowling the streets like that?" he asks,

his eyes twinkling playfully. Butterflies brush the cage of my chest.

"I certainly was not prowling," I say, and scrunch my face up in mock offense. "Anyway, what do you have against Rainbow Brite?"

He raises his hand in surrender. "Nothing. I'm sure she's a very nice . . . person?"

"Right. Sure you're not following me?" I ask, narrowing my eyes at him, and then my cheeks instantly warm with how flirtatious it comes out. For once, I am thankful for how quickly blood rushes to the tips of my ears when I'm embarrassed. They are currently unaffected by the cold.

Bus Boy laughs, but before he can answer, Caleb's car revs into the driveway, almost taking Bus Boy—who is standing closer to the center of the driveway than I am—down in the process. Bus Boy jumps out of the way, shaken. Before I have time to form words, my brother calls out his window, "Why are you standing outside, Addison?"

"Oh my God, do you have to drive like a psychopath? And I'm *talking to someone*," I say, waiting for him to apologize for nearly mowing a person down.

"I was changing songs. I wasn't even that close!" Caleb never stops his car, though, continuing to roll into the garage so that he's yelling back at me when he says, "Can't you talk on the phone inside?"

Caleb doesn't bother waiting for my response, and the garage door gurgles shut behind him.

What? Is he so determined to not see me that he didn't even glance up to make sure I was all right and just assumed I was on my phone?

"Are you okay? I'm so sorry."

"I'm fine," Bus Boy says with a laugh, already back to looking unruffled.

"That was just my asshat brother," I explain.

Bus Boy nods in understanding. I know a lot of siblings aren't best friends and that my distant relationship with Caleb is probably normal. But there are so many days I wish things were different between us. That it wasn't just the two of us, or that we had some kind of middle ground. Right now, though, I sort of want to kick him.

"Hey, aren't you ever cold?" I ask, noticing then that Bus Boy is not wearing winter clothes. Again. His shirt is long-sleeved but far from warm enough to be walking around in.

"I'm not very cold," he says.

"It's, like, twenty degrees," I say, still stunned that he's not shivering or morphing into an icicle right in front of me. Can he not afford winter clothes? He doesn't *look* malnourished or homeless or anything. I don't see holes in his shoes or jeans. "You can't walk back home in that. You'll get hypothermia."

"It's really okay," he says.

I don't know if I sound more like Katy or my mom.

"You'll get hypothermia *and die,*" I say, deciding to invoke a stronger version of their voices.

Bus Boy laughs. A full, rich sound that makes *me* feel a little less cold. "Then I can go to Jimi Hendrix concerts."

"Or not. I bet you still need an invite," I retort. Okay, I'm definitely flirting. It's like channeling Katy a second ago has made her invade my body.

"You know, I have a coat I can lend you," I say, suddenly thinking of something. "Well, my brother does."

Caleb won't like the idea of me lending his coat to a stranger, but it's the least of my concerns.

"It's really okay," Bus Boy is saying, his smile gone. "I'm not even that cold. And I bet it's not my size."

"It's a jacket, not a leotard," I say, and then we both burst out laughing at the mental imagery of either my brother or him in a leotard. *Ew.* Why did I say that?

"Hold on, I'll be right back," I say.

"No, look—" I miss the last of his protests as I race inside the house and set down my music binder. I find an ivy-green winter jacket hanging in the coat closet, still warm. Must be what Caleb just took off. He's nowhere in sight, so I rush back out the front door.

"Okay, you can probably return this tom—" My voice breaks off as I stare out at the empty driveway. I look right, then left, then right again, as if I'm getting ready to cross the road.

Where did he go?

I walk to the edge of the driveway and look to both ends of the street, but there's no sign of him.

I had so many questions for him.

Who are you?

Why do we suddenly keep running into each other?

Once again, I didn't even manage to get his name.

I stand there, clutching my brother's coat as my hands tingle with cold, and I can't believe Bus Boy just left. All I can think is, *It felt like we were at the start of something.*

11

BEFORE
Early July

Every visit to At Home Movies feels like a continuation of the world's longest-running discussion of horror parodies. I start by telling Zach my thoughts, and he counters, defends, concedes before we move on to the next movie. But on the fourth straight day I go into At Home Movies, return the latest DVD (plus its verdict), and await Zach's newest recommendation, he leans across the counter on his elbows and looks at me instead.

"What?" I ask, surprised. "No more Ciano movies? I thought there were way more than four."

"There are," Zach says. "I just have a question for you."

My mouth goes dry as I wait for him to speak. What could he possibly want to ask me? Why does his complete and focused gaze, as if he's scrutinizing something under a microscope, make me a little warm all over? I fold my arms against my chest to steady myself.

"Feel free to say that I've made a hard-core horrody convert out of you, if it's true," Zach says, standing up to his full height again. "I'd *love* it if that's true. But it just seems like you could be doing a million other things instead of indulging some random guy's movie recommendations. If I didn't have to work this summer, I'd be outside hiking and hanging out with my friends and . . ." He trails off, looking out through the glass doors of the store, and his lips twitch up before a warm laugh escapes him. I love the wide-open, carefree sound of it. Like it would never occur to him to contain it. I wish I laughed that way more often. "All right, watching movies. That's what I'd be doing. But you seem cooler than me."

"Excellent," I say. "Then I have you fooled."

Unfortunately, he's still watching me, waiting for a real answer. So I sigh and sheepishly say, "My best friend kind of ditched me this summer. For a trip to New York via *everywhere else* that I was supposed to be on with her. She keeps texting and posting pictures online of how much fun they're having. Like, she just sent me a picture of the amazing food they're having for lunch."

One of Zach's eyebrows skitters up; he does not look impressed. "What they're having for lunch," he repeats pointedly.

"Yeah, but they're, like, in the West Village."

He shakes his head and moves to type something on the computer behind the counter. "Have you ever noticed how rare it is that the thing people are doing that you're jealous of is actually enviable, in and of itself? She's eating *lunch*."

"Somewhere I'm supposed to be," I add stubbornly. "Somewhere I would rather be."

"Okay," Zach accepts. "Sometimes what they're doing *is* cool. You get to ride in the president's motorcade—fine, you win. But most of the time, people are doing completely mundane things and just making them seem better with their enthusiasm. It's all in how you sell the story."

I laugh and shrug. "Maybe *I* want to do those mundane things."

"You should get together with the rest of your friends and send her messages about all the great things she's missing."

"Yeah, that's a good idea. I'll totally do that," I mumble noncommittally, since the alternative involves admitting that, apart from Katy, I don't have that many friends. Acquaintances, casual orchestra friends, and people I could sit with at lunch if I needed to, but not the kinds of friends who think of you when you aren't around. "So, do I get the next DVD or what?"

Zach leads me to the Foreign section of the store, picks up two DVDs, and gives me an eager rundown of both plots. In the end, I go with the one about a town of people who are emitting spiders out of all orifices—ears, mouths, eyes. I'll save the one about possessed machinery for tomorrow.

I'm quiet and awkward around Zach. If he notices, he doesn't say anything, just mentions that he's expecting the full report again as soon as I've finished watching. He waves as I walk out.

The truth about me is that I'm not someone who goes out and has all these great experiences, and I don't know what to think about him calling me on it, four days after meeting me.

I'm not like Katy, with all the boys she falls for and the way she courts attention and drama and diagnoses herself and everyone within a three-mile radius with illnesses. I'm not bright and loud and certain, though I love that about her.

In a way, it feels like I'm waiting for my life to start. Waiting for my life to feel as full and as vibrant outside of a melody as it does in it.

Sometimes I feel like I've sleepwalked through my life so far, with nothing significant or extraordinary happening to me. It's time for that to change.

Even if I was good enough, this is why I've never wanted to go to Juilliard, why I don't want to major in music no matter where I go to college. Music has always been my cover, the thing I hide inside of, and if I let it define me, I know I'll just hide behind it again. And I need my life to get a little bit bigger than that.

12

AFTER
January

Katy is determined to track down the boy from the bus.

We arrive the next day—Thursday—at the movie theater entrance of the mall.

"I can't believe you didn't tell me he *worked* here." Katy has been strangely agitated ever since lunchtime, when I told her about seeing Bus Boy outside my house yesterday. I know she's anxious about hearing back from Juilliard in a few weeks and has been working nonstop on four monologues in the hope that she'll get an audition, but Katy's impatience now seems unrelated.

"Didn't I mention that he worked here before our movie the other day?"

"No, you just said he was here. It's different if he *works* here," she insists.

"Why?" I ask, exasperated.

Before she can answer, Katy is, unsurprisingly, tackled by

a tiny, rambunctious human walking in the opposite direction.

"Ashley!" Katy says, pushing the raven-haired girl off her, slightly irritated.

"Oh my God, I *thought* that was you! I haven't seen you in forever, lover," the girl squeals, bouncing on her toes in front of us. Just watching her tires me. "Your hair is so cute. You're so lucky it's not frizzy like mine. Some people get all the luck."

Katy introduces the two of us. "Nice to meet you," I say at the same time Ashley says, "Didn't we meet at that pool party? You're the one who was dating—"

"No, that's someone else. You're thinking of Elise," Katy snaps. "We have to go, okay, Ash? But I'll see you around, okay?"

"Oh, all right," Ashley says, disappointed. "Text me later, okay? I've missed you! Bye, lover!" she chirps before crossing the road and disappearing into the parking lot.

"Who was *that*, lover?" I whisper once she's gone, and Katy groans.

"She's a junior from Meridian. Total drama queen. But speaking of lovers, let's focus on the task at hand," Katy says as we walk through the automatic doors. "We're getting this boy's name, age, blood type, Social Security number, and mother's maiden name."

"Are we planning to hack his bank account or ask him out?"

Katy laughs, but it sounds oddly strangled. "I *do* like to multitask."

Her agitation is contagious. "Is this even a good idea? I mean, he blew me off last night. He hasn't asked me for *my* name. Maybe this isn't worth it."

"I'll be the judge of that," Katy says. "I just want to see who he is."

With a decidedly smaller crowd of moviegoers than on Monday, when we were last here, I spot him almost as soon as we enter, facing away from us. He's wearing the black CINEX-PERIENCE T-shirt again, his red hair short in the back.

"That's him," I whisper.

Katy, a full head shorter than me, stands on her tiptoes and whips her head from left to right. "Where, where?"

I pinch her arm. "Don't be so obvious!"

"Ouch!" she yelps. She's impatient when she asks, *"Where?"*

I point at the concession area. He still has his back to us.

Katy's immediate reaction looks, strangely, like relief. Then her face crumples with disapproval. "I thought you said he was cute."

I'm taken aback by her response. "He *is*. I mean, you can't see his face right now, but—"

"I can," she says. "And he's, like, fifty. This is really gross, Addie."

"No, no, no," I say, realizing that she's looking to the left of the boy, at a moviegoer whose head is peppered with gray. I take her chin with my hand and force it a few inches to the right. *"Him."*

Katy is very still for a second. Then she says, "I feel like this is an elaborate joke."

"Why?"

"Who are you seeing?" she asks again.

"The tall guy. Red hair."

"Red?" Katy repeats almost too quietly for me to hear.

"Yeah."

I feel Katy's reaction more than see it. She shudders, seems to breathe in but not out. And without my even understanding why, something plummets from my throat to my stomach, a pebble of fear.

Her voice wobbles when she speaks next. "There's no guy with red hair here, Addie. He's not here."

When I look at her, she is trembling and her eyes are starting to cloud. Is she joking? Practicing some bizarre new drama technique on me? I shift my eyes from her to him to her to the boy with the red hair—who I've talked to several times now, who makes my stomach flip, who I can see so clearly fiddling with something behind the counter—and I don't know why she's doing this. I don't know how she can say that when he's right there.

"Katy, he's right *there*," I say, grabbing her wrist. "Come on, we'll go talk to him."

But with a kind of bull-like strength not befitting someone of her stature, Katy digs her heels into the floor and refuses to move.

I leave her there and walk to the counter where he is.

"Hi!" I say too enthusiastically. My heart is pounding and it's not because of a crush. He turns—Bus Boy, all six feet of him—and grins at me. "My friend wants to meet you. Will you come and say hi?"

"Hey," he says, his face lighting up. "You're back."

I nod. "Can you come and talk to my friend for a second?" I point out Katy, whose eyes are bugging out of her head, staring at us. At me? "I want to introduce you."

There's a pause before Bus Boy speaks, a trace of something I can't define in his voice. Apology? Sadness? "I can't."

Then he turns from me, moves away from the counter, and goes back to sorting through a pile of papers.

When I head back to Katy, I feel dizzy.

"He can't come because he's working," I say. Lie? I don't understand what's happening.

"Addie." Katy swipes at a tear on her cheek. "You have to let me call my mom." She's looking at me with a desperation I can't remember ever seeing in her eyes. "Please. She'll know what to do."

I shake my head, and then a burst of laughter that is as short as it is fake escapes me. "Why do you think *I'm* the crazy one? You're the one who can't see him."

"It's not just me!" Katy is saying now. "You said the nurse didn't find him after the accident."

"Because he left! He didn't need to be admitted."

"You've been acting like the walking dead. Not sleeping. Not being able to concentrate. Forgetting stuff."

I look at her, incredulous. "Hello? I hit my head in a bus crash."

"Exactly!" Katy says.

"You think I'm making him up?" I shake my head again and blink a dozen times. He's still there. Still leaning over a pile of papers behind the counter. Still wearing the black CIN-EXPERIENCE shirt. Still existing. "Katy, this is insane."

I can't, he said when I asked him to come with me.

"I know. I know," she says, pushing her bangs out of her face. She looks more panicked every time I look at her. "Okay, look, come here."

She takes my hand and leads me to the concession counter

on the far side of the lobby from where Bus Boy is. There's no one in line, so a woman with light brown hair and glasses—the same one who caught me talking with Bus Boy on Monday—says she'll be with us in a second. I remember now the odd look that she gave me. I thought it was for chatting up one of the other workers.

I was *sure* it was for chatting up one of the other workers.

"See her badge?" Katy whispers to me, and I nod. It says KARI TOEWS, ASSISTANT MANAGER.

"Hi," Katy says when Kari Toews is standing in front of us. "Is there a guy who works here that's about our-age-ish?"

The woman, Kari, narrows her eyes at us, like we want her help to boyfriend-hunt while she's working. I can't tell if she recognizes me. "Yes. There are several *guys* who fit that description."

"Right," Katy says, turning to me. "So describe him. He's . . ."

"Tall," I say, and it is the oddest thing, standing across the room from him and describing him. "Red hair that's kind of messy-looking."

"Smile bright enough to power a city," Katy fills in, looking down at the counter. I shoot her a surprised look. Is she being sarcastic? Did I go on about his smile that much the last couple of days?

"Um, yeah," I say, looking back over at Bus Boy, who still has his back to me. "Skinny."

Kari is shaking her head now. "No. Not unless you mean Vic?" She nods to a tall, muscly guy with long blond hair who's tearing tickets. It's like she missed my entire description.

"Then sorry," Kari says completely unapologetically when I tell her no. "I've been here a year and that doesn't sound like anyone who works here."

"Are you sure?" I ask, desperate. "He's not working today? He's not working right now?"

Kari looks at me, seems to follow my gaze to the exact spot where Bus Boy should be standing, where he is in plain sight, then frowns. "I'm sure."

"She would know; she's the assistant manager," Katy says as we back away from the counter.

"I know," I snap, because my head is buzzing, filling with questions and absurdities. What scares me, what terrifies me, is that I think they are right. Katy. Kari. The problem is me.

Suddenly I'm back on the bus, talking to Bus Boy for the first time, and Goth Guy and the mother with her two children are giving me weird looks. *Who are you talking to?* their looks say now. I didn't know that at the time.

Caleb, yesterday, in the driveway. *I wasn't even that close,* he'd said. And he wasn't—not to me. He nearly ran Bus Boy over because he didn't see him.

On Monday at this theater—the Indian kid who bumped into me and couldn't stop staring, and then Katy dragging me away without seeing Bus Boy. Neither of them saw him then, either?

Oh God.

Katy is speaking. "My mom, she can . . ."

Go to my parents, make them pull my reins in even tighter. Have me admitted into a psychiatric facility? Make sure I never, ever leave Lyndale?

"No, no," I say. "It's just from hitting my head."

"Addie."

"Promise me," I demand. "On my life. You can't tell anyone. I just need more sleep. Let me just try that."

Katy is shaking her head. "I can't take more secrets."

"What do you mean?" I ask.

"I don't know—my, my friends," she stammers. "From Act! Out! and school and stuff. I just feel like I'm keeping everybody's secrets."

I narrow my eyes at her; she looks away.

"Please," I say.

"What if something happens to you?" she asks now, glaring at me. "What do I say then?"

"Nothing will happen," I answer, even as I cut my gaze from her to Bus Boy. "Promise me."

"Okay," she promises, but she looks like she hates herself after she does. "Please let's go home. Please."

He'll go away, I tell myself, watching him as we head toward the exit. I don't know if I'm expecting him to disappear before my very eyes, to turn watery and pale like a ghost. He doesn't.

We leave.

He stays.

13

BEFORE
Mid-July

I can usually find him in the exact same position—behind the counter of the movie store, sorting DVDs or working on the computer. But today he's nowhere in sight.

Having watched nine Ciano movies—and having made nine visits to the movie store—I was dragging my feet going in to return the last one. Trying to think of ways to extend this—this friendship? Discussion group?

I might also have spent more time than I normally do on my look.

And Zach isn't even here.

I'm hovering at the New Releases section, scanning the aisles, when Mr. Laird walks out of the breakroom and past me.

"Hi, Addie! You smell lovely!" *Crap.* I flush at Mr. Laird's comment. My mom is forever telling me to spray only on the pulse points, but (blame the influence of Katy) all over just seems more effective. That is, if I'm trying to attract forty-five-year-old men.

"Thanks, Mr. Laird," I say, hoping to God that Zach is not somewhere nearby overhearing this conversation.

"Is Zach in the storeroom?" That's where he said he'd be if he wasn't at the counter.

"No, he's out back," his father says, frowning at a movie poster and trying to make sure it's straight. He suddenly turns to me. "You march right back in here and tell me if you see him smoking, do you understand?"

"Um, okay," I say, not sure how I feel about ratting Zach out, but glad it seems Mr. Laird is giving me permission to go through the back door of the movie store to "out back." Also, Zach smokes?

Still holding on to the DVD, I head back through a small, dark room that seems to be mostly storage and find Zach outside. He jumps a full foot when I shut the door. And then he smiles, relieved it's just me and, I think, happy it's me.

"Hi, Zach," I say, then shut my eyes.

"Hi?" His voice ticks up at the end, a question.

"You're wondering why I'm shutting my eyes."

"Yes?" Another question.

"Your father said that if I found you smoking I was to—and I quote—march right back in there and tell him." Zach laughs, and I feel myself grinning, stupid, eyes closed. "I have not seen you smoking."

"You will not see me smoking," he says, moving around me, presumably putting the cigarette out, and then stopping in front of me. I sense him close to me, sense his cigarette-y breath. "You may open your eyes."

I do and am blinded by his hundred-watt smile.

"Last one," I say, holding up the DVD case before I forget *all* my thoughts.

"And?" Zach holds the door open for me, then pauses to pull a pack of mints out of his pocket. He offers me one but I shake my head, wondering how much he has thought about the condition of my mouth. Or rather, if he has thought about the condition of my mouth as much as I have considered the thought of his.

"I'm ranking it between *The Mask of Falling* and *Volvo Lost*. The ending just didn't hold up."

"Hmm," he says thoughtfully. "Even with Beppe coming back?"

"*Especially* with Beppe coming back."

"Hmm," he says again, looking at the floor, as we head toward the Horror section. I think for a second that he's trying to figure out what to recommend for me next, but instead he glances up at me. "I have something to ask you."

My heart skips one, two, three beats. What Katy calls a Cardiac Event.

Is he going to ask me out?

"What is it?" I ask, and it's only as I'm whispering it back that I realize that Zach whispered first.

"I don't think," he says quietly but not quite whispering. "I don't think I ever told you that I'm, um"—he seems embarrassed—"an aspiring filmmaker."

I stare blankly at him. Okay, so maybe he *isn't* asking me out.

"God, that sounds pretentious. But I am."

A second of silence passes before I offer, "Like Ciano?"
His fanaticism makes complete sense now.

Zach glances up at me, his eyes twinkling like I *get it*.
"Yes," he says, a tremor of excitement in his voice. "Exactly
like Ciano."

To say that my heart is experiencing a steady fall down-
ward is an understatement. "That's awesome." I hope I at least
sound enthusiastic.

"Well, I have to work on the accent. And the handlebar
mustache," he says, chuckling. "Did you watch the behind-
the-scenes commentary, by the way? Did you expect him to
look like that? I love how he plays into all the clichés. Even in
the way he *looks*. Like, that little Italian director twiddling his
handlebar mustache. Who comes up with that shit?"

I smile. "You wanted to ask me something."

"Yes," Zach says. "I'm working on a little film this summer. My friend Raj and I wrote the script, and I was wondering if maybe you'd be in it?"

"Me?" There's obviously no one else around, but of all
the outrageous things I thought Zach might ask me—for a
date, maybe, or even my hand in marriage—I would not have
expected this, and I can't help wondering if someone else has
popped up behind me.

He nods, smiling at me until my shock wears off.

"I can't act!"

"Exactly," he laughs. "I mean, not that you *can't* act. That
has yet to be determined, but you saw Ciano's stuff. No skill
required."

"But . . ." I try to come up with an excuse, any excuse.

"I think you'd be perfect for it," Zach says, and ugh, his eyes find mine. I don't have the sense to look away.

"I could . . . I mean, I can try, I guess."

"Perfect," Zach says as we reenter the main area of the store. I follow him around to the counter. "Here. We'll be shooting it at my house, so I'll write down where I live, and today's Wednesday. Does Saturday work for you to do a test run, and then we'll start on Monday?" He pulls out a piece of paper, some faded old receipt, and scribbles on it. It's the first time I notice that he is left-handed.

While he's sliding it over to me, a customer—an older man in a business suit, picking something up during his lunch break—comes up to check out a stack of movies. Zach turns away to help him, but the man doesn't have an account, so they have to set up a new one. I'm holding on to the receipt, waiting for Zach to finish, when an idea pops into my head.

I don't know if it makes me desperate or brave or nothing at all, but I decide that, short of straight-up asking him out, there's really only one way to know if Zach even remotely likes me. I mean, maybe he's this friendly and charming to anyone.

So while he's busy inputting the man's details, I tear off the bottom of the receipt he gave me and scribble my cell number on it. Maybe he won't even see it. Maybe he'll think it's just in case he needs to reach me, even though he never asked for it, and my mom's number is on the store's computer system. But before I can change my mind, before I can convince myself that this isn't the kind of thing I would normally do, I put the note down on the counter, stick the pen over it, call goodbye to Zach, and head out.

For the first time in over a week, I leave At Home Movies DVD-less. But with Zach's number and address. A starring role in his slasher film. And an open invitation for him to call me.

14

AFTER
January

I write the note on a piece of paper torn from the back of my Spanish notebook.

Sometimes I write down things I'm desperate to remember. My sheet music is full of notes and PSs to myself.

If I'm asking, then I can't be, is what this one says.

Crazy, is what it doesn't.

Is it true that if you suspect you are, then you can't be insane?

I hope it is, so I keep the note folded in my pocket for six days. For reassurance.

I can't be crazy.

Crazy means stuck here in this town.

But crazy is seeing a boy nobody else can. A person who doesn't exist.

I haven't seen him since Thursday in the Cineplex with Katy, but I am determined not to again.

I steal two sleeping pills from Mom's cabinet and try them, one at a time, because I am still lying awake at night, mind swirling with spinning buses and trees. And now invisible boys. It helps with the sleep, but not the unshakable feeling that something is wrong.

I get onto the treadmill Mom folds up and down in the guest room, since exercise is supposed to be good for your mind.

At dinner, I finish the peas in the salad Mom makes, instead of pushing them to the edge of my plate like I've always done.

I don't know if any of this is working. I only know that I'm exhausted.

It's taking all the energy and concentration I have to focus in school, to follow conversations during lunchtime, to not keep whirling around in my seat, expecting to find my world inhabited by dozens of invisible people. And I think I'm doing a fairly good job of this, of fixing my eyes on things that are solid and certain and close enough to touch.

Until Wednesday, when the boy shows up at school.

I catch only a glimpse from the corner of my eye. A tall, lanky figure at the window of the music room during orchestra practice.

My fingers freeze on the bow and my heart seizes as I whip my head to the right to make sure it wasn't just a shadow, a trick of the light.

It's not.

I'm sitting in the viola section near the center of the room, with Katy and the other second violinists to my right. Only one seat separates Katy from the window, and I can't take my eyes off the glass. I try to blink away the angular crook of his jaw, the clump of hair sticking out from underneath a black beanie. The cloud of air, of human breath, as he presses his forehead against the window, peering in.

It takes everything I have not to grab Katy's arm and force her to look, to see how the mist of his breath stains the glass, how his teeth chatter noiselessly underneath our playing.

Tell me you can't see him, I want to say.

How can you not see him?

But I've told her I haven't seen him since the Cineplex, which is true. I went back there twice without Katy and he wasn't there. I've told her I'm sleeping okay now, which isn't exactly true, and I've tried to stay present when she talks to me, to remember the things she says.

So I can't tell her he's here.

I throw off the orchestra three times on one page.

Katy quirks her eyebrow up at me, silently demanding to know what's with me.

Finally I set down my viola and bow. I ask for a bathroom pass from Mrs. Dubois and hustle out of the room, leaving Paulie rippling a particularly gassy set of notes through the air and Katy giggling behind me.

As soon as I'm in the hallway, I take off running toward the heavy doors that lead to the back of the building, outside the music room. Cold air slaps at my cheeks and chest and fingers, and I think vaguely that I should have retrieved my coat from my locker, but it's too late now. I'm hurtling forward too quickly to stop or turn around. As I approach the music-room window, I see that he's gone. There's no one there.

I come to a stop a little ways from the window so no one from orchestra can see me, and try to catch my breath. I look for footprints or a dropped item or some sign that he was here, but there's nothing.

And then I hear it.

A scrambled noise not far away, like feet crunching through snow.

I know it's him immediately. It has to be.

"Hey!" I call. "Hey, wait!" I take off running again, sprinting on a shoveled walkway in the direction of the noise. I round the corner of the building too fast to stop myself from crashing into someone. He catches my elbows to stop me from toppling over.

"Whoa, whoa, whoa!" he exclaims.

His voice is thick, and his face is wide, weathered by too many hours in the sun. He's also in his forties.

"Where are you going in such a hurry?"

I blink several times, giving the image in front of me a chance to change, but it's still Bert, our school groundskeeper. There's no sign of the boy.

"And you're not wearing a coat. Do you want to catch your death?"

I give a ferocious shake of my head, too out of breath and too disappointed to form words. *I said almost exactly that to Bus Boy days ago.*

"You okay?" he asks, letting me go, and I nod. He continues to give me an odd look, so I force myself to speak.

"Sorry, I thought you were someone else."

He looks like he doesn't quite believe me, but he seems to let it go. "All right. Go back to class." He starts to walk toward the snow-covered football field.

I turn and head back in the direction I just came from,

stopping at the music-room window again to see if there's anything I missed.

I *saw* him.

I freaking *saw* him.

With the adrenaline gone now, the cold sweeps over my skin and I hug myself to keep warm. My teeth are chattering, and I remember I saw his chattering, and I can't be crazy. I can't.

I slide down against the wall and sit on a snowy patch of ground, going over everything in my mind.

Every now and then, I have this one dream. I'm standing in the middle of a crowd—the food court in the mall or the park during a summer festival, sometimes a subway platform I've never actually been to—and suddenly all these things start to disappear. Cars, the grass, tables. People. It's when the sound goes with them—the swirling wind or scores of laughing voices or the marching band that plays at summer festivals—that I start to panic. Force myself awake.

I'm most afraid of the silence.

Of the space that is left by all the lives and people and things I can't hold on to. I don't know what makes them disappear, or where they disappear to. Only that the feeling terrifies me.

I skip back to the accident again, rewind to when he got on the bus, after *I* got on the bus. Fast-forward to the hospital and the movie theater and this window, five minutes ago. I've been doing it a lot the last few days, but I go over every detail I can think of again.

Just one more time. Just so I can figure out what I'm missing.

The weird thing is, he got on the bus before the accident, before I hit my head. Shouldn't it have been after, if he's the result of some sort of concussion? There has to be a way this makes sense.

But I can't come up with anything, and by the time a couple of minutes have passed, I know I really am going to catch my death if I don't go back in now.

I haven't told my parents what I saw, and I've stopped telling Katy the truth. Because I don't want them to think I am crazy. Because I don't want whatever this is—this tangled, itching cloak over my mind—to cost me the things I want most. But I have to understand what's happening.

I need to *stop* whatever's happening.

My jeans are damp from the snow when I stand.

I can't handle this on my own.

There has to be someone I can go to without involving my parents.

The vaguest of plans forming in my mind, I hurry back into the building. My wet shoes squeak against the floor as I make my way to my seat in the music room. Katy points at my fingers, wrinkly from the cold, as I flip to the right page in my binder. *Gangrene,* she mouths. Not frostbite, but gangrene.

"Okay?" she whispers. I nod, not looking at her, pick up my viola and bow, and focus on the sheets of paper in front of me as we wait for the strings to come in.

15

BEFORE
Mid-July

At the risk of sounding crazy, the great thing about being the only member of orchestra without a life is that it gives me plenty of time to practice and possibly get a leg up on everyone else when school starts in the fall.

I've been practicing Bartók's Viola Concerto for nearly an hour, trying to get the tempo exactly right. It goes from steady and lyrical, *andante,* to manic, notes tripping over each other in their hurry to burst out. Then back to calm again. Mrs. Dubois says that all good music tears down walls, shatters glass, shakes the foundations, then puts the house back together. Piece by piece. Brick by brick. Note by note. The strokes of my bow are like blows of a sledgehammer: heavy, violent. I imagine the house I'm flattening is mine—my father's absence, my brother's distance, the way we can't reach each other no matter how close together we are. When I get to the second movement, I picture construction workers reassembling what's been broken. I feel exhausted, like I've been working with them. After playing through all three movements once, I go back and start again. My heart moves at walking pace, then quicker and quicker, the kind of pace that takes you whirling around a corner too fast. It takes a second to slow down again, to *lumber* instead of run. I'm not happy with the first section, so I stop, preparing to start yet again, and that's when I hear my phone ringing. I'm not sure how long it has been going, and when I reach for it on my table, I don't recognize the number on the screen.

I debate letting it go to voice mail, but then an image of the receipt I scribbled my number on for Zach yesterday pops into my mind. I hold my breath as I answer it.

"Hello?"

"Addie!" he says brightly, like *he's* pleasantly surprised to hear me on the line. "I wasn't sure whether this was your cell phone or not, or I would have texted."

"Hey! No. It's my cell phone. So you could have texted. But it's fine that you called, also." *Oh my God. Shut up,* my brain screams at me. "How are you?"

I put my viola down on my bed. What do I say? Why is he calling? Where does one buy stock in Wit and Decent Phone Skills?

Luckily, he doesn't seem completely horrified. "I'm good, especially since I have the day off."

"That's awesome," I say. "Any plans?"

"Actually, that's why I'm calling. I don't know if this is weird or not"—he pauses, and I hear a bit of uncertainty in his voice—"but since your friend ditched you and I don't have to work, I thought I'd see if you wanted to hang out."

Is he asking me out? It sounds like he's asking me out.

"Addie?"

"Oh yeah, sure," I say, trying to sound casual. My heart, on the other hand, beats in syncopated triplets.

"We can do Completely Mundane Things with Unwarranted Enthusiasm," he says. Laughs his joyful, uncontained laugh. I return it with one of my own; I didn't really know I had one.

"That sounds great."

"Yeah? You can say no if you want. As I said, I sense that you are cooler, and I understand if you're not in the market for any more friends."

Friends.

So maybe he's not asking me out.

"You can never have too many friends," I say truthfully. Especially since I've capped off at one.

He offers to pick me up so I don't have to bike, and I give him directions to my house before we hang up. I quickly rifle through my closet for something to wear, settling on my favorite purple T-shirt, cuffed denim shorts, and flats. The real work is taming my hair, which has a hundred percent accuracy when it comes to informing me of when it's humid outside. In the end, I toss half of it into a ponytail and let the rest fall around my shoulders. I'm running down the stairs to wait by the front door when my mother comes in from the kitchen. It's Thursday, but I forgot she has this morning off.

The whole downstairs smells like baked fish, which we usually eat with roasted breadfruit—my dad's favorite. Breadfruit is green and about as big as my hand, and it tastes like a cousin to potatoes. Mom has to special-order it at the farmers' market, but I guess she figures she learned how to bake, sauté, fry, and do a million other things with it in the fifteen years she was married to Dad, so she might as well use it. Cooking is, apparently, Mom's choice of distraction from our familial brand of SAD today. I immediately feel a niggling, familiar guilt for not spending more time with her this summer or looking for ways to cheer her up—Caleb certainly isn't going to—or being as sad as I should about the anniversary of their divorce.

"Where are you going in such a hurry?" she asks.

"My friend is picking me up."

Her eyebrows rise up. "I thought Katy was out of town."

"Another friend," I say.

She folds her arms across her chest. "Someone I don't know?"

The guilt for not spending more time with her starts to dissipate. Resisting the urge to roll my eyes, I say, "They wouldn't let you hold my hand and go to school with me every day, remember? So *yes,* someone you don't know."

"Don't be cheeky, Addison," Mom says. "This is a friend from school, then?"

If she knew I just met this boy in the video store less than two weeks ago, she'd definitely want to meet him. And I can't think of anything more embarrassing than Zach getting inter-rogated by my mother on our first maybe-date.

Because one or two things in the universe are working in my favor, the phone rings right then and Mom goes to get it. She's been waiting for a phone call from Bruce, this guy she started dating a few months ago. I know she expects me to wait there for her to finish speaking, but when she turns her back to me to write something down, I take that chance to make a run for the front door. It's humid outside, but not quite as hot as it's been the past few days. I'm just stepping onto the driveway when an aqua-blue car rattles up in front of the house. Zach waves as I get closer, then leans over to open the door for me.

"Hey!" he says.

"Hi!" I know lots of upbeat people—Katy, hypochondria aside, included—but what's different about Zach is that I seem to match him exclamation mark for exclamation mark. Usually without thinking about it.

The inside of his car smells a bit smoky. The leather seats are warm, as if the car's been in the sun for hours, and it's littered with paper bags, bottles, and empty cigarette packs. There's a pile of DVDs on the floor of the passenger's side.

"Shit, I was going to move that. Sorry," Zach says as the pile collapses around my feet when I get in.

I laugh, picking up the DVDs and moving them to the backseat, which is full of film magazines. A stuffed koala dangles from his rearview mirror. "Is this what it looks like inside your brain?"

"Unfortunately, yes," Zach says, smiling. He's wearing a T-shirt and jeans, same as every time I've ever seen him in his dad's store. His hair is especially remarkable today, the front part of it curling up a little bit, like the tails of little *j*'s. He turns to me, hands on the steering wheel, but doesn't start the car. I have horrifying visions of my mom running out here, furious that I left while she was distracted, and dragging me back in. "So where should we go? What's the most mundane thing you can think of?"

"Hmmm. Laundry. Chores. Post office."

Zach makes a face. "Post office? I thought we were going for mundane, not painful."

I laugh. "Gardening? Grocery shopping?"

"Shopping!" Zach says, pointing at me like I've hit on something ingenious. "That is perfect."

As soon as we drive off, I text my mom: *Sorry. Ride got here while you were on phone! Love you!*

We're near the mall, but we decide to drive a little bit farther to the discount store because it won't be as crowded and, it turns out, we're both cheap. The conversation is steady and normal for the whole drive (we talk about the DVDs he has in his car, which ones are good and worth seeing), but there's this current running through my body the whole time we're talking. It makes me hyper-aware of everything, of the number of times Zach glances over at me as he drives (five), the number of times he laughs at something I say (three), the number of times he touches his hair (seven). I fiddle with my seat belt and fold my hands in my lap, but then that feels matronly and weird, so I unfold them and leave them flat on my shorts, wondering what, in general, people tend to do with their hands.

When we get into the store, Zach pulls out a cart and says, "Have you ever played Bigger and Better?"

"No. How does it work?" It's around noon now and a weekday, so there are only a couple other customers apart from us.

"It's easy. You start out with the smallest thing possible, like, say . . ." He glances around and we're right by the stationery aisle, so he throws an eraser into the cart. "Then *you* pick something else out—something bigger and better—and we keep trading until we wind up with the biggest and best thing there is in here. Then we pay for it and feel awesome."

"Oh, but that sounds like too much *fun* to qualify as mundane," I say sarcastically, and Zach laughs.

"I think we can make it work. Your turn."

I inspect the items closest to us, take out Zach's eraser, and replace it with a pack of yellow Post-its.

He gives me a skeptical look. "It's definitely bigger, but is it better?"

"Of course," I say. "Everybody loves Post-its."

"*I* don't love Post-its," Zach says. "This No Boys Aloud notebook does not love Post-its." He takes out the pack of Post-its and picks up this bright orange book with the four faces of the latest pop girl group to hit the music scene. He shakes his head as he leafs through it. "I'm sorry. The Spice Girls were better."

I snort. "Oh yeah? And who was your favorite, Zach?"

He frowns as if trying hard to recall something. "Thyme?" he asks innocently. His gray eyes twinkle as he tries not to laugh, and something flutters in my chest. "Oregano?"

"Oh my God," I say. "I hope for your sake that you're actually kidding."

Before middle school, one of my many loves was musical groups. I loved the harmonies and the different, complicated histories you could create for each member. Whether they were random bubblegum groups with a five-second life expectancy or Queen, who my dad and I would sing along with in the car. You could never convince us that we didn't have enough voices for the opening multipart harmony of "I Want

It All." I haven't thought about that in forever, and it hurts trying to remember the last time I had that much fun with my dad. Thoughts of the terrible family dinner swirl in my mind, and I suddenly want to go home and blast Queen songs, use them to lure my parents, my brother, myself out of ourselves. I'd wake us all up with Freddie Mercury.

Instead, I pick up a book of crossword puzzles and hold my hand out for the notebook, but Zach refuses to hand it over.

"You can't. A puzzle book? This notebook is clearly superior."

I make a grab for it when Zach isn't expecting it, and our fingers brush, and that electric *zap* surges through my body again. Blood rushes to my ears as I take the notebook from him and drop the crossword book in. I can't tell if he felt it, too, or what exactly that *was,* so I pretend to be thoroughly inspecting the aisles and don't meet his eyes.

We move into the home décor aisle, and Zach takes this couch cushion with French words stenciled in loopy black cursive: *L'amour fait les plus grandes douceurs et les plus sensible infortunes de la vie.*

My attempt at translating goes like this: "Love fate— feet?—big . . . two?"

I glance at Zach and he's repressing laughter, a fist placed over his mouth. "Go on. It sounds like you're on the right track."

"Sensible unfortunate life," I finish.

"So obviously"—Zach pauses, seeking out the right words—"love is for everyone, even Bigfoot."

"Two big feet or two Big*foots* might not be a sensible pairing," I offer.

"Right, because they'd be way more conspicuous that way," he says.

"But a lone Bigfoot is in for an unfortunate life."

"*Yes,*" Zach says emphatically. "We've mastered the French language in, what, five minutes?" He holds up his hand for a high five and I raise mine to meet it, my palm all nerve endings where it touches his.

"And *this* is why French people hate Americans," I laugh.

It's actually fairly hard to find something bigger and better than that, but eventually I go with this oval-shaped plastic storage container. Zach is not having any of it.

"I see your random and flimsy bin and I raise you this broom," he says.

"Um, no way."

"Why not?" he protests.

"It's not bigger *or* better. It's just longer."

"I think that counts, Addie."

"We can't leave here with a broom!"

Finally he relents and then we traipse around the store for several minutes until we find something to Zach's liking. "Yes! My mom has one of these," he exclaims as he approaches the far end of an aisle. "I think I win with this one. It looks like one thing from afar, but when you get close, when you really look closely, it looks like something else."

He says this with such drama that I have to laugh.

"It looks like an umbrella, Zach."

"Wrong," he says. I'm pretty sure he's not allowed to do this, but he pushes the tag out of the way and opens the umbrella up. It flares out with a swoosh, nearly knocking down some stacks of hangers by us. "It's a *giant-ass* umbrella.

88

Functional, therefore better. And"—he points at the container in the cart—"bigger, therefore bigger."

A little boy turning in to the aisle where we are points and whispers something to his dad. Zach turns the open umbrella so that it curves away from us, blocking us from the view of the customers, and he grins at me. "Think they can see us?"

We're standing with our backs to a shelf of items, and when he speaks, I realize how close we are to each other. I almost shiver from how silly and light I feel.

"I think we're in their way," I whisper back, and Zach laughs and closes the umbrella so they can pass. One of the store workers is giving us the eye, and I don't think I can top Zach's item anyway, so we go to the checkout and pay for it.

On the way out, Zach hands it to me. "Yours," he says.

I shake my head. "You won fair and square. I don't need your pity."

But he pokes my arm with the knob at the end of it and says, "I'm not pitying you. I'm having too much fun for it to be mundane. So I'm disqualified."

I don't know if his words land exactly the way he meant them to, because the atmosphere shifts the slightest bit then and I feel myself grinning and he glances away, like he didn't mean to say that. I take the umbrella from him.

"Thanks."

While we were inside the store, someone stuck a yellow flyer under the wiper: OVERTON INC.—CUTTING-EDGE NEUROSCIENTIFIC PROCEDURES THAT CAN CHANGE YOUR LIFE. I hand it to Zach, who crumples the piece of paper and tosses it into the nearest garbage can.

As we climb into the car, Zach says, "So we have the first

part of Doing Completely Mundane Things Exuberantly down, but we're missing a crucial part."

"What's that?" I ask.

"The bragging," he says.

We stay in the parking lot—windows down—while I craft the perfect text to Katy, using the memory of some of her updates as a template.

Just spent an hour shopping and bought nothing but a big-ass umbrella from Two Dollars or Less. Blessed!

Zach is thoroughly impressed when I show him my work, and Katy's response—uncharacteristically fast, considering it's been taking her hours to text back—is great.

??

Huh?

We shake with laughter for a few moments and then I say, "So what's our next mundane thing? Or is one enough for the day?"

"Well, my car is in desperate need of a wash."

We drive over to the car wash and I help Zach throw out his garbage, then lift up the magazines and DVDs so he can vacuum.

I can't help it. I send Katy another text.

Suds. Water. Everything smells like wax. Best car wash of my life. Life is good.

It is not so far from the truth.

THE FUQ?!!! she texts back.

Zach and I erupt in laughter and keep working. He refuses to throw out his broken and therefore unwatchable *Mask of Life* DVD in case anything can be done to fix it. My body hums from feeling for the last three hours like it's been struck by lightning, and I'm afraid to breathe too deeply, to make any sudden movements. I think that maybe this is what it's like to feel wide awake.

When I get home, I send Katy another text, and I know before I send it that I'm going to get a response in all caps, though I don't know when, and all I say is, *So . . . there's this boy.*

16

AFTER
January

He's staring at me, forehead creased with a frown.

The boy from the bus.

Bentley Lake is windy today, the grass in the park around it covered with days-old snow. After a big storm like the one we had over the weekend, the snow stays for ages on the ground, except on roads and highways that have been salted and walkways that have been shoveled. Still, it's one of the warmer days we've had in weeks, and people are strolling along the cleared paths around the park. And there he is, sitting on a bench, long legs outstretched, hands tucked into his jeans pockets. No coat or sweater or anything. He's wearing the same black beanie he had on a few hours ago when he showed up outside the music-room window.

And then disappeared.

I tug on my own wool hat, self-conscious and cold, as I triple-check that I'm really seeing him.

I came here to figure out what to do with the fact that I'm going crazy. To decide who to go to since I can't go to my parents. And then to clear my head and simply breathe fresh air for a few minutes.

But, of course, he couldn't let me have that.

He followed me.

Or showed up here.

Or something.

I fix my eyes on him now as I march toward the bench, determined not to let him slip between my fingers again without some serious answers. I'm trying so hard not to blink—in case he vanishes—that my eyes sting a little by the time I reach him.

"Who the hell are you?" I hiss when I'm standing in front of him. I have so many questions that they come bursting right out of me. "What do you want? Why can't anyone else see you? What happened on the bus that night?"

He blinks at me.

"What the hell is going on?"

He doesn't say anything, just keeps looking at me. I am ready to grab him by the shoulders and start shaking him.

"Hello? *Answer me.*"

"I don't know." He is still frowning, his gray eyes serious as he looks up at me. "I don't even know my own name."

"What do you mean, you don't know?" I ask, my voice rising. I take a threatening step forward till I'm leaning right over him. "I swear to God, if you don't start talking—if you don't tell me everything right now—I'm . . . I'm going to the police."

Instead of calling my bluff—the fact that *I'd* be more

likely to end up restrained than him, since he's probably a symptom of my psychosis—he just says, "Addison, if I knew, I would tell you. I promise."

I breathe deeply as I try to make sense of his words.

The strangest, most frustrating thing happens then. The most terrifying, too, since I've been so sure that if I could only talk to him, if I could only confront him and get him to explain, everything would be fine. But what happens is this: I believe him.

I can *see*—from the earnestness in his eyes, the solemnness of his expression—that he's telling the truth.

It feels like a giant whack to my chest, and I have to sit down on the bench beside him to maintain any semblance of composure. Remind myself to take even breaths, stay calm.

I whirl around to face him. "How do you know my name, then, if you don't remember anything? You just called me Addison! How did you know that?"

"Your brother called you that. That night on your driveway."

"No, he . . ."

Wait. He did.

"My friends call me Addie," I spit.

He pauses a second and then lets it roll slowly off his lips, as if he's trying to see if it sounds like me. Also, there's a bit of a challenge to it, as he's holding my gaze. *"Addie."*

It sounds like a secret, the way he says it.

I lose my train of thought on the way to telling him that he's not my friend.

"So what are you? A ghost? Is that it—are you dead? Or are you some figment of my imagination?"

He laughs then. The full sound sends a wave of warmth up my arms. But it's a short laugh and there's something a little bit sad about it.

And almost immediately he's back to frowning again.

We sit beside each other silently for a few moments. Watching people walking, cars driving by at the edge of the park. "What's wrong?" I ask finally. Grudgingly. It shouldn't matter to me that he looks so unhappy.

"I remember being at your school this morning, and I remember being at the movie theater the other day. Your house and, of course, the bus. But I don't remember anything in between all those things," he says, staring down at his hands in his lap.

"What does that mean?" I ask.

"It means I don't know how I got off the bus, or if I did." He runs his hand through the front of his hair, the only part sticking out, his voice thick with distress. "It means I'm only *around* when you are."

I stare at him silently, watching the cloud his breath makes in the air, and I feel an unexpected twinge for him.

"Maybe it's just a weird type of amnesia," I offer halfheartedly. It's the best I can do through my own disappointment and fury at . . . whatever this is. Just then a woman walks up and places her handbag on the space on the bench next to me, then bends down to tie her shoelace. She put her handbag on the space on the bench *where the boy is sitting,* and only the two of us can see that this purple bag is on his lap, and the whole scene is so ridiculous, so insane, that I have absolutely no choice but to burst out laughing, which prompts Bus Boy to also burst out laughing. The woman jerks up at my laughter and looks at me like I'm crazy—*correct*—and then she grabs her bag from the seat and hurries away like I might attack her or make off with her bag or something.

"I'm not sure she even finished tying her shoe," I say, which elicits another peal of laughter from Bus Boy.

Sobering up, I put my hand close to where her bag was—on his lap—and there's a *human* there. Flesh. Encased in a pair of jeans. I just put my hand on this stranger's lap.

I snatch it back quickly, feeling my ears heat up, and he coughs.

"So I guess you're not entirely human," I say, even though I can feel his body warmth, see his breath, touch him.

He doesn't answer that. What he says instead is, "When you leave, I'll disappear again. If you forgot about me, I'd probably be gone for good."

He says it like he's joking, but I can't tell whether it's the slight chill in the air that makes him shiver or a little bit of fear. Even if he *isn't* real, it must feel real to be him.

I wonder if he's right, though. He doesn't always appear when I want him to, but most of the times I *have* seen him, apart from the first night on the bus, it's been because I was thinking about him. If I could just decide to never think of him again, would he be gone? Could it be that simple? But even if I can get rid of him, how do I know he won't show up again someday, unprompted?

"Could you at least *try* to guess at what your name is? Maybe you're someone's ghost and, you know, we could figure out what's happening if we had the details?"

"Maybe I'm a Matthew," he says.

I face him and try to gauge whether the name fits him.

"Or John?" he offers. "Luke?"

"Are you just naming guys from the Bible now?"

He laughs, sounding more normal than he did a few minutes ago, less sad. "*That* guy looks like a John, though. The one running with his dog."

I find said man: mid-thirties, winter vest and gray tracksuit, running with the leash of a jittery Jack Russell. "Maybe," I say.

"And his dog's name could be Apollo."

"What's that lady's name?" I ask, nodding in the direction of a blond woman walking with a middle-school-age boy.

"Suzanne. Maybe Lorelei."

I raise an eyebrow at him. "If this is so easy for you, you really should be able to figure out your own name."

Just try, I want to beg him. *Please just try.*

He shrugs, but there's that layer of sadness again. I shift to get more comfortable on the bench, and he glances up, like he thinks I'm about to leave and he'll disappear again. The tension in his body decreases when he sees that I'm not going yet.

My fingers tingle from the sharp drop in temperature the last couple of minutes, and I rub them together to warm them. It's the kind of chilly that targets the ends of things: the tips of fingers and noses, ears and knees and toes.

"Cold?" he asks.

"No, I'm—"

But he's already leaning toward me, tugging down my hat so it covers better. His fingers brush the tips of my ears, making them warmer than they already are. He doesn't take his hands back immediately, and it's only when I lean away from him, my heart ticktocking in my chest, that he leans back, too.

"Um, thanks," I say, embarrassed. How is any of what I see or feel real if this—this hearing him breathe out loud, this feeling his fingers on my skin—is not?

"No problem."

I feel so frustrated I could cry. I am sitting with the very person, the very *apparition,* that has tormented me the past few days, and I still don't know a thing about him, about how he got here, why he's here, and what *I'm* supposed to do about it all.

But the other side of it—the unexpected side—is that I feel bad for *him.* He reminds me, weirdly, of myself when I'm with Katy's friends or people at school, of having a family where no one really looks at each other. It's not the same as being an invisible person. But I think *lonely* feels a lot like not remembering your own name.

So I stay with him for another few minutes, naming more strangers we don't know, until it starts to get a little too cold to be outside and the sun starts to sink in the sky.

He doesn't feel all that much like a stranger. It feels comfortable—normal, even—sitting here with him. Still, I notice all the passersby giving me wary looks as they walk, trying to figure out who I'm talking to. And when I finally stand and say an awkward goodbye to him, I know that this afternoon—the strange comfort and understanding between us—doesn't change anything.

I still have to get help.

I still, in all probability, am bat-shit crazy.

17

BEFORE
Mid-July

"You didn't say she was *this* tall."

It is Saturday morning, two days after our day of mundane things, and Zach's best friend, Raj, frowns at me like what he means is, *You forgot to mention she was a troll.*

"Addie's not that tall," Zach says, shooting me an apologetic look, then frowning in Raj's direction.

"She's taller than me!" Raj protests, ignoring the message in Zach's eyes.

"So?" Zach asks, exasperated.

Raj sighs, flopping onto the couch in Zach's (mercifully) air-conditioned basement. Raj has a round face, brown skin, and straight black hair down to his ears. He's dressed almost exactly like Zach.

When I first got here—I biked over and arrived before Raj did—Zach opened the door, out of breath from running up the stairs. We smiled shyly at each other and then Zach said,

"My parents aren't home, but you've met my dad. Kevin will come down in a second, and in the meantime, I can introduce you to everyone else."

We rounded a corner into the hallway, and Zach stooped down to pet a gray Persian cat slinking along the wall. "This is Macy," he said. She stared at us, tail raised, with judgmental green eyes.

"Hi, Macy," I said.

"This is Diego Maradona," he said, pointing up at a framed poster of a soccer player on the wall, next to a picture of two elderly couples I assumed were Zach's grandparents. The poster had a hard-to-read black signature on it and LA MANO DE DIOS typed underneath it. "The first person my dad would save in case of fire."

I laughed. "Wow, I don't think I've ever met a famous person before. Your dad likes soccer?"

"His parents were first-generation Irish immigrants, so that would be a yes."

"My dad is a soccer fan, too. He claims North Americans are the only people on earth who take it for granted."

"Hey, now. Mexico appreciates the beautiful game," Zach said. "And don't let my dad hear you call it soccer."

Dad has tons of stories of growing up playing soccer indoors, on the streets, in random fields with his brother, Uncle Mark, who died before I was born. Their parents let them because that was what they had grown up doing in Vincy. He doesn't tell me these stories anymore; now we talk about furniture.

We walked a little farther into an open-plan dining area, and I followed Zach to a rectangular fish tank with a bluey-green tinge and a bevy of plants and rocks on the bottom. He squinted a bit and then pointed to the glass. "There's Goldie Hawn, Kevin's fish. My mom named him."

An orange tail flicked out from behind a leafy green plant. I imagined it was waving hello.

"Him?" I asked.

"Hey, Goldie's a gender-neutral name for goldfish."

We both laughed.

"So, do you live with anyone who actually talks back to you?"

"I swear I do," Zach said. "Kevin's around somewhere. You're just early."

We went down the stairs off Zach's kitchen into a living-room area in the basement littered with camera equipment and made small talk while we waited.

Now, with everyone present, Zach hands me and Raj about ten stapled sheets of paper each. "Here's the final script. Sorry, we were out of blank paper, so I printed it on lined." Raj sighs heavily as he receives his. I read the copy Zach emailed yesterday, and on first glance, the opening scene looks exactly the same.

"Kev!" Zach calls, and I'm shocked when a skinnier version of Zach—precisely the same color hair, but shorter and not as bouncy—appears.

"This is my brother Kevin," Zach says.

Kevin grins at me, a smile from the same family of smiles as Zach's but—how to put this?—greasier. *"Heeeey,"* he slurs. His greeting is met with a whack to the back of his head so swift that if I'd blinked, I'd have missed it.

"He's *fourteen*," Zach says pointedly, and I smile, kind of enjoying Zach's protectiveness of me, despite being weirded out by his brother's creepiness.

"Fifteen almost," Kevin says, which instantly makes him seem even younger. In trying to bargain for more freedoms, I used to say stuff like that to my mom all the time, and it's only recently I figured out how dumb it is to remind your parents that you can't count (nine months is not "almost") and that you're Not Even [Insert Age] yet.

"Nice to meet you," I tell Kevin, then turn back to Zach. "How many siblings do you have?"

"Three brothers. Two older—both of them live a few hours away. You have just one older brother, right?" Zach asks.

I nod. "It must be nice having a big family. I would love that."

"Believe me, sometimes I would rather just have one brother."

Zach goes to sit on the couch, bits and pieces of camera equipment around him.

I sit on the other end of the couch from Zach, who says, "So I think we need a schedule for shooting and editing this time."

"*I think* we need to get paid. I won't work for free like last summer," Kevin says, flipping through the pages of the script. "Now that I have a real job."

"We can't afford to pay you," Zach tells him.

"Then you can't afford me." But Kevin stays put, continuing to leaf through the script, and minutes later they're talking sets and makeup, which it looks like Kevin is in charge of.

"Why can't we use the trampoline like last time?" Kevin is arguing.

"Because," Zach says patiently, "it was Lindsay's."

There's a momentary silence before Raj says, "She won't let you borrow it?"

"No," Zach answers in a quiet voice. "She doesn't want anything to do with"—he hesitates—"us."

I could have sworn he was going to say something different.

"What a bitch," Kevin says.

"Shut up, Kevin," Zach says, his voice even.

"I'm just saying. If I broke up with you, *I* would let you borrow the trampoline. She knows we need it. How many films did *we* let *her* be in? Beeyotch."

"Kevin," Zach says again.

"Um," I say quietly, "who is Lindsay?"

Heavy silence follows before Raj says, "Zach's ex."

One more beat of silence.

In it, I cling to the word "ex." Zach's *ex*. On the one hand, it means he doesn't have a girlfriend *now*, that our maybe-date the other day still counts as just that. On the other hand . . .

"Not my character, *Lindy*?" I ask.

"Of course not," Zach says, glancing at me as if I've sprouted a second head.

"Your character's a *nun*," Raj adds, implying that Lindsay was not, in fact, a nun. "Zach's quit Lindsay like a bad habit."

It's the first hint of lightness Raj has shown since we met, and he chuckles at his own joke. Kevin roars with laughter, slapping his thigh. "Good one!"

Zach does not laugh.

"You know, Mom and I saw her at the mall the other day and we waved and she just kept walking," Kevin says, shaking his head.

"Maybe she didn't see you," Zach says, eliciting a snort from Raj.

"Oh, she saw us," Kevin insists. "Beeyotch."

"That seems a little harsh," I say, surprising myself by sticking up for someone I don't even know. Someone who *used to be Zach's girlfriend.* But still. I wouldn't want people calling me names.

Raj looks at me, no emotion on his face. "Lindsay's not a bitch because she doesn't want to date Zach," he says. "*No one wants to date Zach.* She's a bitch because she's mean."

Zach coughs and steers the conversation back to the script he's just handed out, but I keep wondering about Lindsay. What she is like, how long they dated (they all seem to know her quite well), whether she was prettier than me or smarter or what.

The three boys continue to talk, referring to past films and ideas for props and scenes.

Zach suggests we do a read-through, and I'm really beginning to question whether any of this is a good idea. Raj (Solomon) and I (Lindy) are the leads. Kevin is the Carpenter, and Zach reads the random parts like Stranger 1, Guy with Ax in Head, and Exorcist.

I feel myself getting nervous as we start reading. Which is so stupid. I'm used to performing in front of rows of people, people trained to hear every note and key change, every mistake. Yet I feel more embarrassed than I can remember feeling for any performance when Zach says, "Okay, Lindy bursts in here."

"Um"—I swallow—"did I hear that you were looking for Little, um, Georgia? Georgie. All the children were picked up last Friday."

My ears are burning so hard they couldn't pick up an ounce of sound if they tried.

Surprisingly, when I glance at Zach, he winks at me. I am not a fool; I know that was possibly one of the worst line readings ever, and I think, *Oh God. No way he'd settle for me if Katy was around.*

It occurs to me that my best friend would kick ass at this.

In the same breath, though, I realize I am glad that Katy isn't around kicking ass. I'm glad Zach chose me to be in his movie, winked at *me*. And with that, I continue my wooden line readings.

To be fair, if I am wood, Raj is metal: "Oh no. My spleen."

I giggle quietly to myself and then a little louder when I see Zach's shoulders shaking.

When we are done reading, I am feeling a little more confident, Kevin is hitting on me again, and the bar, overall, has been set much lower than I initially understood it to be.

Raj, however, is stuck in precisely the same place.

"So how tall are you exactly?" he asks.

"Five seven," I say.

He sighs.

Lindsay, I realize, must have been shorter.

18

AFTER
January

My parents are the very last resort. If either of them finds out what I've been seeing, I'll be in a psychiatric facility so fast I won't know what hit me. I consider driving myself to the hospital, but after the night I spent there after the accident, I'll try anything I can to avoid going back. To avoid the worried look on my mother's face, the plastic food, the stench of disinfectant hiding the smell of worse things.

So after I leave the park, I race home and log on to my computer. I don't know what to search for. Hallucinations? Psychosis? I go with the former, but I'm immediately knee-deep in articles about delusional disorders, and a tremor runs down my back.

I reach into my pocket for the piece of paper, the note to myself.

If I'm asking, then I can't be.

I quickly close out of those pages and frown, struggling to think. I learned in school about a neuroscience facility close to Lyndale, and I've seen a few ads for it. I can't think of the name, though, so I type "neuroscience facility Lyndale" into the search engine. Nothing.

How is that possible?

I know it exists.

After a few minutes of racking my brain, the name comes back.

Overton.

I put it into the engine, but there's nothing.

Did you mean: Over town or Over a ton.

I'm pretty sure it's Overton.

I pull out my phone and try again, but I get the same ridiculous results. Do I have the name wrong?

Neither my phone nor my computer is yielding anything useful. It's not the first time I haven't been able to find something on my computer, thanks to the insane parental controls my mom has had on there since I was in middle school and Channel Sc7en ran some story on child predators and Internet safety. I've never figured out how to get around them.

When I crack open my bedroom door, I can hear my brother downstairs eating dinner, so I tiptoe down the hall.

I don't just avoid Caleb's room because we're not particularly close; I avoid Caleb's room because I value my life. Simply making it the approximately five feet from his door to his computer, I nearly lose my leg. There are clothes everywhere, three bowls with varying levels of moldy cereal, and books and papers covering every inch of his desk. His wall is plastered with pictures of different types of aircraft and a poster of Captain Chesley "Sully" Sullenberger, the pilot who successfully landed a plane in the Hudson River during an emergency.

After flinging Caleb's jeans off the armrest and onto the floor, I sit in his swivel chair and pull up a browser. I type in "Overton," and the website instantly comes up. I know he doesn't have controls on his computer, but I can't explain why mine couldn't even find any results. On the page in front of me, words like "nanotechnology" and "cognitive neuroscience" jump out at me, but with Caleb shuffling around downstairs, I only have time to skim-read. *Having Problems with Your Memory?* a banner at the top of the page asks.

"Yes," I whisper under my breath. From what I can gather, Overton helps people deal with memory problems and emotional issues. The page even mentions sleep somewhere; this is perfect. I grab a pen from his desk and scrawl the number on my palm. I can hear Caleb washing up downstairs, meaning he's done eating, so I close the window and quickly go to his browser history—I don't want him to know what I've been searching for. As I delete the pages I went on, curiosity forces me to look at Caleb's last web hits.

I feel a small kick of delight when I see that, somewhere in between a dozen video-game sites, Caleb searched for "aviation academies" this morning. Is it possible that he *is* itching to get out of Lyndale, after all? Maybe he's finally going to follow his heart.

I'm so busy marveling at this that I don't notice Caleb coming up the stairs until it's too late.

"Addison, what are you doing in my room?"

I jump out of his chair. "I was just, er, looking up New York stuff. School stuff. Some of the pages weren't opening because of the parental controls on mine."

His face is impassive. "You should have asked."

"Fine. Sorry," I say, starting to move toward the door, but then I stop. I know I shouldn't mention what I saw, but I can't help myself. "So, um, I saw you were looking at some aviation academies. Are you thinking of applying?"

"No, I'm not thinking of applying. Who the hell told you that you could use my computer?" Now he's starting to get angry.

"But why not?" I ask stubbornly. "It's obviously what you want to do."

"Leaving Lyndale won't fix anything, Addie."

I can no longer tell which one of us he's talking about. Caleb hates that I want to go to New York. Maybe even more than Mom does. It's like because he can't bring himself to leave, he can't conceive of the idea of anyone else wanting to.

And as happy as they are to clip our wings, it's not as if either of my parents needs us here. Dad only spends a portion of his time in his sad, clammy apartment; the rest of the time he spends doing what he loves. For two years, Mom has been happily dating Channel Se7en's five o'clock news anchor, best known as Bruce "Silver Fox" Landry. Or, to Caleb, as Bruce "Asshole" Landry. I don't think I've ever heard Caleb call him Bruce at any point except when they are face to face. At which point, my brother is the picture of respect.

"So it's better to stay here, forcing yourself to live a life you don't even want?" I ask.

Caleb is quiet and then, in the coldest voice he is capable of, says, "Get out of my room, Addison."

"Fine," I spit. I've barely gotten into the hallway when the door slams shut behind me. I know what I said hit a nerve, and I want to feel guilty—I do—but I just feel irritated.

Caleb and I agree on some things. We both love plantains, fried like my father ate them growing up. We agree on Mom's boyfriend—that he's nice enough and we're glad he makes her happy, but we sure as hell hope she doesn't marry him, because it would break Dad's heart. And also Bruce wears leather oxfords without socks and has his teeth artificially whitened every other weekend. My brother and I feel exactly the same way about this. Sometimes we randomly say Bruce's hammy sign-off to each other: "Hate to leave you hanging, friends, but you'll have to join us in twenty-three hours for tomorrow's news."

We'd been close growing up, but when he was thirteen, right when he became a teenager, Caleb started pushing us all away. Maybe he was angry at the divorce, or maybe it was puberty. Or both—that shivering helplessness at everything changing at once. But the more I tried to include him in my life, the more he retreated from me. Ever since I told him I wanted to go to college in New York, he's seemed downright pissed at me. For leaving, I guess. Which makes no sense, given how little we interact now, living under the same roof.

When I was in elementary school, whenever my brother's friends from the neighborhood came over to ask if he would play tennis with them in the driveway, Caleb would yell, "I call Addie!" Even if they hadn't invited me to play.

Victor would make a face and say, "Caleb's just showing

off. He wants to prove he can beat us, even with a girl on his team."

Both Victor and Job were Caleb's age, and remarkably, Victor had managed to make it to the seventh grade, despite having a pea for a brain. Caleb would roll his eyes at him and tell him to shut up. Which he finally did, when we beat him soundly, even with a boy on my team.

We played pickup basketball in front of Victor's house, and then, too, Caleb would say, "I call Addie." I wondered whether it was because of Dad, flying in another part of the world, and the way he always looked at Caleb before he went and said, "Take care of things on the ground, okay?" I thought that was the reason Caleb looked out for me, keeping his promise to Dad by being nice to me. Or maybe he was saving me the pain of being paired off with either Victor or Job.

Except that when they didn't come out to play and it was just the two of us in the driveway with our rackets, Caleb would ask, "Us against the wall?" And then we'd hit the ball at the garage door and take turns swinging it back.

As we played, Caleb would recite random facts to me.

Did you know that the pilot and copilot almost always eat separate meals, in case one of them gets food poisoning? Dad told me that.

Did you know that there are more than sixty thousand people in the air in the United States at any given time? That's more people than live in Lyndale.

Did you know the longest flight in the world is from Fort Worth to Sydney, Australia? It's almost exactly seventeen hours long.

"*Did you know that the Concorde traveled at more than*

twice the speed of sound? And you could actually hear this massive boom when it broke the sound barrier. Although the first aircraft to break the sound barrier was a Douglas DC-8 in 1961."

After we moved five years ago, there were no more tennis games in the driveway. There were only memories of a time when we used to know each other.

It catches me off guard sometimes how much I miss the relationship we used to have. It happens when Caleb and I are mocking Bruce's sign-off together. Sometimes, when Mom ropes us into watching the holiday movies we've seen every year since we were in diapers, we'll accidentally recite the same lines at exactly the same time, and I feel it then, too. It feels like finding something important you'd misplaced but hadn't really noticed was gone. In those moments, we're shaking dust off something lost and it's like, *Oh, there you are.*

There we are.

Only to lose it again.

19

BEFORE
Mid-July

Caleb is bleary-eyed when he comes down for breakfast on Monday morning. With the exception of Mom's short-lived family movie nights, our paths haven't crossed much this summer. Instead of celebrating the end of high school, making plans for the rest of his life, he's been holed up in his room. Today he's wearing sweatpants and a crusty-looking shirt, but the most offensive thing about his appearance is the dusting of dark facial hair on his chin.

"New look?" I ask, unable to hide my disapproval.

Without looking up at me, my brother pats his chin. "Just something I'm trying."

"I don't think it's working," I say. He doesn't answer, just chews his Lucky Charms silently, obnoxiously. Most of Caleb's friends hightailed it out of Lyndale the second they were done, the way I plan to. I look at him and wonder if he feels lonely, if he secretly hates that he's staying. I want to ask him *why* he is.

I doubt he'll tell me, though.

We never confide in each other.

I remember being fourteen and wanting so much to be included in everything my brother was doing. One afternoon after Caleb had just gotten his license and inherited Mom's old car, I saw him getting ready to go out and I asked to go with him, but he refused. He was so set on whatever he was doing—his jaw stiff, his eyes determined. He was gone for hours, and when he came back, he went straight upstairs. I tiptoed after him, curious.

I found him in the bathroom, his shirt raised, looking in the mirror and flinching like he'd been stung. I moved closer, quietly, so he wouldn't see me through the glass, and I saw him touching his rib gingerly. He looked like he was about to cry.

I stepped into the bathroom before he had time to pull down his shirt.

R. That was all his tattoo said.

"Oh my God!" I exclaimed. "You got a tattoo?"

His face contorted. I was sure he was going to tell me to get lost, threaten me to breathe a word and it would be my last, but to my surprise, he only seemed terrified.

"Please don't tell Mom," he begged me. "Or Dad. Please."

"Okay," I said. I was shocked at what he'd done and, most of all, at his response. I liked the idea of a secret between us, but I wanted to feel fully included.

"Who is she, anyway?" I asked. "R?"

Caleb didn't answer.

"Rachel? Rebekah? Rrrrrandy," I said. Admittedly, I was jealous. I wished I could've thought of something or someone

I cared about enough to mark my skin, my body, with their name.

"Addie, please," was all Caleb said. The lack of disdain in his voice surprised me again. I promised not to say anything.

When I broke a couple of weeks later and told Mom, it was payback for something stupid like Caleb taking too long in the shower. As soon as I saw his face and Mom's, though, I wished I hadn't done it. She was furious with him and, inexplicably, with me.

"I'm sorry," I told Caleb after he and Mom had finished a yelling match behind the closed door of her room. "Is it because you're underage? It's not a big deal. Lots of people have tattoos. I'm sorry."

He stalked into his room and banged the door shut.

"I'm sorry," I called from the other side, but he didn't answer. I knew somehow I'd crossed a line, done something I couldn't take back, no matter how desperately I wanted to.

I caught him on his way into the bathroom the next morning. "Caleb, I'm sorry. It's just a tattoo. Mom will get over it. Should I talk to her or something?"

"Just leave it, Addie," he said with such finality and coldness that it scared me. "Leave it."

I thought of the way I'd found him in the bathroom, running his hand over the curve of the *R* like it was either precious or painful. Maybe both.

Who's R? I wanted to ask him when he was finally speaking to me again, weeks later, but I couldn't. Everything between us felt fragile, tentative.

In a way, it still does.

I force myself to try now, though.

"What's wrong?" I ask.

He takes so long to answer that at first I don't think he will, but finally he says, "Nothing's wrong." But I'm not sure I believe it. "Summer, you know," he adds halfheartedly.

"People still bathe and have normal human contact over the summer," I say, even if we can lounge around the house and sluggishly pass the time.

I'm tempted to ask whether he wants to do something, hang out like we used to when we were younger, but we don't really do that. So instead, I retreat and start getting ready for my viola lesson. Soon Caleb is back in his room, the door shut between us.

"Why didn't you *tell* me?" Zach asks, his mouth open in surprise, moments after I enter his house. It's our first official day of shooting, and he is staring at my viola.

"It never came up," I answer with a shrug. I've just come from my lesson, which I biked to, so my viola is still in my basket.

After a little back-and-forth, Zach has been able to come up with a production schedule that suits all of us. He is working evenings at the movie store this week. Kevin, who landed a job as a dishwasher at Pizza Hut, starts work at four every afternoon. And since my lessons go till ten-thirty every weekday morning, I can only start after eleven, which works well with Raj's request that he not be required to wake up, under any circumstances, before ten.

The great thing is that, with my mom at work, she can't

hover or demand to meet Zach's entire family or something embarrassing like that.

"We were going to use Raj's iPod for the sound track," Zach says now.

"Rajesh likes *honky-tonk*," Kevin adds with disgust. "And not the kind *I* like."

"Kev," Zach says tiredly. He turns to face me again, still wearing the look of shock he had earlier. "Will you play something?"

"Um, sure," I say, even though I am thinking, *Oh God, no.* Maybe it is preshooting jitters, but I can't help feeling nervous whenever Zach's full attention is on me. Our test run the other day went well, but I noticed something. Zach is different when he's behind the camera. He is very calm and focused, and he is almost always frowning with intensity, concentrating. I'm terrified now that somehow I'll disappoint him. Or maybe it's just those gray eyes—twinkling, I can handle, but smoldering, traveling slowly over my face, even with the lens between us, I just cannot get used to.

I sit down on one of the couches, careful not to crush any of Zach's camera equipment, which is scattered everywhere at this point. Then I open my case, pull out my instrument, and begin to play.

I play for a minute, tops, an upbeat melody I hope they'll recognize.

When I am finished, Kevin bursts into applause. "Bravo! Bravo!"

Both Zach and Raj are quiet for a minute, and I watch them, flushed from playing, trying not to be disappointed at their mild reaction.

117

Then, together, they go quietly, "Oh my God." The very first time I met Raj, apart from the fact that he dressed casual and seemed moderately invested in, if a little detached from, their film, it was hard for me to see why he and Zach were friends. But little by little, I'm seeing similarities. Both of them can talk Ciano movies for hours—Zach pro, Raj also pro, but not at Zach's level. Raj, despite appearances, has a dry sense of humor. And for all the heaviness, the *sighing*, Raj brings into a room, Zach's lightness balances it out.

"What's wrong?" I ask now, biting on my lower lip.

"That's fucking *Super Mario*," Raj says, a little inflection— God help us—coming into his voice. "She plays *Super Mario!*"

Kevin laughs. He likes to slap things when he laughs—his thigh, the arm of the couch. Now he slaps Zach's back.

I laugh, too, relieved. "Oh, my brother was obsessed growing up, so I learned to play it."

Raj continues to appraise me, as if I am a deity. "*That* needs to be our sound track."

I realize Zach still hasn't spoken, but he's moved to start putting together his camera equipment.

I am packing away my viola, carefully, because I'm OCD about scratches, when I notice he's stopped what he's doing and is watching me.

"What?" I ask, brushing a strand of hair from my face. I pulled my hair into a somewhat sloppy French braid this morning so that, apart from my bangs, it would be effectively out of my way.

"You play like you're in love with it."

I laugh, but his eyes are so serious that I feel my ears tickle with heat. "Maybe I am," I say back, too quietly for Raj and Kevin to hear. Zach doesn't say anything in response, just watches me for a few more seconds.

The four of us move the furniture out of the way to open up the center of the basement. Zach places a pile of sheets on the ground, which we use to cover the couches just in case. Raj spreads newspaper over the carpet, and I help him, marveling at how efficient they are, how many times they must have done this.

"Okay, makeup," Zach says. "Kev, Mom wants you outside for that."

"The cat stepped in the paint tray that *one* time!" Kevin protests.

"I know, Kev," Zach says patiently. "But it got all over the house."

Kevin turns to me. "Follow me then, babe."

"Kev."

I let Kevin go a little ahead of me, hoping it'll read like a rejection of his romantic overtures. As I'm climbing up the stairs, I hear voices in the basement. Zach and Raj are talking, whispering.

I can't make out what they're saying, and I don't mean to eavesdrop, but I freeze for a second. Kevin has already disappeared through the basement door and is, I assume, outside already.

Figuring Kevin and I are gone by now, Zach and Raj raise their voices a bit.

"Like it wasn't obvious," Raj is saying.

I feel guilty for listening, and Raj is probably about to

come up the stairs to get made up, too, so I start to take the steps two at a time till I reach the kitchen and the side door leading outside.

But not before I hear Zach say, "That violin is one lucky son of a bitch."

Me. They're talking about me.

It barely registers that Zach calls it a violin instead of a viola.

Raj is laughing so hard now that the sound follows me out the door to where Kevin has set up camp.

I'd give almost anything to know what else they're saying, what Zach thinks about me.

It's unbearably hot out, but I hardly notice because I'm already burning all over.

20

BEFORE
Mid-July

The first two days of filming proceed without incident, unless you count running out of ketchup in the middle of a scene involving an ax lodged in someone's stomach.

It's the afternoon of our third day of filming. Raj is at the store, stocking up on ramen noodles and plastic machetes for tomorrow. "I'd have a better chance of finding this stuff if we were, say, in October," I can hear him yelling through Zach's phone when he calls.

Kevin is already at work, and I'm in the backyard, hosing down all of today's stuff before Zach's parents get home.

"Hey!" Zach says, coming outside. We haven't really been alone since our maybe-date last Thursday, but little eruptions keep happening in my chest whenever he so much as glances at me. I've been trying very hard not to let them show.

"Done inside?"

He nods, pulls a cigarette out of his pocket, and lights it.

See, not everything about him is perfect, I tell myself, looking away. *His lungs are probably covered in tar.*

I start to hose off my legs, since having ketchup trickling down them on the way home is something I can live without.

"I think I'm done with hot dogs. Forever," I say, and Zach laughs, breathing out a cloud of smoke.

"Sorry," he says. "I guarantee a couple of weeks after we're done, you'll start to miss all the ketchup."

"Maybe," I say skeptically. I've been wearing my oldest, rattiest clothes the past couple of days. Today I'm wearing a pair of denim cutoffs and an old tank top, with my bikini top underneath. My tank top got soaked through, thanks to my being misinformed about the proper workings of the hose by Kevin just before he left for work. I can't swallow my shock when I see Zach's eyes widen the slightest bit when he notices, and blood rushes to every bit of my skin.

"You know," I say when the silence grows too loud, "I feel like, of the four of us, you have the best end of this deal."

Zach smiles from where he's sitting on the last step of the deck, squinting from the sun. He stabs his cigarette butt into the concrete. "How do you figure?"

"We're all, like, *innards* at this point. All our characters. You"—I step toward him, wielding my hose like a weapon—"are practically unscathed so far." I let the hose spray the grass where his foot is.

Zach laughs, moving his feet up and holding his hands out. "Okay, stay calm. Disgruntled actors should be able to calmly address their grievances with *their director.*"

"I'm actually really, really calm," I say, flicking the hose up a few inches. "Are you?"

"Oh shit!" he exclaims as I let the hose spray his shirt. He's up and laughing immediately. I let the hose spray his face now, taking a few steps back as he runs straight for me.

I laugh maniacally, aiming the water right at his eyes so he's too disoriented to come after me.

"Where is my ketchup when I need it?" he sputters between gulps of water.

It's my overconfidence that does me in, or the fact that Zach is really fast and not as deterred by getting wet as I hoped. Soon he's gotten a portion of the hose and we're fighting for it. Then I'm completely wet, *soaked,* and now I'm the one squealing and looking for ketchup.

After begging for mercy—and Zach double-checking my surrender a few too many times—we wind up on the lowest step of the deck, breathing hard, Zach's T-shirt sticking to his chest just as tightly as my tank top clings to me. We're both still laughing, our knees touching, and then slowly, we grow quiet, listening to the cars passing behind the fence of his house, birds chirping somewhere far away.

My heart is racing even though I've caught my breath, and although it's the oldest trick in the book, I put my hand on the wood between us so he knows it's okay to touch it, to take it.

He doesn't.

"I finished recording the CD last night," I say, when neither of us has spoken for minutes. "I can bring it tomorrow."

"Huh?" Zach looks like he's missed an entire conversation, and it makes me feel better that he's flustered, that maybe he's *thinking* about taking my hand.

"The sound track?" I say, and turn my hand over in the space between us. Just a reminder that it's there.

A couple days ago, Zach and Raj picked out some classic horror music that they wanted me to play and record so we could use it for the movie. Not full songs, but a couple of bars from *Jaws* and something called *Night of the Electric Insects,* lots of minor chords and unresolved phrases.

"Oh, yeah." Zach nods. "Great. Thanks."

"Addie," he says all of a sudden, and I look up at him. "I've been thinking . . . and, I mean, maybe it was fine, maybe you didn't think anything of hanging out last week. You were missing your friend and I . . ." His voice drones out for a second, then resumes. "Maybe I should apologize for it."

"What?" I ask, confused.

Apologize?

No, no, no.

"Lindsay and I only broke up three months ago."

His gray eyes stare into me. I should be wondering why he's bringing this up, but I am busy being amazed that he said *only* three months. Katy has started and ended three "relationships" since she's been on her road trip. Texting me details of one guy, sometimes forgetting to mention that it is a different one now before she launches into the details of another life-shattering but short-lived connection.

"I just think it would be more fair to both of us if we were just friends."

"Oh." *Oh.*

My heart is tumbling down through my body. I can't look at him. I pull a blade of grass from the lawn. Then another.

Zach focuses on a different spot in the grass ahead as he speaks. "I'm not an idiot. And I'm not blind. You're beautiful, and I like hanging out with you. I mean, I do *like* you," he says, continuing to rip out every shred of hope I have, the way I'm doing to the grass in his lawn. I glance quickly at him and see that he is blushing. He has, after all, just admitted to liking me. He just called me *beautiful*. But. "But," he says, "I think I'd be a better friend than boyfriend right now."

I yank one more blade of grass out of the lawn and set it in my lap.

"Why did you break up?" I ask. "You and Lindsay?"

"We were together since we were Kevin's age and I guess . . . that our love was stifling. She said that it was *literally* draining the life out of her," he says. "Which I wasn't aware was something that could happen. I mean, with real love." He says this wryly, but I can tell that he is mostly serious. Our eyes meet and then flicker away from each other again, and because I'm in the process of being devastated, I don't tell him I agree with him. That I think love wakes people up. Even the idea of it. Even the whisper of the idea of it.

My body is thrumming, a timpani beat of want and disappointment and embarrassment.

"So I guess it's for the best that she ended it," Zach says. "But it still feels so recent."

He waits for me to speak and I don't. Silence is my only recourse.

"I'm trying to be honest, Addie," he says softly, and I nod, feeling like a world-class idiot. Feeling like a jerk for wanting to say, *Three months is a* lifetime *ago!* To ask what is so great about Lindsay anyway. Lindsay, whose refusal to lend her trampoline had, just this afternoon, led to Raj sighing heavily with him and Kevin having to hoist me (in nun costume) up at every third count from Zach. When that had failed, they

125

bring in a spring mattress from the guest bedroom for me to jump up from to make it look like I was flying through the air.

But instead, I say, "Thanks for telling me, Zach," the way my mother has taught me to, and then plot word for word the text I will send Zach later tonight, informing him that I rode into a postal truck on my way home from his place and have broken too many bones to continue filming. Or, alternately, that I've developed a sudden and ferocious allergy to anything red—ketchup, his *hair*—and, as such, can no longer be part of anything with which he is associated.

21

AFTER
January

I call first thing in the morning and make an appointment with Overton for after school. The receptionist is a woman with a crisp European accent, and when she asks what I'd like to see the doctor for, all I can think of to say is a checkup. I'm expecting her to ask more, but she just takes my name and tells me to get there fifteen minutes early for my appointment at four. If I have to pay for anything, I'll have to dig into my savings.

I'm hurtling out the front door, swallowing the last bite of my bagel, when I see him. Bus Boy. I'm not exactly surprised, because I've been thinking about him. Wondering where he is when he's not with me. I mean, he has to *go* somewhere, doesn't he?

He's pacing along the sidewalk, a cigarette in his hand, when I step outside. He freezes and smiles when he sees me. The hundred-watt smile from the bus. A smile of the tummy-turning, heart-teasing variety.

Get a grip, Addie, I scold myself when I realize that I'm grinning back.

This is exactly why I need medical help.

Loose flakes are falling from the sky. It's the kind of snow that won't stick and looks like salt being sprinkled from a shaker.

Bus Boy takes one more drag of his cigarette, then puts it out and lets it fall on the ground.

"Hey," he says.

"Hey," I say. "Want a ride?"

"Don't know how I'd get anywhere otherwise," he jokes. But it's too soon, and an awkward silence follows as we slide into my car.

I start the car and back out of the driveway, letting my wipers swat away any snow on my windshield.

"So, uh, how was your night?"

"Fine," I lie. I didn't take a sleeping pill, and the tossing and turning I did last night had less to do with post-accident insomnia and more to do with the Overton appointment. Worrying about whether I could actually get one and if I'd be on hospital lockdown by the end of it.

I shoot a look over at Bus Boy and consider throwing him out of my car. I shouldn't like the manifestation of my insanity so much.

The lingering smell of cigarette smoke makes my throat feel parched.

"Mind if I turn on some music?" I ask so we don't have to talk. So I can start preparing myself for when I stop seeing him, which will hopefully be after my appointment.

Bus Boy looks disappointed, like he can tell I'm trying to create distance, but he says, "Sure."

The car fills with Bartók's Viola Concerto. A few seconds in, the boy muses, "Wow, you're really dedicated to your violin music." I can hear the smile in his voice.

"It's a viola," I correct him as I'm changing lanes.

"Right. Jimi Hendrix," he says. "Sorry."

When we pull into the parking lot at school and climb out of the car, he looks a little anxious, knowing his disappearance is imminent.

"See you later?" he asks as I'm pulling my schoolbag over my shoulder.

"Yeah, sure," I say, already striding away from my car. "Bye."

"Don't, uh, forget about me," he calls, almost shyly, forcing me to turn around. Meet his eye. We hold each other's gaze for a long second, his eyes twinkling some message that neither of us can understand. The skin on my back tingles like it's being brushed with a feather, and I *really* don't know what's wrong with me. He's invisible, for God's sake.

I feel torn at his words, but I'm also running late, so I force myself to turn around and keep walking. When I steal a glance back at my car, just before entering the school building, he's gone.

All day I fight the urge to tell Katy about my Overton appointment. To ask her to go with me. But she has been acting weird for the last few days—irritable and distant, always preoccupied with something or some*one*.

I told her I've stopped seeing the boy, but whether she

believes me or not, she doesn't seem to want to hear more about it. I wonder if she thinks Crazy is contagious.

So after school, I check my phone for directions and climb alone into my car. Apart from a few dustings here and there, we're not supposed to get any major snow today, or my mother wouldn't have let me take my car this morning. Still, I go slowly for the entire fifteen miles out of Lyndale and am constantly passed by impatient drivers.

Finally I come upon a cluster of nondescript gray buildings, a giant *O* in front of each of them. I'm so busy trying to figure out which of these buildings I need that I don't see the massive green gate blocking me from them until I'm right in front of it.

A bearded security officer sticks his head out the window of a small booth. "Do you have an appointment?"

"Um, yes," I say, looking from him to the buildings again.

"Name?" he asks.

"Addison Sullivan." I swallow as he types something into his computer screen and then nods. The huge green gate slides left so I can drive through. The whole thing suddenly seems a little ominous. Maybe seeing my family doctor or the school nurse should have been my first step, even if they would go straight to my mom.

"Thank you," I say, and drive my car into the complex. Immediately I spot a green arrow sign that points me to the clinic. I follow other signs like it until I enter the parking lot. Then I climb out of my car and walk toward the entrance, feeling anxious. Maybe I should have done more research before coming.

Different from the gray, impenetrable concrete of the surrounding buildings, the clinic is mostly glass. Inviting. I can make out a reception desk from here, and a woman is sitting behind it, holding a phone to her ear.

My fingers are tingling from the cold, with uncertainty, but the automatic glass doors slide open, beckoning me in, before I've come to a stop.

Inside, the clinic is exactly like any doctor's office I've ever been in. Chairs against the walls, a table of outdated magazines in the center. A man and a woman sit beside each other, the woman on her phone, the man flipping through a sports magazine.

Still, there's a difference in the air, an edge I can't quite put my finger on.

The receptionist behind the desk is a friendly middle-aged woman with the same vague European accent I heard over the phone. Beside her is a man in his twenties. He must be new here, because she's explaining what she's doing as she enters my name. After a few seconds, she passes me a clipboard with two forms. Standing off to the side, I fill out questions about my contact information, medical history, and health insurance. Thankfully, she doesn't mention anything about payment.

I hand the forms back to the receptionist. She tells me to take a seat and Dr. Overton will be with me in just a minute.

As I sit, I still feel nervous. A baroque piece by a composer I don't know plays through the speakers in the corners of the room. I don't understand why classical music is used for waiting-room music, elevator music, hold music. It makes me restless, makes me want to do something, and since there's nothing to do, I tap my fingers on my knees, imagining I'm playing this concerto.

I hope this appointment is actually useful. That the doctor doesn't just tell me to take my vitamins or exercise, the types of clichés you normally hear to help strengthen your mind.

A nurse dressed in scrubs, a purple streak in her dark brown hair, comes to get the couple. She smiles at me while she waits for them to stand and then leads them down a hallway.

On the table beside me, next to a pile of magazines, is a stack of booklets, all with the same oval *Os* as those on the buildings. For the first time, I notice the tagline underneath the company logo: *Because Your Past Should Never Stand in the Way of Your Future.*

I flip to the second page.

Ask Your Doctor About Limbic Shaving! it says in bold letters, the way pamphlets at my family doctor say things like *Ask Your Doctor About Cholesterol Management!* Or at the eye doctor: *Ask Your Doctor About Lubricating Eye Drops!*

I turn to the back of the booklet and read the title on the last page: *A Brief History of Overton.* Two men in their sixties are pictured, smiling and wearing lab coats.

It was more than three decades ago when two highly revered neurobiologists formerly employed by the University of Maine conceived of a cure for military personnel suffering from post-traumatic stress disorder. They researched, experimented, and conducted longitudinal studies. By the time the Gulf War ended in the early 1990s, it was more than an idea. The theory: that the soldiers were held captive not by PTSD itself, but by memory.

132

The cure: memory splicing, a technique that could wipe clean the worst of their memories, while preserving the best. After years of thorough trials, the Overton technique, as miraculous as it was exact, was made available to the general public. A number of refinements to the Overton technique have since been implemented, including limbic shaving—a tweaking of the emotional components of memories, the feeling and connotations of certain memories.

A chill runs down my spine. They can change the way your memories feel?

What is this place?

I thought they'd give me memory exercises or teach me techniques, that they'd make recommendations to improve my concentration. Wasn't that what it said online? Something about improving your memory and sleep?

I glance up, and the receptionist smiles at me. Feeling weirdly like I've been caught doing something bad, I quickly look away and keep reading.

Since its development, the Overton technique has saved and improved countless lives, and it continues to do so. Since 2013, a team of highly qualified doctors led by Dr. Stephan Overton has maintained the private clinic cofounded by his father.

I skim to the bottom of the page.

Rhys Overton, MD, and John Salisbury, MD, continue to oversee the research portion of their facilities. Over twenty memory-splicing clinics have opened around the world, adhering closely to the Overton method.

I'm starting to feel a little claustrophobic. When we learned about Overton in school, we learned that they helped people with memory problems and trauma. I know I saw online that they could also help sleep and cognition. But removing memories completely? Altering them?

And it's dawning on me just how *deliberate* everything is in here. How much it's *supposed* to look and sound and feel like you could come here for a flu shot.

My hand is shaking by the time I hear my name.

I jerk my head up to find a man in a button-down shirt, glasses, and loafers smiling patiently at me. Dr. Overton . . . Jr.? He must be. He's younger than the founders in the picture, forty at most.

"Hi," I say, standing. I can't exactly run out of here, can I?

"How are you today?" He holds out his hand, and I shake it. A male nurse hands him a chart—mine, I assume—and whispers something to Dr. Overton, who nods and peers at it for several seconds. The doctor instructs me to follow him to an office down the hall, where he slides behind a desk and motions for me to sit, too. He seems a little distracted, still reading my chart. Do all doctors have access to a person's full medical history? Because the chart he's reading is way thicker than the forms I just filled out.

Finally he glances up and smiles at me. "So how can I help you?"

Dr. Overton picks up a half-eaten granola bar and finishes the rest in one bite. The music from the waiting room—a piano piece by Schumann—drifts in under the door of his office. "Sorry," the doctor says, scrunching up the wrapper and throwing it at the small garbage can against the wall. "Low blood sugar."

I'm surprised by how casual he is. How friendly and informal. I relax into my seat across from him, trying to let the unsettledness from a few minutes ago pass. It's not like he's going to operate on me.

"I've been having some issues with my memory," I tell him. "I was in a bus crash twelve days ago."

He sits up straighter. "Not that one up by Greenvale? I heard it was very scary. How are you doing?"

"Um, not so good," I say. "I mean, that's why I'm here. I've been having . . ." I can still hear whispers of piano music outside, the very deliberate lilts and lurches in the tempo. Can you usually hear the waiting-room music in the doctor's office? Do they want to make sure the appointment is as soothing, as uneventful, as the wait?

"I haven't been sleeping well since the accident. And I keep, like, losing my concentration and forgetting little things."

"And this just started after the accident? It's not something that's been ongoing?" he asks.

"No," I say. "Also, I've been seeing things."

There's a long crease down his forehead now. "What kind of things?"

The music is still slipping in from under the crack of the door. My nails are digging into my palm. Why am I here?

Tall. A boy my age. Big smile. I see him, but nobody else does.

Instead of giving him the description I gave Katy or the manager at the Cineplex, I say, "Just, um, things."

"Hmm," he says, still watching me with concern. Then he asks if I've been having headaches.

"No," I say.

Nausea? Auras? Blurred vision?

"No."

"Hmm."

135

He is silent for a few moments, then he explains that they specialize in memory procedures, not more general problems like mine. They wouldn't be able to do anything without a guardian's consent, anyway, because I'm only seventeen.

"It's possible you have a concussion that wasn't detected at the hospital," he says. "And I'm happy to do a very basic test for that, but I'd really make an appointment with my family practitioner if I were you."

"You're not a doctor?" I ask.

Hearing the alarm in my voice, Dr. Overton laughs. "I am." He points at the MD certificate and a dozen others on the wall to my left. "It's just that we don't practice family medicine here, and the medical community is quite uptight—no, let's go with 'stringent'—about these things."

"Oh," I say.

"But let's have a quick look at you anyway," he says.

He has me sit on the edge of the exam table and shines a light into my pupils, just like the doctor in Greenvale did after the accident. He checks my reflexes, has me read from an eye chart, asks me random trivia questions—what day it is, who is president, when I was born.

He tells me at the end that I have no signs of a concussion.

"A CT would give us more certainty, but . . ." He trails off, thinking. "I think we'd better leave it up to your doctor. I'll send him a note. It's Dr. Langley, right?"

I nod, realizing I won't be able to keep this from my parents any longer. If he can't help me, what choice do I have?

"I wish I could have been more helpful," Dr. Overton says, giving me a rueful smile as I leave.

When I get back to the reception area, there's an old man in the waiting room, flipping through a magazine. And suddenly it hits me that there are people in this town who come to a place like this. I try to imagine a world of normal-looking people who've visited Overton. I try to imagine them all being okay with the words I read in the pamphlet while I was waiting—"splices" and "removals" and "shavings."

The man who's training is sitting at the computer while the receptionist fiddles with the coffeemaker on the far side of the counter. She sees me and starts to come over, but the man shakes his head.

"I can do this one," he says. "Hi, Addison. So you saw Dr. Hunt today?"

"No, I think it was Dr. Overton."

The man frowns at the computer screen, his face scrunched up as he clicks around. "Oh, my mistake. Dr. Hunt was last time. Okay, so did Dr. Overton give you . . ."

Everything freezes.

"Last time?" I croak.

The man's eyes widen. He barely has enough time to blink before the receptionist is back, pushing him out of the way.

"Brendan, you have the wrong patient's file open." She looks at the screen, then smiles at me. That same warm smile that somehow makes me feel like I'm doing something wrong. "He had the wrong file open," she repeats, apologetic. "Did Dr. Overton say you needed a follow-up?"

I shake my head, but my throat is closing up. "What did he mean, last time? Have I been here before?"

Her smile stays in place. HEIDI, her name tag reads. "Like

I said, it was the wrong file. I can't reveal anything about other patients."

"I had the wrong file open," Brendan blurts out again.

"Nice meeting you, Addison," Heidi says, smiling broadly, but there is something tight about it now. Something off.

Nice meeting *you.* She says it with such force, like she wants to convey more than she's saying.

This was your first time here.

We've just met.

I mumble a goodbye and stumble outside, through the parking lot. I sit in the car, blinking at the setting sun, and now it's Brendan's words echoing in my mind.

Dr. Hunt was last time.

It wasn't another patient's file. I saw it in their reactions.

Heidi's immediate coolness, Brendan's panic.

Dr. Overton's chart that was thicker than it should have been.

I've been here before.

I've been to Overton before.

22

BEFORE
Mid-July

Because I am a glutton for punishment, or because the nineteen uses of the word "conscientious" on my report cards over the years are true, I don't send Zach a text to say I'm dropping out of his movie. Yes, I want to keep my word. But I also imagine Zach's disappointment, him scrambling to find a new Lindy, Raj sighing as he dons my nun costume, Kevin calling me a *beeyotch* for abandoning them when they need me the most. I don't have great reasons—the most convincing is that I've been having fun with them, feeling like I belong somewhere during this Katy-less summer—but they are enough to bring me back for the final two days. I won't die from another ten to twelve hours of filming. And more importantly, I can't fall any harder for Zach in that amount of time than I already have. Can I?

On Thursday after filming, I present Zach with the CD, and he plays it as we clean up for the day.

"This is fantastic!" Zach says, eyes wide. He reaches out and hugs me, a normal three-second thank-you hug that my body misinterprets as permission to get warm all over and tingle. When we pull apart, he's beaming at me. And I realize right then that I was wrong—I can fall harder for Zach, and I won't even need ten hours.

"I like a woman who can plaaaay," Kevin says, wiggling his eyebrows as he helps Raj push the furniture back into place.

"Kev," Zach sighs.

On Friday, our last day of filming, nostalgia hits. Raj asks if I want to keep the nun costume when we're done or if I plan on "breaking the habit." I tell him I do—plan to break the habit. Kevin asks if I'll miss him when we aren't spending hours in a basement together every day.

I feel a twinge of sadness. We are having a viewing party tomorrow—Zach is editing all the footage overnight—so it isn't goodbye yet. But still, I wonder when I'll get to see them, *if* I'll get to see them all again. We haven't spent so much time together that Raj or even Kevin and I are friends. And Zach . . . well, it probably isn't a good idea to *try* to be friends. But I hate the thought of not seeing him every day, even if he is just recommending a new slasher or we are washing his car or I am thrashing violently on the floor while he bends over me, filming every twitch, every tic. I'm not even self-conscious anymore.

And despite that awful talk with Zach, being around him still makes my cells shiver, tremble like the vibrato of my viola strings. A song too quiet for anyone but me to hear. Whenever it's playing, I don't feel like I'm sleepwalking.

Zach seems distant the whole time we are setting up. I wonder what he is thinking, if he is thinking the same thing I am.

And then, as he and Raj sit on the floor, putting together the camera equipment, he says, "Do you think we should send Lindsay the DVD?"

"Are you *kidding*?" Raj asks.

"It's just," Zach says, "she paid for half the ketchup."

"So?" Raj says.

"She didn't even give us the trampoline!" Kevin interjects.

"I didn't ask her," Zach says quietly. "Maybe she would have."

Raj snorts. "She would not have."

"Okay, but she's seen every single one," Zach continues.

I busy myself spreading sheets over the furniture, smoothing them out, tucking them in, smoothing them out again.

Raj gives the longest, heaviest sigh I've heard him give yet, and that is saying a lot. "It's too weird, man. Give it up."

"It's *weird*?" Zach repeats, genuinely surprised.

"It's *fucking* weird!"

"Kevin."

"Yes, it's weird," Raj confirms, then whirls around to face me. "Ask Addie. She's objective. Is it weird?"

"Sending her a DVD?" I ask, as if I've only been casually listening. Oh, Katy should see my acting now. One week in the horrody genre and I am an ac-*tor*.

Raj nods, but Zach only watches me, gauging my expression with interest.

"If I was Lindsay," I say slowly, measuring my words, "I'd call the police."

Kevin giggles.

"You can't send your ex a slasher in which a thinly veiled version of her is nearly decapitated. You just can't," I finish.

"Lindy isn't—" *Lindsay,* Zach starts to say for the fiftieth time since we've started filming, but he stops himself. "She's the only one who survives."

"Minus the left part of her body!" Kevin reminds him, slapping the carpet with his palms.

"See?" Raj says triumphantly. "It's *weird.* Send her a box with all her stuff cut up like a normal heartbroken lover."

It is crazy to associate the word "heartbroken" with Zach, with his impossibly bright smile, his dancing eyes. Only when he mentions Lindsay, when he speaks about her, can I see it. His eyes get a little dimmer, his shoulders less square, his smile less bright. Lindsay must be a bitch after all. Who the hell would do that to the world?

I notice that Zach is still staring at me, watching me, and I say evenly, "That's just me, though. I'm not Lindsay."

I don't watch his face to see if he gets the dig. Instead, I hold out my elbow for Kevin, saying, "I'm ready for the chair." And we go up the stairs to start makeup.

While he's mixing face paint—lots of black and blues, since my character, Lindy, is barely hanging on at this point—I say, "Kevin, what's Lindsay like?"

"Eh," he says, concentrating hard as he dabs makeup on my forehead. "She has kind of a horse face."

"Kevin!"

He plunges a sponge into a tray of paint and then applies it to my cheek. "I'm just sayin'," he drawls, "her jaw doesn't hold a candle to yours."

I don't know if it's true or not. But Kevin beams his Zach-like smile while I try to hold still, and somehow I feel the tiniest bit better.

23

BEFORE
Mid-July

On Saturday, with no lesson and no filming—only the viewing party at Zach's tonight—I decide to sleep in. It's past eleven when I get up and pad down the hall to the bathroom. I see that Mom's door is open, and it sounds like she's talking to one of her friends on the phone, so I stick my head in to say good morning. But she doesn't see me, and she's still in bed, phone cradled between her head and neck. What catches me off guard is the tremor in her voice, like she's been crying.

I quietly step out of view and listen for what she's saying.

"It's always hard around this time." There's a pause, and then she says, "I know. And sometimes I think we're not being careful enough."

I keep listening, but the conversation turns to some project she's doing for work, and I keep wondering why she can't get over reliving the divorce this time of year.

It's weird because Mom is the one with the boyfriend;

she's moved on far better than Dad has, so why is she still so shaken about the divorce after so many years? Is it because he was the one who left?

I ride over to Zach's around six, excited to see the finished product but sad that filming is over. I let myself in and take the stairs down to the basement. Zach meets me at the bottom of them.

My hair is wet from the shower, falling in damp curls over my dress. Zach blinks at me and then blushes as he realizes he's staring. At which point I remember that he's used to seeing me in a ketchup-drenched habit, my hair sticky and frizzy and awful. If he *doesn't* think I look better, I should be worried. Plus, I might have put in a little more effort than usual, some mascara and my favorite watermelon lip gloss.

"Um, where is everybody?" I ask, looking around.

"Kevin's working an extra hour, but Raj should be on his way. Raj should *be* here." He glances at his phone like he's expecting his friend to spring out of it. "I called him an hour ago and he'd completely forgotten, but that was an hour ago."

"Oh, okay," I say. I glance at the couch, where Zach's laptop is surrounded by a clutter of cords and CDs. "Did you get all the editing done?"

"I did," Zach says proudly. "I wasn't going to sleep until I did."

"And?" I ask. "What's the verdict?"

"*I* like it," he says. "It's no Ciano, but definitely an improvement over our other stuff."

Zach walks to the couch and sets his laptop on the floor, then swipes the CDs and everything else off. "Wannasit?"

"Thanks." I walk over to the couch and sit.

"Yeah, no problem. Do you want popcorn? Or something?" he offers, picking things up, moving as he's speaking. He is strangely fidgety.

"Popcorn would be great," I say. "Can I help?"

"No," he says quickly. "Relax. I'll be right back."

While he's gone, I look at some of the CDs he has lying around and realize from the pictureless covers that they are DVDs of Zach's past films.

He returns, bringing with him the aroma of buttery popcorn. "Here you go," he says, and he sets a big bowl down in front of me. And then he's moving to do something else, *moving* something else. It almost seems like he's afraid to be alone with me; I don't know whether to be hurt or flattered.

"Can I watch some of these while we wait?" I ask, holding up a DVD.

"Good idea," he says. He turns each of them over, trying to decide which one to start with. Then I realize he's looking for one without Lindsay, and I wonder if it really was a good idea.

Apparently, he finds one, because he pops it into the DVD player. Before he starts it, he says, "It's one of the very first ones we did."

"Okay."

"And," he says, remote control still in hand, "thematically, it's a little all over the place. Also, my older brother Rob is in it. He's not all that comfortable with cameras."

I giggle. "Okay."

"And," Zach says, stalling, "the music is shit. It's Raj's."

"Anything else?" I ask, and Zach is about to answer before he catches my sarcasm, grins, and plops down next to me.

"Don't judge me," he says.

"I won't."

Zach's older brother appears on the screen, walking down what appears to be their street in a suit that is three times too big for him. He is swinging his briefcase a little too aggressively to be normal, and he looks right at the camera as he walks.

Zach and I laugh.

There's a bang, and all of a sudden a younger version of Kevin falls from a tree. Lifeless and soaked in ketchup.

"Oh my God," I say.

I glance at Zach and he is watching me, a small smile on his lips.

It takes all my effort to face the screen again.

"Oh no!" Rob cries, and leans over Kevin, trying to resuscitate him. Suddenly someone is screaming, a girl. I hold my breath, thinking that maybe it is Lindsay after all, but a girl who looks just a little younger than Kevin runs into the frame, pointing at Kevin's lifeless body.

"No! Don't touch him! Don't touch him!"

"Why not?" Rob asks, his expression lifeless and flat.

I laugh.

"I told you it was bad," Zach says, chuckling too.

"Shut up, I'm watching the next Ciano," I say. The movie is about twenty minutes long and includes a cameo by a couple-years-younger Zach. When it's done, I break into a rousing round of applause.

Zach laughs at my response, and my stomach twirls. Is it that easy? If his smile will stay put, I'll keep clapping until it fills the room.

"Your hair was so much shorter," I say.

He self-consciously touches it.

"No puff," I add.

"*Puff*," Zach repeats, like it's the first time he's heard it. He laughs, still touching his hair. "It's kind of a pain."

I sit up straighter, surprised. "I like your hair."

Zach's eyes hold mine and I don't want to let go. "I like *yours*," he says.

"No," I say, shaking my head now, my voice thick with conviction. "I'm not being nice. Your hair has character."

"I like your hair," he says gently, like it's too precious to say out loud. And when his hand reaches out to touch it, to roll some strands between his fingers, I hold my breath.

I lean a little bit closer; Zach leans a little bit closer.

Then he's breathing on my lips. He kisses me slowly, a lock of my hair still between his fingers. And then he pauses, his lips still on mine, and when I open my eyes, he is frowning. It startles me because I'm used to him smiling.

He's still frowning when we kiss again. And he draws it out, like he's figuring something out, thinking and exploring. His hands haven't left my hair; they're all over it now, working their way in, carefully but confidently. With his hands in it, I believe it when he says he likes my hair.

My hands are in *his* hair, which is surprisingly soft.

"Zach!" We jump apart at Raj's voice. Luckily, it's coming from the top of the basement stairs.

"Um, down here," Zach says, patting himself up and down. I stand and run a hand through my hair, smooth down my dress, but then I realize Zach has also stood up and is smoothing out *his* hair. So we both sit down. Too quickly. Guilty.

"Hi, Raj," I say.

"Hey, man," Zach says.

Raj squints at his friend. "You're mad I'm late? I had to wait for the car. Plus, my mom was making rajma because my cousins are coming over tomorrow, and I needed to taste it."

"No, not mad," Zach says casually, throwing the remote control up once in his hand.

Raj looks between the two of us, squinting still. I'm not sure what he sees, but he flops onto the beanbag chair near the wall and sighs.

24

BEFORE
Mid-July

Even though I was *in* it, I have no idea what happens in our movie.

Zach's parents come down for its "world premiere," and they laugh and cringe and react with Kevin and Raj. Afterward, we put on a bunch of horrodies that Zach ordered off the Internet and no one has seen yet. My stomach is doing somersaults the entire time, just turning and turning, making knots inside me. Zach and I are suspiciously quiet throughout the evening, though he does a better job of hiding his distraction than I do. I hope being the new kid gives me a pass.

About eight, I get a text from my mom asking if I'm still at the address I gave her (Mom has a long-standing rule about leaving the address of where we are going on the fridge whiteboard) and whether she should come and pick me up. She knows now that my new friend is a boy and that he works at the video store. She knew Zach's dad from getting movies there the past few years. Strangely, her reaction was to stare at me quietly for several seconds and say, "You seem happy." And then I scrambled into my room before she could make any rules about me seeing him or ask for his Social Security number to run a background check. Her meeting Zach and his parents, though I don't think she'd dislike them, is just not something I'm prepared to deal with tonight. So I explain to them that I have to head home and, since I'm riding my bike, want to beat the sunset.

"Do you drive, Addie?" Zach's mother asks. She has gray hair and looks a little older than Zach's dad. She has the warmest face, eyes that have a way of drawing you in, and an easy laugh. I can't pick out whose exact smile Zach has, but I can see how if you put Mr. and Mrs. Laird's together, you might get Zach's.

"I have my permit, but my mom wants me to wait till seventeen to get a car."

"Well, Zach can give you a ride," she says.

"In his piece-of-shit car," Kevin supplies.

"Kevin," Mr. Laird warns.

"It's okay, I enjoy riding," I say.

"I'll walk you out," Zach says, jumping up.

Everyone calls goodbye but thankfully seems too invested in the movie Zach put in to notice anything out of the ordinary or to offer to come with us.

I'm freaking out as we silently take the steps up from the basement and then leave the house. I'm freaking out that Zach is going to decide it was all a big mistake and it shouldn't have happened, because even though my lips are still buzzing, electricity zapping through them from before, I think I've already forgotten what it felt like to kiss him.

"Um," Zach says after he's watched me silently unlock my bike. "Thanks for being in the movie."

"Thanks for letting me be in it. I had fun." *Oh God.* Does it sound like goodbye? We have no other excuses to see each other.

"Me too."

We're standing in front of the garage, watching a sea of pinks and oranges start to flood the sky. I can't believe I sometimes think it looks empty.

"Addie," Zach says.

"Yeah?" I'm getting ready to counter whatever he says, to tell him what I should have before: *Three months ago is forever. I like you. It's not that complicated.*

"I think I'd like to kiss you again." He says it softly, facing me now.

Oh.

I stand on my tiptoes and kiss him before he has the chance to change his mind. And holy freaking crap, does he kiss me back.

His kiss is more urgent this time, my back against the garage door, his kneecap against it, too. He cradles the back of my head with his hand, and I kiss him feverishly, and he doesn't stop, either, and I wonder why three days ago he said it was better if we were friends.

He doesn't kiss me like we're friends.

25

AFTER
January

On the way home, my hands are trembling so much I can barely grip the steering wheel. I feel like I've slipped outside my own body. I'm still at Overton, thinking about every single detail of that place. The gray walls of the complex. The *O*s stamped on every building in case you forget. The very deliberate way everything was set up, from the music in the waiting room to the warm, unreadable smiles of all the staff. The nurse with the purple streak—did she know me? *Have* I been there before? Was the doctor so nice because he recognized me? Apparently, he wasn't my doctor last time, but what about the receptionist? She made me fill out all that paperwork when I first came in, as if I was new.

I rack my brain trying to think of anything I recognized in there—the pattern in the carpet, the setup of the waiting room, anything—but nothing stands out.

And yet—they *erase* memories there. Does it mean anything that I can't remember?

As soon as I pull into my driveway, I whip out my phone and dial Katy's number.

Dr. Hunt was last time. The words ring continuously through my mind over the ringing on the line.

I deflate as I hear Katy's familiar voice mail recording.

Hi, you've reached Katy. I can't come to the phone right now, so leave me a message and I'll call you back. Unless you're Jason or Mason or Grayson from Music Fest. I only gave you my number because I couldn't think of any other way to get rid of you. Anyway, bye!

As she says bye, you can hear me crack up laughing in the background.

"Oh my God, Katy!" I'd said after she flung her phone away from her.

"What?" She'd shrugged, looking innocent. "At least I'm being honest."

The thing is, we both knew she wasn't. Jason (not Mason or Grayson) was a cute guy from Music Fest, a regional music festival that our orchestra had gone to in December. A bunch of other musical groups from Lyndale to Raddick combined for two days to "share our mutual love of music." Or, if you were Katy, to hide in the shadows and make out with the best bassoonist in the tri-state area. And she *had* liked him; she'd whispered, cheeks flushed, to me about him nonstop on the bus trip back to Lyndale. They'd talked about visiting each other and had exchanged phones to put their numbers in with such solemnity that you'd have thought they were exchanging promise rings. But a week after we got back, Jason still hadn't called, and Katy insisted *he* needed to call *her*. A miserable week later, he was either Jason-or-Mason-or-Grayson and she recorded that message. Katy was hurt but not heartbroken. She moved on, two weeks later, to a guy my brother's age who worked at the music store downtown, and she genuinely forgot Jason's name. It was just that easy for her—people came and went in her world, an ever-rotating cast of characters, each one replaceable.

As I'm shivering in my car, waiting for her to call or text me back, it hits me that I've lasted a long time but might be next.

I dial her number again. Voice mail.

I text her: *Call me ASAP.*

I stay in the driver's seat, my hands still shaking, watching the screen of my phone. But she doesn't call.

Maybe because of her distance the past few days, it's not hard to imagine this silence being as deliberate as her voice mail message, as the waiting-room music in Overton.

I'm on my own.

I climb out of the car and burst into the house, going over everything that happened at Overton again.

They said I needed a guardian's permission for any procedures. Does that mean . . . Could my parents . . .

It's just after five, but my mother isn't home from work.

I take the stairs two at a time, and before I know it, I'm knocking on Caleb's door. Letting myself in.

He's on his computer, but he turns to face me as soon as I enter.

"What's your problem?"

He's not asking why I barged in. He's asking why I'm shaking. Why I'm pacing.

"Addie?"

I never go to my brother with problems. It feels like we're hardly ever on the same side.

And yet . . .

He's staring at me, confused. He actually looks concerned.

"I drove out of town today," I say.

"Where?"

"Overton. It's that facility for brain research and *memory procedures*." I hiss the last part. They don't help you remember. They make you forget.

I'm pacing across his room as I speak, stepping over clothes and shoes and books and model airplanes and possible human remains. "You've heard of it, right?"

Most people have heard of it. But I've *been* there. As a patient.

God.

I need to sit down.

"I guess." Caleb shrugs. He's looking at the ground. At his unwalkable carpet. There's a rumbling downstairs—the garage door opening. "Is that Mom?"

It must be, but I'm too caught up in what I'm saying to acknowledge his question.

"I think I've been there before," I say, sounding like a balloon whose air is rushing out. "I think I had a procedure there. The guy at reception told me. I don't think he meant to, but he was training and . . ."

My brother is not looking at me.

"Caleb."

He doesn't look up. His eyes are magnets, gripped by the carpet at his feet.

"Caleb?"

I take a step toward him.

"You know something!" I gasp.

"Addie, you have to talk to Mom about this," he says, shaking his head. Still looking at the floor.

"So I *have* been there." He's not even denying it. I lean back against the wall, needing to feel something steady. The world seems to be spinning suddenly, shifting beneath my feet. "Tell me what you know."

"Addie, seriously. Just . . . just go to Mom. Shut the door when you leave." If he wasn't frozen in place, he'd be pushing me out of his room. Letting the door shut in my face.

"No," I hear myself say, suddenly ferocious. He's my brother. Why are we never on the same side? "I don't want to hear it from Mom. *You* tell me."

"For fuck's sake, Addie," Caleb says, annoyed, snapping out of his frozen state the slightest bit.

Good, let him be annoyed. Now we're evenly matched.

"I don't know anything about Overton, okay?"

"Yes, you do," I say. "And I need you to tell me everything. Right now."

He's shaking his head.

"Addie, I—"

"Please," I beg. *Please.*

It's the same tone he used when he pleaded with me not to tell Mom about his tattoo, when I pleaded with him to forgive me. Somehow, though I don't know how, I suddenly understand that we've been talking about the same thing for years, a continuation of the same conversation. Except it's one I don't understand.

Why aren't we ever on the same side? It's an unspoken question, but my brother seems to hear it and then he's standing. Walking toward his closet. Digging around. Opening some kind of box and pulling something out.

A photo.

Small, like a Polaroid.

When he gives it to me, his hands are shaking.

It's of me and Caleb. I'm leaning over Caleb behind a couch I don't recognize, and Caleb is sitting on the couch, gingerly holding a chubby-cheeked baby with tight black curls and skin the same warm shade of light brown as ours.

My heart instantly beats a little faster.

I look about eleven, Caleb twelve or thirteen. It's *definitely* us. But I don't remember anything about it. I don't recognize where we are, what we're doing.

"What is this?" I ask him.

"What do you think it is?" he asks, a genuine question.

"That's us," I say, my thumb hovering over our faces. My mother always says not to touch people's faces in printed pictures or they'll smudge, leaving headless bodies.

"Who's the baby?"

"Turn it over."

I do, my hands clammy with sweat. On the back, in black ink, it says *Rory.*

R.

Who is R?

The world starts to spin even faster. "He looks just like you," I tell Caleb, remembering all the baby pictures I've seen of my brother.

"Yeah," he says at last.

"He's . . . I don't remember this picture." My voice is starting to falter, on the verge of breaking.

"I know," Caleb says.

What is this? Who is the baby?

"What the hell is this, Caleb?" I ask. Now everything is shaking. I don't know if it's me or just the whole world. I don't know if I'm on ice, if I'm still on the bus, plunging headfirst into something horrible.

I need to sit down. *I don't understand.*

"You have to ask Mom, Addie, okay? I . . . I can't tell you any more."

"Caleb, he looks just like you." My eyes are blurring now. "Is he yours?"

"Addie, *no!*" Caleb says, then lets out one guffaw. Laughter. Shock. *"God."*

"Is he *mine?*" Caleb laughs again. I'm not within a slingshot of puberty in that picture. But if I'm joking with that question, then it's only a little bit. In the last hour, I've lost all comprehension of what is far-fetched or true or impossible.

"No," he says.

Then what?

What?

"Ask Mom," he says, and pushes me out the door, but his voice is shaking now, too. "Make her tell you the truth."

26

AFTER
January

"Mom." My voice wobbles as I stand in the doorway of her bedroom, my entire body shaking, too. She's setting a stack of work papers on her desk, her back to me. "Don't lie to me. Tell me about Rory."

The name feels strange and loaded on my tongue, a bullet with a target, and she flinches when it lands.

Slowly she turns around to face me. "Where did you . . . how . . ."

"I found out about Overton. Then Caleb showed me a picture."

Her eyes widen, her face a canvas of emotions. First she gets angry. At Caleb. At Overton. They weren't supposed to tell me. Next she's defensive—deny, deny, deny—and then she looks worried. Finally she exhales, long and slow. She takes a seat on the edge of her bed, posture impeccable, shoulders set on a ramrod-straight back.

"He's my . . . brother?" I ask, my voice barely more than a whisper. I'm half expecting her to laugh, to blink and ask if I've lost my mind. *Say he's some cousin I don't remember. There's still time.*

"Yes," she says, folding her hands in her lap.

I take another step into her room, my whole body feeling like jelly.

Her face and impeccable posture crumble. "He died when he was a baby. Eight months."

I can't wrap my mind around what she's saying: I have a brother other than Caleb.

Had.

"What happened?" I am still whispering.

She shakes her head. "I can't—"

"Stop *lying* to me. I'm going to find out somehow. I'm not going to stop until I find out. You have to tell me," I insist, savage, angry, scared.

She blinks at me.

"It was an accident, Addie. It wasn't your fault." *My fault?* I sit at the edge of her bed, the whole room spinning. "Your father was away for work. Caleb was out that morning. And I'd just put your brother—Rory—down and gone to take a quick nap. It was ten minutes, at most.

"You'd just started lessons after months of begging and were in the basement, practicing a piece." I picture our old house—light green walls, a ceiling fan in the landing, my room next to Caleb's. I used to stand at the top of the stairs and belt out show tunes. I don't remember why we moved. "And that's when he started crying, and I didn't hear him. So you went up to his room and took him out, and . . ." She inhales almost painfully and I can tell she doesn't want to tell me this, but her words are coming out in a rush. It feels like I'm a priest and she's at some sort of confession.

What did I do? I'm scared to ask it out loud.

"You took him out of his crib to play with him because you knew I was tired and we were the only ones home. You put him down in the kitchen to get something. He had just started crawling. You didn't remember the basement door was open."

She gulps, tears streaming down her face. "I heard you scream," she says, shaking her head, eyes wild with anguish, like she's still hearing it all these years later. And I get this crazy image of her being locked in a chamber where the sound of my scream is played over and over again. And I'm wondering how this could be true—how any of this could be true. I would know if she was telling the truth. Wouldn't I?

My mother is leaning closer to me now, grabbing at my wrist, desperate for me to look into her eyes. "It's not your fault. It was never your fault, Addie, but you blamed yourself. No matter what we said or did, you blamed yourself. The months afterward were hell." Suddenly she is sobbing so hard that it sounds like she's suffocating on her words. "One night—your dad wasn't home then, either—I was cleaning out the medicine cabinet in our bathroom and I realized his pills were missing. He had the ones he took every day for depression." *Vitamins,* I think, remembering what he told me when I was little and asked him about them. *They make me better,* he'd said. "Those were missing, as well as the ones he took for migraines and when he was jet-lagged. They were all gone, and I don't know how, but I *knew* I would find them under your bed."

I feel like I am being ripped apart as she speaks, like all my ligaments and tendons are being stretched in opposite directions and I'm going to explode from the pain of it.

"I asked you about it and all you could say was that it hurt too much and you thought your father's pills would help you. They could have *killed* you," she says. "You were so young. Still my little girl. And I decided right then that we couldn't let you bear it. We *wouldn't* let you bear it." She shakes her head with such ferocity that I can only watch her blankly, trying to remember how the pieces of my life, of everything I've ever known, fit together. Wondering whether they do, or ever did.

I was twelve when my father left. When he stopped having anything to say to me, when I started having to remind myself he loved me. When Caleb and I stopped being allies.

"So you *erased* him?" I can barely breathe as I say the words. I feel like I'm in a dream—a dream inside a dream—or some badly scripted TV show.

Tears continue to trickle down her face. "We used Dr. Overton's procedure on you."

For a second, the whole world is silent. Neither of us breathes. The air is static.

Of course I'd deduced this, but it stings to hear her admit it. *My parents erased my memory.* All the air has been kicked out of my lungs.

"This is why Dad left," I say quietly. "Because of Rory . . ." And when she looks at her hands, then at the carpet— anywhere but at me, just like he would—I know I'm right.

"It's so much more complicated than that, Addie," she says. "He was so against you having the procedure. To this day, he thinks . . ." Her voice trails off, and she shakes her head, as if to shake off a memory. One I don't have. "It caused a lot of friction in the whole family. But you understand why it was necessary, don't you? Rory's death was impossible to survive. For any of us."

Rory.

I feel like I am back on the bus during the accident, everything swirling around me. I sink deeper into the edge of her bed.

"And what happened to your younger brother wasn't your fault," she says again, like the most important thing is for me to understand this. But I don't. I don't understand any of it.

After a few moments of silence, my mother, sounding like herself again, says, "Many people are having the procedure these days. For much smaller things. It's very safe, it's very affordable, and sometimes it's the best option. People might frown on it, say it's unnatural or act like it doesn't exist, but it works."

She's speaking like she's on an infomercial, pitching a product she's toiled over for years or one she's tried that has finally cured her impossible case of bacne.

I am still stuck on several seconds earlier.

I am still stuck on "your younger brother."

On two lives I never knew existed—Rory's and my own.

"Caleb knew all this time?"

"He was in as much pain as you were—losing his brother, watching you suffer. I thought he should have the splice done, too, but he was set on not forgetting. But the procedure seemed like the only thing that would help you. And you were willing to try it. You were a mess, Addie. You weren't eating or sleeping. It was like living with a ghost. It killed me to watch you sinking deeper and deeper into your grief every day."

It killed *her*. Where was Dad?

Gone, almost immediately, I guess.

She talks for several minutes, hours even, and when she's done, she waits for me to ask something meaningful or do something significant.

But all I can do is whisper, *"What?"*

And let her start again. Keep starting again.

I had a brother named Rory.

My parents erased him from my mind.

I'm the reason my family fell apart.

27

AFTER
January

After I leave my mom's room, everything is in fragments.

The whole world feels shredded, like strips of paper with all the sentences out of order.

Soon my shock gives way to anger, to paranoia.

I can't focus on my homework. I can't eat. I can't look at my mother or at Caleb.

How can any of this be true?

Does it matter that they did it to protect me? That they figured they didn't have any other options? That I agreed to the procedure?

Would I really choose to forget?

No.

No?

I have no answers. I don't even know the girl my mother was telling me about. The girl whose brother died because of her mistake.

The worst thing is that it makes sense. It explains the fog over my memories after age eleven. It explains my dad, my mom, my older brother. The way Mom sometimes reacts around little kids. The summers where it felt like our house was sinking from the weight of sadness in it—Mom said Rory died in June, five years ago.

How did I not know?

How?

Hours after Mom's revelation, Caleb finds me in the kitchen, holding a glass of water and staring blankly ahead.

"Addie, I'm sorry," he says, even though it is Mom who stalks around the house with swollen eyes and the shadow of a dead baby. She has done it for years now. Caleb, too, in his own way. I think of the *R* on his chest. I remember it raw, the black-purple of bruised skin, and I feel like I am made of freshly tattooed skin. It hurts. I want to go back to before it.

R is not for a Rachel or Rebekah or Randy.

It's Rory.

My other brother.

"How could you?" I ask, not sure what I am asking.

Erase him? Lie to me for six years? Tell me the truth?

The glass of water sweats around my palm.

"Did Mom drag me there? Did they even tell me what they were going to do?" I ask.

Caleb nods. "Mom sat down with you before she made the appointment and told you what it was for, why she thought you needed it."

"And I told her I didn't want it, right? I must have."

He runs a hand over his head. "You told her you could try harder, that you could be stronger, that you didn't want to

167

forget him, but then she asked you—we were sitting at the dining table and I'll never forget it—she asked what you wanted more: to feel better and move forward, or to remember."

I chose moving forward.

"Even after you had it, I wanted to tell you, but you were destroyed by Rory dying, Addie," he says, looking down, remorse palpable in his voice. "That's the one thing they got right—you needed some sort of help, and months of therapy wasn't helping. Mom was sure it was the only way to save you, and what was I going to do? I was thirteen."

"So you just silently hated me instead."

He frowns. "I didn't—don't—hate you. I hated the pretending. I hated that we couldn't talk about Rory. All those birthdays . . . he'd be almost seven now. I hated that we had to pretend like everything was fine. And then after all the bullshit and the pain, all you wanted was to go away and live like it never happened."

"I was already living like it never happened."

"Do you really think that's true?" Caleb asks.

I mentally rifle through anything and everything that has ever seemed out of place. My parents' divorce. Mom's overprotectiveness. The invisible boy.

Oh God, the invisible boy. How can he be a coincidence, some fluke bout of crazy, after all this? Is he . . . could he be connected to Rory somehow?

People don't spontaneously appear and disappear; something makes them. And in any case, they have to come from *somewhere.* Somewhere like the past.

Who is this guy?

I look at Caleb.

I want to say, *Do you know why I went to Overton today? Because I'm seeing things. Because just like everything outside me, something is broken inside me, too.*

But I look at my older brother, and even though I've known him every day of my life, I don't recognize him.

I'm not telling him about Bus Boy.

I slip past him and head upstairs.

My mind is racing a million miles per hour, and I can't even think about sleeping, though it's past ten and I have school tomorrow.

I think about texting Katy again, but what would I say? *Guess what, my parents are crazier than we thought—they erased my dead little brother?*

I can tell from Mom's and Caleb's reactions that it wasn't easy, that it hurts them just to say his name after not doing it in so long. Or did they do it in private, when I wasn't around? Did they think about him at birthdays, random days of the year to me that made them want to crawl under the covers and hide? Did seeing me happy, normal, when they couldn't be make them hate me? Is that what Caleb meant about me getting to live like it never happened?

My chest hurts at how random things I never thought about must have devastated them.

But I don't have enough space to feel sorry for them. Not when the corners of my room seem to be crowding in against me.

Not when there are tiny storms erupting in my head, thoughts of packing my bags and leaving and never coming back home, questions about what I can trust and who I can trust. Not when everything feels like a lie.

169

I want to call my father and scream at him, scream and not have to see the hurt in his eyes.

This is why he stopped loving me.

But he's probably in the air.

I put on headphones and listen to my favorite piece from the concert, "Air on the G String."

Now the melody snakes its way around me. Every instrument's part tangling and interweaving with the rest, like clasped hands tightly tucked within each other. One hand tracing the lines on the other's palm; the webs between the fingers damp with sweat. This song makes me feel close to something, to someone nameless and faceless.

I don't want to feel close to anyone tonight, though. I want to be unreachable.

So I pull out my viola, despite the hour, and play a different song.

I play loudly and recklessly. I play angrily, for so long that I push the corners of the room further back and hold them there. Mom doesn't dare ask me to stop, even though she has to get up early for her six-thirty report.

My fingers tremble from the music or anger or fear, and I keep playing. Playing away the ghost of a brother I didn't know I had, playing away all the questions that I still can't answer.

I keep thinking about Bus Boy, about the night on the bus. I can't shake the feeling that everything that happened tonight, everything since the accident, started the moment that boy walked onto the bus.

But how does *that* make any sense?

Rory would be six now, not seventeen. How can they be connected?

I don't have any of the answers, so I play away the questions. Caleb pounds twice on my door, begging for quiet. I play harder.

And then I stop.

28

BEFORE
Mid-July

To say I float into At Home Movies the day after our kiss is an understatement.

I blow in with the wind, weightless and airy and tangled up in the sunshine that beat across my face as I rode here. A stupid pop song is matted into my wind-battered hair, trickling into my ears and head and throat. I am *buzzing*.

I find Zach in the Comedy section, kneeling beside a stack of DVDs on the ground, sorting them.

I wait for him to notice me, my hair particularly thick and wild today and the pair of peach-yogurt-colored short shorts that prompted Caleb to make a face when we collided in the hallway this morning.

On the ride over, there was a tiny bit of fear that last night never happened, or that Zach regrets it and will now try to steer us back into friends territory, but it dissipates almost immediately when I see him.

Zach notices my feet first, and then his eyes travel up the length of me, twinkling by the time they reach mine, a smile already stretched across his face.

"Dad?" he yells across the store. "I'm taking my break now!"

And then he grabs hold of my hand and pulls me to the back of the store, tripping over the DVDs on the ground in the process.

"Walking hazard!" he says as we run out the door, both of us giggling.

"Hi," he says when we get outside, his grin impossibly wide.

"Hi." I grin back, feeling the muscles in my face stretch, finding a new normal.

And then we kiss behind his father's store. It's almost exactly the same as last night, only against the wall of the building instead of the garage door this time. The air is urgent and humid but perfect. And Zach's one hand is at the back of my neck, while the other plays with the edge of my shirt. The skin on my stomach burns from his touch.

I don't ever want to stop kissing him. And happily, he doesn't seem to want to stop kissing me, either. Kind of the opposite.

"So, listen," he says, playing with my shirt still, when we come up for air. "If we're going to keep doing this, I think we should go out on a date."

"Are you saying you'd like to keep doing this?" I ask, husky-breathed, signaling at the space between us. I can't believe the words that are coming out of my mouth. Confident words. Flirtatious words.

Zach responds by leaning in to kiss me again, but I retreat a little and ask, "What made you change your mind? About being friends and all that."

He scratches his head now and grins. "I was *trying* to be friends, but last night—last night I kind of realized that I'm not interested in being just friends. I think the first kiss did it."

"Funny, I feel like they just keep getting better," I breathe.

"Should we test that theory?"

When we kiss again, I loop both arms around his neck, and Zach's hand feels like fire on my lower back.

After what seems like mere seconds, the back door flings wide. We jump apart.

"Zach," Mr. Laird says in an even voice. "I will kick your butt to Timbuktu."

"I'm not smoking!" a red-faced, red-lipped Zach protests.

"Damn straight you're not," his father says. "You are also not taking a twenty-five-minute *break* on my watch."

Twenty-five? Zach and I look at each other, incredulous.

"Fine," Zach says, but he's smiling as his father goes back inside. We follow Mr. Laird, still holding hands, and tingles travel up my arm.

I help Zach finish stocking the DVDs, and then he mans the counter while Mr. Laird has his lunch and watches TV in the breakroom. He keeps the door open, though, presumably to keep an eye on us.

"Can I ask you something?" I'm standing on the other side of the counter, leaning against it as Zach does inventory. When he nods, I ask, "What's with the smoking?"

He glances up at me, as if he's surprised that's what my question is about.

He puts down his pen before he answers me. "I went to an all-boys boarding school at the start of ninth grade. Fincher? It's just outside Raddick. My dad and my older brothers went there. *Everyone* smoked at Fincher. All my friends, the teachers. Students weren't allowed to smoke on school property, but we would literally walk half a mile out to where the school's sign was and smoke right in front of it. As long as we weren't *behind* it, we were fine."

I laugh.

"The first time my roommate, Dean, offered me a cigarette, after I'd been there, like, two months, I tried it just to see what the fuss was about. It was *horrible*. Like, I-nearly-hacked-a-lung horrible."

I giggle again.

"Then Dean got caught smoking in the locker room one time and wound up with an expulsion warning. I hid his last two packs in my suitcase, hoping it'd deter him."

"Did it?"

Zach shakes his head. "He gave me this." He leans forward to point out a tiny scar on the side of his right eye. The scar isn't raised and it looks old, but I reach out to run my finger over it.

"Violent boy." Zach tsks. "Anyway, I forgot all about the two packs and came home for spring break." He drops his voice, like he doesn't want his father to hear this part. "And then my parents sat me down and said they couldn't afford another year of tuition for me at Fincher."

He speaks louder again, but not quite as loud as when he started the story. "I was pretty devastated. I was making all these friends. My brothers had both gone to Fincher and graduated; it was supposed to be, like, a rite of passage for my family."

"That sucks," I say, and he nods. He rips open a bag of gummy bears and sets them between us.

"It does. But at least I had the one year." He chews on a bear. "Kevin probably won't even get that." It's the first tinge of real sadness (non-Lindsay-related, anyway) I've ever heard in Zach's voice, and it makes something twitch in me, too. "Kevin might not *need* that, since he already curses like a sailor."

I laugh, reaching for some gummies.

"All *my* bad habits I learned at Fincher." Zach picks up the pen and checks something off on his piece of paper. "Anyway, it's spring break. Dad tells me I can't go back the next September. I try to act cool about it, but I sit in my room, moping all week. And you know what I find? Two packs of cigarettes. I smoked both of them in a weekend."

"*Zach,*" I scold, as if it's happening now.

"I'm trying to quit, though. I'm way better than I used to be," Zach says, looking proud. "Dad has promised to get me a Sonic CXX if I'm down to two a day by the time school starts in September."

"That's"—I pause, searching for the right word— "nonjudgmental of him." I imagine the Cerebral Event—aka stroke—my mother would have if she ever caught me with a cigarette in hand.

"He's worse than *me!*" Zach laughs. "Or he was. But he finally stopped at the end of last year, all these years after he picked it up at Fincher."

"Well, I hope *you* stop," I say, unable to hide the disapproval in my voice.

"So what about you?" Zach asks. "What's *your* vice?"

"Hmm," I say with mock thoughtfulness. "I'm weirdly addicted to gummy bears. This is practically poaching." I pop one into my mouth as I speak.

Zach smiles, but he appraises me seriously before saying, "You love your viola more than you do people."

I'm so taken aback by it that it takes me a while to answer, and I remember that he said something similar at his house last week, too. "You've only seen me play once."

"I know," he says.

There's a long pause before I say, "Well, maybe I just haven't found the right person to love."

Zach's lips are tilted up at the corners. "Yet," he says.

"Yet," I say, and eat another gummy bear.

29

AFTER
January

After Caleb's and my mother's lights go out, I pull on my jeans, sweatshirt, coat, and boots, and then I grab my keys and quietly leave the house.

Bus Boy is not out front. The cigarette he dropped on the sidewalk this morning is gone, too. But maybe someone kicked it onto the grass, or a gust of wind blew it to another street. Maybe it never existed to begin with.

A headache is building behind my eyeballs from running on so little sleep the past two weeks. I rub my temples and try to remember what I was thinking of when he appeared before school—Overton, the bagel I had for breakfast, the humanness of his thigh on the park bench yesterday—but none of that works, so I decide to go to him.

I drive first to my school, to outside the window of the music room, because I'm not sure where else to start.

But nothing is there.

I drive around the perimeter of Bentley Lake and the park surrounding it, but there's nothing.

Then I try the mall, because he "works" there, and presumably he could be there now, even if it is nearly one in the morning. I climb out of my car and wander around the closed mall entrance.

No sign of him. The parking lot is deserted, covered in a layer of snow and tire prints.

At this point, I'm at a loss, so I whisper, "Bus Boy?"

There is, of course, no answer. And I jump, terrified at the sound of my own voice, and hurry toward my car, a little relieved there's no answer.

I have no idea where to go to find him. How to find him.

I've never actively *tried* to make him appear. Am I just not trying hard enough?

What was the last thing he said to me?

Don't forget about me.

Still holding on to the door of my car, I shut my eyes and try to think back to the night I first saw him. I think about the concert and the bus. His bright, contagious smile.

No sooner do I hear footsteps crunching in the snow than I jump into my car and lock all the doors. My heart thumps hard in my chest as the red-haired, smiling boy only I can see, nowhere in sight a second ago, walks toward me. He has his hands in the pockets of his jeans, a shirt too thin for the cold, and a completely casual expression.

As if he's been waiting out here for me. As if I did not just conjure him up out of thin freaking air.

He raps twice on my window, and I take a couple breaths and then slide it down an inch. My skin is littered with goose bumps.

"You okay?" he asks.

No, I think. *No, I'm not even* almost *okay.*

But what I say is, "Tell me you've figured it out by now. Who you are. Something."

He gives an apologetic shake of his head.

"Nothing?" I say, exasperated. "Not even a little bit?"

But, of course, I know in the back of my mind that this isn't about him. It's about me. If I can conjure him up, if I can see him and nobody else can, if I can speak to him and hear him when he's not really here, this is all on me. *I* have to figure out what's going on.

I stare at him, trying to superimpose the image of the baby that Caleb showed me over this tall, red-haired boy. He looks nothing like my brother. They don't even have the same color skin.

And yet, they have to be connected somehow.

Is Bus Boy just some kind of beacon? A signal meant to make me question my sanity, to lead me to Overton and the truth about my family? But now that I know, why is he still here?

Apart from looking nothing like my brother, I can't be related to him because of the butterflies in my chest when he's nearby, that turning of my stomach at his smile. I know I'm crazy, but having a crush on someone I'm related to would just be another level of insanity. Not to mention repulsive.

If Bus Boy and the brother I lost are related, it's not in that way.

"Can I get in?" His breath is visible in the night, and his nose is bright red. I must've said yes, because Bus Boy jogs around to the passenger side door and waits for me to unlock it. And the whole time I wonder if I'm imagining this—seeing him, speaking to him, letting him in my car. My head is spinning with so many thoughts I have to fight the urge to scream.

The car feels so much smaller with him inside, like we're inches apart and not a couple of feet. His long legs take up too much room, and I hear his hand fumbling in the dark, struggling to push his seat back. I lean across him, trying not to breathe him in—laundry detergent, sweat, cigarette smoke— and press the lever under his chair that makes it slide.

"Thank you," he says, and I'm thinking he means for his seat, but he adds, "for coming back."

That mixture of confusion, guilt, pity—I don't know what—at the way I seem to make him come and go stirs in my chest and all I can do is stare straight ahead through the windshield.

"I found out tonight I had another brother," I say quietly. I don't know why it comes tumbling out, but it does and it feels okay. It feels right.

"What happened?" Bus Boy asks, no lightness in his voice.

"He died," I say. "Almost six years ago."

"I'm sorry," he says. He touches my shoulder, and through my layers of clothing, I feel a surge of warmth in my arm. From an imaginary boy.

I don't say anything for minutes, my mind spinning, spinning, coming to its inevitable conclusion.

I'm not imagining him.

A burst of cold air comes into the car, and when I face the

boy, he has a cigarette in his mouth, a lighter in his hand, and the window rolled down.

"What?" he asks, his eyes wide.

"That's disgusting," I say slowly. As I continue to speak, my voice gradually rises. "If you're going to smoke, get the hell out of my car."

I'm angry, yes, but it's not just because he's smoking. It's not just because of what seeing him has put me through. It's the way I can feel my life shattering, a tightly confined case of glass dismantling all around me, and there's nothing I can do about it. Who do I trust? What do I do next?

To my surprise, he pushes open the door of the car and climbs out.

I watch him start to walk off, cigarette in hand, and I wonder where exactly he's planning to go.

If a tree falls in the forest and there's no one there . . .

He knows that when he leaves my sight, he'll be gone again. And maybe I've annoyed him enough that it doesn't even scare him at the moment.

But then it hits me that if he goes, and of his own will for once, I might not be able to find him again. Whatever mind-conjuring voodoo I did to get him here might have just been luck, and I still have too many questions to let him be gone forever.

"Hey!"

I start after him, but he's walking quickly and making a point of ignoring me.

"Hey, come back!"

"Why?" he yells over his shoulder, not stopping.

"I think I know who you are," I yell back. I see him freeze, his back to me. And then he turns around and looks at me.

We are both holding our breath. Even from this far away, I can tell.

"Who am I?" he asks. A challenge.

I don't yell it because I am confident. Because I am afraid. Because I feel it in my bones.

Don't forget about me, he said before.

"A Memory," I whisper.

30

BEFORE
Early August

Our first-ever date is at Schiavoni's. Since we already have *some* things established—the kissing, the fact that this is actually a date, the location—I'm excited and not nervous about tonight. Selecting an outfit is terrible and nearly worthy of an emergency phone call to Katy, but then I remember that Zach has seen me with a face full of *ketchup* and this is still happening, so I pick out a navy blue dress with a halter top and sailor-like stripes at the bottom and top. I pair it with my favorite cork wedge sandals and keep my hair down.

Zach picks me up at six, and he's wearing an oxford shirt, brown tailored pants, and sneakers. His hair is slicked back and looks almost unrecognizable, except for a tiny portion at the front that rebels and sticks up just a little bit.

My mom is at an event for Channel Se7en, but Caleb is in a surprisingly good mood tonight. He's out of his room and still sporting facial hair, but he's wearing clean clothes. He bolts for the door before I reach the bottom of the stairs. "Do *not* embarrass me!" I say, hurrying after him. When he's not sequestered in his room, Caleb's ratio of asshole to nice older brother is still a paltry 7 to 3, and I'm worried about which one he'll be tonight. Which one he'll be to Zach.

When I reach the entrance, he's let Zach in and is asking, "So what are your intentions with my sister?"

"Caleb!" I hiss at him, and he bursts out laughing. Zach is smiling, too, but his face is the deepest shade of red. I punch my brother's arm. *Nice.* He's going to be nice to him.

"I'm *kidding*," Caleb says, leaning against the wall, arms crossed. He is enjoying this, and I suddenly feel like there's so little I understand about my brother. *What makes you sad and happy and angry at random times?* I wonder. "So you go to Meridian?"

"Yeah. Go Titans," Zach says, trying to sound normal, but he seems nervous. Even though they're about the same height, Zach seems smaller and more subdued in Caleb's presence.

"Wrong answer. West Lyndale Wildcats," Caleb says.

"Hey, we kicked you guys' ass last year in football."

"One game. Psh," Caleb says. "What do you have to say about our three-year streak before that?"

Zach laughs. "We called it the Reign of Terror."

"Damn straight it was."

"Okay, glad we had this talk. We're going. Bye," I say, pushing Caleb aside to get to the front door.

"Seriously, though, where are you two going and when will you be back? Mom's going to need that information when she gets home, unless you want her to send out a search party."

Zach tells him the plan and then Caleb finally lets us

leave. I watch my brother shut the door behind us, a hundred unanswered questions circling the air around him.

"Hey, you," Zach says when we're outside. He leans down and kisses my cheek. "You look beautiful."

"You too," I say, and he laughs. He *is* beautiful, with his Zach hair and Zach smile and Zach eyes. He has become an adjective.

The meeting with Caleb behind us, I expect him to relax, be back to his normal, springy self. But Zach's face is still flushed and he's fidgety as he drives, and I think, *He's nervous about our date,* which makes me feel good in this sadistic, wonderful way, and when we get out of the car at the restaurant, I take his hand and thread my fingers through it. They are warm and bigger than mine, rough and a little bit dry, like my dad's hands.

I feel like everyone is looking at us when we enter and Zach gives them his name for the reservation. *He made reservations.* But, of course, they are all just eating dinner, going about their business as usual. Except that Zach seems to stiffen a little as soon as the hostess approaches us, and if he was nervous before, now he seems to be waging some internal battle. I don't know what to think, and I stare at the short, blond woman in front of us, younger than my mother but older than us, and she says, "Your usual table?"

And I get it.

They used to come here before.

Him and her.

This is their place.

Lindsay.

My hand goes limp in his.

Zach is shaking his head. "Um, no." He points somewhere far across the room. The hostess looks at me, sees that I'm a stranger, smiles apologetically, and leads us to a table for two over there.

I slide into my seat across from him, the heat of the lights making my face feel hot, or maybe I'm wearing too much makeup. Our waitress, Taryn, places two menus down in front of us. Zach immediately picks his up and starts to read, but his expression is still strained, still distant. She returns seconds later with a plate of steaming garlic bread, and my stomach rumbles, but I don't reach for it.

The tips of my ears start to get a little hot, and my neck, too, and I feel stupid and so, so embarrassed.

"We don't have to do this," I say, and am surprised to hear my voice coming out angry.

"Do what? Order?" Zach says stiffly. "I don't think they can read our minds. Unless you know something I don't."

I don't laugh, though I know he wants me to.

"Any of it. We don't have to do *this*." I gesture at our table, at both of us. "I'd rather know now if that's the case."

I'm expecting him to feign confusion or something, but he just puts down his menu and sighs. "I'm sorry, Addie," he says. "This is the nicest restaurant I could think of, and it didn't even occur to me that . . . I mean, I feel like an idiot."

Zach leans across the table then and asks, his voice earnest, "Do you want to . . . we can leave if you want."

I think about it for a few seconds, my face and neck still warm, the glare of the lights still too much. But then I focus on Zach's eyes, gray and deep and apologetic. Even though I'm annoyed at him, they send a jolt through my body.

If I storm out, make him take me back home, I'd be ruining something I've wanted since practically the moment I met him. Not just getting to *date* Zach, to spend time with him under the full disclosure that we like each other, but also that vibrant, inextinguishable feeling coursing through my veins whenever we're together.

It's like he pries my eyes open with his smile, with his touch, with his presence.

"And let perfectly good garlic bread go to waste?" I say, still a little bit angry, but Zach smiles slowly, relieved.

"I'm an idiot," he says.

"I'm not going to argue with you," I say, and he laughs. I order for both of us—the chef's special—which neither of us has ever had before: corzetti stampati al limone. The pasta is round and flat, shaped like coins, with lemon sauce and cheese sprinkled over it. It is hot and cheesy and lemon-tangy, the best thing I've tasted in years.

"Hmmm."

"Mmmm."

We take turns making increasingly questionable-sounding murmurs of appreciation over the food, and as I do, I'm conscious of the fact that I rarely do this—let go, enjoy myself, wrap myself in a happy moment, even if it means being silly.

I make a concerted effort to indulge myself, to dip myself in the buzzing, happy, warm Zachness of this moment.

"Good."

"So good."

"You should be a professional meal orderer."

"Only if I got to eat everything I ordered."

"Of course," Zach says.

"I'd try something new every single day," I say.

"I like that about you."

"You like what?" I glance up at Zach, but tearing my gaze away from my food for too long seems like blasphemy, so I quickly go back to it.

"That you try things. That you haven't made up your mind about every single thing," he says. "When I offered you a horrody, you went for it, which not everyone would. Some people would leave with only what they came for. And then you watched it—and went for all the rest."

I chew more slowly now. "I was kind of swayed. . . . I mean, I don't promise I'd have done the same thing if you were really unattractive." This isn't untrue, but I am suddenly feeling emotional about what Zach has just said.

I've never thought of myself as open. I think of myself as somehow incomplete, desperate to find things that will fill me, make me feel like I'm really *living*.

I blink rapidly because, oh my God, I can't cry in here. On my first date with Zach. Over something so stupid.

He doesn't notice what's happening, and he's grinning at what I last said. "And then when I asked you to be in my movie, you were game. And you were up for everything. Even the mattress-hoisting thing with Raj. Sorry about that, by the way."

And as if the only way to prevent the crying is to channel all that emotion into the exact opposite feeling, I start giggling. It starts in my chest, little ripples of laughter, rising, *frothing* upward. Unfortunately, I'm still chewing, and a small piece of food gets caught in my windpipe, so now I'm choking a little and laughing a lot. Which sets Zach off. Which makes me laugh harder.

I reach for my glass of water and gulp it down, but it seems to go down the wrong way, so now I'm *actually* coughing and my face is hotter than ever—both from the coughing and the awareness that we're making a scene—and it's completely embarrassing. Zach is laughing so hard he's wheezing, but then he abruptly stops and his eyes go wide and he says, "Wait, you're actually okay, right? You're not actually choking?"

But with all the coughing and laughing, all I can do is nod. The couple at the table next to ours looks over at us and I lose all composure again and I think the last time I was this silly was in, maybe, fifth grade, but the laughter is like the contents of a bottle whose cork has sprung off. I can't stop it. I can't push it back in.

Zach, no longer laughing, says, "It's not like you're about to die on me, right?"

I shake my head, sobering up the slightest bit, the coughing receding a little, but I still can't trust myself to speak.

"Wait, is that yes, you're fine, or no, you're not?"

I nod, and when I see Zach's wide eyes, I dissolve into a fit of giggles again, which makes the coughing resume. And then Zach is dragging his chair around to my side of the table, like all the way around, so our chairs are touching, and then he puts his hand on my arm and says, "I need you to nod if you're okay, Addie, and shake if you're not."

Get a grip, Addison, I chide myself.

The hysterics cease for a bit, and though my eyes are still watering, I nod.

"O-kay," I wheeze out, except it sounds like *oke*. Maybe *oh*. There's not even really a hard *K* sound.

Zach shakes his head at me, fingers still on my arm, still sending jolts of current through my bare flesh. "Shh," he says, to discourage me from more attempts at speaking. "And good," he says. Then, more quietly, his eyes dancing as a smile slides across his face, "You're, like, my favorite person right now."

There's a second of nonsensical neuron firings in my brain, and I'm glad I don't have permission to speak, because my heart is tingling and blood is coursing through my body so quickly I think it would sound like an ocean if I tried to speak. Just a roar of currents and waves and things I can't control, threatening to come up or apart. Have I always had this much inside me?

It's not that I don't feel like myself, either; I do. I just feel like a different version of myself at exactly this moment.

So instead of speaking, I just lift three fingers up at Zach.

He frowns, trying to comprehend. "Three . . . top three?"

I point at him, then raise three fingers again.

"Me," he says. "Top three?"

I shrug, and he bursts out laughing.

His full, uncontrollable laugh that feels as warm as the temperature of the sun on my skin. "God, you're really pissed about this restaurant, aren't you?"

31

AFTER
January

"So I get that I'm remembering you, but why like this? *Are* you a ghost?" I ask him, cranking up the heat in my car when we're back in it.

I guess the pieces started falling together while I was playing in my room earlier. Hundreds of questions and guesses moving in slow motion until they collided with one another just now, until the single most messed-up day of my life finally started to make a crumbling kind of sense.

"The *real* you," I clarify when he still hasn't responded.

I obviously don't remember Bus Boy. The "real-life" Bus Boy.

But I know I am asking the right questions. It's the only version of things that makes sense and that doesn't make me a complete lunatic.

If I'm right, though—if he is a memory—I have a million of them, and none of them are like this. Life-sized, real enough to talk with, to touch. Could he be a ghost?

I shoot a quick glance at him, his long legs cramped in my small car, and wonder exactly what he was to me. What *I* was to *him*. Blood rushes to my face and I feel angry with myself. Of course, I'm crushing on an invisible boy. The fact that I know I didn't *completely* make him up offers some relief, but it is mild at best.

"Well?" I prompt, impatient for his response.

"Well." Bus Boy pauses thoughtfully. He sticks his arm out and flexes his hand so his fingers press against the cool window. "I can't go through objects. But maybe that means nothing. I wouldn't call myself an expert on ghosts."

Or anything, I think bitterly. I mean, if we were to tally up the number of things he does know, particularly on the subject of himself, we'd be firmly at zero.

I cross my arms over my chest. "So, then, you *might* be dead?"

"I suppose."

"In which case, you'd be a ghost."

"I . . . could see that," Bus Boy says carefully, and I roll my eyes, but my heart is starting to feel like a rock in my chest.

What if the real him is dead?

Did my parents know about him? Did they remove him intentionally when they removed Rory's memory?

But if that's the case, why didn't my mother mention him when she told me about my little brother?

We don't seem to be getting anywhere, sitting in the car, watching our breath mist the windows, so I drive home. Bus

Boy and I say goodbye in my driveway. Then he climbs out of the car and starts to walk down the street. I watch him for as long as I can, his figure growing tiny before, in one blink, blending into the darkness. *Did he disappear? Or did he just get too far away to see?*

I hate that I can't tell.

I quietly slip into the house, ready to endure another night of tossing and turning, my mind whirring with too many things.

In the morning, the atmosphere in the house is nearly as cold as the one in my car last night. Neither Mom nor Caleb seems sure of what to say to me. I leave without saying anything to them, without even having breakfast.

I corner Katy at her locker before first period. I know she's used to determining the duration and continuation of her relationships, but she can't do that with me. I won't let her. And I need backup. I need my best friend.

"Oh, hey!" She looks surprised, caught off guard when I corner her at her locker. "Sorry I didn't call you back last night. Working on those monologues is *killing* me. Literally killing me. You're so lucky that you don't have to perform a piece or anything for NYU. You've applied and it's done, but my process is just *starting*. So that's why I've been so busy." I fold my arms across my chest and let her dig herself into a hole with her explanation. "Plus, my throat has been killing me. Maybe it's all the practicing, but I told my mom to produce proof of my mumps vaccination by the time I get home today, because I am not one hundred percent sure I've had it. And this is *not* a regular sore throat."

"I need to talk to you," I say.

"I'm serious. Cough drops aren't helping. Am I running a fever?" She grabs my hand and puts it against her forehead.

"You feel fine."

"I feel *awful*," she says, but a second later, she's waving violently at Mitch Enns, who is en route to class with his football posse but breaks away to pretend to reel her toward him. She laughs and flicks her wrist, dismissing him and the rest of his crew.

"Maybe Mitch gave you something," I say pointedly, and her eyes snap to mine, hurt at my impatient tone.

She decides to ignore it. "Did I tell you Mitch found my bracelet? It was in his car."

"I thought you said you drove *your* car the day you hung out?" My voice is still sharp, accusing.

Katy's cheeks flush. "That was a different day." She tucks her hair behind her ear. "He looked all over for it—he looked through all the dressing rooms at Act! Out! because he didn't know which one was mine. He checked all the classrooms and the girls' bathrooms after school and told the custodian I'd lost it. I didn't even know he was doing all that, but it ended up being in his car the whole time. Can you belie—"

"Katy, you've been avoiding me," I say, cutting her off.

"I've been busy," she says, proving my point by avoiding eye contact.

"I need your help. Urgently," I say, and my throat tightens as everything I've learned rushes into my mind.

Rory.

I'm not imagining Bus Boy.

I have pieces, but I need help ordering them, figuring out where the corners go.

195

She frowns, gauging my no-nonsense expression, and scans the hallway. "Okay. Where do you want to go?"

We sneak out of the school building as the warning bell rings and wind up in my car, Katy in the same seat Bus Boy was in only hours ago.

"What's up, Buttercup?" she asks, dropping her backpack on the floor. "Why's the seat so far back?"

I blink back the memory of my invisible boy's long legs cramped in here last night, blink back the tears building in my eyes.

"My whole family is so fucked up, Katy," I say, which was not where I intended to start, but it now seems as good a place as any.

"Hey," Katy says gently, leaning over to hug me. "What happened? What's wrong?"

"I had a baby brother. Rory." Even now the name feels poisonous and big and small. It means nothing and everything at the same time. "He died when I was eleven because of a mistake I made. And you know Overton? That brain facility outside of town? My parents—well, my mother—had him erased from my mind there. *Erased.*"

I feel Katy's body go rigid beside me. Her arm over my shoulder becomes wooden. After a second, she slips it off and puts her hands in her lap.

"Oh my God," she whispers. "Oh my God."

"I know," I say. "I went there yesterday to ask if they could help with my memory lapses and not being able to sleep."

She looks at me, surprised, all color drained from her face. "You said it was better—that you were sleeping. That you weren't seeing him anymore."

"I lied," I tell her sheepishly.

"Oh God, Addie." She says it over and over, under her breath.

"I *know*," I say, and I want to reach across and hug her again because she understands. Because she's my best friend and the only person I could tell this to—tell that my whole life has been a lie—and she'll understand how much it hurts, how awful everything feels.

"Anyway, I think Bus Boy is related to Overton and to Rory. I thought for a second that maybe he was my brother, but he can't be. He's too old and they look nothing alike." *Also, I think I like him.* I'm rambling now, only vaguely aware of Katy turning white as a sheet beside me. "So now I think maybe he got erased along with Rory when I was eleven. I mean, I could be wrong. Maybe I have brain damage from the crash. Maybe it is a Psychological Episode and I've imagined up some guy, but I don't think that's what this is. He feels familiar. I think I'm remembering him."

"Addie," Katy says, and when I look at her, I see that she is weeping now, the kind of crying where you can't draw in enough breath. I'm confused because I know she's shocked about everything I just told her, but that can't explain her reaction.

"What's wrong?" I ask her.

She's shaking her head, struggling to find words and air. But finally both start to tumble out. "I told you to let me go to my mom. Oh God, Addie. You made me promise. I didn't know about Rory. Obviously, you didn't, either. I n-n-never would have let you if I'd known. We thought it was the f-f-first time. You wanted it to get over what happened."

She's saying words, stuttering them, but not one is making sense. I grab her arm to calm her down.

"What are you talking about, Katy?"

"We didn't know, Addie," she's saying now, bawling again. "We didn't know you'd had it done before."

"I don't understand," I say, even as some of her words are starting to catch like burs on socks.

We didn't know.

We thought it was the first time.

"I don't understand," I say again.

Katy takes a deep breath and looks at me.

"We went back, Addie," she says, her words and voice finally clear. "You had the procedure done again."

32

BEFORE
Early August

"Addie, what do you know about goldfish?" Zach asks, in lieu of saying hello, when I pick up the phone.

"Don't they forget everything? Or is that a myth?" I ask.

"I think that's a myth," Zach says. It's around eleven-thirty in the morning. I've just come back from today's viola lesson and quickly fallen into a William Primrose wormhole. Most of the recordings online are fairly old because he died in the 1980s, but he's probably the most expressive violist I've ever heard. He plays the way you use your fingers or vocal cords, thoughtlessly, naturally, like his viola is part of his body. I would kill for his dexterity. Even after all these years, playing is hard for me. The easier I need a piece to sound, the harder I have to work on it. But it's worth it, if only for that moment I can play the piece all the way through without thinking about technical things and lose myself in the music completely.

"Well," I say now, trying to unwind from practice mode

and answer Zach's question. "They're gold. They're fish. Freshwater, I think. And you have one."

Zach sighs. "Had," he says. "He was floating at the top of the fish tank, just, like, *sitting there,* when I woke up this morning. I tapped on the glass, trying to wake him up, and then used the net to nudge him, and that didn't work. His gills aren't moving. Also, his eyes are this weird concave shape and gray, which they never used to be. I looked online and those are all the signs."

"That sucks," I say. "He seemed . . . like a good fish."

"Oh, he was terrible," Zach says. "We actually started out with him and another fish—a yellow molly called Molly. But Goldie ate him within, like, six hours of both of them being brought home."

"Oh my God," I laugh. "Still. That sucks."

"I mean, he was my brother's, but . . . yeah." I hear what sounds like movement on the other end of the phone. "So, listen, Kev is spending the day at his friend's place and he doesn't know yet. And I thought maybe you'd like to help me find an exact replica of Goldie Hawn before he gets home. I hate to overhype it, but it's going to be pretty mundane."

I laugh. "I don't know. I was going to spend the day doing nothing and maybe practicing for a bit and then going back to doing nothing," I say. "But I guess I might be able to take some time out of my busy schedule."

"Excellent," Zach says, and I can hear the smile in his voice.

When he picks me up, half an hour later, he's wearing a faded green T-shirt with a tiny hole in the neck, and his hair is exceedingly messy. The whole effect is so hilariously disheveled that it makes my stomach flutter. I run my fingers through his hair, because *I can,* when I kiss him hello in the car.

"I have to work at four," Zach says, glancing at the clock on his dashboard. It says 9:12, which I've figured out means it's roughly twelve-something, as it tends to run three hours behind no matter how often Zach resets it. "So we're going to have to make good time."

I shoot him a confused look. "I thought we were picking out a goldfish, not a house. We have three hours."

But Zach is right; three hours does leave us pressed for time. Because, as it turns out, we are not looking for a goldfish. We are looking for Goldie Hawn's identical twin. In the first pet store we go to, there are dozens and dozens of fish, and we press our faces up to the glass and Zach shakes his head in dissatisfaction. "No, he had this one white stripe just under his eye."

"White stripe? You're sure it's not a *clown* fish you're looking for?" asks the spiky-haired teenager who is helping us.

Zach gives him an unimpressed look. "Yeah, I'm sure. It wasn't a long stripe. Not even a big one. Just, like, a white mark."

We try another store, where the manager is this super tall guy, like quarterback big, except in his forties. He is very knowledgeable about all things goldfish, and maybe even a little judgmental. "Sure," he says after we explain what we're looking for. "I'll show you our troubling and we'll see if there's one that meets your very specific criteria."

"Troubling?" I echo.

"A group of goldfish is a troubling. Like a herd of cows."

He flicks his gaze over us, like he's not sure what they even teach in school anymore. I'm not, either; I thought all groups of fish were called schools. "I bet you didn't have him in a big enough tank. That's always it. And to think some people put them in *bowls*. They can grow to be over a foot. How would *you* like to live in a bowl all your life?"

I know he means "you" in the general sense, but it sounds pretty accusing. Zach and I exchange a glance, and I bite my lip to keep from laughing. I wouldn't like to live in a fish tank, regardless of the size, but I don't see the point in saying this out loud.

Being in a pet store reminds me of how animal-crazy I used to be in elementary school. Before music, horses were the great love of my life—my room and notebooks were covered in cutouts of ponies. Since I couldn't have a horse, I'd drag Dad into a pet store whenever I could and try to convince him I desperately needed a gerbil or rabbit or parrot. We owned a tiny gray Lhasa apso for a whopping twenty-eight hours once. Mom freaked out because Caleb was allergic and the dog wasn't hypoallergenic, so we returned it, and there was talk of going back in the next few months and getting one that shed less. I'm not sure why we never did.

Zach peers into the giant aquarium full of goldfish that look, to me, exactly the same as the fish I saw in his house.

"What do you think?" I ask when the guy goes to attend to another customer, leaving us to decide. Personally, I am starting to wonder if Zach is crazy. Maybe it's too good to be true that I would like a normal, well-adjusted boy who likes me back.

"They just seem very obviously *not* the same fish."

He sighs and walks around to the other side of the aquarium to look more closely at a particular fish that is in the process of eating something.

"Zach," I say, realization dawning on me as to why a person could possibly be this obsessed with replacing a goldfish. "Did you do something to Goldie Hawn?" I drop my voice so Judgy McJudgerson doesn't overhear, even though he's about two aisles away. "Did *you* kill him?"

Zach's eyes widen. "What? No!" he says, and I laugh, not believing it for a second.

"No, I swear," he insists. "I just found him that way this morning."

"Right. Well, you seem awfully invested for *just* having found his body."

Zach shakes his head and looks at me. "It really had nothing to do with me," he says. "I just . . . Kev—for how annoying and mouthy he tries to be—is actually kind of a sensitive kid. He is. Don't look so shocked."

"I'm not," I lie.

He straightens to his full height now and runs his hand through his hair, which just makes it look even more like he might have been electrocuted. "I mean, Kevin is *fourteen* and obviously knows about the circle of life and all that, but even I was sad when I saw Goldie just lying there floating at the top of the tank. It just sucks to watch something go from being alive to being dead. No warning, no in-between. And we've had him for three years. I just hoped Kev wouldn't have to know."

Zach shakes his head when the manager comes back to ask if we've found what we're looking for.

We leave and try another store, the last pet store in town, and the fish area is close to the loud, squawking bird area, which doesn't seem like the best idea if those birds ever get free, and we circle the tanks over and over again, looking for the right fish, but Zach keeps coming back to one that has sidled up to the glass and is peering right back at us. With our heads pressed close together, I can smell citrus laundry detergent and sweat and the slightest hint of cigarette smoke on Zach. I watch him while he nods at this fish. He runs his hand through his hair worriedly as he leans against the counter while he's paying, continuously looking back at the water-filled bag we're taking Goldie Hawn's twin home in and asking if I think it's fine that *this* fish's mark is closer to the mouth than the eye. I think it's kind of the sweetest thing I've ever seen in my life.

But when I mention this to him, he says, "Nah, you'd do the same if you had a younger sibling," but he's smiling a little bit.

And I don't know if it's true—what I'd be like as an older sister—but I remain firm in my conviction of his sweetness.

Later, once Goldie Hawn II has been acclimated to the tank and Zach has gone to work and I'm back at home, arguing with Caleb about cleaning the bathroom, I get a text from Zach.

Sooo. Mom saw Goldie this morning before I did and she picked Kev up on her way home from work this afternoon and told him the fish had died.

WHAT, I text back. *I hope you pretended he'd had a miraculous resurrection or this was his ghost, back to clear up his unfinished business.*

Ha ha! Zach replies. *I should have done that, but I just told him the truth. . . . He said he'd have preferred a turtle.*

HA HA HA, I text.

And, *You're a good brother, Zach.*

Hey, thanks, he texts back.

We keep texting for the rest of the night, through dinner and practice and right up until it's midnight, and my lips hurt from smiling. I thought I needed something to wake me up. Like a city full of things to fall in love with—people and places and monuments and tastes and sounds. Not just one person, not just a *boy* who lives across town. I want my life to be more than that. And yet.

I feel idiotic and silly and funnier than I am, and my heart kicks in my chest every time my phone vibrates with a new message. I feel crazy, charged with electricity and exhausted and slightly panicked at each text I send that goes unanswered for a few minutes. Or when he *does* write back and I have to figure out something funny or clever or flirty—or, oh my God, all of the above—to say back.

It feels a little bit terrible. Like walking across a shaky bridge with the world laid out before you. You might fall off any second, but you have to know what's on the other side. There is not much to hold on to. And I don't know if I would, anyway, if there was.

33

AFTER
January

"I'm so, so sorry. Please don't hate me," Katy says. "As soon as you told me he worked at the Cineplex and then when you described him, I realized you were seeing *him*. That's why I asked if you'd let me go to my mom. I thought something had gone wrong."

That's why you started avoiding me, I think, but don't say the words. I'm leaning forward, head bowed on the steering wheel, eyes closed. Trying to get a grip on reality.

"I hoped it was just a glitch. Just some temporary thing because of hitting your head. After everything we'd done so you could forget what happened, after how devastated it made you, I wasn't just going to blurt the truth out to you. And then you said you'd stopped seeing him and you were feeling better, so I thought it was fine. . . . I don't know."

I still have a million questions.

Who is he?

What happened?

You knew? All this time I thought I was crazy, and you knew who he was?

How can this be true? How can any of what has happened over the last twenty-four hours be true?

"Who is he?" I ask, deciding to go in order.

"Zach," she says.

Zach.

The name tugs at something quick and sharp inside me. It's like a jolt of electricity, a pinched nerve.

His name is Zach.

I picture Bus Boy. His weather-inappropriate clothes, his wide smile. His name feels like a balm on a burn.

And yet. Katy hasn't given me much. Who the hell *is* Zach?

"What happened?" I ask.

She is tentative. Unsure. "You were so sad. I had never seen you like that before. It scared me. So when you looked up Overton and you wanted to get your memories of him erased . . . I mean, it seemed extreme and scary, but I wanted you to be happy. You're my best friend, Addie—I've never been friends with someone as long as I have with you. I supported whatever you wanted."

I stay silent.

What?

This isn't my life.

It can't be my life.

Who is Zach?

"How did it work?"

"The procedure? I'm not too sure. I know they use

207

electrodes—these black patchy things hooked up to a machine. Or do you mean how we were able to get them to do it without your parents knowing?" She pauses, but I don't answer, so she addresses the latter question. "We used our fake IDs. You had it done as Kathleen Kelly. They thought you were nineteen."

I glance up at that. So we *did* get use out of them, like she wanted.

"Who was my doctor?" It's such a stupid question. Mundane.

"Overton. The old one."

Dr. Hunt must have done the procedure when I was twelve. Overton Sr. removed *Zach*. And Overton Jr. really had never met me.

"But how?" I ask again. "Nobody else knew him? My parents have never even mentioned him. *How?*"

"We never told your parents you got the procedure done. You were really upset after everything with him, and they knew that. So when you asked your family not to bring him up again, they were only too happy to agree. None of our friends at school really knew him. The biggest problem was his dumb-ass friends would approach you and try to talk to you—mostly at the beginning."

People I thought were Katy's friends.

The girl at the mall—Ashley—who said she'd met me.

God.

Oh God.

Still leaning over the steering wheel, I bury my face in my hands and cry. Quiet, heavy tears that start from my chest and weave their way up.

This is not my life.

None of this can be true.

And yet—here are the pieces, falling together, interlocking. Making sense.

My whole life is a lie.

"I'm so sorry," Katy says. "I only wanted you to not be so sad. I didn't even want you to have the procedure, but you were so sure. I'd never seen you so upset."

I can't even answer her. I can only continue weeping, shaking silently.

Oh God.

What do I do now?

"I'll tell you everything you want to know," Katy says, squeezing my shoulder. "Everything I remember. Stuff you told me. I'll tell you how you met and everything you told me."

Everything she *remembers.*

What about *me*?

Somehow Katy has one giant chunk of my life, and my family has the other. What do I have?

What have I done?

"No," I say, lifting my head from the steering wheel. I don't want her to tell me what happened.

"O-okay." Katy seems surprised. "Addie, I'm really, really sorry. I swear I didn't know about Rory. And I should have told you right away when you started seeing the . . . Zach, but I was just . . . I didn't know how to handle it or whether it was the right thing."

I nod, but say nothing.

I feel numb, like a stranger in a completely new and

foreign world. Katy gives me the closest thing to a hug she can manage with me sitting catatonic, leaning over the wheel and looking out the windshield.

"Will you be okay?" she asks.

I nod again, and then she is reluctantly opening the door, scrambling out of the car. I stay there for minutes, hours, staring out the window. Trying to make sense, for the second time in twenty-four hours, of an entirely new version of my life.

34

BEFORE
Early August

Zach is working today, and I've just ridden over from my viola lesson. Since his dad is at a dentist's appointment and the store is dead, I am sitting cross-legged on the counter, wistfully scrolling through the latest pictures Katy has sent of her trip.

"Did your dad always want to own a movie store?" I ask as Zach works on the computer a few feet away. He's ordering some new horrodies.

"No way," he says. "We used to sell mostly music back in the day, but the only thing selling worse than DVDs is CDs. It's all digital."

Then he points at the screen and says, "Look at this one." I squint at a picture of a man in a business suit, his pants rolled up to the knees, holding a briefcase and standing in a literal pool of what is quite obviously ketchup. Of course.

"It's by a British dude named Moyer. He was number one on *Cinema Tomorrow*'s list of up-and-coming directors, and his first film was pretty good, but obviously not as good as what Ciano was making when *he* first started. Do you know what's so great about Ciano, like, specifically?" Zach says.

"What is so great about Ciano, like, specifically?" I ask.

"He nearly died." Which is not what I'm expecting him to say. "*Rotary Windclock*—you know, the third one I gave you—was inspired by it. When he was nineteen and in college, he was out late one night alone when he got jumped by four guys, mugged, beaten to a pulp, and left for dead."

"Holy crap," I say.

"I know. There was no one around, and by the time they found him, he was unconscious. He had to relearn how to walk. Like, he still walks with a cane because of it.

"Anyway, the point is that when he made it into a movie, he decided not to make it heartwarming or depressing or a story about overcoming or whatever. He didn't even aim for funny, which is at least the respectable cousin of silly." Zach opens up another web page while he talks, pauses to read its synopsis of a movie, then closes it. "He said in an interview that his producing partner wanted him to do a documentary about his journey back, like regaining his locomotion and stuff, but he refused."

"That might actually have been pretty interesting," I say.

"Yeah, but that's his point." Zach focuses on me now, his eyes intense, voice passionate, the way he always gets when he talks movies. "That was his *power.* You take the worst thing that's ever happened to you and you tell it any way you want to. You make it silly. You reclaim it. The point is that it's *yours.* And everything that happens to you, not just the bad stuff, is like that. Make it whatever the hell you want it to. be. The entire interview is a fucking revelation. I should find the article and email it to you," he says.

"Do it," I say, reaching for my phone, which has just vibrated in my pocket.

I show Zach the picture Katy sent. "They were *literally* outside Carnegie Hall."

Zach squints at my phone, then stands and stretches. His T-shirt jumps up, revealing his stomach and the waistband of his underwear peeking just above his jeans.

"You're making yourself miserable," he says, playing with a strand of my hair. I untuck my feet and let them dangle so Zach is standing between my legs. "Maybe *Katy* is having a horrible time but she's taking Ciano's advice and making it sound wonderful."

I roll my eyes at him but hold his shirt between my fingers and pull him in closer.

"I'm not that miserable," I breathe against his lips.

"*Now,*" he says, smiling. His lips are so soft, his tongue warm inside my mouth. His breath is a little cigarette-y, but he's always chewing mint gum lately to decrease the taste. I wrap my legs around him and kiss him harder. If this is misery, I want to be miserable for the rest of my life, *die* miserable.

We are tangled all around each other when the door of the store suddenly bursts open, a faint breeze—the first real hint of summer passing—wafting in.

I twist my upper body around to find Raj gaping at us, his jaw a few inches lower than normal.

"Hey, dude," Zach says casually.

I spin around so my legs are on the counter again, no longer locking Zach's body around me. "Hey, Raj."

213

He stands there for a good thirty seconds, not speaking, before he says, "So I hit an electrical pole on my way over."

"Holy shit. Is your mom's car okay?" Zach asks.

"I was on foot," Raj says, speaking in this slow, dazed way I've never heard from him before. "Anyway, now I realize it must have been a person."

Zach and I exchange perplexed looks.

"A person," Raj repeats. "Because my glasses are old and my eyes keep playing tricks on me. It's happening right *now*." Oh—he's talking about us. I guess Zach hasn't yet told Raj that we are more than friends.

Zach evades his friend's eyes, looks down at his computer, and says with no emotion in his voice, "Really."

"Really," Raj echoes, still looking at me, stupefied. I feel my ears get a little hot. And then he seems to shake off the bewilderment and strides toward the counter. "I was playing *Dungeon World 2* last night, and I think I have a new idea for our next film."

"Sweet. What is it?" Zach asks.

Raj launches into a tale about dragons and a mall cop and a blood-vomiting sea animal with the ability to exist on land so long as it has mated.

"That's really disturbing," I say, glancing up from the exclamation-laden text (*Omg, so cool!!! You must be having the BEST time!!!!*) I'm sending back to Katy.

"Right?" Raj says, misunderstanding my use of the word "disturbing." "It's genius."

"It's almost the exact same plot as that Van Durgen movie *Truth or Troll*," Zach says.

"That movie was shit," Raj says, and I'm not a hundred percent sure, but I think he means it as an insult.

"And still the highest-grossing Swedish movie last year."

"So that's a no?" Raj asks sadly.

"That's a definite no. If we're going to follow in the footsteps of someone, we could aim a little higher than Van Durgen. Especially if we have a CXX in September," Zach says.

"Whoa, you're down to two cigarettes a day already?" Raj asks.

"Working on it," Zach says.

"Nice." Raj nods. "But seriously. Unequivocal no to that idea?"

"Unequivocally," Zach says. "Sorry."

The phone starts ringing then, and Zach turns to get it. "Sure" he says, "let me see if we have that." He heads to the back of the store. I'm still staring at my phone when I feel Raj's eyes on me.

"What's up, Raj?" I ask pointedly.

"So you and Zach, huh?" he asks.

"Yeah," I say, fighting the twitch of a smile in the corners of my mouth. "You seem . . . shocked?"

"Yes and no," he says, then shrugs. "No, because that kid is not subtle. I knew he liked you from the second he told me he was thinking of asking you to join our movie. And he was *jealous* of your viola."

I laugh. "Yes, because?"

"Yes, because I wasn't sure we'd live to see a Lindsay-less day. Even when Zach went to Fincher for a year, they were solid."

This information is not exactly surprising, but I still flinch a little at her name. Why does she always seem to come up?

"You don't seem to like her very much," I tell Raj as Zach's voice on the phone carries to where we are.

"*She's* the one who doesn't like *me*. I mean, whatever, we're friendly. It's fine. But she doesn't like me or Kevin or any of Zach's friends. She doesn't even like horrodies."

"But she's starred in almost all Zach's movies," I point out. And how does she not like Kevin? He's Zach's *brother*.

"For the acting experience and because she respects his work ethic when it comes to movies. She actually said that." Raj shakes his head. "She hates *Dungeon World 2,* the smell of Indian food, and puppies."

"Puppies?" I repeat, incredulous.

"Fine, not the last thing."

Now I'm frowning, leaning forward on the counter. "Then . . . what did Zach ever see in her?"

I'm expecting him to say that only God knows, but Raj sighs. "It's not like she's a bad person. She just doesn't give things a chance. She's very quick to form an opinion, and then she doesn't change it." I suddenly remember what Zach said at Schiavoni's. That he liked that I tried new things, that I hadn't made up my mind about every single thing. Unlike Lindsay?

"And then she's also convinced she's just a little bit better, more mature, than everyone else. She thinks *we're* bad influences on Zach, when—for the record—she smoked all the time with him."

"Lindsay smokes?" I don't know why this shocks me.

Raj nods. "Where there's smoke, there's Lindsay. She

thinks it's sophisticated or something. And she likes that it makes her voice raspy."

"Wow."

Before I can ask more, Zach reappears. "They're coming to upgrade our systems next week. Dad finally put together enough money to make the jump."

Zach pulls up a few more movies he's thinking about ordering and reads out their synopses. After a few minutes, Raj heaves a heavy sigh and asks if he can open a bag of cotton candy.

While he goes to grab it, Zach leans toward me and kisses the flap of my earlobe. Every inch of my body tickles.

"Stop." I writhe, giggling.

"Do you know you tug at your ears when you're feeling shy?" he whispers. I didn't, but it's because they constantly heat up when anything remotely exciting happens. Katy thinks it's a condition.

They warm when I'm angry or embarrassed. *When you look at me,* I think. *When you touch me.*

I think now about what Raj just told me, and I wonder whether I make Zach forget her—Lindsay. And whether I like or hate that.

But what I say is, "You're the first person ever to notice that."

35

BEFORE
August

We hang out almost every day, before Zach works and after I'm done practicing. So that I don't completely neglect my viola, I implement a rule for myself wherein I am not allowed to see Zach unless I've practiced for at least an hour that day. We make a point of doing the sorts of mundane things people who are not obsessive cinephiles and viola players would do and tell great tales of. Summer things and outdoor things.

I introduce Zach to the strawberry-kiwi milk shakes—the Oreo pieces sprinkled in are the key—that Shake Attack only makes in the summer and Zach quickly falls victim to my addiction. We go there roughly five times a week. One time twice in one day.

We play Bigger and Better in At Home Movies when I visit Zach at work. Somehow Ciano always comes out on top, which is the best evidence I have that the game is deeply flawed and rigged.

We have a picnic on the grass by Bentley Lake, though it is a little bit traumatizing because these white and gray birds keep swooping down a few feet away from us, begging for crumbs. They never actually get within a foot of our basket, but that doesn't stop both me and Zach from ducking our heads and yelling whenever one dive-bombs out of the sky and lands not that far from our picnic blanket.

"Okay," Zach says, "they're just birds. It's fine. They're not even getting that close."

"So it's fine for them to just sit there and stare us down while we eat?"

"Should I give them a piece of my sandwich?" Zach asks.

"No! What if they all swoop down for it? Or that gives them the courage to come closer? Let's just try to ignore them."

Which is impossible to do on account of the fact that they make quite the entrance when they land one by one and then they *all* just sit there, watching us threateningly. Soon seven are clustered on the grass to the left of us.

"Oh God, I'm breaking, Addie. I might have to give the closest one a cracker, just to leave us alone," Zach says.

"Do not!"

"I have to! It's like that bigger, older kid that bullies you for your lunch at school."

"Exactly. Ignore him and he'll go away."

"That is *terrible* advice," Zach laughs, shaking his head. "I have to listen to my heart. I'm sorry."

"Oh my God, don't!" I order him, but he's still trying to break up a cracker, so I lunge at him. We start laughing and I'm trying to pry it out of Zach's hands before he throws it, and he's trying to keep it out of my reach, crushing it in his

palm. We're both laughing too hard to do either thing effectively, and then we're toppling over backward. The sun is warm against my skin and we're both lying on the grass, facing upward, and I have to squint against the sky. Who cares about some dumb birds?

If a stranger walked by, they would think we were having simultaneous asthma attacks. My stomach hurts like I've been doing crunches. Shaking with laughter, I find Zach's hand, warm and only inches from mine, and the feel of his skin still makes a current rush through my body every single time. I lace the fingers of my right hand between the fingers of his left hand, which is unfortunately where he's crushed the cracker but I don't care, and our palms are sweaty and warm on each other's, with hundreds of tiny little pieces crushed between.

And maybe we would lie there for a few minutes, maybe all afternoon, just cracking each other up over things that are not even that funny, our bodies rising and falling with each breath. The sun is making me drowsy and I could fall asleep with my head on Zach's chest, and I probably would. But just then another bird dive-bombs us even closer than the last, and we jump apart. Quickly and without discussion, we start to pack up our picnicking stuff.

We put the food away in Zach's mom's basket, hoping that will deter the birds, at least while we make the trek back to Zach's car. I carry the folded-up blanket under my arm, Zach takes the basket, and we make a run for the parking lot.

"We're almost there we're almost there," Zach says as we run with a hand over our bowed heads, the way you do in a thunderstorm. Once we make it safely into the car, we discuss the possibility that maybe we are not picnic people.

"Do you know what would have helped?" Zach says. "A giant-ass umbrella. Maybe one from Two Dollars or Less."

It's tempting, but we don't give up on the outside-summery stuff all together.

We go bike riding through town, coming up with names like Otis and Horatio and Michèle for the people we pass. We try one of the hikes out by Calamore, which is long and hard and sweaty, but still somehow fun. We go out boating once with Zach's family. They borrow their neighbor's boat and take it out on a lake two hours from Lyndale, and Raj actually agrees to come, even though he spends the whole time sitting on the boat in a giant straw hat that Zach's mom made him wear because he didn't bring one. He sits there, unimpressed by the sights of nature, by the glistening nearly green water, by Kevin's dirty jokes, or by Zach and me holding hands. He just sighs deeply.

"Dude," Zach says, tugging on the black beanie he's wearing today to keep his hair under control. "I say this because nobody else will, but you're reminding me of a cranky old grandma right around this second."

"A cranky old grandma at a rave," I add. "Or a college party."

Zach laughs but Raj rolls his eyes. "I only came because my cousins are *still* staying with us, and I needed to preserve my sanity." He flips the brim of his hat up to give us a put-upon look. "But I think I went about it wrong."

We try some new non-Lindsay-exposed restaurants and wash Zach's car (he cannot keep it clean to save his life). We talk on the phone, text, and hang out with his brother, and everything is ordinary and normal and slowly summer starts to turn into fall. There is a little voice in the back of my head that wonders whether people like Katy who post about great and exuberant normal lives are not pretending. If they are not embellishing the happy. Maybe their exuberance is even warranted.

Maybe mine—newly found and not broken in yet—really is.

36

AFTER
January

Long after Katy leaves my car, the tears finally stop coming and I pull out of the school parking lot and drive in aimless circles around Lyndale. I turn off my phone so no one can reach me and turn the music up so loud I can't think. It doesn't work. My mind whirs with the same thoughts: *You erased him. Bus Boy. Zach. You chose to remove him. How could you do that? Why would you do that? You erased him. . . .*

Over and over and over.

I don't know I don't know. Why would I do that?

I think of what Caleb told me last night about Rory, about how I chose to move forward.

I erased my brother, too.

I drive around Bentley Lake and the park. I drive to the east side of town, weave through the streets, until I find the place where we used to live. Our old house, its walls light green on the inside, the outside made of dark red brick. There is a silver-blue minivan in front of it, in the driveway where Caleb and I used to play tennis with the neighborhood kids. Otherwise, it looks the same. I want to knock on the door and go inside. To stand at the top of the stairs, toes sinking into the carpet, and belt out show tunes like I'm a kid again. I want to be eleven so I can meet Rory and hold him and smell his skin and know what it's like to be a big sister. I imagine my whole family still lives there—not us now, but like we used to be. We haunt the house with our laughter, with Caleb's dream of flying, with my music, with the way my parents used to love each other, because I like the thought that things keep existing where they once were, where you leave them, even when life changes. I like the idea that the things we did and thought and felt are entities that go on existing outside of us.

My parents erased him.

Why did they do that?

Why did I let them?

How could I do it to myself again?

When I finally head home, it's almost dark out.

Dad's car is in front of our house. Mom's and Caleb's cars are there, too, which means they are all waiting for me.

I enter as quietly as I can, hoping, somehow, I'll be able to slip upstairs without anyone noticing.

I almost make it. Dad has his back to me. He's talking to my mother, his voice tired and gravelly, an indication that he hasn't slept since arriving from work. Mom, her face in her hands, is on the couch farthest away from him.

It's odd to see my parents in our living room, like we are five years in the past. What is different now is that the secret they've been keeping, the weight that has quietly torn our family apart, now sits exposed and obvious in the center of the room.

In this light, I wonder how I missed it. All the weird looks my family got over the years. I thought then that it was because of my mother's mild celebrity or my parents' breakup. Obviously, it was because people still remembered our tragedy. Most of them were too polite to say anything. Maybe they mentioned Rory at first and the name meant nothing to me. Or they said other things in a way I didn't understand.

Let us know if you need anything and how are your parents doing could mean anything. I'd wonder self-consciously, *How do they know my dad hasn't been home in three weekends?*

Now my question is this: How did I never figure it out?

The answer, of course, slaps me right in the face, as it has been doing all day.

My parents quite literally hid it, wiped it clean from my mind.

And then I did it again to myself.

"Addie, how could you!" my mother exclaims, asking the very question that is haunting me, before I have a chance to get upstairs unnoticed. "You went to Overton on your own? You *lied* to get your memory erased? Do you know how dangerous it is to have a procedure on your *mind* without your full medical history? Do you know all the things that could easily have gone wrong and we wouldn't have even *known* about it? For a whole year?" Her voice is breaking. My mother has cried more in two days than she has in years.

I want to point out that the procedure seemed perfectly safe—convenient, even—when *they* had it done on me, but I bite back my words. "Katy told you?"

She must have called and told them everything right after she left my car at school.

"Katy called me," Mom says. "But when your father landed, he already had several missed calls from Overton. Apparently, some of the staff recognized you when you went in yesterday. After you left, they put together that you'd been there both as Addison and under that other name. They realized that if you were only seventeen now, you had to have been underage for the procedure last year. That the information they had for you under the other name didn't add up. When they figured this all out, they only had your father's cell phone number and the disconnected number from before we moved."

"I came over as soon as I got into town," Dad says now.

Which staff members recognized me? I wonder. *The receptionist? The nurse with the streak?*

"They can't believe you've had two procedures," Caleb says. "It's really rare."

"And now you're hallucinating? Why didn't you mention what was happening right away? Why would you do something like this?" Mom asks.

Dad looks at the wall behind me. Even now, with everything out in the open, he can't force himself to look at me. It makes my chest hurt. It infuriates me.

"Why would *you*?" I shoot back, since I can't answer her question. *I don't know why I would.*

Maybe it's true that they succeeded in protecting me—I don't remember my brother's death—but they've also taken away the most valuable thing I had: the ability to know myself.

Dad surprises me by speaking then, instead of leaving it to Mom, as usual.

226

"Addie, there's more to the story than you realize. But we can get to that later. Dr. Overton wants you to come in right away for a scan. When I called the clinic back, he said when you saw him, you didn't tell him anything about the boy you were seeing."

The boy.

Zach.

Zach, Zach, Zach.

I suddenly wish I was with him right now, my apparition. That I could tell him what his name is so he'd have a little bit more of himself.

Then a pang of something I can't name slams into my chest. My parents know him, too—Katy told me that.

Zach.

He is my memory, and yet I'm the only one who doesn't remember what happened. Who he is.

"There is no way," I say slowly, "that I'm ever going to Dr. Overton again."

"Addie," Caleb says, "you have to."

"I don't have to do anything."

I turn and start for the stairs.

"Stop being dramatic, Addison," Mom says now, following me up. "We need to know why you're seeing him. It could be something really serious."

"Or something not so serious," my dad adds quickly. Mom is always jumping to conclusions, anticipating the worst.

"Most likely it has something to do with the bus crash," my brother says.

"I'm not going," I say again, and slam my door shut. I fall onto my unmade bed, my whole body heavy from exhaustion.

That sinking feeling I sometimes have, of watching every-thing around me vanish, wraps around me and won't let go. I ache for sleep, the kind of peaceful, uninterrupted sleep I haven't had since the bus crash, but it won't come.

I think about reaching in the dark for my viola, but for once, I am too sad to play.

37

AFTER
January

My father stays the night. Or arrives bright and early the next morning to begin the work of wearing me down. I'm not sure which.

He knocks several times on my door, begging me to please open it.

I ignore him until at least midday. It's Saturday, after all.

Finally I don't hear his voice, but I see a shadow under the door, and I hear him breathing in and out. I draw the door toward me and put my face through the crack.

He is dozing, sitting on the floor with his knees pulled up, his mouth slightly open, but he jerks awake immediately.

"I need to tell you some things," Dad says, getting to his feet. I open the door, even though I'm fairly certain I don't want to hear this.

"If you're going to lie to me, we don't have to bother with this conversation."

"I'm not going to lie to you," he says, actually holding my gaze. I step back and let him in.

He sits on the edge of my bed and surveys my room like he hasn't seen it in years. I don't think he has. He looks like a giant sitting on a piece of furniture that's too small for him and might break at any second.

I lean back against the wall by my door. I have so many questions for him, but I'm afraid I might cry, so I let him go first.

"You're built too much like me," he says.

I shoot him a weird look. What is he talking about? We're nothing alike.

"It's always been my biggest fear," he continues, "that you might end up in some of the places I have."

I'm too much like him? Does he not see how much Caleb looks like him? How much Caleb wants to fly?

"Dad," I say impatiently, but he holds up a hand.

"I'm getting there," he says. "I've suffered from pretty bad depression all my life. My brothers, too. You know about Uncle Mark." I nod and glance away. He killed himself his second year of college, before I was born. "I had dark times, too. Your grandmother would look at me and say, 'Open your eyes. Wake up.' And for the longest time, I had no idea why she said that. I thought she meant that I always looked like I was falling asleep."

I bite my lower lip.

"For the most part, after your mother and I were married, I was better. Most airlines need you to be stable for a minimum of a year before you can fly, and I was. I started—and am still on—meds, but I was finally happy. And after you kids were born, I was really happy. And then Rory died. . . ." He takes a breath in like he's been punched.

"That's why you left," I say. "You blamed me."

He glances at me, surprised. Then he says, like he's having trouble picking out his words, "It was a lot of things." He doesn't deny it, though—that maybe he had trouble forgiving me. And in his non-denial, I find more truth—painful and sad—than I have since I found out about Rory. "We walked around in a fog for months. We tried for a year to get past it. All of us. Me, your mother, Caleb.

"But you were the worst, Addie. You were carrying so much blame around it was like it had contorted you. That little girl who was bursting with so much life, who burst into every room. Your eyes were glazed over. Your passion for everything, for music—it was just gone. I couldn't bear looking at you and not recognizing you. I wanted to say the same thing my mother had said to me: 'Open your eyes.' To tell you it was going to be okay. And I believed that you would be okay. I really did. I thought it was possible to live through depression, because I was doing it."

He shakes his head now. "But when your mother told me about my pills and where she'd found them—she was so convinced that if you *didn't* have to live through it, then you shouldn't. I knew she'd never forgive me if something happened to you. And honestly, I wouldn't have forgiven myself, either. So I let her decide."

He looks me in the eye again. "Caleb didn't want it and I understood why. If I couldn't imagine having it myself, then I couldn't force him to."

You fought for Caleb, but not for me.

"It would have been a betrayal, unnatural," Dad continues. "A parent doesn't forget a child. I—we—had a responsibility to remember him."

"So it wasn't unnatural when you let me forget him?"

And they hadn't just betrayed Rory by doing it; they'd betrayed me, too.

"I don't think it was the right thing to do, Addie. Some days it eats me up inside . . . ," Dad says, squinting, looking past me. "Whether it was right or wrong, your mother and I just wanted you to be okay. We had a chance to take away your pain, and we did. I wish sometimes someone could have done that for me."

His voice breaks a little then, and I swallow.

I want to shout a million things at him, to yell what that tiny voice in my head is saying: *I could have done it. I could have gone through it and come out okay.* But my throat burns and different words form.

"I had it done again. I *chose* to go back a second time. I didn't know how much I had already lost," I say, tears spilling unbidden down my cheeks.

He looks for a second like he's going to walk across the room to me and wrap me up in his arms like he used to do.

"I know. We set you up for that. Whatever happened with the boy—you never told me the details—it tore you up inside. Anyone could see that."

I swipe my hand across my cheek.

"Rory was the first major loss you had, and the boy—"

"Zach," I say. I want him to say it, acknowledge the apparition I've being seeing.

"Zach. Because you never really dealt with the grief of

232

losing Rory, this second heartbreak felt like it was the end of the world to you. I think the way you learn to deal with one hard thing affects the way you deal with the next and the one after that. You didn't remember what it felt like to lose anything and come through it." It reminds me of what Mrs. Dubois always says. About firsts and how they set the precedent. "How you learn to cope with it and *live through it,* that's important."

Is he saying Zach is dead, too? Lost the way Rory is? Why didn't I let Katy tell me everything she knew?

"Dad, do you know *anything* about me and Zach?"

He shakes his head at me, like now is not the time.

"Addie, your mother was right that a number of things could be causing what you've been seeing," Dad says. "Figure out why you made the choice you did to have the procedure on your own. Let's find out what's wrong—why you're seeing him—first."

38

BEFORE
Early September

"Come here, you love-bitten mothertrucker," Katy says, sweeping me into an inescapable embrace. "Don't you ever leave me again!"

"You left *me*," I point out, laughing into her shoulder as I hug her back just as tightly.

"Why? Why did I do it?" she hisses. "I nearly fell into a Depressive Episode, I missed you *so much*." Which, of course, is not true since not one of her hundred messages made mention of said Depressive Episodes, or even of missing me. But her hug tells me now what her words when she was away didn't.

I step back and say, "Zach, this is my best friend, Katy."

Keeping one hand on my lower back, Zach reaches forward to shake Katy's hand and grins at her. "Hi!" he says, speaking loudly to be heard over the music at the pool party we're at. "Addie tells me you're an actor."

And I want to hug him because if there ever was a perfect way to introduce yourself to Katy, that was it. Not "act*ress*," because she finds the *-ress* ending to be sexist, plus Zach's comment indicates that I've been talking about her, which she loves.

One of Katy's eyebrows shoots up and she shakes hands with Zach, clearly impressed.

"I am." She smiles back. "It's nice to meet you, finally!" Zach and I have been official for more than a month, but since she only got back last night, having spent the past three weeks with her cousins in Long Island, this is the first time we are all together.

Katy attaches herself to my side and says much louder than she realizes, "Okay, you were right about the smile. My God. But where is *the friend*?"

Zach laughs, clearly making out her every word. "Raj said—and I quote—'I would rather die a slow and merciless death at the hands of one of Van Durgen's whimpering characters than put on a pair of pants and go to a *pool* party when I can play *Dungeon World 2 and* my mother's making aloo gobi.'"

Zach and I laugh hard and Katy stares at us in fascination, especially at Zach's smile. She pinches my side just under my rib cage.

"I got, maybe, three words of that, but you two are *revolting*," she says, giving Zach and me her crucially important seal of approval.

Most of the party passes uneventfully. Katy is one of about seven people who strip out of their clothes and actually get into the pool—or rather, she cannonballs in. Everybody else dances and talks, loitering around the pool or on the grass. Some people are even on the roof or the fence.

Usually I'd be trailing behind Katy at a party like this, or halfheartedly conversing with one of her the-*yo*-ter friends while Katy chats up some guy, gets wasted, or tries to convince me to loosen up. ("If you're going to New Yawk, you're going to have to learn how to party like you're from New Yawk.") She's diagnosed me as having *at least* a mild form of agoraphobia, loosely defined as the fear of public spaces and crowds. For once, she might not be far from the truth.

That, coupled with my mom always wanting to know my whereabouts, makes me a not-so-frequent attendee of house parties.

Now, though, Zach introduces me to a few of his friends and then we find ourselves a spot underneath a peeling tree in the yard and lose track of everyone else.

We're playing One-Up, a game that Kevin, of all people, taught Zach. It's actually pretty similar to Bigger and Better. You say one thing that scares you, and the other person one-ups you until you can't think of anything worse. Our first topic is fears.

"Drowning," I say.

"The dark," Zach counters.

"The *dark*?" I repeat, incredulous.

"Not, like, scared-to-turn-out-the-lights dark," Zach laughs. "I mean, like, *abject darkness*. The kind of dark that can swallow something whole. I honestly can't think of anything worse."

"Good thing it's *my* turn. Hmmm. How to top that? Let me think of something truly scary. Oh, I know!" I say, flicking something off his jeans. "Lint. It's so terrifying. And, like, fluffy."

"Fine. Laugh it up," he says, rolling his eyes. "But I guarantee you that you'd freak out if you could only *fathom* the kind of darkness in my mind."

"Okay, this is getting creepy, Zach."

He laughs. "I'll put it in a movie someday and *then* you'll understand."

Zach suddenly stiffens, his face rigid.

"Shit," he murmurs under his breath.

"What's wrong?" I whirl around, following the direction of his eyes. They're right on Katy, who is leaning over the edge of the pool, still in it, and talking to a girl in a short black summer dress. As we watch, Katy talks animatedly and then gives a little squeal, putting her hands up. The girl, whose hair is midnight black with a big red flower in it, bends down to give Katy a hug.

I've seen her before, at one of their community-theater events.

The girl laughs now and steps back, the front of her dress wet from Katy's hug.

"Do you want to go?" Zach asks very quietly. The girl is moving across the lawn now, toward a group of girls lying on towels on a patch of grass. And they squeal and hug her when she reaches them. One of them pats the flower in her hair.

"Sure," I say with feigned lightness as we both get up and dust our clothes off. "I'm going to quickly say bye to Katy, okay?"

Zach nods, still distracted, but he's no longer watching the girl. He's staring down at his sneakers.

When we leave the party a couple of minutes later, Zach is holding my hand, leading the way so we don't lose each other. We both say hi to a few people we know as we pass—Zach to people who go to his high school, me to people who go to mine. Mostly band people.

I glance one last time over my shoulder, trying to make out the red flower in the dimming light. I find it in almost exactly the same spot I saw it last, and I notice that she's a hand-talker. Her hands wave animatedly as she recounts a story to her friends, which has one of them grabbing at her sides and doubling over.

Whatever lightness or end-of-summer giddiness I entered this party with has dissipated.

Lindsay is not, in fact, horse-faced.

39

BEFORE
Early September

"Your mom is *nice!*" Zach whispers as my mom heads up the stairs. After weeks of me hanging out with Zach, Mom has finally insisted I bring Zach home to meet her. I think she's been fairly lenient because Caleb gave her a decent report about him and because she knows his dad.

When he came in, Zach shook her hand and introduced himself. She asked all these questions about his family, and everything was going okay until Zach mentioned that his older brother's wife just had a child and he tried to bring out his phone to show Mom a picture of baby Russell. I could have sworn her face crumpled just a bit, and then she mumbled something about having work to do and raced upstairs. It turned out Zach didn't have a picture on him, but I have no idea why she reacted that way. She tends, in general, to leave a wide berth around little kids at the mall and stuff, and when I ask her about it, she says it just feels like a long time ago since me and Caleb were little. Or she says kids are draining, too energetic. I know this can't be totally true, since sometimes I catch her dabbing her eyes during diaper commercials.

Still, if Zach noticed her strange behavior, he didn't say anything.

But he is right; she *was* nice to him. I doubt Dad is going to meet Zach anytime soon. I've seen my father once this summer, for the joint birthday-graduation dinner, and I can't even imagine maneuvering the here's-my-boyfriend meeting with him. Too much awkward in one place.

"You made me think she was scary. You were freaking me out!" Zach is saying.

I laugh. "She's both. I mean, she's fine. But she can get weird sometimes."

"In what way?" Zach asks, flopping down on the living-room couch.

"Like, completely overprotective. You know how I've been biking around the entire summer?" Zach nods, his hair falling against the brown sofa, as he stares up at me. I pop a movie into the DVD player and go back to the couch. "Two days ago, she freaked out about me 'incurring a head injury' while biking and why couldn't I drive like a normal person. I don't even have a car!"

"And isn't driving more dangerous than riding?"

"Exactly!" I say. "I mean, I always wear a helmet. Tomorrow she'll have a problem with driving, *too,* but the point is that she just up and decided it was too dangerous and I can't do it anymore, and I was like, 'I've been doing it all summer.' I know everyone thinks their parents are a little insane. I think mine actually might be."

Zach laughs. "And your house isn't as depressing as you made it sound."

"What did you expect? Black walls and emo music?"

"Pretty much," Zach says. It's true that the house is significantly less depressing than it's been this summer. Caleb is even out with some friends today. I rest my feet against the center table—hoping Mom stays upstairs awhile. He rests his head in my lap.

"Hey, Zach," I say, playing with his hair. It's so soft I wish I was small enough to burrow in it. "About last night . . ."

"Sorry about making us leave in such a hurry."

It's okay, I'm tempted to say, but it's not. As a rule, we don't really talk about Lindsay. I hate thinking of Zach kissing her, doing mundane things with her. I hate thinking that Zach's power to wake me up, make me feel special, worked on her as well.

I texted Katy this morning telling her about Zach's reaction to seeing Lindsay last night. Katy had never met Zach but she'd heard about him since she and Lindsay have been in community theater together forever. It was only when I texted her that she put together that my Zach is her theater friend's Zach.

She seems nice, I said, trying to find something neutral, a gateway for further conversation that was respectful of the fact that Katy and Lindsay are supposedly friends.

Always so PC, Sullivan. I know what you meant by that was: Holy shit she's hot af what do I do?

I texted back, *That was not what I meant! . . . You think she's hot af?*

She's not my type ;)

241

What were Zach and her like together?

Umm . . . Never saw them together, but all the Meridian kids say they were joined at the hip. He was always picking her up in his super old car and stuff, and judging by how bummed she's been about the breakup (even though SHE initiated it), he's a good one. You're lucky! Is his friend single???

LEAVE RAJ ALONE.

But is he???

Addie??

Ugh, you're no fun. Whatever. I'm still texting, like, four guys I met on the road trip ;) Though I'm now concerned one of them had ringworm??!

"Are you still in love with her?" I ask Zach now, because I need to know.

"Of course not," Zach says, almost too quickly. Maybe because he knew I would ask. "I mean, we have history. We always will, but that's all it is."

"Okay," I say, feeling more at ease than I have since last night. And then, because I'm a masochist, "So what's she like?" I ask. "Lindsay?"

All Katy had for me was that Lindsay is good at improv (though sometimes slow to her mark) but bad at physical comedy and has killer taste in boots. I guess spending a couple of hours a week together makes them friends, but not super close.

242

Zach sits up and looks at me. "Why would you ask me that?"

Because I'm a masochist.

Because sometimes she feels like a ghost, haunting us.

I shrug. "I want to know. You've known her your whole life, right?"

"Since third grade," he says. He pauses a second, like he's debating whether to tell me more, then finally he sighs. "She was nine going on nineteen at the time. Her parents are lawyers; they let her stay up late with them, watching documentaries about genocides and global warming and old Hollywood movies, and she'd come to class and bring them up during discussion time. It blew my mind—all our minds." I feel the hairs on my body stand up as he talks about her. There's a mixture of wariness and pain and respect in his voice. "She was the kid that got put in charge when the teacher stepped out of the classroom for a minute. But it wasn't just that grown-ups treated her like an adult; she *acted* like an adult. She wanted to be taken seriously. She always has."

"Is it true that she doesn't like your friends? Raj said that."

Zach looks surprised.

"I don't think she . . . I mean, she . . . she doesn't *hate* them. But yeah, she thinks they can be a little immature. She thinks *I* can, too, but fortunately—or unfortunately—she was in love with me."

She was in love with me. There's no doubt in his mind, no questions; he knows she loved him.

"So why did she break up with you, then?" *And why is she still sad about it?*

He runs a hand over his face. "In eighth grade, people

hooked up or went out for a couple of days and then broke up and made out with other people. Lindsay wasn't interested in that kind of relationship, and I wasn't, either, really. I liked her. I wanted to *be* with her. I knew that." Now it feels like something sharp is grating the inside of my chest. I hate the certainty with which he talks about her. "So we were instantly serious. We made plans. We talked about our lives and our families and, well, it was serious. . . ." His voice fades. "But when everyone was starting to *really* think about college for the first time and Lindsay started looking into college drama programs, it was like she freaked out. She suddenly realized she—we—are sixteen. It hit her how much life would change in a couple of years and how much time she had spent trying to be an adult, trying to be older. How serious her whole life and high school experience had been, how serious *we* were. And I guess . . . well, I guess it stifled her."

After a few seconds, Zach shakes the glazed expression and says, "She was probably right. I mean, what do you know about love or relationships in high school, right?

"But enough about Lindsay," Zach says. He goes back to lying down, head in my lap.

"Did I mention," he says, purring a little bit as I start running my hand through his hair again, "that you're my favorite person? Especially with whatever it is you're doing right now."

I tell myself his saying this has nothing to do with the conversation we just finished having about his ex-girlfriend.

"Finger combing is your turn-on? Who would have thought?" I say, and we both laugh.

"How am I doing in the rankings, by the way? Am I anywhere near the top of your list?" he asks. "Or am I still top three?"

"Top two," I say.

Zach feigns despair. "Who is this mystery person I'm competing with, anyway?"

"William Primrose. Famous violist."

"Old?" he asks.

"Dead," I say. It's not true that Primrose is in my top two favorite people; I'm just being difficult. The truth is, I don't know how I'd rank the people in my life. Apart from Zach, I mean, and he's doing much better in the rankings than I let on.

I hit play and we start to watch what I refer to as my New York Experience. Really, it's *New York Stories,* an anthology of films made and set in New York by famous directors; the 1954 version of *Sabrina;* and everything Nora Ephron ever made. "My mom loves them, too," I explain about my love of Nora Ephron films, "but I think she likes to come off as having superior taste, because she *always* opts for some schmaltzy foreign stuff even though her eyes are so bad she can't even read the subtitles."

I look around to make sure she's not lurking close by, eavesdropping, and when Zach laughs, my whole lap shakes.

The other thing about the foreign movies is that my mother always remarks that she wants to go to *that* place, or that she's heard the food there is excellent, or that Greece has the most perfect weather in the world, but when I ask why she doesn't just go, then, she'll say something about how dangerous it is or ask what will happen to my brother and me while she is gone, like we're four and six instead of sixteen and almost nineteen.

We're finished with *Sabrina* and on to *New York Stories* (payback for all the Cianos, I tell Zach) when Mom does come back downstairs, causing Zach to bolt upright. She acts like she's looking for something, but it's obvious she's spying. She must be satisfied with what she sees because she goes back upstairs and shuts her door.

I go to the kitchen and come back with snacks and cold drinks.

While we're eating, Zach says, "I read this editorial Ciano wrote last year about hating all those throwback trends that are coming back. Handhelds and Super 8s. Directors are doing that just to get the vintage label."

"It's nostalgia," I say, though I know nothing about hand-helds or Super 8.

"That's exactly Ciano's point. Nostalgia is a form of pre-tentiousness."

"Maybe they just like that style," I say, offering a counter-point because I like to hear Zach's voice. I love how passionate he gets about movies. And *horrodies,* for that matter. It never occurs to Zach to not be ecstatic about the things he likes.

"But that's the thing—it's *before their time*. You can't be nostalgic for something you didn't experience. How do you miss something you don't remember?"

"You don't have to have been there to appreciate some-thing, though," I say, taking a sip of soda.

"Exactly!" Zach says, beaming as if I've just made his point. "That's precisely Ciano's argument. If you like something, pay homage. Don't try to cheapen it by, like, re-creating it."

And even though that wasn't my point at all, I let the conversation end there because we're up to some of my favorite parts of the movie. I'd warned Zach earlier that it wasn't the stories I loved this movie for, but the fact that it was a total New Yorkasm, as Katy puts it.

"So you're in love with New York and your viola," Zach says, chewing on a handful of trail mix. "What gives?"

I shrug. "I like the way they make me feel," I say.

I've never really told anyone about this, but when I see Zach looking at me, his eyes attentive and patient, I take a deep breath and decide to tell him about how I've sometimes felt like something was missing. Like maybe I wasn't living the life I was supposed to.

"So when I started finding things that didn't make me feel that way," I explain, "I clung to them."

I hear Zach's even breath as I continue. "After all the years I've played, I know I'm supposed to be a serious *musicienne*," I say with awful French affectation. "I'm supposed to be into all these little-known underground classical composers."

"Underground classical composers?" Zach laughs. "Is that a euphemism? Because they're all old and dead?"

"*No,*" I say, laughing too. "I'm supposed to be above liking something as overexposed as Vivaldi's *The Four Seasons,* but I love that piece. I love how the seasons change and different instruments, different voices, come in and out. Every season is different, but so vivid and vibrant and full. If my life was a song, I'd want it to sound like that."

"If your life was a song in New York, you mean," Zach says, tickling the underside of my foot until I retract it, giggling.

"Anyway, I stand by my assessment: in love with New York, in love with your viola."

And maybe someday with you, I think but don't say. I know I might be falling for Zach—he makes me feel more alive, and I like everything about being with him—but I haven't given myself permission to actually *be in love* with him. I still worry that it will get taken away.

I've only known him a few weeks.

Something is happening inside me, but maybe there isn't a word for it.

And maybe I don't need one. Not yet.

Still, assured that Mom isn't coming down the stairs again for a little while, I lean across the couch and kiss him softly once. Then I rest my head on his shoulder, turn up the volume of the TV, and spend the rest of the day educating him on more of the things I love.

40

AFTER
January

The scanner is essentially a large donut that I slide through on a bed, while staring aimlessly at the plastic white ceiling. It only takes about fifteen minutes. Afterward, Dr. Overton smiles and tells me that I can change back into regular clothes and he'll meet me and my parents in his office in a minute. There are not as many staff members or patients around today because it's Saturday and the clinic is only open for half the day. I fill out a long questionnaire about my sleeping pattern, or lack thereof, since the doctor is sure it's related.

My mother fiddles with the hem of her skirt while we wait. "I just hope he's *sure* that the machine doesn't use much radiation."

Dad sighs, rubbing his eyes. "I'm pretty sure he went to school for that."

"A lot of good all his credentials are when they let an underage child come into this place and get a procedure. She doesn't even *look* nineteen. And why didn't he do the scan as soon as she came in on Thursday so we could be sure there's no damage?"

"He said they needed consent, seeing as the machine uses radiation," Dad says.

"If it's so much, then we *should* be concerned."

With my parents' back-and-forth, I almost can't hear the waiting-room music today.

The doctor arrives then, holding not an X-ray but several pieces of paper. "Thanks for your patience." He smiles before sitting across the desk from us. "Your scan looks perfect. Even with the two procedures, there doesn't seem to be anything of concern. There are no lesions; there's no irregular activity. I think at this point we just want to monitor your symptoms— the sleeping, the appearance of the boy, any headaches, that kind of thing. But as far as we can see, your brain looks healthy."

"Thank God." Dad sighs again.

"So what's the problem, then?" Mom asks, not ready to be relieved yet.

"Well," the doctor says, a thoughtful expression on his face, "it's hard to say. It's hard to say if it even *is* a problem."

"You said you've never had this happen to a patient," Mom says.

"That's true." The doctor nods. "I don't know if you know much of our history, but Overton started primarily to treat post-traumatic stress disorder. One of the key symptoms of PTSD is re-experiencing the traumatic event, whether through flashbacks or spontaneous memories. When you think about it, reliving things that have happened is not just associated with severe trauma; it's something we all do, and depending on how we are built, we can do that to different, sometimes clinical extents. So when it becomes a source of distress or impairment, that's when we treat it. We target the memory itself."

I can't help myself—I have to interrupt. "Okay, but Rory wasn't just one memory. He was alive for eight months. How did you erase all that time if I still remember things from that year, from around the time he'd have been alive?"

"Good question. The answer is a little technical, so bear with me," he says. "You see, every memory has a focal point. The procedure completely removes all memories where the person you want to erase is the focal point—where your primary attention was directed toward that person when the memory was formed. In memories where the person we're erasing is part of the background, a secondary figure, the memory simply gets a little hazy. For example, you might remember what was said, but not who said it. Or you'll remember the gist of an event but not specific details about it."

This explains why my memories around eleven are so hazy and vague. Why I don't remember my mother being pregnant. Why I don't remember arguments between my parents after my younger brother died or them taking down his pictures. I only remember that suddenly things were changing and I couldn't wrap my head around why. Not all the memories of my life in the time frame surrounding Rory's life are absent; some are just cloudy.

Dr. Overton continues to speak now. "My father

believes—always has—that memory is like a string of DNA. Linear building blocks, linked to one another to form an entire molecule. He's going to be *very* interested in your case."

We gape at him as he keeps talking. "My belief—no empirical evidence, mind you—has always been different from my father's. I'm not sure memories are particularly distinct. One common theory is that memory is not localized in the brain but distributed among various neural circuits. Which means that even when we are able to isolate specific events, specific memories, the other components accompanying them, such as spatial recognition, emotional memory, or even implicit memory, as the case may be . . ."

It's only now that he has the sense to look up and realize he's lost us. "Let's try that again," he says with a light chuckle. "I like chocolate granola bars way more than is good for me," he says, pointing to a crumpled wrapper beside his computer. "Obviously, I *remember* them. I have a stored and existing recollection, a database of chocolate granola bars."

I shoot my parents a skeptical look. Are they following this?

"And," Dr. Overton continues, "if I wanted to forget granola bars, I could splice out every instance of ever having had one. Every time I tasted one, every time I saw one. Every memory where a granola bar is the focal point, and every memory where it is part of the background—everything. And theoretically, I should not know what a granola bar is."

None of us speak, but he goes on.

"The possibility stands, though, that if I were ever to taste a chocolate granola bar again, even after the splicing, it might feel familiar. And it's not a failure of the technique or equipment or my mind or any nameable source; it's just one conceivable way the brain works. So I might forget the instances—*all* instances—of eating a granola bar, but perhaps not the experience." He looks right at me. "I think this might be what has happened in your case, Addie. You've forgotten every specific instance you shared with this boy, but not the experience. The million-dollar question is, Why now? My first guess would have been that the accident played a role—"

"I told you it started before," I say, and Dr. Overton nods.

"Right. Well, that leaves us with a question: What could have happened to trigger your Memory?"

The room is silent, and I can hear Dr. Overton's and my parents' minds whirring at the possibilities.

For once, I think I might know the answer.

On the night I first saw the boy—before the bus crash— some of the music at the concert made me feel something I couldn't place, something that felt like waking up.

But there's no way I'm going to tell them that.

I don't know why, but I think all this is because of a piece of music.

41

BEFORE
Mid-September

"Why does violin music always sound so *sad*?" Zach asks, glancing around the gym of Lyndale Community College, which tonight is a makeshift auditorium. Mrs. Dubois sent out an email to all her students, like she always does when there is a music event happening close by. She saw me from across the gym when Zach and I entered and was beaming and waving so wildly I could almost hear her bracelets clinking from all the way over here. As usual, I am the only one of her students who actually came.

I shift in one of the plastic chairs that line the whole back of the gym. "Classical music isn't always sad. It's expressive."

". . . -ly sad?" Zach says, but he's grinning at me, his eyes playful. I smile back. My hand is wrapped in his, our fingers tangled around each other's in a way that feels natural but still sends an inexplicable tremor along my arm, then throughout my body.

Ever since I asked him two nights ago whether he wanted to come with me, I've wavered between regret and doubt.

Zach isn't the biggest fan of classical music, and though I wish it would, a community college orchestra certainly isn't going to change his mind.

But I know what is most important to him—movies, *horrodies*—and I want him to know what's most important to me.

The concert is two hours long, and even though the orchestra is relatively unpolished, they are good. I can tell they've been playing together a long time.

The good news is that Zach doesn't fall asleep. The bad news is that he shifts uncomfortably every now and then, trying hard to be attentive but failing. I feel the slightest twinge of disappointment. I know he doesn't have to like the same things I do, or even understand them—and he *is* trying—but it still makes me sad. Especially when the performers start on the second-to-last piece on the program. It's Bach's Orchestral Suite in D Major. I've heard the most famous movement on its own before—the one later arranged as "Air on the G String"—but hearing it in the context of the whole suite, the way the story was meant to be told, takes my breath away.

So I do something I never thought I'd do.

I break one of Mrs. Dubois's cardinal rules of concert etiquette. I lean up and whisper into Zach's ear, tugging slightly on his hair to bring his face closer to mine. "What do you think of this song?"

"It's, uh . . ." Zach seems to search for words. "Very good. Very violin-y."

I giggle, steal a quick glance around to make sure we're not annoying people with our whispers, and then say, "It reminds me of a boy who likes Ciano movies, and a girl who likes his puff."

I swear his smile starts at his eyes, and if we weren't in public, I'd have no choice but to kiss the crap out of him.

But even Zach, his closeness, his smile, can't eclipse the music. The melody is so hopeful and warm, deliberate but unsure. It's true that it makes me think of me and Zach. Not because anything about it sounds like us, but because *I* decide it does. I picked it right now, this moment. I close my eyes and picture us ducking under the arch of the cello's trembling string. Crouching, lingering. Who will think to look for us here?

The long-drawn-out violin notes are how long it takes for breath to rise from the base of my lungs and out of my body when Zach is around. And the bop of his hair, his cheerful twinkling eyes, they're hidden inside this piece, too.

When my parents separated, music became my safe place. Where I stowed pieces of myself I couldn't express or bear for anyone to see. Everybody's parents broke up. It was as run-of-the-mill as losing your baby teeth, being picked last in gym class, or getting a growth spurt at eleven. You were supposed to shake it off and keep going if it happened to you. When it happened to you. But the pain at the thought of two separate rooms and two toothbrushes and two birthday cards didn't feel so collective. It felt so distinctly mine that it made the hairs on my body stand up when I thought about it too hard, stung the back of *my* eyes and made *my* throat close up.

I looked for things in the pieces I played, for the yelp my mother would give when Dad jumped around a corner, surprising her by flying in an hour early because of unbelievably good weather in the Keys. I looked for that feeling of certainty, of everything right and in its place, instead of broken and scattered and *wrong*. For an explanation of why everything had fallen apart without warning, why there seemed to be holes and cracks in my life I couldn't explain.

But mostly, I found things in my music. Hope. Distraction. Happiness. I found those things and held on to them as long as the piece lasted, and then I tucked them back inside a melody, where they'd be unreachable.

I explain this to Zach after the concert. If he thinks I'm crazy, he doesn't show it.

We talk about that Bach second movement the rest of the drive home. I stop short of calling it *our* song, because Katy once told me that sharing a song with someone is on par with sharing a pet. It just should not happen. For everyone involved.

But Zach says, "Air on a Thong. I kind of like it."

I throw my head against the headrest when I laugh.

But I think he agrees that somewhere in the second phrase, in between the tremor of the violin strings, there's a little bit of us.

42

AFTER
January

After me and my parents get back from Overton, I spend the next three hours tearing my room apart. Searching every drawer of my dresser, every corner of my closet, under my mattress, beneath the rug. I throw all my clothes out of my closet and search the pockets of pants I haven't worn in years. Looking for a note, a T-shirt I don't remember, a picture.

A memory.

Bus Boy is one thing: his full-wattage smile, the weird ease I feel around him. And I want to see him, I *like* being with him, but even being with him is so incomplete.

His first name is a start, but with more, I could find *more*. I feel disgusted at myself for ever walking into Overton voluntarily. Why would I do that? What could have happened?

Why would I knowingly rob myself of a life that had real experiences? And if it's true that I did, then I owe it to myself to figure this out, to piece everything together myself.

I could ask Katy to explain it to me, to tell me what happened as *she* remembers it, but I don't want her version of the truth. I don't even know how much I can trust it. I want to find all the pieces that have been lying around me all this time—that must *still* be lying around somewhere—and fit them together to rebuild the scattered fragments of my life.

And I need to do it alone.

I keep searching through everything I own, looking for a clue.

Maybe two initials scribbled on the back of my sneakers, or a name etched into the wall behind my headboard.

I come up empty.

Of course I come up empty.

Did I throw out everything that would remind me of him—of Zach?

There are so many gaps in my life—missing pieces. There always have been.

And I barely even noticed. How is that possible?

It's past nine, late enough that I could conceivably go to sleep, but I'm sick of lying awake at night, tossing and turning.

I want answers.

My mother is upstairs in her room, talking to Bruce on the phone, so it doesn't take much to escape the house unnoticed.

It's dark out, night creeping in where evening was, and though the roads are icy, I drive faster than I need to.

Without having a particular destination in mind, I wind up at this park my parents used to bring Caleb and me to when we were little. I would hang upside down, pretending to be a bat, and stare up at the sky, which was the brightest shade

259

of blue. I'd stay that way till I felt the blood rushing to my head, and then I'd pull myself right-side up, and even without the pumping and swirling of blood between my ears, there was never a doubt in my mind that I was alive.

The park is completely deserted. I climb out of the car, snow crunching underneath my shoes.

The too-small swing is wet, and I wipe it down with my sleeve. It sinks from my weight when I sit. Instead of actually swinging, I just close my eyes and twist and twist around, the chains that hold up the swing wrapping around themselves.

Eyes closed, I spin and spin and spin until my head feels light and my stomach turns. The air is so cold it makes my ears hurt.

I hum a song with a melody that feels like getting lost, every phrase a new path, and none of them lead back home. Then "Air on the G String," the piece that I think first made me see the boy. In my mind, in the night of my closed eyes, I imagine that I'm playing it instead of humming. Feel the weight of my viola underneath my jaw. My bow, weightless, as much a part of my body as my own fingers.

Zach.

I don't need to say it out loud.

I plant my feet on the ground, pulling myself to a stop, though the world continues to spin around me, the park whirling like a merry-go-round, circling me.

On the first turn, I see a red-haired boy with his hands shoved deep into the pockets of his jeans.

On the second turn, he grins at me and steals all the night.

On the third turn, I breathe in, adjusting to the still world. "Are you okay?" he asks as I try to refocus on him.

How are you here? Who are you? Why do I feel this way with you?

"Zach," I say out loud this time, slowly, matching his face to the sound of his name, the cadence of the person in front of me.

He smiles at me, his gray eyes wide. "That's it. That feels like mine."

I know he can't really make that call, that it's *my* mind confirming that the face of this boy I'm seeing fits the name I've been given. A flicker, maybe, of my memory.

A wave of loneliness rushes over me then, because there is no Bus Boy. There's only me and my mind and what it's been trying to tell me all this time, without finding the words. The details. The facts.

But the air is still warm with his breath, and his eyes catch the moonlight, twinkling at me. He still *feels* real to me.

This invisible boy is still here, to me.

Even if he's a figment of my imagination.

Even if he is a ghost, gone, just like Rory.

He stretches out his hand, the wind making his hair tickle his forehead. I stick out my hand and let him pull me up from the swing.

Are you dead? I want to ask, but he can't tell me that. I slip my fingers between his and he squeezes, his palm warm.

You can't be dead.

We sit on a bench, damp with moisture, and I can't stop looking at him. Zach. Memory Zach.

"What?" he asks, quiet in the dark.

"It drives me crazy the way you're dressed," I say, even though it's the last thing on my mind. "I get that you're not

261

really cold, that you won't die from hypothermia"—*especially if you're already dead*—"but it's still really bizarre that you're wearing that shirt when it's so cold out."

I unzip my puffy coat and peel it off. Then I hold out the left side to him. "Here."

One of his eyebrows skitters up, but he takes it, amused. Scoots closer. Closer.

The warmth of his body against mine makes me light-headed.

I wrap the right side of the coat around me. He pulls his half of the jacket around his body the best he can, which is ridiculous because it is much too small for him, not to mention both of us. But we are sharing it just the same, our bodies pressed close to each other, our breaths loud and warm, indistinguishable.

"Better?" he asks, the hint of a laugh in his voice, but his face is weirdly serious. And his eyes seem glued to my lips.

It makes me self-conscious. It makes me think too much about *his* lips.

"Better," I whisper, and his face is suddenly even closer than before. He smells like a mix of mint and cigarettes.

"Zach?"

Zach. His name is Zach. In the car yesterday, Katy didn't talk about him like he was dead. Neither did my parents. He can't be dead.

"Hmm?" he says, still so, so close.

"I want to find you. The real you."

43

BEFORE
Early October

Once school starts, it gets harder and harder for Zach and me to see each other. Especially since he's just gotten another job, working at the Cineplex at the mall. When we're not at school, he's either working or doing something with Raj, and I'm at orchestra practice or viola lessons or doing something with Katy.

So when Zach tells me his parents are going out of town for the weekend, and Kevin is at work, *and* he doesn't have to be at the store, it feels like fate is screaming at us.

I make up something about going to study at Katy's and then wait outside for Zach's piece-of-shit car. I've grown to appreciate its tacky bright blue color, the way it whines every single time Zach hits the gas.

"Hey, you," Zach says as I climb into the passenger's seat.

I lean over and kiss him. "Hey, yourself." A drop of water

falls on my chin and I giggle, then brush Zach's wild *and* wet hair up.

The car smells like cologne, and my ears warm as I realize he put some thought into what we'd be doing today. We hadn't *said* it in so many words, but we had both clearly been thinking it. I'd brought a small bag with a toothbrush and hairbrush and makeup and other very important items.

"Where did your parents go again?" I ask Zach.

"To Caldwell. They can't get enough of Russell." The last time I was over, Zach's mom had insisted Zach show me something of the hours of footage he'd taken of his nephew when they'd gone up to Caldwell the week before. Zach blushed and pulled out his phone, showing me a pink-skinned baby with brown hair.

"He's adorable," I whispered, staring at the video of a cooing, wriggling newborn. I felt a tug at my chest, an overwhelming desire to reach through the screen and grab hold of Russell's tiny pinkie. I like babies, but the thought of babysitting has always terrified me. *What if I do something wrong? What if something bad happens and there's no one to help me?* Maybe I inherited Mom's slight aversion to little kids, or maybe it's because, being the youngest, I haven't had much experience with them.

Russell *is* adorable, though, if only because I know they have a bunch of good-looking men in their family and he'd have to go seriously wrong to not wind up at Adorable.

We drive the rest of the way to his house, talking about school and his dad's store and the solo Mrs. Dubois gave me a week ago.

"So," Zach says when his car belches to a stop outside the garage. "What shall we do today?"

One side of his lips is tilted up, his gray eyes warm and twinkling, and I lean over and slide my hand up, up his thigh.

"Oh," he says, fully smiling now. "I can get behind that."

"Oh my God," I say, laughing, and lean over even more to kiss his neck.

"What? I didn't mean it like *that*," he says, laughing too. He slides his seat back from the wheel and starts to pull me into his lap, and the idea of doing anything else but *that* seems impossible.

And then there is a loud rap on the driver's window.

Speaking just loudly enough for us to hear with the glass still up, Raj says, "What are we doing today?"

44

BEFORE
Mid-October

Life continues to be very cruel to us and then one day, about two weeks later, I'm sprawled out over my bed, surrounded by Spanish homework, with zero desire to tackle it. So I pick up my viola and am playing an elegy by Stravinsky, a deceptively slow-moving piece that is bittersweet and sounds like falling or watching a shadowy graveyard or the kind of heavy storm that rolls in cloud by cloud, when I get a call from At Home Movies.

"Hello?"

"Hey, *baby*. I got let go from Pizza Hut. Which, I'm told, means fired."

"Kevin?" I ask after a moment of trying to place the voice.

"You know it, babe."

In the background, I hear Zach yelling something.

"You got fired? What happened?" I ask.

"I called my boss a fox. I guess that's not allowed," he says dismissively.

"Oh my God," I say, swallowing a laugh so as not to encourage him. "That's terrible."

"Eh," Kevin replies, and I can picture him shrugging.

I am about to ask why he called—other than to tell me he got fired—when he says, "Zach says hi."

"Say hi back," I tell Kevin.

"She says hi," I hear Kevin say. "Zach also says that friend of yours, the blond one, is a babe and would be perfect for me."

"Kevin," I hear Zach say, and then there's some sort of scrambling, scratching sound. And then a slap that is followed by Kevin snort-laughing and continuing to slap what sounds like the counter.

"Oh God, sorry about that," Zach says, sounding a bit out of breath.

"It's okay. I can't believe he got fired," I say.

"Can't you?" Zach deadpans, and I laugh.

"So, listen, my parents are going to Caldwell again, and I was supposed to watch Kevin until they get back tomorrow, but now he's *fired,* so he's going *with them.*"

"Okay," I say, mimicking his tone, "*that's* good to *know.*"

"No, no," Zach says, and I can hear the smile in his voice, picture him bringing the phone closer to his mouth as he speaks. "They're gone till *Saturday.* With Kevin."

Oooh. Now I'm catching on. "What about the store?"

"It might be closing earlier tonight. You never know."

I faux-gasp. "Can you do that? Your dad will freak."

"We haven't had a customer in *six* hours. Somehow I doubt in two—"

A scrambling sound, Mr. Laird's voice, a pause, and then, "So where were we, babe?"

"Kevin, stop flirting with my girlfriend!" I hear Zach say, and I can't help smiling. *My girlfriend.*

Zach's *girlfriend.*

"Zach's back pretending to stock shelves now," Kevin informs me. "He says please let him know of your decision."

"Tell him yes," I say.

"She says yes."

"Zach said to tell you that just so you know"—he pauses while Zach passes on a message I can't hear—"he has sent a strongly worded text to Raj."

More mumbling from Zach.

"With threats of dismemberment and/or"—more mumbling—"Raj wearing the nun costume for the next ten films"—more mumbling—"if he comes within a mile of our house tonight."

I laugh into the phone.

"Why can't Raj come to our house?" Kevin asks Zach.

"Tell Zach," I say, "that I do not condone dismemberment or threats of any kind, but that sounds perfect."

Kevin relays the message. I'm already texting Katy to cover for me and pretend I'm spending the night at her place.

U slotmachine! she texts back instantly. *But done.*

"Have a good trip to Caldwell tonight," I tell Kevin.

"It would be better if *you* were going," Kevin says.

"Kevin," I hear Zach say on the other end. "Didn't you get *fired* for this?"

45

BEFORE
Mid-October

I haven't been this nervous about seeing Zach since the day we met. When he opens the front door, we stand there and grin awkwardly at each other. Then Zach holds the door open for me to come in, and I do.

So we continue smiling awkwardly at each other in the foyer until Zach laughs and says, "There is no way to be smooth about this. Do you want to come upstairs?"

I laugh now, too, and he leads me up to his room, holding my hand.

I tell him how I only just managed to get here. Despite the pains I'd taken to create an alibi with Katy, Mom set up camp in the living room tonight and patted the couch as I approached to ask if I could borrow her car. Caleb was already in the chair across from her, his hairy feet on the ottoman, and his eyebrows went way up when I mumbled something about wanting to meet Katy to practice for orchestra and how we had a chem project and also she was tutoring me in English. I was *not* a good liar.

"I did pretty well in *English*," Caleb said. "Want me to tutor you?"

"That's okay," I said quickly, and shot him a pointed look. A part of me was worried; Caleb might decide to call me out just because, just to remind me that we aren't allies. But he only smirked at me. To my surprise, Mom was relatively easy to convince, but she made me promise to spend next weekend at Dad's, since Caleb had been there the last two, and I'd seen my father once all summer.

"Sure, I promise!" I said, a little too quickly and brightly to be believable. How had I made it into Zach's movie again?

Zach cracks up as I relay this to him.

His room is cleaner than I've ever seen it. All the DVDs usually strewn on the floor everywhere are stacked against the wall. Some of the posters that were half falling off the walls are taped on properly, and his bed is neatly made. I feel honored that he picked up for me, and then I feel nervous that he picked up for me, and then I don't know *how* I feel, but my heart beats an unsteady staccato against my ribs.

I put my bag on the table, which is full of books and camera equipment.

"You know," Zach says when I turn around again, "we don't have to do anything tonight." I can almost feel the heat drifting off his face; his cheeks are a warm red. "We can just, like, watch movies. Or . . ."

While he's trying to think of another suggestion, I press my lips against his. He looks caught off guard but recovers quickly and kisses me back. We back up until his legs hit the bed. He lies back against the mattress, with me on top of him, our lips never losing contact.

We kiss like we don't have enough time in the world. He's out of breath and I kiss him, filling up his lungs, and then I'm out of breath and we volley the tiny amount of air in this room back and forth and back and forth and somehow it seems to be enough.

When we stop to catch our breath, I sit up, my legs on either side of him, and he props himself on his elbows while I try to take off his shirt.

He helps me yank it over his head and then he flicks it away. His lips move all over my neck as he tries to undo the zipper of my dress.

"Son of a bitch," he hisses after a few unsuccessful attempts. He pauses for a moment, concentrating hard to get it down, and I laugh.

He gets it halfway and his hands are like fire on my bare back.

I climb off his legs and take a step back; he stands, unbuckling his belt. We watch each other as my dress falls past my hips and hits the ground and his jeans fall past his hips and he steps out of them.

I feel warm everywhere just from his eyes. I feel their fingers travel the length of my body, from my head to the tips of my toes, to my ears and neck and everywhere.

His face is flushed, too, and I think, I hope, I'm having the same effect on him.

Zach frowns, looking away suddenly. I crawl into the bed, still in my underwear, while he searches for his wallet on the ground and comes away with a small silver packet.

He crawls under the covers now, too, and we're facing each other, breathing on each other's lips but not kissing.

His voice hitches like it's hard to swallow when he says, "You're beautiful." And I believe him, because he looks at me as if I am.

We kiss again, and seconds later, he is on top of me, all our clothes gone now. Nothing between his skin and mine.

He props his elbows on either side of me.

"Have you ever, um, done this before?" he asks, even though we've already talked about it. I mean, he knows he's my first real boyfriend; I guess he just wants to be sure.

"Tons of times," I joke, and we laugh despite our trembling. Both of us a lot smaller, more fragile, without our clothes on. Zach was with Lindsay for two years, and I know his answer to this question.

"There was Stu. Kindergarten. He pulled my hair, so that's one," I continue, even though I just want to be quiet so this can happen. *Shut up shut up shut up,* a voice screams in my head, but I'm a prisoner to whatever is happening to my mouth, which won't stop moving all of a sudden.

"And then there was, in seventh grade, Grant. Acrobat-Tongue Grant. He had the tongue of a serpent," I say.

Zach rumbles on top of me as he laughs, but he's still holding himself up, leaving only inches between our bodies.

"There was also Eric Johns and he got to second base and oh God I don't know why I'm still talking." I cover my face with my hands.

Zach laughs and kisses the center of my chest. "I'm not sure I like this Eric Johns." He looks up at me again. "And after that?"

The air in the room has shifted again, more serious and so still that I feel like I can hear both our hearts beating.

"It's all you," I say.

Zach nods and kisses me gently. He is careful and keeps asking if I'm okay, if this is okay, if I'm still okay, and I bite my lower lip, nodding yes, when the truth is that we're both trembling.

46

AFTER
January

"It makes zero sense," I say, "that you are sitting right here and we can't work out anything else about you."

Now that I understand why he's here, now that I have some sort of lead, I figured I only had to ask the right questions for the rest to become clear. It's why I haven't broken and done the obvious thing—ask Katy. I was sure I could piece it together myself. It's *my* memory, after all. I knew him—Zach. The name still seems magical after days of not knowing.

But after an hour of grilling him for information, I've learned exactly one thing about him. And it didn't even come from him; it came from going over and over the details of the night I started seeing him. It came when I remembered what was sticking out of his backpack when he got on the bus.

A folded tripod.

His backpack contained camera equipment.

It is late at night and we are at Jolley's, an old-timey diner just off the highway. I cradle my cup of coffee, blowing on it while I watch Zach, who's sitting across the booth from me. As we've been talking, I've forgotten numerous times that I am the only one who can see him. After a few odd looks from strangers, I've started pretending to be on the phone or reading the menu aloud when someone walks by.

"It seems like I can only tell you what you already know," he says now, and I roll my eyes. He's kept repeating that one all night. His explanation for why he knew I'd gotten his name right but couldn't tell me any more. "You have to find the things they couldn't explicitly wipe. Like a feeling, things you associate with . . . the other me."

"Uh-huh." I already tried listening to "Air on the G String" on my phone, and that feeling of recognition, that warmth I got listening to it at the concert the first night I met Memory Zach, came back, assuring me I'm on the right track. But while it might have triggered my memory of Zach the night of the accident, it's hardly going to give me his last name. I am starting to lose patience with myself now, starting to think I might need to go crawling back to my parents or Katy for answers.

I'm staring absently over the rim of my coffee mug when I feel Zach's gaze on me.

"What?" I ask. I can't read the expression on his face.

"What do you think happens when you find him?" he asks, fidgeting with a chip in the wood on his side of the table. "You know, to me?"

I shrug. "Why would anything happen?"

Zach nods, seems to shake off his worry, and leans forward. "Okay, go back to the tripod and camera stuff. Can you use it in any way?"

"Maybe you're a photographer?" I ask hopefully, and Zach says, "Maybe."

I sigh, pretty sure this is what it is like to talk to an amnesiac. Someone who knows absolutely nothing about himself. I push aside the thought that, in some ways, that's exactly who I am. Who I've been.

"Okay," I say, and type "Zach Lyndale photographs" into my phone's browser. Also "photography," "pictures," "photos." "There are a surprising number of Zachs in Lyndale who happen to be photographers. Most of them over the age of fifty."

Zach laughs and I am startled again at the warmth in his voice, the fullness of it. I glance up at him, wondering if maybe that was a memory—if, somehow, I am remembering the real him. And I am surprised to find him already watching me, his eyes twinkling. I glance away quickly.

One thing that is *not* going to make my life easier?

Falling in love with the Memory of some boy I used to know. The *invisible* memory of some boy I used to know. Everything I see him do happens only in my head, and I *like* him. Tonight, when we were on the bench, our bodies so close it was like we didn't need the coat at all, it felt like something heavy had lowered itself onto my chest. It was the realization that I was inches from kissing an invisible stranger, and I wished the space between us was less. But more than that, I started to get the sense, to understand for the first time, that I might have loved the real Zach. The breathless, pulsing kind of love that you can't recover from. The kind you can't forget.

So why would I have erased him?

"What other types of cameras are there?" Memory Zach asks, mercifully drawing me out of my thoughts. It takes a second to remember what we're talking about.

"Video," I say, scribbling down the names of three Zachs I've found without pictures who could conceivably be the one I need: Zach Easton, Zach Thomas, and Zack Neil. "Maybe you even *sell* cameras. Do you sell cameras, Zach?"

"Your guess is as good as mine," he says.

"But what do you *feel?*" I intone, making the corners of his mouth tilt up. My stomach twirls at it and blood rushes to my ears.

I glance at the screen of my phone again.

"Okay, let's try . . ." I type in "Zach cameras" and get mostly useless hits.

"Hey!" I say all of a sudden. Someone glances over at me from across the diner, and I duck my head, bringing my voice to a whisper. "What about that job you were 'working' at the Cineplex that day? What does *that* mean?"

Zach narrows his eyes, thinking. "Camera. Cinema. Movies?"

I type in "Zach movies Lyndale" and take a sip of my coffee while I wait for the search results.

"What's wrong?" Zach asks. I'm frozen, staring at the screen of my phone. "Addie?"

"I think this is it."

It is an article, nearly three years old, about a local fifteen-year-old boy with an interest in filmmaking. Making *horror* movies.

"Meridian High School students and best friends Zach

277

Laird and Raj Gupta celebrate after their third-place finish in a national short-film contest," a caption says.

What has stolen my breath, though, is the picture. In it, an Indian boy faces the camera, looking very solemn. He's the boy who bumped into me and couldn't stop staring at the theater that day. Next to him in the picture—next to *Raj*—a tall, red-haired boy stares at me with a grin as wide as the sun.

"Are you sure?" Memory Zach asks, moving around to my side of the table so he can see.

But I only gape at him, fighting to keep my breath steady and my mind calm, and then stare again at the boy who looks exactly like him. Who *is* him.

Zach Laird.

The name forms in my mind, wrapping around my brain in a way that is familiar and foreign and confuses me.

I look at the picture again.

I don't know the first thing about him, the *real* him, but the steady ticktock of my chest, the bomb racing to an inescapable explosion, confirms something I haven't been sure of—only suspected, only feared.

And it speaks with complete assurance.

I once loved this boy.

47

BEFORE
Late October

Zach and I see each other in spurts. For minutes between viola practice and the store and the Cineplex and my dad's apartment and his trips to Caldwell. Since he's much busier than I am, I'm usually visiting him at one of his two jobs or at his house.

So when I stop by at the Cineplex after school one day and one of his co-workers says Zach is taking out the trash, I head outside to the back of the theater and literally pounce on him.

His back is to me, and when I wrap myself around his waist, he jumps. "Holy shit, you scared me," he says, turning around to face me.

I cough and feel my eyes water as he exhales smoke directly into my face.

"Sorry," he says, giving me a wide smile. "I was literally plotting ways to kidnap you." He kisses my top lip.

I don't kiss him back, just stay frozen, unable to erase the frown on my face.

"What's wrong?" Zach asks.

"You smell like a chimney."

Zach holds his cigarette far away from his body for dramatic effect. With his other hand, he reaches to cover my eyes. "You did not see me smoking."

"I *smell* you smoking," I retort, taking his hand off my face. "I thought you were quitting. Your dad bought you a CXX." *When it's all your family has been able to do to keep At Home Movies running the past few months.*

Zach seems surprised, his eyes wider than normal. "I didn't know it bothered you so much." He puts out his cigarette.

"It's just gross," I say, wishing we were spending the first time we've seen each other in a week making out, but I don't feel like kissing Zach at all right now. Also, weirdly, I remember what Raj said once: *Where there's smoke, there's Lindsay.*

He nods, still watching me. "Sorry." He runs a hand through his hair. "I *was* really down to two a day, but then with school. And Raj keeps wanting to make something to enter for the Valley Con Short-Film Contest, and I'm avoiding him because that's all he talks about. I feel like shit."

I take a step toward him now, put my hand on his shirt. "Why don't you want to enter?"

"I *do*," Zach insists. "I just . . . can't think of anything good. And then my dad pays eight hundred freaking dollars for a CXX that I can't use."

"Maybe," I say thoughtfully, "maybe you're thinking too

narrowly. Like, a while ago, I felt so sick of my playing, and then I borrowed some of Katy's music, transposed it down a fifth, and learned a couple of *her* pieces. I was pretty bad at them, but it made me feel better."

"Addie, you don't get it." Zach's voice is impatient. "I think I just need time or something. I need to figure it out on my own."

"It seems like you've been having a lot of that," I say.

"What do you mean?" Zach frowns.

"Time on your own. I've seen you, like, twice in two weeks?"

"I've been busy with school," he says.

"I have school, too. And practice and a bunch of other things."

Zach looks like he's about to protest—he has two jobs *and* school—but then his face softens. "You're right. Sorry. What were you saying about trying Katy's songs?"

"Maybe do something totally different," I say, consciously letting the tension slip from my voice and body. I proceed a little more carefully now. "Like, horrodies are great and Ciano is brilliant, but maybe you could try something new?"

Zach takes a strand of my hair between his fingers. "You think so?"

"I do."

I wrap my arms around his neck and stand on my tiptoes to kiss his chin.

"Sorry about my cigarette breath," Zach says, looking into my eyes. And I shrug like it's no big deal. Truthfully, I've started carrying perfume in my purse so I can spray myself after I'm with Zach to prevent my mom from asking questions. Not knowing that he smokes is not going to kill her.

"Maybe you're right," he says, slowly now, glancing above my head. "I just feel . . . stuck."

I wrap my arms around his waist, and our chests heave in sync for a few moments before I put my hand in the back pocket of his jeans and promise, "I'm going to help you." Then I muse, "How do we unstick you, Zach?"

48

AFTER
January

I can barely concentrate at school on Monday.

Between my continuing insomnia and my eventful weekend, my brain feels close to short-circuiting.

I am so restless, so ready for answers, that it takes everything I have not to tackle Katy for them when I see her. But the one thing I'm sure of, the one thing I *know*, is that I want answers on my own terms, so I don't go to her.

She corners me before orchestra anyway, during the time when she would usually be socializing.

"Are you mad at me for calling your parents?" she asks, fiddling with the end of her French braid.

"No." *Yes. No.* I don't know if I care about my parents knowing I chose to have Zach removed from my mind. I care that I did it. That I made that choice. It makes me sick, makes me want to shake myself every time I look in the mirror.

"Well, then, can we talk?" Katy asks. More softly, she says, "I miss my best friend."

I hesitate before nodding.

For the first time in recorded history, Katy and I skip orchestra and huddle in my car with the heater on.

"So what are you going to do?" she asks.

I tell her Caleb told me where Rory was buried and I want to work up the courage to go there soon. I tell her about today's plan, too—to go to Meridian after school to find the real Zach. Katy's not thrilled about it, but I think seeing him might bring it all back. It has to. At the very least, I'll finally understand what happened between us, and I tell myself that knowing how and why might somehow fill up this giant hole that the truth has ripped in my life.

From the moment I got to school today, I've been second-guessing everything. Every weird look or strange conversation I've ever had with a person. Is there more I don't remember? Is there something they know that I don't?

Do I know something *they* don't? I must have run into people at some point who have had Overton procedures before, too.

Do people at school know what I've done? The thought that they might—that they might have been whispering about me, gossiping about me all these years—is unbearable.

"Everything is so . . ."

"Absolutely shitty?" Katy finishes for me, and as I nod, we both burst into laughter. At this moment. The sheer absurdity of it. Then the laughter morphs into sadness.

There are people in this town, this stiflingly bland town,

who know I had a baby brother. Who have known for years that he's gone. And I just found out days ago.

There are people in this town who know all about the first—the only—boy I've ever loved, and I just found out his name.

"You said nobody else knows that I got the second splice?" I ask Katy. *Please say nobody else knows.*

"I swear," she says. "I'd never do that to you."

I believe her. I know this is not her fault—she was trying to do what *I* wanted—but why would she let me go through with it? How could she let me erase such a big part of my life?

When I ask her that, she says sadly, "I know you want a better reason, but all I have is that it was what you wanted. It was going to help you. It felt, at first, like an adventure. We planned out how we would do it, the IDs, what we would tell different people. We cleaned out your room, removing every single thing that was related to Zach. It felt like this daring, secret thing I got to do with my best friend, and it seemed kind of . . ."

"Kind of what?" I push.

"Special. That you were trusting me to keep this secret for you for the rest of our lives." She chews on her nail. "That even when we were in college, hopefully both in New York"—in the absence of wood, she knocks on the dashboard—"we would always be linked by this one thing."

"I thought you said the other day that you were already keeping a million secrets for your other friends? That you were sick of too many secrets?"

Katy rolls her eyes. "Um, I was *covering my ass.*" She laughs now and I manage to force a laugh too. "And please, Sullivan. Are you new here? Best friends come before the-*yo*-ter friends. By definition, that means I like your secrets better than I like theirs." She laughs again now, but adds, "Yours feel like mine."

I want to keep pushing Katy for more and more answers, but really, there's only one person I want to hear the truth from. The real Zach.

"Speaking of secrets," I say, and urge her to tell me about Mitch Enns, and how her bracelet got to be in his car, and just how often they've been "hanging out." It turns out to be quite a lot, and she doesn't even seem ready to start referring to him as Rich or Fitch yet.

"The second he seems bored, his new name is Glitch," Katy says, and I laugh.

"I don't think he'll get bored, Katy." I hope she stays with him long enough to find this out herself.

"Everybody does eventually," she says, and I think she means her dad and Jason and all the other boys she's dumped before they had a chance to get sick of her and do it to her first.

"You can want things, you know," I tell her now. "Other than Juilliard."

"Shut up," she says, half laughing.

"It's true," I insist. I want to say, *You can want a boy to call, and cry about it when he doesn't, or you can call him yourself. You can want solos and your parents' love and you don't have to passive-aggressively fight for them or invent crises.* But what I say is, "When you first came to Lyndale, I bet Mrs. Dubois would have given you more solos if you'd asked."

"And robbed you of your billions, Chosen One? I doubt

it," she says dismissively. "Did I mention Mitch has a special ringtone for me?"

As she talks about him, her cheeks redden and she plays with her braid again.

I wonder if I was this embarrassed the first time I told Katy about Zach. I wonder when I knew I loved him.

"Hey, Addie? There will be other boys, okay?" Katy says just before we climb out of the car and head back for the rest of the day.

I swallow and nod, then shut the car door and follow her.

I know she must be right, but I can only think of one boy at the moment. Well, two, if you count Memory Zach.

All through last period, I keep glancing at the clock. I might as well have not even come to Spanish for the amount of attention I am paying. But I decide to wait it out. Then, with thirty minutes left in the period, I hand Mr. Hilton the note my "mother" supplied about my dentist's appointment and leave. I feel Katy's eyes on me as I walk out, that one perfectly trimmed eyebrow with its acrobatic curve. She's worked for years on getting it to tilt up just like that to show surprise or curiosity, and it does so now, like, *Dentist's appointment, huh, young lady,* even though she wrote the note herself. Fighting a laugh, I run—or slide, thanks to the snow—all the way to my car, crank up the heat, and drive the fifteen minutes to Meridian High. Massive trees, white with snow, leaves bitten off by winter, guard the redbrick building. A few cars wait in front of the entrance, and a couple of students are already walking toward their cars or talking to each other, but school hasn't let out yet.

My heart is staging a stampede, each beat a heavy-booted kick to my chest, and I have to fight with myself, argue with my fear, to step out of the car at all. I drag myself toward the building but stop under a tree. I try to blend in, to look like a student who has gotten out early and is waiting for a friend or a ride or a sibling.

I thought about bringing Memory Zach with me to do this, but I could see things getting awkward quickly. I don't know if my mind can take the real Zach and the invisible version of him both in one place.

I try to figure out what I'll say, what I'll do, when I see Zach. Should I just walk up? Should I let *him* walk up?

I'm turning over seventeen different scenarios in my mind when a sharp trill pierces the air. Instantly the heavy doors of the school burst open and people begin to pour out, laughing, talking, yelling to be heard over each other.

A couple is holding hands. One very tall boy launches himself onto the shoulders of another boy with an Afro, and they stumble down the front stairs, struggling to stay upright. Everyone around them laughs or bolts out of the way.

As kids flood out of the doors, my heart is beating, beating, pounding so hard that I stop being able to hear them.

Then I see him.

Not Zach, but his best friend, Raj. The one with the glasses and the serious expression from the article. The one who looked like there was so much he wanted to say in the theater that day. *That* was the expression on his face, I realize now.

Raj walks down the stairs, and holding my breath, I

288

scan the crowd around him for Zach but don't find him. No red hair. No tall, thin guy. No hundred-watt smile. Raj has paused now, looking around, probably for his ride. His eyes skitter over the tree I'm still under, then around again, like he can't find who he's looking for.

Zach?

Raj gives no indication that he recognizes me. Maybe he can't see my face this far away.

Raj pulls out his phone, and his fingers move a mile a minute. Then he sticks his phone back into his pocket and keeps waiting, no longer looking around.

I'm about to venture out of my hiding place, to brave walking up to him and asking if he knows where Zach Laird is. I don't know how Raj will react. He obviously recognized me that day, so we know each other. But could he know about Overton? Did he tell Zach he saw me? Have we run into each other before? And what do they think happened to me—why do they think I didn't recognize him?

I take a deep breath and decide to approach Raj.

But before I can take my first step, I see him.

Zach.

He's walking through the doorway, staring down at his phone. He walks until he meets Raj. They talk for a second, then start walking again.

They have to be able to hear my heart from here.

I watch them as they cross the parking lot, watch until Zach throws Raj a set of keys and gets into the passenger seat of a bright blue car that makes a loud wailing noise when they start it.

I let out a small noise as I watch them drive off, because I feel this tightness in my chest, this pain that I can't explain. I want them to hear me or see me or *know* me.

I want to know them.

I did know them once.

I keep staring at the spot where the car was.

I wonder when Zach cut off all his hair.

49

BEFORE
Early November

The day after Halloween, I go over to Zach's house at his mother's request to help finish the leftover candy before it settles on her hips. Her exact words, as transmitted by Zach. I'm spending the weekend at my dad's, but since he's catching up on sleep and things are as uncomfortable as ever between us, I'm happy to oblige.

"Lookin' fine!" Kevin purrs after he swings the front door open for me.

"Hey, Kevin," I say.

"Maybe you could get your own girlfriend?" Zach suggests, turning up behind him and ruffling his brother's hair. "Cassie Swinton keeps giving you the eye."

"Ew." Kevin frowns. And I laugh, surprised by his reaction.

"He only *thinks* he's a ladies' man," Zach explains. I lean in to kiss him.

"Well, well, well," someone bellows. We break apart, and standing behind Zach is his older brother Rob. He's eyeing us and carrying a plate that is, quite literally, heaped with food. "What do we have here?"

He is surprisingly less wooden in person than on camera.

Zach is blushing hard when he says, "Addie, this is my brother Rob. Rob, Addie."

"Nice to meet you," Rob says. "I'd shake your hand, but"—he shows me his food-stained fingers—"Mrs. Gupta sent over a ton of Indian food and I got carried away."

"That's okay," I say, smiling at him. "Nice to meet you. I've seen some of your, er, work in Zach's films."

He bursts out laughing then. Definitely not as wooden as on camera. "I like this Addie," he says to Zach, who is still beet red and not showing a hint of a smile. I don't have to wonder what he's thinking for too long, because Rob says, "This is all very interesting. All this time when you were skipping trips to Caldwell, saying you had to work or whatever, I figured you were just moping around. Nursing that broken heart."

I can tell from the glint in his eyes that he's teasing Zach, but Zach does not look amused.

"I did have to work," Zach says quietly. "Besides, if you didn't let your phone go to voice mail so often, you might actually know some things."

Rob laughs again. "Point taken," he says. He glances at me, then back at Zach. "But still, you could have told me you had a *girlfriend.*"

I glance at Zach then, ready to ask why he didn't tell his brother about me, but he's already following Rob to the basement, where his parents, Kevin, and Raj are all assembled. In addition to the food, Raj has brought over *Dungeon World 2,* and for hours everyone takes turns playing.

I'm always aware, when I visit, how different Zach's family is from mine. There's this sense of ease, a lightness that reminds me of how my family used to be before my dad left. They laugh often, and each of them genuinely cares about the others.

After a couple of hours of snacking and everyone screaming at the TV and each other, Zach and I stand to go upstairs.

"Ooh!" Kevin says as we take the first steps up from the basement. "Just so you know, the house is not soundproof, so we'll hear if there is any screaming or headboards shaking!"

"Fuck off, Kevin," Zach says quietly, but still loudly enough to be heard. I've never heard him genuinely mad at his brother, and I've certainly never heard his father use with him the warning tone everyone in their family usually reserves for Kevin.

"Zach," his dad says.

Zach does not apologize, just keeps going up the stairs, never letting go of my hand. My face gets warm because now everyone downstairs *has* to be wondering what we're doing in Zach's bedroom, which obviously means we can't do anything, even if we still wanted to.

"Are you okay?" I ask Zach after he shuts the door and sits on his bed. I've never seen Zach this weird before, this moody.

"Yeah. I just have to tell you something." He doesn't look up at me, doesn't give me that stomach-flipping smile to reassure me that everything is okay. And for the very first time,

I'm not so sure everything *is* okay between us. We see each other less now than we ever have, and sometimes Zach forgets to call or text me back. But I figured that was all just busyness.

I lower myself into the rolling chair beside his desk.

"Lindsay's been texting me," Zach says grimly.

The air freezes all around us.

"Why?" I finally ask.

He looks up at me, meeting my eye for the first time since we've come upstairs, and says, "At first it was just to discuss our bio labs, but eventually she—"

"You're lab partners?" I blink twice.

Zach's turn to blink. "Technically. I mean, there's a whole bench of us."

"Why is Lindsay at your bench?" I ask, trying to sound cavalier but not exactly pulling it off.

"It's not *my* bench," Zach says, a hint of exasperation in his voice, as if I'm missing the point of this conversation. "Anyway, we're both *L*s. She's Loach."

"Loach," I repeat.

What kind of bullshit school still uses alphabetized seating charts, I think, while also trying to calculate how close Loach would be to Laird.

"How long has she been texting you?"

Zach shrugs. "A couple of weeks. Addie, the—"

"A couple of *weeks*?" I repeat. "What has she been saying?"

"Well, I told you, at first it was just questions about our labs and some calculus problems"—*Oh, now it's calculus, too, for God's sake,* I think, but don't interrupt—"and then she was more . . . I mean . . ." He stares down at his hands.

"She was more?" I repeat.

Zach sighs, says softly, "You realize you're just repeating what I'm saying now."

And since I can't repeat that, I ask, "Does she know you have a girlfriend?"

"Of course she knows," he says. "I mean, I told her I did."

"Well, that's kind of a bitchy thing to do," I say. "To text somebody else's boyfriend."

Zach sighs again and brings his right foot on top of his bed, even though he's still wearing his sneakers. "I don't think she's trying to be bitchy. She just"—*is a bitch*—"is going through some family stuff."

"Zach," I say, like, *Please God, tell me you're not actually falling for that.* "Katy told me in September that Lindsay *missed* you."

He shrugs without meeting my eye, then continues.

"I told her that her family stuff isn't any of my business anymore," he says. "I promise. I just wanted you to know."

Now he reaches forward and pulls my chair toward him until I'm right in front of him, only a couple of inches between our faces. The smell of smoke hangs between us.

"*Please* change your last name," I tell him, and his gray eyes twinkle as he laughs. "Or move to my school."

He kisses the base of my throat. "Move into my *room*."

He keeps kissing me, but I can't concentrate, can't do anything but think of Lindsay and her slutty flower and her curvy body in that black dress, dissecting frogs in a skanky lab coat.

"Stop freaking out," Zach breathes against my jaw.

"She's texting you advances!"

"And I'm *telling* you," he counters, not denying the advances part.

"But she obviously wants you back. How can I *not* freak out?"

He pulls his face away from mine, frowning. "Because you trust me?" he says.

"Of course I *do*," I say, sliding my hand over where his sits on his lap. "But girls like Lindsay . . ."

"You've never even met her," he points out. "You've met me. You know *me*. If that's not enough, then . . ."

He ends it there. *Then.*

Then I climb in his lap and kiss him. I do trust Zach.

At least, I want to.

It's just that I know you don't date a girl for two years unless you're crazy about her. Or *Zach* doesn't, anyway, because that's who he is.

And sometimes, at the most random times, like when we're riding our bikes through town or watching a movie or getting something to eat, her ghost will flit right in between us. Zach will get distant or a little sad or flush a little, and I'll know it's because this thing reminds him of her. A lot of things remind him of her.

It's like the first time we were at Schiavoni's or the night Zach showed me his homemade movies in his basement and at first he couldn't find one that didn't include her.

I wish I could kiss him and make him forget.

I wonder, as his tongue works its way into my mouth, if he wishes that, too.

And even though I am too wrapped up in him to say it, too out of breath to breathe it, I know there's a word for how I feel about Zach. Even without my permission, it's there. Even though we haven't been together all that long.

My body works overtime to tell him.

My heart beats in triplets, in syncopated rhythms, stopping and starting as he kisses me.

I like your hair, Zach.

Your smile makes it easier to breathe.

Everything about you is beautiful.

I love you, Zach. I really do.

50

AFTER
January

The real Zach was right in front of me yesterday and I let him slip by.

"You'll do it today," the other Zach—Memory Zach—says from the passenger seat beside me. "He's not going anywhere."

"I know," I say, but I'm feeling the anxiety bubbling up inside me. Both at the prospect of meeting real Zach and at where I'm headed to beforehand.

I left school today thirty minutes earlier than I did yesterday, skipping last period entirely, and this time I'm driving north instead of south, toward Lyndale Heights Cemetery.

When I pull into the parking lot of the cemetery, my stomach does a few somersaults. I've never been here in my life, only driven past it, either completely unaware of it or with a fleeting thought, sometimes a prayer, that I'd never have to walk through it.

It hits me even as I think this that remembering has nothing to do with it. I might have been here before, for the burial.

When I shut off the car, I turn and face Memory Zach. Look into his eyes, which are kind and concerned.

Come with me, I want to say, but no, I need to talk to my brother on my own.

Make a joke about concerts for the dead. I want to think about music, the happiest song I know, and I want the little brother I never knew to be hearing it right now, to be somewhere or something that is not dead.

"I'll be right back," I tell Memory Zach.

He reaches for my hand and squeezes.

"Okay," he says, instead of what he must want to say: *Don't forget about me.*

It is a given, by now, that I won't, so I don't bother to say it. Just take a deep breath, gently untangle my hand from his, and climb out of my car.

Some part of me might already know where Rory's grave is, but if that's the case, my mind is certainly not in any hurry to share that information as I glance left and right, trying to figure out which direction to go.

I spot a sign with a map of the cemetery and find the section containing the newer graves. It's several yards north of where I am. I follow a concrete path to it, then walk between the graves, searching for a stone with his last name. My last name.

And then I find it.

I'm expecting his grave to be empty, devoid of flowers, like many of the headstones around it, but a bouquet of fresh hydrangeas sits in front of it. The flowers seem to shiver in the cold.

I kneel on the ground in front of them.

My fingers trace out the words on the granite stone.

The *R.*

I see it on flesh instead of on rock.

RORY DAMIEN SULLIVAN. OCTOBER 18, 2009–JUNE 9, 2010. Instead of a poem or quote, it simply says WE WISH WE'D HAD YOU LONGER.

My hands are trembling as I continue tracing out the letters, and my eyes cloud with tears.

"Hi, Rory."

I have no idea what to say or if I'm doing this right. How do you miss—someone you don't remember?

Didn't I love him? How is it possible not to miss someone you once loved? Or is it possible that I *have* missed him, just without knowing? Is it possible to miss someone in a quiet, unspoken way, the most hushed of whispers instead of a shout? Is the world shaped a little differently for me because I once had someone I loved, someone I lost?

Some of my anger toward my parents returns, but it's overridden by a sadness I can't shake and guilt that something in me didn't just *know* without having to be told.

"I'm sorry," I say, choking a little on my tears. "Sorry for not watching you more closely that day. You should still be here. With us."

I sit back on the ground now and dig my fingers into the snow. "You know, I obviously don't have the details, but I'm pretty sure I liked being a big sister. Being *your* big sister. I bet I liked carrying you around and playing games with you and watching you toddle around. I bet I played my viola for

300

you constantly. I was kind of obnoxious about it back then." I laugh a bit as I speak. "So, sorry if you didn't like that."

It hits me then that he used to be a *person,* not a concept, not something that happened to us. He liked and disliked things; he took up space and had a particular voice and smell. He was going to grow up and do stuff someday that people would have remembered him for. It feels unfair that he will never get the opportunity, that he's been hidden here, buried without having had a chance to expand his world. To make friends and go to school and find people who wouldn't forget him.

It is the saddest thing in the world that you can take away a person if you take away the people who knew them. And we basically did that to my brother. By not talking about him, my parents and Caleb erased him twice; it's like he never existed.

Suddenly I am crying again, full-on sobbing in a way that forces me to gasp for breath. I just keep thinking, *I'm sorry. I love you. I don't know how I know, but I do.*

All those moments when I've wished for a more complete version of my family, less broken, I've been missing the brother I lost. My parents' separation, me and Caleb's relationship. His absence has been all around me every single day.

"I think I've missed you my whole life," I tell him now. "I always will." *Consciously, from now on.* And although it feels stupid and like not nearly enough, there is a little relief, a little comfort, in knowing that. Missing a person every day for as long as you live is not something everyone has the right to. But he is my brother, and I am entitled to miss him, and I finally understand that I have, in a way, all along.

"I would have come sooner," I say now. "And more often, if I'd figured it out. I *will* come more often."

I take a deep breath and touch the granite stone again.

"I wish I knew, Rory." *How to change what happened. What to say. You. If you were as much like Caleb as you look in that picture.*

I wish I'd known all along that I missed you.

51

AFTER
January

Memory Zach is gone when I return to my car, but I decide to wait until I've seen the real Zach before I bring him back.

After I leave the cemetery, I get onto Park Avenue, retracing my steps from yesterday exactly, and wind up outside Meridian High again ten minutes before school lets out. But this time I stay in the car and wait for students to start trickling out to the parking lot.

I keep my eye on the bright blue car that Zach and Raj drove off in yesterday.

This time, they burst out of the building together, talking and laughing as they walk toward the parking lot.

I slouch in my seat while they climb in the car and it wails to a start. Zach pulls out, drives to the exit of the parking lot, rolls to a stop at the yield sign. I watch him roll down his window, and his upper body pops out of it as he yells something to a boy on a skateboard. The boy turns around and gives Zach the finger, laughing.

I see Zach laugh, too, as his window goes back up. I can't tell whether his smile is the same as my Zach's smile, the Zach I've been remembering or conjuring up or whatever the name for it is.

Then they get out onto the road, and before I think about it, I'm pulling my seat belt across my body, starting my car, too.

At a stop sign about a block away, Zach signals left. I let a car between us and then follow them.

I know what I'm doing is crazy—illegal, even—but I can't bring myself to stop.

I desperately want to know this Zach.

I want to know what he knows about me.

Following them starts off fairly easy, straightforward. And then, just like that, I've lost them.

I'm on a one-way street, silently kicking myself for trying to play detective and letting a car between us, when a flicker of bright blue catches my eye.

I heave a sigh of relief and keep my eyes fixed on the car.

Zach is not a good driver, if this exhibit is anything to go by.

He speeds up unexpectedly, turns wildly, suddenly slows down. At one point, it almost seems like we're driving around in circles, but eventually he and Raj end up in front of a string of restaurants downtown. They turn into what seems to be an alley. I'm almost a hundred percent sure that there's no exit from it, so I pull up to the curb. I'm trying to decide what to do next when someone raps three times on my window. I jump so high I nearly slam my head on the roof of the car.

It is Raj. He is speaking, but I can't make out what he's saying.

He signals for me to roll my window down, and although I'd rather say "no thanks" and speed the heck away from here, I do.

"Hey," he says sternly. "Can I ask why you're parked here? You're not allowed to be here."

He gives no indication of remembering me from the theater or from when I used to date his best friend, but I notice he's craning to see into my car, that his eyes are narrowed at me in suspicion.

I stare blankly at him and then scan the street, desperate for an excuse. "Oh," I say. *Why are you acting like you don't know me?* That's what I want to say. Instead, I say, "Food. I, uh, this restaurant." I point at the nearest restaurant. It has a BRAND-NEW! TRY US! sign in the window. "Is new. I wanted to see."

Raj looks in the direction I just pointed. "That's my mom's new restaurant. You're going there?"

"Yeah," I lie. *No, you idiot.* I should say no, but I nod stupidly. "Yeah, so where"—*is Zach?*—"do I park? Legally?"

Raj frowns, hesitating. "Over there," he says finally, pointing across the street at an empty parking spot. I maneuver my car into the space, take a deep breath, and climb out.

Raj has already gone through the doors of Real New Delhi, and I follow behind him, eager to find out where Zach disappeared to. Or, worst case scenario, leave with a belly full of Indian food.

The smell of curry envelops me as soon as I walk in, and

my stomach rumbles, reminding me how little I've eaten the past few days. I can feel saliva building up in my mouth, and I'm beginning to think this is the best decision I've made all day. That is, until I see Zach in the doorway of the kitchen. He's concentrating on tying an apron around his hips, over his jeans, and there's a yellow pencil in his mouth. When I walk in, he glances up and meets my eye. We hold each other's gaze for a long moment, and then he turns, expressionless, and heads into the kitchen.

"Ma, we have a customer!" Raj yells, materializing behind the counter.

"Sit them!" a woman, presumably Raj's mother, yells back.

Raj sighs heavily and walks toward me reluctantly. *You're not allowed to be here.* For some reason, I'm not wanted here, and it makes my throat tight. "Please sit. Can I get you a drink to start with?"

"Um, some lemonade?"

Why aren't they acknowledging me and why do they seem to hate me?

"Okay." Raj nods and disappears into the kitchen. I'm scrambling to leave when Raj's mother, a short, skinny woman with a warm smile, appears. She convinces me to try today's special. She asks whether it's still cold out and if anyone else is joining me, and then Raj places a glass of lemonade in front of me. His mom returns to the kitchen, but Raj leans against a wall, arms crossed, pretending not to watch me.

It's difficult to swallow with the feeling of hostility all around me, and even though my meal is incredible, all I want is to get out of here.

Then Zach appears again. His hair is so much shorter in

real life that it makes it look darker. My breath is trapped in my chest.

Zach whispers something to Raj as they pass each other, then opens up the cash register. He mutters to himself as he counts, glancing up at times to write something down, but he won't look at me.

Raj's mom calls for him then, and he goes into the kitchen.

I can't get down the last third of my food. All I want is to leave.

I've accepted the fact that I don't know Zach—not really—but I wasn't the least prepared for him to hate me.

Did I *do* something to him?

Maybe I don't want to know how this ends.

Suppressing the fountain of emotion bubbling inside me, I push some words out at Zach. "Can I get my check?"

Screw finishing this meal.

He nods when our glances meet, and I can't read anything in the eyes that have haunted me for days. It's all I can do to keep it together.

He brings the check to my table—gives me a toothless smile, that pressing together of the lips reserved for strangers—and goes back behind the counter.

I put a few bills, plus a tip, under my cup and am trying to hightail it out of there. I'm almost at the door when I suddenly hear him speak.

"Hey, Addison," Zach says, looking right at me. "Are you following me?"

52

BEFORE
November

"This is a conversation for when I have pants on," Zach says groggily, burrowing his face into his pillow. I roll onto my side beside him and prop myself up on my elbow.

"I'm serious, Zach," I say. "You could *totally* get into NYU."

Zach doesn't respond, except to make a low, groaning sound into his pillow.

"They have a really good film program, and all you'd have to do is apply. I mean, I'm sure it's competitive, but you're good, and I bet you could get something together, an application package, before their early-decision deadline."

Zach is out of bed now, wriggling into a pair of jeans that has previously on the floor of his room. I wrap the sheet around me and place my head on his pillow. It smells like the cucumber shampoo he's just started using, and I close my eyes for a second.

"I doubt they're going to be impressed by homemade parody films."

"You never know," I say, opening my eyes now.

Still shirtless, Zach brings a glass of water to his lips and sets it back down on his table.

"It doesn't matter whether they like it or not if I'm not even sure I'm going to college," Zach says, and I sit right up in bed. "And why would I go to NYU, of all places?"

Because that's where I'll be?

My hair must be crazy at this point, but I don't even bother patting it down or anything.

"You won't go to college at all?" I ask, shock in my voice. "Because you can't afford it?"

"Because I might not want to go," he says with a shrug, bending down to retrieve my jeans from the carpet and placing them on the foot of his bed.

"Zach," I say.

"Addie," he says.

"You're going in with a defeatist attitude. College admissions committees can smell that a mile away," I say, half joking.

"God, Addie," Zach says suddenly, "could you drop it? It's easy for you; you're a fucking prodigy. You can get into whatever school you want."

I blink at him, my face slowly heating up. "That's not true."

"It *is* true," he says. "You could get into Juilliard but you won't even *apply* because you're desperate to hang on to this anti-conformity thing. This idea that it's expected of you or you can't stand to be like all *the other* fucking prodigies."

"That is *not* it. At all," I say, raising my voice now, too. I'm stunned by what Zach's saying. He's the only person I've ever told about why I chose New York, about wanting it to fill something in me. How can he say that? "It's not *easy* for me. You know how hard I've worked to stand a chance of getting into NYU—how hard I work to make good grades. I was reading books for the next school year in the *summer*. And even if any of what you're saying is true, what's your point? What does that have to do with you not wanting to go to college?"

"I didn't say I don't *want* to," Zach says, more softly now.

"You did!" I exclaim, not reducing my volume. "You just said that!"

"I don't know what I want," Zach says. He pauses for a moment, as if he's trying to figure it out right now, and then he goes back to picking stuff up from the ground. "Anyway, I'm pawning the CXX."

"Are you serious?" I ask.

Zach nods. "My parents can barely afford to keep the store open. And here's eight hundred dollars rotting on my table and I can't even *use* it. And I'm back to smoking a fucking pack a day."

He sits on the bed, his back to me. And even though I'm pissed off at him and hurt at the things he said, I see the tension in his slumped shoulders. His frustration as he bends over, elbows on his knees.

"We'll figure it out."

"I have to sell it," he says, mostly to himself now. "I shouldn't have accepted it in the first place. I *knew* I shouldn't, but I couldn't say no."

"Zach," I sigh, and put my chin against his bare back. "It's okay. We'll figure it out."

We stay like that for several minutes, and then Zach says, half twisting so I can see his face, "Sorry for being an asshole. You *are* a prodigy." A hint of his signature smile appears, but it doesn't quite fill his face. "But I shouldn't have said any of the other stuff. I'm just jealous you're talented."

He turns around fully and kisses me.

I say, "I'm just jealous you're hot."

He bites my lower lip. "You do *not* need to be jealous about that. Trust me."

53

BEFORE
November

Meridian High is putting on a Thanksgiving production that Zach has been coaxed into videotaping for the drama department, so I have seen even less of him the past two weeks.

Katy has informed me that Lindsay is in it.

"If there's any justice in the world," I say as we are getting ready to attend opening night, "she's playing the turkey."

Katy snort-laughs. "She certainly has the chin for it."

"What? She's tiny!" I exclaim, laughing even though I feel guilty. But I want Katy to know I appreciate her loyalty. Soon after finding out that Lindsay had been texting Zach, Katy promptly dropped her, explaining that best friends come before the-*yo*-ter friends. She broke into a rant about how Lindsay's blatant pursuit of Zach exemplified one of the major problems in show business: actors relinquishing their human characteristics in favor of more cowlike-slash-female-dog behaviors. Since they have many mutual friends, Katy is still keeping tabs on Lindsay, and she updates me on her activities from time to time.

"Oh, honey," she says now in a posh British accent. "As a victim of Big Belly on Tiny People myself, I can't deny that skinny people with double chins do exist."

"She does *not* have a double chin," I say, because it is true. Katy just laughs.

Zach and I haven't talked too much about Lindsay since the day after Halloween, except for me asking a couple of times if she was still texting him and him saying no, that he'd told her to respect his decision. With how little we see each other lately, everything feels a bit harder between us than it used to, and bringing her up would only add to that.

I glance at my phone several times before the lights go down. I texted Zach my seat number and asked about meeting him afterward, but he hasn't responded.

Sadly, it turns out Lindsay is not playing the turkey. We don't even get the satisfaction of seeing her in an ill-fitting Pilgrim costume. Her character is a refugee from an unnamed European principality who transfers to an American school in time for Thanksgiving and must traverse the high school social hierarchy while learning about deeply held traditions and the legacy of our forefathers.

"Deep shit for a Thursday night," Katy whispers, forcing me to break into an uncontrollable fit of giggles.

I spend the whole intermission scanning the auditorium for Zach. Just afterward, I finally find him way at the back, up in the viewing balcony, working the camera. He's wearing an orange T-shirt and large headphones. We wave at him from our seats below, but I don't think he sees us. He's concentrating hard, his attention never leaving the stage.

I keep glancing back, glancing up, not expecting him to see me since I'm just a spot, just another seat in the sold-out auditorium. But I watch the careful way he works, the stillness of his body as he goes entire minutes without moving once.

I look back at the stage, at Lindsay's riveting monologue, then back at him. Then back at the stage again. I can see his shoulders rising slightly with each intake of breath, falling when he exhales.

It's only when Katy nudges me that I realize what I'm doing.

I'm mirroring his movements, tilting left when he does, inching forward, moving back.

But minutes after Katy flicks my arm, I go back to doing it again.

Inching forward, watching the stage, watching him watch her.

And for the whole last act, I can't breathe.

Because he's holding his breath.

54

AFTER
January

I can't breathe.

Are you following me?

Zach's—the real Zach's—words hang in the air between us.

"No. Yes. Maybe." My words tangle together.

"I was pretty sure it was you yesterday," Zach says, arms folded over his chest. *Oh crap. They* did *see me.* "And I was *definitely* sure today."

"I'm sorry. I just need to talk to you."

He nods, but he's frowning, staring at me. "So you remember me?" His words are laced with bitterness, his posture still rigid.

"I don't," I admit. "It's kind of a long story. Can we talk?"

He doesn't answer right away, just holds my gaze, and then his expression softens the slightest bit. "I might be able to take a break now. Let me ask Mrs. Gupta."

I watch him disappear into the kitchen, already peeling off his apron. I think about running away, think about leaving before I open another can of worms, one I might not be able to close again. One I apparently couldn't live with.

Zach comes back and I follow him out of the restaurant. It's chilly despite the sunlight that's making us both squint. I breathe in and face him, and I want desperately to know everything. To start fresh. I feel like we should introduce ourselves.

"Hi," I say at last. *You're real. We're having a conversation.* I smile at him and he hesitates but finally, finally smiles back. This time, his teeth show. And his smile is bright. And it is beautiful, but still reserved, stiff. *Memory Zach smiles at me with his whole face. He fidgets less than the real-life boy in front of me.* I almost wish I was telling my Zach about this, explaining how it went and watching his reaction, rather than living this moment. I know he'd laugh at the part where I ended up stuffing my face with Indian food instead of confronting Zach.

"Where do you want to go?" Zach asks. "My car's still a piece of shit, but it's probably warm." *Still.* He's watching me, wondering whether I get the reference, whether I remember ever being in it.

When he first got on the bus, Memory Zach said his piece-of-shit car wouldn't start.

My ears ache from the cold. "Sure."

Zach unlocks his car and we slide in.

I glance around. It's a mess, full of film magazines and old bottles and DVDs. A koala dangles from the rearview mirror.

I want so desperately for something to be familiar. The smell, the warmth, anything.

"What are you doing here?" Zach asks, and behind the defensiveness, I hear the genuine curiosity in his voice. I think his eyes look a little bit sad. "Katy told me you had gotten the procedure done."

"Katy told you? She said no one else knew." Did she think I'd be angry that she told Zach?

"I guess she felt she had to tell me to keep me from bothering you. She told me what you'd done, that you would never remember . . ."

"Us," I offer, and he nods. "I don't. But I found out about the"—I swallow—"memory splicing."

"I didn't know about it at first. You didn't even tell me when . . ." He shakes his head, and the hurt in his voice is palpable. "You just did it without saying anything. Like everything that happened between us didn't matter." He runs his hand through his hair. "I still don't understand."

That's why he's been so cold to me. For erasing him.

I suddenly feel ashamed. Because he cared about me. It's obvious that he did. So why *would* I do it?

"I'm sorry," I whisper.

He shrugs. "Katy said you wanted me to stay away from you, that I needed to act like we didn't know each other if I ever saw you. I tried calling you anyway, and I even came to see you at school, but Katy threatened to beat my ass if I didn't leave you alone.

"She said this was your way of trying to let go, and that I didn't have to like it, but I had to respect it. So Raj—he's

317

the only person I told—and I weren't sure what to make of it when you suddenly started following us." Most of his anger seems to have dissolved now, to have been replaced by hurt. "And it's one thing if we'd run into you, but I don't understand what kind of sick game you're playing. Is Katy behind it? I know she's not my biggest fan. You're coming into Mrs. Gupta's restaurant, and to my school, just to what? Show me I still mean nothing to you? That I never will again?"

It feels like he's pushing pins into my chest. "That's not why I came. I would never do that."

"Well," Zach says, and runs his hand over his head like he's expecting for there to be more hair. "I've seen you a bunch of times since . . . we broke up." He glances at me. I stare back. "And since the procedure. Usually you don't even look at me."

"At all?" I ask, a little incredulous. Because even if I didn't know Zach, surely I would still notice him. That smile, those eyes. I guess maybe with the shorter hair, but . . . "I feel like I'd still notice."

His cheeks get a little pinker and he laughs. "Thanks, but no. It's been"—he searches for the right expression—"kind of a mindfuck. And now you're . . . here."

"I was in an accident almost three weeks ago," I say. "On a bus from Raddick."

"Oh my God," Zach says, his eyes widening. "I heard about that. Are you okay?" I see his hands twitch like he's tempted to reach out, but they stay put on his lap. And all his concern remains on his face.

"I'm fine," I say. But then I tell him what happened after. About the boy on the bus who's more than a boy on the bus now—who's *him*—and his face goes ashen.

"That *is* a mindfuck," he remarks.

I tell him about the brother I never knew I had, about how figuring out that the apparition I was seeing was a memory led me here.

"Sorry about stalking you," I finish.

"Yeah, likewise," Zach says, looking spooked, and we both laugh awkwardly. He seems—looks—older than the Zach I've been seeing, and I feel a twinge of sadness, realizing I know neither of those Zachs. It's funny how the way I remember him is both different from and completely the same as the real him.

"All anyone keeps saying is that I was"—I pause—"like, depressed after whatever happened with us."

Zach looks at his hands. "Yeah, I heard. I mean, Katy sent me some pretty strongly worded death threats."

I give him a smile, but it is a small one.

"The whole thing was . . . I mean, I got why you did it, why you hated me. But even if things were reversed, I would *never* want to forget you." His voice is deep with hurt, but insistent, like he's wanted a chance to tell me this for a long time. "I still can't believe you went through with it. It just seemed like such a cowardly thing to do. And I'd always thought of you as brave."

My face is burning now with embarrassment, with anger at myself. Having no memory, no context, I can't defend myself.

I am a coward.

Was.

Am?

"What happened?" I press after a moment. "Why did I do it?"

Zach's expression is wary as he appraises me. "I don't know if . . . I mean, I'm probably not supposed to tell you. And I'm not sure I *want* to." His face is a deep red now.

"Zach," I say, feeling a surge of anger rising up in me. I'm sick of people keeping things from me, lying to me—myself included.

"Did something happen?" I ask him.

"Um, yeah?" he says, like he's not entirely sure what I'm asking.

"Was I there?"

"I . . . yeah, of course you were."

"Then you don't get to be angry with me without telling me why, without letting me understand. Tell me everything. Please."

55

BEFORE
Late November

"Do you like the idea or not?" I ask Katy the day after sitting through Lindsay's Thanksgiving production.

"Yes, yes, I love it. I bow to you. The only conceivable way you could be a better girlfriend would be if you cloned another version of yourself and *both* of you banged Zach at the same—"

"Ugh, okay. Stop!" I say. "Help me carry this thing."

"That looks like one heavy-ass overhead projector," Katy says, blowing on her newly manicured nails—short, though, so they don't affect her playing—as she steps around me. "I'll bring the popcorn."

I sigh and carry the projector by myself all the way to the front door of Zach's house. I set it down on the ground and go back for the nine DVDs I picked up at his father's store this afternoon, then shut the door of Katy's car. I enlisted her help to set up, Mrs. Dubois's to borrow the projector that sits in the corner of the music room but nobody ever uses, and Zach's family's to use the basement. Kevin has even put sheets over the furniture, just like the old days. All I have to do is set up the projector, and Zach's perfect night will be a go.

I am doing it partly because, between play rehearsals and performances, I've hardly seen him the past week and a half. It feels longer than that, since we've both been busy the past month with the things we always seem to be busy with that aren't each other. I am also doing it because of my promise to unstick him.

"Eww," Katy crows when I tell her this.

"Get your head out of the gutter," I laugh. "I mean inspire, motivate, encourage."

"Whatever," Katy says, slurping on the milk shake she insisted we get from Shake Attack on our way here. (I'd snorted when she said, "That's what you get for making me drive. And though all signs point to my being spectacularly lactose intolerant, I need sustenance for all the heavy lifting we'll be doing.")

It turns out the only person doing heavy lifting is me.

I pull down all the Ciano posters from Zach's room— twelve—and with them line the walls of the basement.

Katy waits with me for Zach to arrive. The performance is supposed to finish at eight, with the cast party going till nine, but Zach told me in his last text that he's exhausted and doesn't plan to stay more than a few minutes or he'd have taken me.

"So, Katherine," Kevin says, sitting on the couch next to Katy. "If I were to pick up a musical instrument, what would you recommend?"

Katy shoots me a skeptical look. "Um, I don't know. What kind of music do you like?"

"All kinds," Kevin says, wriggling his eyebrows. "And personally, I think I'd be fantastic at the harmonica."

"Kevin," I say in that warning voice I've heard everyone use so often with him, even though I'm not a hundred percent sure where he's going with this.

"Or should I say," Kevin continues, "the *mouth* organ." He makes loud kissing sounds, then throws his head back and releases riotous laughter, slapping the arm of the couch.

"My God," Katy whispers to me. "How old is this kid?"

"I'm fifteen literally in two weeks," Kevin supplies. "Old enough to date."

"Good Lord," Katy says with disgust, and I laugh. I would tell her she's finally met her match, but then Kevin would probably take that the wrong way, and the last thing I want is to encourage his out-of-control flirting.

"Where is *your* boyfriend?" Katy asks after a minute. "There is a world of post-pubescent boys waiting for me."

I check my phone again. Still no message from Zach. I've sent him a couple of texts, but I don't want to send too many or he'll suspect something is up.

"It's eight-thirty," I say. "He's probably on his way as we speak."

"Hey, Raj left his *Dungeon World 2* here. Do you wanna play?" Kevin asks all of a sudden.

"What's *that* a euphemism for?" Katy asks me.

"I don't think anything."

"Fine," Katy says to Kevin. "But I don't actually know how to play."

"I'm more than happy to show you, babe," Kevin says, and proceeds to explain the game quite patiently. The three of us take turns playing for about half an hour, and then we are all bored again.

"Where *is* he?" I say out loud, and send him another text asking just that. Five minutes and zero responses later, Kevin pulls out a tray of face paint he got recently and convinces Katy it will be hilarious for her to jump out at Zach looking like a zombie when he arrives.

So we sit mixing colors, Kevin relishing the opportunity to touch Katy's pimple-free face, for about another half hour.

And then it is nine-thirty and Katy is stretching and saying, "I love you, Sullivan, but Gilbert has to go. I don't know what convinced me in the first place that it would be *cute* to watch you two suck face when he sees your surprise, anyway. And you know that is what all *this* is an excuse for."

I scoff. "As if I need an excuse to suck face with my own boyfriend."

"Ew," Kevin says, sounding tired, too.

"Thanks for helping me out," I say, hugging Katy.

I glance at the time again. The plan was for Zach and me to pick a movie and then spend a couple of hours watching it (or not watching, as the case may be) and then come back tomorrow and continue the marathon, but soon *I* will have to leave. My mother is at a dinner party tonight and I've been counting on making it home before her, but I've also been counting on Zach showing up before ten.

"Let me walk you out," Kevin says, rushing ahead of us up the basement stairs.

"That is *quite* okay," Katy says. "Seriously, kid, hit on people your own age."

Kevin just snorts and disappears down the hall.

Katy and I continue out the front door and start toward the driveway. Katy is the first one to freeze. She goes completely rigid beside me.

I stop because she has and then follow her gaze, follow her eyes to the driveway, where a car I've never seen before is parked.

And inside it is Zach.

And I can see her hands in his hair, her fingers sifting through it, her fingers all over him. She has his back against the passenger side door, and she is basically in his seat. She is kissing him.

He is kissing her.

There is a frenzy of motions, an urgency. They are never just doing one thing: not just kissing, but kissing and touching each other's hair. Or touching each other's hair and talking, their lips shivering as they say something only they can hear.

I watch them for days.

I drag one of the couches from the basement and fall into it and watch Lindsay kiss Zach. Watch Zach kiss Lindsay.

Watch Katy grab hold of my elbow, like she has to stop me from running, like I am going to move. Like I am going to leave this couch that I've fallen into and am watching them from, two people removed from my world. Strangers.

One I love.

One I love oh God so much.

"Those sluts, those sluts, those sluts," Katy says under her breath now, or maybe she's screaming it, because Lindsay seems to respond to those words. She jumps away from Zach, her eyes wide, and then he's scrambling out of the car, moving toward me.

Oh God.

I want to close my eyes so I won't see.

See his gray eyes filling, hear him promising he is sorry. She was just giving him a ride because his car wouldn't start.

See my fists pounding his chest, once, twice, over and over again.

"You are un-fucking-believable, Lindsay!" Katy is shouting at her ex-friend, and Lindsay looks startled, terrified, since Katy looks like a zombie. "How are you even a human being?"

Lindsay wraps her arms around herself, safely behind her steering wheel, and stares down at it.

Katy keeps shouting.

Suddenly Lindsay slams on the horn, making us all jump. "Leave me alone!" she yells now. Which just makes Katy start yelling all over again. Which makes Lindsay yell back.

Zach and I stand off to the side of the car, a foot apart, dazed, watching Lindsay and Katy have the altercation we should be having.

My voice is hollow when I finally speak. "You told me you weren't in love with her anymore. You told me it was over. And like an idiot, I actually believed you."

"Addie," Zach says taking a step toward me. I take a step back. "I made a mistake. I wasn't thinking. I'm sorry. I'm so sorry."

His voice is thick and muffled. In the wind, his hair, his *puff,* rattles and dances. Mocks me.

The terrible thing is that I still want to kiss him, even as I want to kill him. I want to scream at him, but I want to do it close to him. I want to tell him I love him.

But what I say is, "I hate you, Zach."

He shakes his head, pained, willing me to take it back.

I don't. I won't.

The world is blurring around me now and I start to walk toward Katy's car. I can hear her wrapping up her argument with Lindsay, and by that I mean they are still screaming strings of obscenity at each other but without referring back to past events or even current ones. Just "bitch," "slut," "ho bag," "assface."

Zach is following me toward Katy's car now, still pleading.

Maybe there's an alternate version of this where I take him back, where I hear his remorse, where I forgive him. Maybe it doesn't matter that all his films include her or are about her or that I played a thinly veiled Lindsay in one of them and possibly all along. Maybe I'm so desperate to love someone, to love *Zach* and have him love me back—so desperate to be pried awake by how I feel about him—that I can forget this.

But *no.*

I can't.

I whirl around and face him, not caring if tears are streaming down my face, not caring that tears *are* streaming down my face.

"Stay the fuck away from me," I say, pulling open the door of Katy's car and climbing in.

56

AFTER
January

It doesn't feel like it belongs to me. He tells me the start, the middle, and the end as he remembers it, but it could be the story of any two strangers, two people I don't know and never will.

Even when Zach says, "I'm sorry, Addie. Really sorry," it feels like it belongs to someone else. I nod vaguely, blankly. "I know you didn't want to hear it before, but I *am*."

And I nod again.

He mentions in passing a night I spent at his house when his family was away. Though neither of us says it, I know what it means.

We slept together.

Me and Zach.

Really, it's her and Zach. Another Addison. I don't feel different, I haven't noticed anything different, and I would have if it was me and Zach.

I would have.

"I screwed up," he says now in a soft voice, a voice that forces me to look up at him. His face is red. His eyes squint a little bit, like he's still mad at himself. "But I *did* love you. I hope you know that."

His gray eyes rest on my face as he says that, and I feel the air vacuum out of my lungs, confirming, I guess, that his words do belong to me. Or I want them to.

I want Zach to have loved me. I want to know that.

"So that was it?" I ask after I trust myself to speak again. I mean, it isn't hard to see how I might have been crazy about him, how much he'd meant to me before. I could see myself being upset at the breakup, but according to my family and Katy, I'd been devastated.

Was it because we had sex? Was I even more in love with him than I can comprehend? Or was I just too weak to move on?

"That was it," Zach says.

He was right. I am a coward.

To erase my memory over a breakup?

I frown, staring at the dashboard and wishing I could find some way to claim the things Zach has told me, to make whatever I felt before—love, betrayal, sadness—belong to me again.

"I'm really sorry. I can't imagine being in your shoes," Zach says.

I stare at my hands in my lap, suddenly embarrassed to think this boy has seen me naked. He's the only boy who has. And once upon a time, I bet, I could trace the contours of his body.

How is it possible to forget all that?

"So when did you start working at Real New Delhi?" I ask, changing the subject to ward off the heaviness, the hopelessness, settling over my whole body.

Even if how it ended was awful, I just want it to feel familiar. I want *him* to feel familiar.

Zach grins at me now, and my stomach tickles. It might only have been familiar from the invisible Zach, Memory Zach, but I still like recognizing it. And *oh my*.

"A whopping five days ago," he says with a laugh. "Could you tell?"

"Not really," I say. "I saw that the restaurant was new."

I'm captivated by his smile, the way his lips tilt up, and my face gets hot as the thought of having kissed those lips—having done more and more—fills my mind.

"Yeah. My parents closed the store months ago, and I quit at the Cineplex not long after we broke up. The owner is kind of a hard-ass, so pretty much everyone I worked with there has left. Then Raj's mom asked if I'd work for her restaurant. Free food. No way was I turning that down."

I laugh, and he smiles but doesn't laugh this time.

When his eyes get this faraway look, I wonder if he's thinking about a version of me I have no memory of. I fiddle with the partly open little ashtray of his car because I feel restless, feel like I need my viola, but also I'm still trying to find something I know in this car.

"Oh, I haven't used that in ages," Zach says, looking into the tray. "Ever since I quit smoking."

"You quit?"

And when I face Zach, he is nodding and beaming, the car getting at least five shades brighter.

"That's so great!" I say.

He laughs. "I knew you'd be impressed, still." He feels me keep watching him, so he adds, "You weren't a fan of the smoking."

"Well, there's one thing that sounds like me. Finally."

Zach gives me a sad smile.

His phone suddenly vibrates in his pocket, and when he pulls it out, he says, "Shoot. My break was over ten minutes ago!"

"Oh," I say, feeling myself deflate. The car is no longer warm, but I don't mind the idea of sitting in this car with Zach for hours.

We climb out anyway and he comes around to my side. "If you ever need me," Zach says, "you know where I am."

I nod, a lump the size of a house growing in my throat. And I blink rapidly to keep my eyes clear.

"Hey," Zach says, gently wrapping his arms around me. And that, *that*, feels familiar. The tips of my ears burn and not from the cold.

I let my head rest on his chest, hear his heart beating steadily through his T-shirt, and I'm already dreading the moment he'll let go.

It comes too soon.

And I realize as we step back that it didn't come hurtling back—the memories, what it felt like to be with him. Secretly, I hoped it would. That being in his presence, touching the real Zach, would bring it all back.

"I hoped seeing you would jog something, but . . ." My voice fades. "I guess I'll just have to take your word for it that that's how it happened." I'm half laughing, even though it's not funny. Even though a tear has escaped down my cheek.

Zach frowns, at least a foot between us again, and looks sad for me.

"I'm okay. I promise," I say, swiping at my cheek with my hand.

He nods, keeps watching me, then glances back at the restaurant. Finally he starts to walk in that direction.

And then I feel something, a realization, like a forceful kick to the chest. I loved this boy. Memory Zach isn't real; if I rest my head against his chest, it's my own heartbeat I'm hearing. When he speaks, it's my voice, my own mind, I'm hearing.

But here is the real Zach. He still gives me butterflies. And if I let him walk away . . .

"Zach!" I call. He stops and turns around.

I take a couple steps toward him. "Do you want to . . ." I swallow. "When your shift is over or something, maybe we could hang out?"

I watch the blood drain from Zach's face. He glances quickly at his fingers, then back at me, and I feel my heart plummeting.

"Or we could *not*," I say, trying to make my voice light, trying to save face.

"No, it's just . . . ," Zach says, glancing down, glancing back at me again. "Just that . . . Lindsay and I are still together."

All the air falls out of my body.

Oh.

"Oh God," I say, my whole face burning now. "I'm sorry. God. I swear I didn't know."

"I'm sorry, Addie," Zach says, not for the first time today, and I nod, even though I don't know for which part he's apologizing. For breaking my heart in the first place. For me not remembering any of it. For still being in love with Lindsay, after all this time.

57

BEFORE
Late November

It's the night after Thanksgiving, eight days after I found Zach and Lindsay in her car, and my chest still hurts from the thought of it. From how stupid and blind I was.

But I miss him.

I miss his full, joyful laugh. I miss his hair between my fingers. His breath, even cigarette-y, against my cheek, against my mouth. I miss being in his arms, the feeling of his body next to mine.

For the first couple of days, I turned my phone off. I wouldn't listen to his messages or read his texts, and I asked my mom and brother to send him away when he came over.

But allowing myself to listen to one, just one, message was like falling into a vortex. Soon I was listening to all of them. Some three or four times.

He kept saying the same things.

I'm sorry, Addie.

I screwed up.

If you would just let me explain.

It wasn't supposed to happen. I swear it was the only time.

Sometimes I played them for Katy and we thought of the worst names we could for him. She called him Zach-or-Mac-or-Jack, trying to make me laugh. I did, but it felt hollow and false.

The last message is from Tuesday, three days ago—the longest he's gone without trying to reach me—and I wonder if he's given up. Has he accepted that it's over? Have I?

Do I *want* it to be over?

Foolishly, I call him now while I'm lying awake in bed. He picks up after four rings, sounding out of breath, like he raced for his phone.

"Hello?" he says. I breathe into the phone, don't answer. My heart fluttering in my chest.

"Addie," he says seconds later. I know it's caller ID but I want to believe he recognizes the sound of my silence, the shaky intake of my breaths as I fight back tears. "Addie, hey."

"I really hate you right now," I whisper into my phone.

"I'm sorry. I never wanted to hurt you," and it sounds like he's near tears as he says it.

"It was one time? A mistake?" I ask, paraphrasing the messages he's left for me.

"One time," Zach promises. He doesn't repeat the second half of my statement.

"I think you were never over her. Deny it."

Our voices are gentle on the phone, like we're exchanging secrets in the dark.

"I think because we were together so long I just . . . It's not that easy to cut her out of my life. I thought it would be, but it wasn't. She's still my friend and I thought maybe that would be okay and I guess, I don't know, it wasn't."

I feel my blood warming as he speaks. "So what do you want, Zach?" I hiss the question. Who *do you want?* I don't want it to be his choice, I hate that, but my heart is betraying me, sitting firmly in his pocket, the one I slid my hand into and promised to unstick him.

"I want you to not hate me," he says. "I want us to meet face to face and talk and—"

"What do you *want*?" We are both silent, and then I say, angrily, "Figure it out," and hang up.

Another two days pass.

I keep trying not to think about him or the phone call or the fact that he couldn't answer when I asked him what he wanted, who he wanted.

He hasn't called since I hung up.

Today, on my drive back from seeing my dad—he was away on Thanksgiving, so Caleb and I went over there this morning—there is a force against my chest, relentless and sharp, like I've broken a rib or something. It's been there for the past ten days, but I realize now that as angry as I am at Zach, I'm not close to being over him. Maybe seeing him face to face like he wanted would help. Maybe, just maybe, there's somehow still hope for us.

He doesn't know I'm coming because I didn't plan to. As soon as I pull into the parking lot of the movie store, my mind is already filling with uninvited questions: Will he be behind the counter? What does his hair look like today? Will he grin at me when he sees me, that bright, disarming smile? Or will he be contrite, apologetic, nervous?

Then, as I get closer, climb out of my car: What if he's not even here? Today is Sunday. What if he's working at the Cineplex instead?

But as I step on the concrete, before I even reach the all-glass front of the store, I have the answer to my questions. He is working today. And he's not behind the counter; he's on a stepladder on the far end of the store, draping tinsel over the shelves, decorating for the Christmas season.

She's standing next to the ladder, in a pair of jeans tucked into brown riding boots, and she's holding it steady with one hand, gesturing with the other.

I can't move.

I can't do anything but watch them through the glass.

He climbs down and hands her a bunch of tinsel, and she flings one piece back at him. Wraps the other piece around his head.

He laughs and says something to her. He touches her back, her waist. It's only for a second, and then he drags the ladder over a few feet and climbs on again to add some more tinsel.

It doesn't mean that they are together, or that they are almost together or not together.

It doesn't matter and I can't tell and I don't want to.

I told him to figure out what he wanted.

And he did.

He did.

As I stand there watching them, that pain in my chest

stretches and expands until it's a tidal wave of sadness, of anger.

It hurts to draw in my breath, to stay standing, to turn back and head to my car. And all I can think is, *It was always her.*

Why did I let myself love him, let myself be with him? Everything I felt with him, felt for him—all the things I told him that I'd never told anyone else—in spite of all that, I wasn't and would never be enough for him. He woke me up, he made me come alive, but Lindsay did that for him.

Did everything that happened between us mean anything? Was our whole relationship a lie?

I fall into my car and the world roars with too much silence, and it ends right outside where it began. In Zach's father's movie store.

Because he still loves her.

It was always her.

I don't remember when anything has hurt so much.

58

AFTER
January

I pretend to busy myself with something in my car until Zach disappears back into Raj's mother's restaurant. And then I sink lower in my seat and close my eyes.

"Zach," I whisper, and wait for the sound of his voice.

"Zach," I say again, more loudly. Open my eyes and he's still not anywhere around. I think of "Air on the G String." Our song.

I hum it, and there is still nothing.

"Zach!" I yell into my car.

"*My* Zach," I say. "Memory Zach?"

Nothing.

He doesn't appear in my passenger seat out of thin air. He doesn't appear across the street and walk toward me.

Not his flapping red puff of hair, not his crazy bright smile, not even his cigarette. Nothing.

And suddenly I'm remembering what he asked me in the

diner on Saturday night: *What do you think happens when you find him?*

And what he said that morning we drove to school together.

Don't forget about me.

How nervous he was that he wouldn't exist anymore if I found the real Zach.

But I didn't forget. I didn't. Just because I talked to the real Zach, I . . .

I never meant to make him go.

We didn't even say goodbye.

He didn't know it would be the last time he existed.

Zach, Zach, Zach.

"Where are you?" I say out loud, feeling a surge of panic begin to build in my chest. "Come back."

The noise of my car's heater whirs a warm silence back at me.

"Come back," I whisper to it. To no one.

To myself.

59

AFTER
January

The tears hit me with force when they come. I wrap my arms around myself and lean my hand against the headrest, and all I can do is heave and sob because I can't stop thinking about all the things I've lost without knowing.

I'm still parked outside the restaurant, but I can't stop thinking about what it might have felt like to have a younger brother. A pink-toed baby brother who maybe cooed at the sight of my face and danced around in a high chair and smelled like baby powder and new life.

I can't stop thinking about the day we put him in that tiny grave and how it's been there all these years and how I never went back. How I should have gone back.

I can't stop wondering about the first time I met Zach, and whether I liked him from the moment I laid eyes on him. And why don't I remember what it felt like to kiss him the first time? To lock my fingers in between his?

I lost my virginity to him and it's supposed to make you different, and all this time I didn't know. And even now I'll never really know.

What did his hair feel like in my hands, and what are all the truths I told him, *gave* him, about myself that I'll never get back?

Who was I when I loved him? Did being in love make the air feel light and musical? Did I have more good hair days and better playing days, and was I any surer of who I am? Were my eyes wider, my lips different, from having been kissed? Was I that girl who couldn't stop grinning, couldn't stop telling strangers about this boy I liked, or was I quiet and cool and coy like I always hoped I'd be?

I don't remember anything about being with him, or not being with him. Did it really make me different, did our relationship really mean anything, if he's still with her?

I would take the sting of brokenheartedness, of being betrayed, if I could somehow get back the knowing, the feeling, of all those days. The weight of them, certain and clear in my mind. I would give anything to have them back. I'd even take his invisible replica, the boy who wasn't Zach but who led me to him. And to a version of myself I might never have known existed.

The impact of everything I've lost, all the things I've lost forever, hits me again and again until I can't breathe.

60

AFTER
January

"I need your help please I need your help." I mumble a run-on sentence once I reach the counter where the receptionist is. It's Heidi again, and the man who was training is nowhere in sight. I drove to Overton right after losing it in the car, and I was expecting to have to plead or grovel my way into the clinic since I didn't make an appointment, but apparently Dr. Overton has granted me temporary emergency access because of my "symptoms," the unexpected side effects I've been experiencing.

"Please," I say again. I must be loud, because while Heidi is trying to calm me down and the other patients are staring, the nurse with the purple stripe in her hair hurries in with Dr. Overton, who's holding a half-eaten chocolate granola bar, his eyes wide with surprise.

"Addison!" he says. "What are you doing here?"

"I need you to help me."

He and the nurse exchange a glance, and I determine

definitively that, yes, she does know me. Then I follow Dr. Overton to his office and sit across the desk from him for the third time in a week.

"What's wrong?" he asks, looking genuinely concerned.

"The boy I was seeing? The memory?" Dr. Overton nods. "He's gone. I can't get him to come back."

I see some of the tension release from his shoulders.

"Well, that's good! Right?" He watches me carefully.

I shake my head. "No, that's not *good*. He's all I have."

Of the first time I fell in love. Of the two people who were erased from my mind.

Dr. Overton's forehead furrows and he seems unsure what to say for a second. Finally he chuckles. "He's not *all* you have, Addie. You have two parents who would do anything for you and—"

"You don't understand," I say, speaking over him. "I feel like there's a giant hole." I hear my voice catch as I continue. "And I don't know how to fill it. How to go back to being normal and happy. How to look at my family again."

To know that they're not who I thought. That I'm not who I thought.

The crease remains in the middle of Dr. Overton's forehead.

"I want *you* to fill it," I say slowly. "I want you to give me my memories back."

He is silent for a long moment before he exhales through his nose. He gives me a sad smile then, like he actually understands, genuinely feels for me.

"Addie, I wish I could, but I'm afraid I'm not in a position to do that," he says.

"That's not good enough," I say, my voice rising. "All I hear about is how easy memory splicing is, how easy it is to take away the past. So it must be just as easy to bring it back. Saying you can't do that is not good enough."

I know I've crossed the line into disrespectful, but when I finish speaking, he looks shaken, not angry. His eyes are full of something like empathy, like conflicted feelings.

"Addison, I know you've been through a tough few days. I know you're upset—and you are well within your rights to be. If I were in your shoes, well . . ." His voice fades out. "Do you know what I love about this job? What I love about our minds?"

Thankfully, he doesn't wait for me to respond.

"I love the idea of us carrying around fragments of places and people and things we've experienced. It's so unlikely and almost miraculous, when you think about it. All the things that matter stay with us. They take up space inside us. Sometimes *outside* us, too, I suppose." He smiles at me then, and I know he's talking about Memory Zach. The apparition I was seeing.

He runs his hands over his eyes, and I can see that this is something he has thought about a lot. "Every now and then, *often* in fact, I'm reminded that I'm not playing with neurons or electrodes or even memories. I'm playing with fragments of people's lives, people's hearts. And I don't take that lightly. I really don't."

There's a long silence between us then, and I take the opportunity to say, "So help me? Please?"

"I wish I could. I really, truly do. But we've never done a successful retrieval procedure. My father is working on it, but it's years away. There's nothing I can do."

I bury my face in my hands.

Memory Zach is really gone. My brother is really gone.

And what was the point? What was the point of the last few weeks? Only to make me more aware of what I was missing, what I'll never have?

How will I ever feel anything now that's not incomplete or hollow or a shadow of what's real?

How do I go back to dreaming of New York, making plans for college and the rest of my life, when massive chunks of it—of who I am—are gone forever?

How do I move forward?

All I have in place of my past is brokenness. This sadness that nothing can lift, a fog I can't see through. This knowledge that my family lied to me for years and years, that I lied to myself. That I'm the reason my family crumbled. That if I had done something different, my little brother might still be alive.

I can't take it.

It's too much.

How do I move forward? That's what I want. To *move on*—it's, in a way, what I've always wanted. After Rory died. After Zach broke my heart.

It's why I've been itching to leave Lyndale my whole life.

I want what's next.

"Addie, I'm so very sorry," Dr. Overton says, sounding like he means it.

I can't stop shivering, but then a thought hits me.

I pull my fingers away from my face and look at him.

If there's no way to bring back my memories, to fill this

new and ugly void in my life, maybe there's something else I can do.

"If you can't bring them back," I whisper, "can you take them away? For good?"

Now it's not just my hands shaking; my voice is, too.

"What do you mean by 'them?'" The line of concern down his forehead is even more etched now.

"Everything I've figured out. Everything starting from when the boy got on the bus—no, *before* that. I don't want the Bach suite—the concert, either."

Dr. Overton looks confused, but he lets me go on.

"I don't want to know about Rory or about Zach. I don't want to know that I erased him or to remember meeting him today. I want everything from the last three weeks gone."

He's shaking his head. "That's three procedures. We're still monitoring for the effects of the accident. I don't think we can do that."

"It's not dangerous. All the pamphlets and stuff say that. And you said my CT was clear. It's what I want. Please." I'm practically hysterical at this point.

"But, Addison," he says now. "You do realize that you won't get them back? That these memories will be gone for good if we go through with what you're asking for?"

The thing I want most is to move on. And the procedure helped me do that before, didn't it? Maybe not completely, but mostly. That's why I came back for the second one. Why I'll do it again now.

"I know," I say, still shaking.

"Okay," Dr. Overton says. "Okay."

The waiting-room music is slipping in under the door, and I dig my nails into my palms. I don't want to think about anything right now.

"One problem," Dr. Overton says. "You're still only seventeen. There's absolutely no way we can proceed without a parent's permission. And given the circumstances surrounding your last . . . Well, one of them has to be with you for the procedure."

61

AFTER
January

Bruce, Mom's boyfriend, is the first person to see me when I enter the Channel Se7en building. "Hey, little miss!" he exclaims when I hurtle into the office area, full of cubicles, where he's standing reading a sheet of paper. He's wearing a checkered sweater vest, gray dress pants, and black oxfords. No socks, as usual. "Everything okay? Where are we going in such a hurry?"

"I need to talk to my mom," I say. "Do you know where she is?"

He frowns at me, concerned, then glances down at his watch. "She's probably in a meeting. It's in the boardroom, but I can run over and stick my head in for you and we'll tell her you're looking for her, okay?"

"Thanks," I say as he starts down the hall to get her.

Bruce is fond of the royal "we." If, God forbid, he

impregnated my mother, he'd be one of those men going around announcing, "We're pregnant."

But he's always been nice to me and Caleb.

I pace around now as I wait for him to return. It's past four. Less than an hour till Overton closes. And what if Dr. Overton changes his mind about attempting the procedure?

Mom's clicking heels announce her presence before she rounds the corner. "What's wrong? What is it?" she asks, hurrying toward me. "Bruce said you looked like something was wrong."

"I want to forget all this. The past few weeks. Finding out about Rory," I tell her once she's stopped in front of me. She glances around and then leads me into her office. She shuts the door after us. "Dr. Overton is willing to do the procedure as long as you'll sign for it and be there."

"Addison," Mom says. She looks stunned. "But you were so adamant that it was the wrong thing, that we should never have done it to erase . . . your brother."

Even now it's hard for her to say his name to me.

Rory, Rory, Rory.

I do it for her while I still can.

I do it for him, too, before I betray him a second time. A third time.

He's dead because of me.

I wasn't even strong enough to remember him.

In the cemetery, I promised him I'd remember him from now on, but Zach was right.

I'm a coward.

"Well, I guess you were right the first time. I'm not strong enough for the truth." I burst into tears now, and she wraps her arms around me. Smooths my hair from my face.

"Oh, honey," she says. "Oh, Addie."

She's quiet for a second, tracing circles over my back, and then she says, "You know, you were different after the first procedure."

I remember that feeling of things vanishing, the feeling of wanting more than I had. Did my mother feel guilty because of what she'd taken away from me or because she was finally sleeping for the first time in months, knowing that I was, too?

"I remember," I say.

"You know your father won't support this. You know how he feels about Overton."

"Well, he's not here, is he?"

"And what about the side effects from when you erased the boy? That had never happened to a patient before. What if it's not safe? What if your side effects are even worse this time around?"

"Mom, please," I say. My mother has always tried to protect me because, I realize now, her biggest fear is that she can't. So I appeal to the part of her that hopes something else will help me, even if it's not her. "*This* is the worst thing. Having some of the pieces but not all. Knowing the worst parts and not the best. I don't want it anymore. *Any* of it. I just . . . I want to be able to move on. I want to forget."

62

BEFORE
December

"Doesn't it seem a bit extreme?" Katy says, and she shivers a little. "They'd be messing with your *brain*."

"Maybe my brain needs to be messed with," I mumble, afraid it is true.

I'm lying on my side on my bed, eyes swollen and puffy from crying. Katy is lying on the floor, facing me.

"I want to knock his effing teeth out but I still can't stop thinking about him," I tell her, feeling myself beginning to tear up again. And then I want to knock my *own* teeth out, because why am I still crying? It's been days since I saw Zach and Lindsay at his father's store. More than two weeks since I first saw them together. Days of my mother worrying, hovering and stone-faced like she's seen a ghost, and even Caleb feeling sorry for me.

And I'm feeling this panic, like I'm falling into a hole that I can't get out of. That I don't know *how* to get out of.

"I must have been wrong about the whole thing. All along, it was probably just in my head."

Katy shakes her head. "It wasn't in your head. If anything, he led you on. Maybe he led himself on."

I don't know if it hurts more because being with him made me feel like I'd always wanted to, made me hum with electricity and lightness and life. And maybe most of that wasn't even Zach, not specifically the boy, but the way love pries your eyes open and forces you awake.

"Everything reminds me of him. Food tastes awful. I don't get it," I sniff. "What does food have to do with him? I didn't eat *because of* him, you know? I was never anything *because* of him."

"Except a Ciano fan," Katy points out with a smirk, but gently, like she's been doing since Zach and I broke up.

"Well, maybe that," I admit, turning onto my back. "God. Why did I date him when he *told* me he was still in love with her? Before anything happened, he told me."

"Bad move on your part, but still his fault," Katy says. "Keep your freaking tongue in its trap. It's not a hard concept."

I stare at the ceiling, the tiny cracks and dips.

"My mom is worried that there's something, you know, *clinically* wrong. Or that there will be soon. Poor appetite, bouts of uncontrollable crying, eternal desire to live in sweats." *I'm* worried that there's something wrong. I've never felt like this before. I turn to Katy. "What's *your* diagnosis?"

She pretends to think long and hard about it. "Clearly, a Depressive Episode. Unanticipated heartbreak, not otherwise specified. Moderate to severe, but definitely curable."

"I don't think I've ever heard you give a positive prognosis," I say, trying to sound lighthearted. But I'm doubting her prognosis. Every cell that zinged with happiness and excitement now throbs with a sharp, awful pain.

I just want it to stop.

"Well, you know, atypical circumstances. You're my badass best friend. And you can do so much better. You're *going* to do so much better. I don't know why you're even entertaining the notion of . . . what's it called? I've already forgotten the name. The memory sprite thing."

"Memory splice," I say, remembering all the pages and pages of information I've read about it. I remember finding the ad on Zach's windshield on our mundane day. Ironic.

The splice means I'll forget everything about Zach. His eyes, his face, his smell. I'll forget filming our movie and falling asleep in his arms and laughing so hard in the park while we got chased by birds. Plus, it seems safe and fast. Legit.

"Addie, I know places where they do *legit* amputations, but it doesn't mean I have to have one. And what about your parents, anyway? They'll never agree to this."

"They don't necessarily have to know."

Katy gasps. "How would we manage that?"

"*We* wouldn't, but maybe Beatrice Lane and Kathleen Kelly could."

"Addie . . ."

"It's supposed to be super safe. And it's not that expensive—I could cover it with my savings."

"As in all the money you've been saving up to leave this town? You can't!" Katy sits up and looks me in the eye. "I know it hurts right now, Addie, but are you sure it's worth it? Are you sure it's what you want?"

"If I don't have it . . ." *I'll be stuck here, trapped reliving the pain and heartbreak and anger over and over again.* It's like something is wrong with my mind.

And I can't imagine running into Zach and Lindsay, seeing them together again.

"You'll be okay. I know you will," Katy says.

But I don't. I can't remember ever feeling this broken.

"If I could only stop thinking about how hard my heart was beating the first time he kissed me or the way my stomach kept doing somersaults for the first week after. He was the first boy I was with," I say, swiping my eyes with the back of my hand. "I think I'd feel better if every single thing I ever felt for him or with him wasn't running through my body every second of every day. I wish I'd never met him."

My heart feels shredded and raw and small.

Maybe I'm not strong enough. Maybe I can't handle the full spectrum of good and bad, the blunt surfaces and sharp edges of life. Of love.

Maybe my mother is right to always be so overprotective.

Maybe the only way to feel better now is to forget.

63

AFTER
January

Mom drives fast—we left my car in the parking lot at Channel Se7en—so we can get there before Overton closes. I'm glad that there's no time to talk more about it. No time to *think* more about it. If I did, I'd doubt myself. I'd hear Zach's words in my mind telling me that erasing him was cowardly. I'd question whether maybe in time I'd be grateful for the pieces of my life I got back—Memory Zach, Rory—and for understanding finally why my family is the way it is. Why *I* am the way I am.

But there's no time for that.

Dr. Overton is finishing with his last patient when we arrive. I fill out a form about my medical history while my mother fills out a consent form. Did they make me fill out something like this the last time I had this procedure? Did I put Katy down for my emergency contact, and did it feel this scary, this strange, signing away part of my life?

I think of Katy.

What will she say when she finds out I did it again?

Will she be disappointed? Angry? Relieved?

And what about Caleb? What about Dad?

What about Zach?

I push them all out of my mind.

An imaging technician comes to get me after I've changed into a green cotton gown.

"First we're going to do what we call a baseline scan," he says, then explains how the machine works and how I'll be positioned in it. "It tells us what your brain looks like in its neutral state and also lets us double-check that it's safe to perform the procedure. I want you to focus on the pictures that come up on the monitor while we capture the images. Any questions?" I shake my head and then slide into the same donut-shaped machine as last time. This time, the technician pulls down a small white monitor, and pictures of different shapes—chains of triangles and circles and polygons—dance across the screen while the machine purrs quietly. Afterward, I'm sent into a room where a nurse I haven't seen before helps Dr. Overton run the computer, then watches as he puts the electrodes on my head. Mom sits in a tiny attached room, like those for X-ray technicians, watching through the glass, fidgeting like it's the night of the crash and she's in the hospital beside me again.

Did she sit there, too, the first time I was here? When they erased Rory?

"Sleep is our main tool for the consolidation process, so we'll be giving you a sedative and you'll feel fairly groggy afterward." Dr. Overton goes through a list of things to expect during the procedure, then some side effects: the worst are headaches, a rash from the electrodes, nausea, and drowsiness. I get to go home afterward, but because I've had complications in the past, he's given Mom his number and will be on standby for the next forty-eight hours in case anything goes wrong.

"It's not an invasive procedure, so I truly don't expect any problems," Dr. Overton says to reassure me.

Finally I am lying on a hospital bed, all hooked up to electrodes, Dr. Overton and the nurse looking at the computer, which shows an active picture of my brain. My fingers tingle with nerves, with fear.

I tell myself I am ready to forget. That I am ready to start again.

"I want you to think of the first thing you remember from that Saturday, the Saturday from the bus," Dr. Overton says.

I grasp for the moment I woke up the morning of the crash, before I met the boy.

"Just relax. You're doing great," Dr. Overton encourages in a soft, distracted voice.

"Picking up the cingulate cortex," the nurse whispers.

"Posterior?" the doctor asks. "Are we getting a read on the hippocampus?" They quietly discuss whatever they're seeing on the screen.

"Doing great, Addie," Dr. Overton says again, and out of the corner of my eye, I see him nod at the nurse. I'm thinking about packing up my viola case and my mom dropping me at the bus stop the day all this started. And then the nurse wipes something cold on my arm and there's the prick of a needle and everything slowly gets a little blurry.

Dr. Overton says, "I had a Zach once."

I manage to glance sleepily at him, surprised.

"Her name was Nina. First girl I ever loved," he says. And I relax again, realizing he's just making small talk. I wish he wouldn't talk about Zach, though. I wish he would talk about something that doesn't matter.

"Shift a little left, Leslie," he says, peering at the computer screen. Then he keeps talking to the nurse or me or maybe to himself. "I haven't seen her since senior year of high school at *least*," he says. There seems to be a tinge of sadness in his voice. But I'm feeling so foggy from the procedure that it's hard to say.

"Every now and then, I'll think I see her in the market or at the gym. It's the oddest thing." He chuckles, and the nurse laughs with him.

"Sometimes I'll think about her, wonder if she looks the same. What she did after college, whether she ever thinks about me, wonders about me." His voice gets fainter and fainter. "Where she is right now." He pauses. "And what she's done with her piece of my heart."

64

BEFORE
December

In the car outside Overton, I'm shaking and terrified and beyond grateful Katy drove. Beyond grateful she's doing this with me.

"Here," she says, dropping an envelope in my lap after she cuts the engine. "For today."

When I open it, I find a whole bunch of bills. After a moment of confusion, I understand what she's doing and shake my head vehemently. "I can't take this, Katy. No way."

"Well, you *can't* use all your savings and then get stuck in Lyndale. I'd have to go to New York by myself. That's not happening."

"It won't. I'll figure it out, but there's no way I'm taking your money. Where did you even *get* all this?"

"Robbed a boy—I mean a bank," she says, and I snort. "Fine. I pawned something my dad sent me. Some stupid pearl set that would work if I was the First Lady or something."

"Katy!" I exclaim. "Why would you do that? A gift from your dad? You have to go get it back!"

"I don't *want* it back. I want you happy. I want you in New York. And I don't want shit that reminds me of how little my dad knows about me. I mean, it's fine he doesn't remember my exact birthday, but he's, like, three decades off with my age."

I point to her wrist. "You like the silver bracelet, though. You never take it off."

She shrugs. "'Cause it's cute, which means his new wife probably picked it out. I can pretend he knows me well enough to know it's something I'd like. But a *pearl set*? Anyway, I might have enough money left over to get a new Stentor. I've had my violin for, like, four years." She faces me now and says, "Just take it, okay? If you're going to do this, if you absolutely *have* to, then I want to help."

I eye her for several seconds, blinking to hold back tears, then throw my arms around her. "I'm paying you back."

"No, you're not," she says.

"I am," I argue as we both undo our seat belts.

"*Forget* it, okay?" Katy says, laughing at her own joke, but our laughter is strained and I wonder if her heart is pounding as hard as mine, her stomach turning as quickly, her mind racing as fast, as we climb out of the car and walk toward the clinic.

Minutes later, when the nurse comes to get me, I leave Katy in the waiting room, holding my phone and hers, since electronic devices are not allowed in the procedure rooms. Before I leave, my best friend gives me a look that is fearful and knowing and something else I can't define: maybe regretful.

Why are we here?

Let's get the hell out and go home.

But the nurse is waiting. She's short and young, with a bright pink streak in her hair, and I follow her down the hall, clutching the pen and form I started filling out in the waiting room. She hands me a hospital gown and directs me to a changing room.

As I get undressed, I chant the same thing over and over in my mind: *Don't think, don't think, don't think.*

If I did, I might run out of here. I might go find Katy in the waiting room, and I'd call her Katy instead of Beatrice, and she'd call me Addie instead of Kathleen, and we'd go to her house or mine and talk about music or Juilliard or NYU. I'd try to forget Zach by filling my mind with other things, other people, not by erasing him.

But what if that's not good enough? What if I can't get over this?

My chest still throbs from just the thought of him.

And yet, I can't stop wondering if this is wrong. If this is stupid.

If I'll regret this.

My heart is racing now, my palms are clammy with sweat, and panic is swelling inside me, rushing up. *Don't think, don't think.*

"Almost done in there, Kathleen?"

"One second," I call back, but as the nurse's footsteps retreat, I see the pen and clipboard with the form I should have handed her sitting on top of the clothes I just took off.

And despite the mantra echoing in my mind, I think, *What if I hate myself for this afterward?*

The nurse is back again, hovering outside, but I pull my

jeans out of the pile of clothes, letting the rest drop. And I don't put them on, because I don't think I'm strong enough to live with this pain, because forgetting is still the easiest way to move forward.

But I turn my jeans inside out and start to write, scribbling as fast as I can.

I write all I have time to. All I can think of to say to the girl I wish I was, a girl who I hope will be a little braver than I am.

"Dr. Overton is ready whenever you are," the nurse calls, and then I am picking up my clothes again and opening the door and I am handing the nurse my form. "You're going to be okay," she promises me, and smiles in a way I don't want to forget. Another woman takes a scan of my brain, a baseline scan, she calls it. And then my nurse with the pink-streaked hair is back, leading me to a room where a doctor in his sixties shakes my hand and explains what's going to happen. The sedative, the side effects.

"How does it work again?" I ask in a moment of panic, stalling. I expect Dr. Overton to be annoyed, but he clearly never tires of talking about his life's work.

"Well, every time any of us remembers something, we don't just pull it out of the box and then put it back. We're actually reforming the memory of that thing. It's like every time you open a document on your computer and make changes— you save it anew. You write over the file every time you access it. Same with memory—anytime you access a memory, you write over it and then re-save it. We call it reconsolidation. And I think that's why sometimes it feels like we're reliving things that we remember. We are constantly re-creating or

363

re-saving memories in our mind." I nod and think of every memory of Zach, of how it feels too real and too much. "So what we do is we ask you to start off thinking of what you want to forget. You access it so we can locate the neural connections involved, and then we interrupt the reconsolidation process; we interrupt the process so the memory *doesn't* save. Does that make sense?"

I nod again as I lie in the bed, gripping the sides to stop myself from running out. I think of Katy in the waiting room, my mother at work, my father somewhere far away.

And Zach.

Before I forget him.

His hair, his smile, his scent, his laugh, his movies.

"Let's start with the day you met him. Do you remember that?"

I think of the heat the day I rode over to At Home Movies, pushing the door open, a boy with twinkling eyes springing out from behind the counter.

Zach, the boy I love.

The doctor and nurse discuss what they're seeing on the screen, throwing out words that are completely foreign to me.

"We've got it," the nurse says finally, pushing something into my arm. "Relax now, Kathleen. We'll take it from here."

Don't think, don't think, don't think.

As the sedative starts to kick in, it becomes easier not to.

65

BEFORE
December

"You're probably starting to feel quite foggy by now, a little sleepy, which is perfectly normal," the doctor says. "Try to relax."

"She's so restless," a woman says now, the nurse, I think. The fog makes it hard to tell.

"Here," she says, and takes my hand, squeezes.

It helps. It stills the tremor coursing through me, vibrating like a plucked string.

I can still feel the warmth of her grip as I fall into a cloudy, quiet state. And as I feel things starting to disappear, *see* things starting to dull in the window of my mind, I panic. The cars go first. Round-faced vehicles with headlights shaped like bulging eyes, on a street I recognize vaguely. The grass goes next. Tables, then people. Random strangers in different parts of different scenes.

It's when the sound goes with them that I start to panic.

What am I doing?

I try to squeeze the woman's hand, to tell her to stop it. I don't want to forget.

I don't want to forget.

Not even how it felt.

Not even how it hurt.

Not yet.

Because it mattered and it made me different and maybe I was wrong. Maybe I can handle it.

I can handle it.

But my hands don't seem to move, don't seem to convey any sort of message to the nurse, and the people and things and memories keep vanishing.

So I search for something I can hold on to. A sturdy, firmly planted pillar in the middle of a tornado.

A piece of music. Bach.

I've always hidden things in my music. I don't know if it will be enough.

Still, I grab on to it. I don't let go.

66

AFTER
January

As I'm falling under, I start to panic.

At that feeling of things disappearing, the edges growing dim, the spot left vacant by things I can't hold on to.

"Just relax," a murky voice says to me, and I tell myself to.

It's okay.

You're going to forget.

You're about to start over.

But I still can't stop the storm in my chest, the feeling in my body saying that something isn't right.

I try to form words, but I can't. To ask for a minute or five.

I was glad there wasn't enough time before, but now I want it.

Now I need it.

My mind begins to blur with images, spinning. The accident.

Spinning.

Goth Guy.

The hospital bed.

Spinning.

The theater.

Zach on the bench next to me, sharing my jacket.

Rory's gravestone.

Spinning.

These are the things that happened to me.

These are some of the things I did.

I think of "Air on the G String." This is the piece that reminded me.

I don't want to lose it.

I don't want to lose any of it.

But what if I am not strong enough? To take the pain of having just fragments, of knowing that I'll never truly have all the pieces of my life? What if I am not strong enough even to make out words now, in this fog? To tell Dr. Overton that I don't want to forget?

I try to form words, but it doesn't feel like my lips are even moving.

"S . . . sss . . . s . . ."

Stop.

Spinning.

Stop.

Please, please stop.

Spinning.

The things I know about my life are just shards of broken glass, the aftermath, what I've been told and pieced together. They are just a shadow, a replica of what happened and how.

But I deserve to know them.

I deserve to keep them.

Stop, stop, stop.

I'm not strong enough.

I've never been strong enough.

I cave when things get hard. I prefer to live vicariously, to live other people's stories because I am not brave enough to live my own.

That is who I am.

"S . . . sst . . . o . . ."

Spinning.

"Addie?" a voice says now. I still can't tell whose it is.

Did they hear me?

Am I imagining it?

Am I strong enough?

"Stop," I say.

Stop.

Finally—finally—they do.

67

AFTER
January

"Open your eyes. Wake up," my dad whispers as I stir.

When I open them, my parents are on either side of me, and my mother wraps her arms around me.

"Did they do it?" I ask, my voice muffled, pressed into her shirt. "Did I lose everything?"

"No," she says. "They stopped just as they were targeting the first memory, but you were already sedated, so they let you sleep it off."

Dad blinks at me. "Your mother called just after it started. She asked me to come."

"Oh," I say, squinting at him. Then I look away because we never have anything to say to each other. Because he's probably hurt that I didn't tell him I was doing this, because I don't want to face his disappointment right now.

But a few minutes later, when Dr. Overton gives us the

okay to go home, Dad asks if he can drive me, even though I came with Mom.

Mom shrugs when I look at her. "Maybe I'll go with Caleb to pick your car up from my office."

In the car, I stare out the window, not saying a word. It started snowing while we were in the clinic, and it's still falling in thick and heavy clumps. Sidewalks are already nearly completely white with it. It's hypnotizing watching it fall, watching it restructure the world by hiding edges and rocks and stairs and roofs.

"I'm glad you didn't go through with it."

I make no sound, don't turn to look at my father.

"I know you've had a lot to deal with the last few days, Addie. And I'm sorry for how everything turned out."

I had thought that I wasn't going to say anything to him, that I had as little to say to him as he had to say to me the past few years, but I suddenly break.

"How could you let me have the procedure the first time? You fought for Caleb to have a choice, but you didn't do the same for me. Why? Why did you just give up on me? Even if I agreed to it, you had to know that it wasn't really what I wanted. You didn't even *try*."

"I fought your mother on it for a long time."

"Obviously, it wasn't long enough. Obviously, you gave up."

"I . . . I knew I wouldn't be able to live with myself if she was right—if you did sink to a place so deep you couldn't recover," he says. *So he agreed with her that I wasn't strong enough, that I couldn't deal with losing Rory.* "I also somehow

371

convinced myself that by walking away, by leaving, I was having no part in it. I wasn't complicit in the lie."

Tears are stinging my eyes now. "But you were! You lied to me for years and years." *I am a big sister. "Was" or "am"? What is the word for things you were and no longer are but always will be?*

"I know," Dad says, and he seems on the verge of tears himself. "I realize that now. And not just for Rory, Addie, but for letting you believe you weren't strong enough. By doing what we did . . . by me letting it happen, your mother and I were the first ones to tell you that. And eventually you told yourself that, too; you believed it. But it wasn't—*isn't*—true."

He sighs now. "I've lived with depression all my life, Addie, and I don't have the words to describe how difficult that life can be. It's not *just* sadness. For me, at least. Some days it's a combination of the worst things I've ever felt in my life—fear, sadness, apathy, loneliness, sorrow, restlessness, hopelessness. And some days it's absolutely nothing—empty, turned out, like my brain doesn't even turn on. I don't know if you will live or would have lived the same life, but I couldn't take seeing you at eleven, seeing you now, and wondering if I've passed that on to you—my inability to deal with pain."

I look at him and glance away again, still fighting tears.

"But you are dealing with it," I say quietly after a moment. "You lost Rory and you lost Mom and you haven't given up. Why didn't you think you'd given me that part of you, too?"

He pauses, then nods. He's leaning forward in his seat, driving slowly on the slippery road.

"While you were asleep, I was talking to Dr. Overton and he was telling me how experiences reshape the brain. Whether

372

it's depression or joy or love, you can see how they physically reform someone's mind. By taking away the first tragedy you ever went through, we also erased the way your mind was learning to face it. Sure, maybe you were learning too slowly for us, maybe you needed more help and counseling or medication, but your brain was rewiring to deal with that pain, and we prevented it. So when this thing with Zach happened, your first instinct, even without knowing it, was to remove the source, not to cope with it.

"Addie, letting you believe that you weren't strong enough was one thing—and it was wrong—but the biggest lie is that there are things that aren't survivable. That there are things not *worth* surviving. I never, ever want you to believe that. That you can't keep going or that you can't overcome the thing you're facing." He pauses. "I'm sorry that I had a hand in teaching you that."

My eyes are completely cloudy now, but I shrug. "I had a choice a second time, remember? And I chose it again."

"Well, today you had a choice a third time, and you chose to move forward. I hope you keep doing that."

I blink at him. *Move forward.* Just a few hours ago, I thought that meant erasing every moment after the bus crash, but now I realize it means leaving the past behind. *Choosing* to leave it, to move on, instead of living like it didn't exist.

There is a difference.

And it means there's something I have to do.

68

AFTER
January

The front of Zach's house is covered in snow and nearly indistinguishable from all the others on this street. Which is why I'm glad for Katy's presence in my passenger seat, directing me.

It took some convincing for my mom to let me take the car.

"This was the scene of the crime," Katy whispers as we walk up the driveway. "Where we found them."

"Oh," I say, looking around, but there's not a trace of recollection. The disappointment only lasts a millisecond before it is overshadowed by the task ahead, the reason we're here.

I ring the doorbell, and after a few seconds, we hear footsteps getting closer and then the door is flung open. For the briefest moment, I think it's Zach. Maybe even Memory Zach, because this boy is younger, shorter, and skinnier than the Zach I talked with yesterday. But then his eyes widen and the boy grins, a different smile from any in Zach's collection.

"Well, *hello, ladies.*"

"You're repulsive, Kevin," Katy spits before I can work out who this is and why he is here.

"Is Zach around?" I ask, and Kevin's eyes wander back to me. He knows me. Some version of me knows him.

"Zach! Addie's at the door!" he yells, eyes still fixed on me. "Thought you hated him now?" He smirks, and I realize he doesn't know about the splice, the erasure. To Zach's little brother, we had a completely normal breakup.

When Zach comes out to meet us, his eyes are wide with surprise.

"Um, hi," he says uncertainly, looking between the two of us. "Is something wrong?"

"Yeah, your moral compass. How dare you call her a coward, you cheater," Katy hisses, and I grab her elbow to restrain her. Both Zach and Kevin look shell-shocked. Katy's clearly been itching for a showdown with Zach for a long time, because when I asked her to come with me to his house, she was only too happy to go running for some pitchforks and firewood. I shoot her a look now—*down, Katy*—and take over. She relents, remembering our discussion on the drive over about how I'd get to do the talking.

"Can I talk to you in private?" I ask a red-faced Zach. With him here now, the familiar turning in my stomach is starting, the lure to his gray eyes, the desire to touch his hair. Why didn't I touch Memory Zach's hair before he was gone?

"Um, yeah, okay," he says, scratching the back of his head.

I remind myself that this is not Memory Zach; this is the boy who broke my heart. They might look and sound and act the same, but one is gone and one is someone I *used* to love.

I start to follow Zach, and I hear Kevin's voice behind us, telling Katy, "I'll keep you company, babe."

I can't hear what she says back, but the acid in her voice is hard to miss. I fight a smile.

As I follow Zach through the hallway—passing family photographs and an autographed picture of a soccer star—I strain my mind for something familiar. The house feels warm, like I could imagine feeling comfortable here once, but I don't remember it. Not in the detailed, specific way you recall places you've been to.

Zach leans against the island in the kitchen and offers me a stool, but I shake my head. "So," he says, a question in his voice.

Across the room, a goldfish bigger than my hand swims across the tank, its tail waving some kind of greeting.

I try to think of all the things Past Addie would want Zach to know. All the things she might have felt or wanted to say, but didn't give herself the chance to. But I don't know enough about her or enough about what she knew to speak for her, so I take a breath and tell him how I feel now.

"You said I was a coward," I say, jumping right in— starting in the middle of a thought because I can't think where else to start. I don't have much context for so many things in my life, but I can't keep waiting to gain it. I want my life to be more than that. "For erasing you."

Zach hesitates. "I meant—"

"I was," I say, cutting him off. "But it wasn't your place to tell me that. It was a stupid choice, but it was *my* bad choice. The way you acted yesterday in your car was completely unfair. *You* broke my heart. *You* lied to me. You don't get to act like I'm the one in the wrong or like I'm the one who owes you an apology. I'm not obligated to remember you."

Hurt flickers over his face, but he doesn't speak.

"I *want* to," I admit, feeling my voice shake a little bit. "But only because it mattered to me. Because it changed everything. You're the first boy I ever loved."

"I'm sorry, Addie. . . ."

"It's my fault I don't remember. And I'll live with that for the rest of my life."

I continue. "But *you* were a coward for not telling me you were still in love with Lindsay. For treating me like I didn't matter."

"But I *told* you I was. At the very start. I said we should be friends."

I . . . don't remember that.

"Then why did you change your mind? Why did you let things go further and further with us?"

"Because . . ." Zach sighs, pushes his hand into his hair like Memory Zach used to, but there's so much less of it. "What I liked about you was how open you were, how ready you were to try new things. And I wanted to be a little bit like you. I didn't want to keep moping about Lindsay. I wanted to be open to something new, to forget about her."

So I wasn't the only one who was trying to forget someone.

He looks me in the eye. "I know now that it was wrong

and I wasn't being honest with you or myself. But even though I wasn't over Lindsay, I *did* like you and I told myself this was the way to move on."

Move on.

There it is again.

"Can you at least understand how much pain I was in and why I would want to erase you? You didn't have to cheat on me. If you weren't over Lindsay, if you wanted *her,* then you should have been honest with me. You could have just *told* me."

He looks ashamed, but he holds my gaze. "I know, Addie. I'm sorry. I fucked up. Some days I hate myself for what I did."

I am silent for a few moments, and then I tell him, "You shouldn't have used me as a crutch, but I think to move on, you have to deal with the stuff behind you, to let it go. That's why I came here."

And I'm not exonerating him.

I'm letting him go.

69

AFTER
January

Katy is still talking about it as we pull into her driveway. As we wave hi to her mom, watching a crime-investigation show in the living room, and take the steps two at a time to her room.

"I mean, of all the things, who would have thought what that little skeeze responds to is, 'I'm in a relationship.'" By "little skeeze," she means Kevin. "He backed right off."

"Sure it had nothing to do with your rant on *A Vindication of the Rights of Woman,* which you have never even read?" I ask as we enter her room, which smells just like my best friend. Like lavender. When I'd finished talking with Zach, I'd walked back to find Katy giving a purple-faced Kevin a piece of her mind. ("Do you know what girls *ACTUALLY* do at sleepovers? They talk about the pervy guys who catcall and lick their lips and how nobody likes them. Do you want that to be you, Kevin? *DO YOU?*") I guess she needed to blow off all the steam she was holding in at Zach.

Now Katy drags a chair up to her closet and retrieves a cardboard box.

"Nah. I think the brat just knows Mitch has the hardest thighs in Lyndale and could crush him in a fight."

"Oh God, Katy," I say as she cackles at her own joke. "Ew."

She shrugs and climbs down, handing the box to me. It is full of all the things we took from my room before the procedure, full of things that are in any way related to Zach. Pictures, horrody DVDs, notes. The clothes I wore on the day of the procedure.

I hold up a DVD with a person covered in what seems to be a whole lot of ketchup. It has Zach's name on the spine.

"Maybe I should mail this to him?"

"How do you know he didn't give it to you?" Katy says, dismissing the idea. "Anyway, half my belongings are from exes. Remember Marvin Mouth?" I nod, and she points to a lamp on her desk. "And Josh What's-His-Face?"

"MacPherson?"

"Whatever. These are his gym shorts. And, God, I wouldn't own any T-shirts at all if I gave back stuff," she says. "No, no, Grasshopper. You wouldn't listen to my wisdom when you were heartbroken right after the Zach-or-Mac-or-Jack thing, but now I will teach you my ways. You borrow stuff from other people—books, clothes, DVDs, mannerisms, jokes— and after a while, you break up, and you stop remembering who it's from. It all melds together and it doesn't even matter, because now it's yours. Such is the circle of life."

"I think that's called stealing," I say, eyebrow quirked in skepticism, mirroring her signature look.

"It's called *appropriating*," Katy argues.

"Also theft."

"Fine. Maybe I have a condition," she concedes with a shrug. "But I thought the rule was that you get to keep one item for every time his tongue has been down your throat."

"Ugh."

"Oh, and there's this!" she says, reaching back in her closet and giving me the biggest-ass umbrella I've ever seen in my life. "Part of the Zach Pile."

"What's it from?"

"Two Dollars or Less," she says. "And the day of the best car wash of your life."

I don't understand what that means.

Zach told me the highlights of our relationship, but he obviously left out some things. And maybe the details he thought were important are different from those I did.

"I'll tell you what I know," Katy says, squeezing my arm. "Whenever you want."

"Okay." I nod, fighting a sudden swell of emotion in my throat. I throw my arms around her. "Thank you."

We hug for a moment, and then Katy fake-pushes me off her. "Love you, Sullivan, but *I'm in a relationship,* or did you forget? Who knew that line was so powerful? God, no wonder normal people date for ages!"

"You mean other people don't date for *rock-hard thighs?*" I ask, feigning surprise as I back out of her room, the box in my arms. Katy's pillow just nearly misses my head, but she's blushing. Happy.

I drive home as quickly as I can in the snow, desperate to go through the box. I grip the box tightly as I carry it carefully up the stairs. I sit on the floor in my room and start taking the items out one by one. There are two ticket stubs for a concert at the community college during the September I was with Zach. Is that where I first heard "Air on the G String"? Does the real Zach know that was our song? I'll never really know.

I hold the stubs close to my chest, missing Memory Zach, and then take them away.

There are a bunch of DVDs, a nun habit. There are pictures of me and Zach. In one, we are sitting in a room I don't recognize—his?—and he's smiling at the camera while I kiss the side of his face.

Something stings the inside of my chest.

There's a picture of me and Zach and Raj, and I miss them, some kind of friendship I don't know.

There's so much I don't know.

I look through the last items: the clothes I wore on the day we went to get Zach erased. A pair of light jeans, black kitten heels, a white button-down, and a blue blazer. Did we think these would make me pass for nineteen, for Kathleen Kelly? I can barely walk in heels.

Too soon, there's nothing left to discover. Nothing that tells me more about who I was and what happened. These things are something, but I want more.

I want artifacts. Proof that I lived another life, a way to remember.

And what about Rory—what do I have of him? Why aren't the walls lined with pictures of his face? Why don't I have a box full of things to remember him by?

I allow everything to sink in—the things I've just seen that give me hints about my relationship with Zach, the things

I'll never know about being with him, about having a baby brother—and the force is so great I have to lie on my bed.

I keep drawing in breaths, even though my lungs feel like they are full of too much air. Several minutes pass like this, and then I reach for my viola. I hold it by the neck, fingers fumbling over its strings, over its curves, like following the ridges of words written in braille. I bring it to my chin and play. Just a few bars, a few seconds of the Prokofiev piece I've been working on the past month. Its sound is really more suited for a violin, and the piece I have is actually Katy's, transposed to a lower key, but its mood—its wistful, desperate, heavy sound—is made for my viola. It does something to steady me, to help me find a kind of rhythm in the rushed staccato of too many and too few faces and seconds and emotions that are crammed in tightly packed corners of my mind. And then I improvise, making up my own melody, one about getting lost and finding your way home, about the thickest fog you can imagine and pushing, fighting, breaking your way through it. About waking up.

It's not so good yet, but it's familiar. And I can work on it—I can start writing my own story. One where no one thing—music, a boy, my broken family—is my *whole* story. Anyway, Mrs. Dubois says what's important is how joyfully you play.

Later, I head across the hall and knock on Caleb's door.

"Hey," he says when I walk in.

I hesitate. He hesitates, too. Then I sit on the edge of his bed. I know I'm making a face as I survey his room, but I can't help it.

"When was the last time you picked up this room?"

"You can have it if you want," Caleb says.

"What?" I frown at him.

"That day you used my computer, I was applying for aviation academies. Well, starting to fill out applications and then chickening out and then starting again. Around and around. But a couple of days ago, I sat down and forced myself to do it. To finish." He shrugs. "Maybe I won't get in anywhere. In which case, I'm keeping my fucking room."

We both laugh.

"But you applied?" I repeat, shocked, delighted. He nods. He looks happy.

"Why didn't you before? I mean, I know you felt like you had to stay and make up for my not remembering or something. . . ." I trail off because it sounds stupid. Why *did* Caleb stay?

"Everyone talks about the day Rory died," he says. *Nobody talks about the day Rory died,* I want to argue, but I let him continue. "Dad was at work. Mom was sleeping. But where was I? Nobody ever talks about where I was."

I ask the obvious question. "Where were you? Mom said you weren't home."

"I was at the Lyndale Air Show. Me and Victor from next door rode our bikes to the grounds that morning, even though Mom had told me not to go." There's a pause, and then Caleb continues. "Before he left the night before, Dad told me to 'look after things on the ground,' because he always did. Because I was the oldest."

"Caleb," I say, hearing where he's going with this. "You were thirteen. Why *shouldn't* you have been out with your friend? And what would you have done if you were home, anyway?"

"Maybe *I'd* have taken Rory out of his crib when he started crying. Maybe I'd have seen that the basement door wasn't shut before it was too late. I don't know. I've always felt like I had to stay. Like I was atoning for something by sticking close to home, by never leaving Lyndale. And I wanted to look out for you, too, but when *you* started making plans for New York . . ."

"It made you angry."

"You were going to leave me here, and none of it had fixed anything. Rory was still erased and you were going to have a life and I wasn't." He shrugs again. "After everything, I kind of just want to get out of here. Even if I don't go to aviation school straight away, I'm ready to leave Lyndale."

"To move on?" I offer.

"Sure," he says. It feels a little bit sad to think of being in this house alone with Mom. Dad gone. Both my brothers gone.

When I say this, Caleb snorts. "Maybe the Asshole can move in, if you feel like you need a strong male figure."

I pretend to gag.

"You'll be out of here soon enough, anyway. You're going to go off to New York, become so big with your music that the Asshole will be name-dropping you to get tables everywhere— though, God, I hope Mom's not still dating him then."

"Nice, Caleb," I say.

We both laugh and I like this. I've missed this. The sound of us getting along, sharing a conversation we both understand.

"Caleb," I say. "Tell me about Rory. One thing you remember about him."

Caleb has to think about it for a while, and then he leans back and says, "Well, little-known fact, but Rory was kind of a klepto."

I guffaw. "What?"

"It's true. One time—Rory was about six months—we were driving with Mom and she'd stopped at Gas Fill. While she filled up, we three went into the convenience store to get some grub. I was pushing him in his little carriage, and we were walking around, arguing over which type of beef jerky to get. And then we paid and were leaving when the old man behind the counter started yelling at us to come back. Rory had a pack of gum in his carriage."

"You think he grabbed it?" I ask.

"You swore you didn't and I swore I didn't. I mean, maybe it got knocked off the shelf and into the carriage."

"Or Rory was a klepto," I say, laughing.

"Exactly." Caleb grins, remembering. I feel a pinch, wishing I remembered, too, but I'm happy to have this. To have a picture in my mind. "The guy didn't believe us and kept us in there, yelling at us, till Mom came and paid for it and explained that it must just have been a misunderstanding."

I don't know whether the cloudiness in my eyes is from laughing or crying now.

"Another thing was that Rory hated your music, your

practicing, a little less than the rest of us." Caleb says this softly, like he knows that it will mean a lot to me. "He had this bouncing, body-wriggling dance." I giggle at Caleb's attempt to demonstrate by bopping on his computer chair. "We could play all kinds of music and he'd wiggle his toes. Country, rap, electro—he was no snob. He'd nod or clap or flap his wrists."

Caleb is smiling, and I wonder if he's been waiting for this, waiting for the time when we could talk about our little brother together. Miss him, remember him.

R for remember.

"But when you played, that kid got down. He loved it. He loved you."

I am doing both now—laughing and crying.

The difference is not clear.

It's not important.

70

AFTER
January

When I head back into my room after talking to Caleb, I feel lighter and heavier. I feel sad, but certain that I made the right choice yesterday in the clinic.

How could I have ever thought forgetting was the way to move forward?

How could I have done it without hesitating?

I am packing all the Zach things back into the box—all the memories I have, will ever have, of him. I'm folding up the clothes I wore to erase him when I see a four-petaled flower drawn in blue pen on the jeans. I frown because I never draw on my jeans.

When did I do that?

Then, for a reason I can't explain—I guess just to double-check that they really are mine—I turn the waist part inside out to check the tag. Yep, my jeans.

And then a line of blue pen again catches my eye. And I see that there's writing down the thigh of my jeans.

I turn them completely inside out and hold my breath as I read, in my own writing, *Your name is Addison Sullivan.*

My breath shudders, but I stay calm and read it again. *I wrote this. Before Zach was removed from my mind.* I feel so light-headed that I can barely breathe.

Your name is Addison Sullivan and you are sixteen, but you will remember that. What you won't remember is Zach, the boy who broke your heart.

I did remember, I want to tell this past version of myself. In a way, I remembered. I force myself to think of Memory Zach. His smile, his hair, the night I met him on the bus, but I can't make him appear.

He's gone.

The sadness stings, but I think I'd rather have a fragment of the real truth than an illusion of it, a hint of it that isn't the same as the real thing.

I think of what Katy said in my car a couple of days ago: *There will be other boys, okay?* Other Zachs. And I know she's right.

When I start reading again, I say the words out loud, claiming them for myself. I've been told and given a lot of details and information from people over the past few days, but this time, I tell myself my own story, my own facts.

I don't know where or who I heard it from that when something happens to you, whether it's the best or worst thing that's ever happened to you, you can tell the story any way you want.

The point is that it's yours.

Your name is Addison Sullivan and you are sixteen, but you will remember that. What you won't remember is Zach, the boy who broke your heart. You don't want to remember it today, but maybe someday you will.

So find him and make him tell you.

It matters. Who you were, who he was, who you were with him, and who you were after.

Or maybe don't find him—it's your choice.

Find everything that comes after.

There will be so much that comes after.

But open your eyes.

Acknowledgments

This book would not exist without my agent, Suzie Townsend, who has been a tireless champion of my work. *Everyone We've Been* started as a messy, ill-conceived *thing,* and you knew exactly what to do with it. To my editor, Julia Maguire, working with you has been a joy. Thank you for caring about Addie and Zach's story. To my sisters and my parents, I am forever grateful for your love and unwavering support. Thank you also to Ray Shappell for a one-in-a-million cover, and to Heather Kelly, Artie Bennett, and Dawn Ryan as well as everyone at Random House and Knopf. A million thanks to all of Team New Leaf, particularly to Kathleen Ortiz and Sara Stricker, the GIF Queen. Infinite hugs to my writer friends, especially Mariah Irvin, who read one of the earliest drafts of this book and didn't run off screaming. Last but not least, thank you to my colleagues, friends, and family, who have seen me through these last few years. You have made all the difference.